VITRO

JESSICA KHOURY

razOr
bill

An Imprint of Penguin Group (USA) LLC

Praise for Jessica Khoury's *Origin*

"Khoury's debut captures the lush rhythms of the rainforest. . . . The plot moves at breakneck speed. . . . Utterly refreshing."   —*Kirkus*

"This well-written first novel concerns 17-year-old Pia, who, as the result of advanced genetic engineering, is invulnerable and immortal. . . . [Khoury's] descriptions of the rainforest and the native people contrast beautifully with the laboratory setting . . . and Pia is a fascinating protagonist."   —*Publishers Weekly*

"This first novel is a gripping read . . . with a clever blend of elements. It is an adventure story with romantic overtones, has a lush exotic setting framed by science, turns the eternal-love concept on its head, and rotates around a compelling moral quandary."   —*Booklist*

"Readers will be thrilled with the page-turning adventure/survival scenes in a descriptive and imaginative setting, and will root for Pia and Eio to the end."   —*SLJ*

"*Origin* is a startling mystery played out in the vivid and lush Amazon jungle. In this deadly clash of science and nature, a heroine emerges. Pia clawed her way through the pages and left her mark on the landscape of my imagination as the almost tangible danger left me breathless."
—Colleen Houck, *New York Times* bestselling author of *Tiger's Curse*

"I loved *Origin*'s action, romance, and mystery—and I couldn't stop thinking about the questions it raised."
—Beth Revis, *New York Times* bestselling author of *Across the Universe*

"Is this science fiction? It feels too scarily real. This spellbinding tale of the horrors of genetic engineering gone mad is both thriller and love story, breathlessly paced and beautifully told."
—Judy Blundell, National Book Award–winning author of *What I Saw and How I Lied*

"A lush, dreamy page-turner that will live forever in the hearts of its readers. Pia may be the perfect antidote for those suffering from Katniss withdrawal."
—Josh Sundquist, author of the national bestseller *Just Don't Fall*

FOR DADDY

razor
bill

A division of Penguin Young Readers Group
Published by the Penguin Group
Penguin Group (USA) LLC
345 Hudson Street
New York, New York 10014

USA / Canada / UK / Ireland / Australia / New Zealand / India / South Africa / China
Penguin.com
A Penguin Random House Company

Library of Congress Cataloging-in-Publication Data

Khoury, Jessica, 1990-
 Vitro / Jessica Khoury.
 pages cm
 Companion book to: Origin.
 Summary: "On a remote island in the Pacific, Corpus scientists have taken test tube embryos and given them life. These beings—the Vitros—have knowledge and abilities most humans can only dream of. But they also have one enormous flaw."—Provided by publisher.
 ISBN 978-1-59514-606-9 (paperback)
 [1. Genetic engineering—Fiction. 2. Science—Experiments—Fiction. 3. Science fiction. 4. Youths' writings.] I. Title.
 PZ7.K5285Vi 2015
 [Fic]—dc23
                                    2014029528
Printed in the United States of America

3 5 7 9 10 8 6 4

From: ghkg874a@mcnwr.com
To: misdefyinggravity@gmail.com
Date: 09 July 23:46
Subject: Come

Sophie,
I need you. Please come at once. I'll look for you on Friday. Do not reply to this e-mail.

Emergency.

—Mom

ONE

SOPHIE

"*Skin Island,*" Sophie said for what felt like the hundredth time. "I know what I'm talking about. It's called Skin Island, and it *has* to be nearby. Please, can't you just check again?"

She'd spent the last twenty hours in airports and cramped planes, nearly missing her second connecting flight after getting lost in the Tokyo airport and almost arrested for having a pair of scissors in her backpack, and she felt she would collapse if she took another step. She planted her hands on the travel agent's counter and refused to move until she had an answer. Behind her, the lobby of A.B. Won Pat International Airport basked in the afternoon sunlight that streamed through tall glass windows. Sunburned tourists and TSA agents navigated through the network of cordoned-off aisles and piles of suitcases, oblivious to the turmoil churning in Sophie's stomach. Her flight to Guam had landed an hour earlier, but she still felt as if she were caught in a wave of turbulence.

The travel agent's eyelid twitched. Sophie could tell that the man was nearing the edge of his patience. "I've checked every list, every database I know of, young lady. There simply is *no* Skin Island. It doesn't exist."

He spoke with a tone of irritated finality, and leaned back in his chair and folded his arms over his chest. Sophie guessed the man was in his fifties from his balding scalp and drooping jawline. He had sweat stains under his arms and smelled of garlic.

"I can pay you, I swear. I know it exists! My mom's worked there for *years*."

"You could hand over the key to the national treasury, wouldn't make a bit of difference. It's *not there*, I'm telling you! I'm sorry, miss, but I can't produce an island out of thin air."

She drew a deep breath to steady herself, feeling like a torn flag whipped and battered by a hurricane. "If you can't help me, then who can? There must be someone local who knows the surrounding area."

"I'm telling you, there's no—"

"Look . . ." She glanced at his name tag. "Randy. I did not come halfway around the world just for kicks. Give me *something* to go on—a name, a map, a fricking rental boat so I can go find the place myself." She glanced over the counter, at the desk he was sitting at, and spied a laminated map folded up and tucked between a mug of pens and a stapler. Before he could react, she lunged across the counter and snatched it, dancing backward when he tried to grab it.

The Mariana Islands marched in a gentle crescent from southern Guam to some speck of an island called Farallon de Pajaros on the northern edge of the paper, but none of them was called Skin Island. There were, however, several small, unlabeled islands—perhaps one of these was the one she sought.

The map disappeared as the travel agent plucked it away, and she found herself staring at her own empty hands. He had risen from his chair in the effort, and now sat down again, making the chair squeak beneath him. Heaving a sigh, he methodically refolded the map and tucked it back into place.

"You might check with the local charter pilots," he said. "Might be your island is too small to be listed with me, or goes by another name. Get a taxi, go to the Station—it's the bar where they all hang out. If they don't know your island, then it really doesn't exist."

"*Thank* you," she said. They exchanged scowls of mutual annoyance before she turned and walked away.

Outside the airport, she stood on the curb and waited for a taxi. It was the first moment she'd had since landing to stop and breathe and take it all in. Guam was a mixture of strange and familiar; strange, because for the last nine years she had lived in Boston, and the warm, damp air and tropical views seemed hardly real. Familiar, because the first seven years of her life had been spent on this island. It was home to her, but a home that was a distant, sepia-toned memory, a life that was folded between the pages of a dusty scrapbook. Now that she was back, she felt oddly shy, as if she were calling up a friend she'd not seen in years. Would anyone here remember her? How much had this place changed? *It doesn't matter*, she thought. *I'm not here to stay.* She was just passing through. Her mother didn't live on Guam anymore; she'd moved to Skin Island when Sophie was seven, and a month later, Sophie and her dad moved to Boston.

A taxi finally pulled up. She tossed her backpack inside, slid into the crackled leather seat, and told the driver her destination.

When she got there, Sophie thought she'd been played for a fool. She'd asked to go to the Station, and the taxi driver had dropped her at a rusty, tin building that just looked . . . well, *cranky.* Like it wasn't any happier to see her than she was to see it. She didn't remember this section of the island, but then, she'd remembered much less of what she'd seen on the ride here than she might have guessed.

She was doubtful, but then she saw THE STATION painted on the tin in faded, chipped green letters. The small window in the metal door, though dirty and streaked, revealed a dimly lit room within. She stood on the toes of her worn pink Chucks and pressed her nose against the glass. There was a bar, after all. She could see it against the far end of the room, complete with a tired-looking bartender and a small television playing an old '90s sitcom.

Sophie hitched her backpack higher on her shoulders, then turned the metal handle on the door. It was heavier than she'd expected, and she had to push it open with her shoulder. Once she was through, it slammed shut with a bang, as if offended by her intrusion. Only one table in the room was occupied, by a group of men playing poker. They all stared up at her. Feeling intensely self-conscious, she wondered if one of them might be a pilot she could beg for help.

To be certain, though, she first went to the bar and stood at the counter. "Excuse me," she said. "I'm looking for—"

The bartender had his back to her, and he threw up a hand for her to wait. She bit her lip and glanced at the men in the corner. They'd gone back to their game, but were watching her between plays. She looked away. On the other side of the room, an A-frame ladder was set up between two tables. Someone stood on top of it, his jeans dirty with grease and rumpled over a pair of work boots. The man's upper half was concealed by the ceiling; he'd removed one panel and seemed to be working on something electrical she couldn't see.

Sophie turned back to the bartender, who was intent on polishing a set of shot glasses and seemed happy to ignore her. She drifted further down the bar, to where a small metal fan oscillated on the corner. The building was not air-conditioned, and it was hotter inside than it was outside—and it even felt more humid. She wouldn't have thought it possible, from the way her clothes had instantly adhered to her skin when she walked out of the airport.

Now she was standing just beside the ladder, and peered curiously up. Whoever it was on top of it, his reaching into the ceiling was making his shirt lift, revealing a stack of abs and a hint of plaid boxers.

"You gonna wipe that drool off my counter when you're done gawking, young lady?"

Sophie jumped. The bartender leaned over the counter and grinned at her with gleaming, perfectly aligned teeth. They didn't look real, not in his stubbled, pudgy face.

"The guy at the airport said a local pilot might be able to help me find the island I'm looking for. Are there any pilots here? He said this was where to find them."

He nodded to the table in the corner. "There's Jordy and Pete. Ty'll be along later, but Nandu's out flying some tourists."

There was a sudden clatter overhead, and Sophie instinctively ducked, but it was just the guy messing around in the ceiling. The fan turned her way and blasted her hair across her face. "Thanks."

She made for the table in the corner. Two of the men had gray hair and deep tans, and the third was entirely bald. Sophie stood beside the table and waited. The poker players glanced at her casually, but didn't give her their attention until she cleared her throat and tapped the table. Then they turned away from their game and stared at her silently, each of them looking offended that she'd interrupted the round.

"Sorry to bother you," Sophie said, doing her best to keep a rein on her frayed and weary temper. "I was told one of you might know the location of Skin Island, and could fly me there?"

They exchanged looks. The bald man laid his cards face-down on the table and twisted his neck, making his spine crack. "Skin Island," he said slowly, drawing the words out in a low tone that Sophie barely caught. The other two stared at Sophie again, but this time, there was a guarded look in their eyes. The one who'd spoken was American by his accent, and the other two looked Polynesian.

"Maybe I've heard of it," the bald man went on. "Maybe I haven't. But I'd sure as hell not fly you there."

"Wouldn't fly the president himself to Skin Island,"

growled one of the others. He tossed a five-dollar bill into the pot. "Raise you five, Pete."

"I see you," the third man said. "And I raise you five back. Look, little lady, what my friends here are trying to tell you is that nobody flies to Skin Island. Nobody. I don't know what you want with that place, but you'd best just turn around and go home." He glanced around the room, as if afraid someone had heard him speak.

She started over. "Listen. My mom works on Skin Island. I don't know what you've heard or what your deal is, but I *have* to get there. Please. It's an emergency."

They were unmoved. If anything, they looked even stonier.

"Nandu flew out there a few months back," said Pete. "Didn't he tell you about it, Jordy?"

The bald man grunted. "He'd run into engine trouble and had to put down. Skin Island had the nearest airstrip. Said he was met by an armed welcoming committee—they welcomed him to leave. He got a good look around, though. That old resort—Halcyon Bay or something like that—they'd taken over a few of the buildings, had a bunch of doctors running around, real secretive. They marched him back to his plane and sent him packing. Would have shot him, he said, if he didn't go. He took his chances with the faulty engine." He shook his head. "He barely made it back in that old junker he calls a plane."

The story seemed stretched to Sophie, a tall tale told by a pilot to impress his friends, perhaps. Then again, her father had always told her she'd never be allowed to visit Skin Island, no matter how many times she begged her mother to let her come. The security around the place was Code Paranoid, which Sophie found a bit melodramatic considering the focus of her mom's research was finding cures for psychological conditions like Alzheimer's. "What are you scared of?" she'd asked her mother once on the phone. Moira Crue had replied, "Our work has the potential to make billions of dollars, Sophie. People have committed genocide for less. Now stop asking questions."

"See, girl? You're better off getting a flight to the moon," said Pete.

"Forget about Skin Island," said Jordy, and he folded, leaving the third man to collect the pot.

"Is there *no one* who will take me there?" Her voice pitched upward. *I will not panic. I will not panic.* But as many times as she told it to herself, it didn't quench the riot of nerves sizzling like cut wires inside her. She clenched the paper in her pocket as if it were a rabbit's foot to bring her luck. She had to get to that island. It wasn't just the e-mail. It wasn't just her mom. *I can't go back now. I'd look like an idiot. Dad will murder me for this as it is!*

"Well . . ." Pete yawned and drummed grease-stained fingers on his Heineken bottle. "There might be just one guy stupid enough to—"

"Pete." Bald man's voice was low, cutting the pilot off midsentence.

"Can't hurt to ask," Pete replied genially. He peered up at Sophie from beneath wispy white eyebrows. "If there's anyone who might fly you to Skin Island, it's Jim Julien."

"Jim Julien," Jordy grunted disdainfully as he shuffled the deck.

"Jim Julien," replied the third man with a thoughtful look. "You know, I think Pete may be right. Jim might take you."

"Jim Julien," Sophie whispered. A little bell began to ring in the back of her mind. *I know that name. . . .*

"Jim!" the bartender yelled suddenly. "Get down here. Someone for you."

"Not the IRS, is it?" asked a voice.

Sophie spun to see the work boots making their way down the ladder. Her eyes trailed up, over the jeans and sleeveless gray undershirt, to a tan, square jaw and a pair of deep, golden-brown eyes. He was no older than she was, from the look of him, and he was not what she'd expected at all. After talking to the poker pilots, she'd imagined every aviator on Guam was ancient, grizzled, and half-sunk into a bottle of beer. This one was anything but. And the moment she met his gaze, it all fell into place: golden afternoons spent splashing in the shallow blue bays around the island, star-speckled night hikes through the jungled mountains, hours of playing hide-and-seek at the Chamorro fiestas that were held on an almost weekly basis around the island.

Jim Julien. She knew him, all right.

His housekeeper Ginya had practically raised the pair of them while Jim's mom taught at the university and his dad flew tourists around the islands and Sophie's parents did their research on Skin Island. Though he figured prominently in most of her memories of Guam, she hadn't really thought about him in years. He hardly looked like the energetic little boy who was always dragging her into trouble, but there was a trace of mischief in his eyes that was the Jim she remembered, and she found herself grinning ear to ear.

"Oh," he said, looking Sophie up and down as he pulled a

red bandanna from his back pocket and used it to wipe sweat from his forehead. He didn't seem to recognize her, and the fuzzy feelings in her stomach faded a little. "You don't look too dangerous." He pocketed the bandanna and jumped to the floor, then stuck a hand out. "Jim Julien. Can I help you?"

Sophie realized her jaw was open. She snapped it shut and took his hand. It was warm, callused, and she noticed how defined the veins on the back of it were, tracing up his wrist and over the muscles in his arm. *Definitely not the little boy I remember.* He had an Adam's apple and stubble on his jaw. The Jim she'd known had had a childish plumpness to his limbs and gaps where his baby teeth had fallen out.

"Hi. Um, my name is Sophie. I was hoping to get a—a ride." She watched him closely, to see if he'd recognize her, but he just nodded and leaned on the counter, ran a hand through his hair—not, Sophie thought, without some idea of the impression he made when he did so. She narrowed her eyes, irrationally indignant that he didn't seem to be keeling over with sudden recognition.

"Sophie, huh? It's hot out there. You want a drink?"

"I don't drink. I'm just seventeen."

He gave her a bemused look. "Just a Coke. Porter?"

The bartender tossed a can to Jim, who cracked it open and handed it to her. "You sightseeing?" He looked her up and down and grinned. "I know some great spots for sunbathing. You a sunbather?"

"You a pilot? You seem kind of . . . young." She was being snappish, wondering why he didn't seem to know her. *We used to weave hats out of palm fronds and strut around the neighborhood as if we owned it, stealing bananas from the fruit vendors. Ginya used to let us take naps on the grass, but when she fell asleep we'd sneak off and you'd steal matches from the kitchen and teach me how to light them.* They'd set the neighbor's chicken coop on fire, and then Jim had tried to convince Ginya that the chickens had done it.

"I'm twenty-two," he said casually, stretching his arms and giving her the full benefit of his biceps. Sophie rolled her eyes. She knew it was a lie. And since when had he been a pilot? His dad had taken the two of them up in his plane on several occasions, Sophie recalled, and he'd let Jim sit up front and pretend to fly. The memories were swarming back like sparrows taking flight, startled out of hiding by the unexpected appearance of this strangely grown-up version of her childhood friend. *Best friend*, Sophie thought. *When I was four, I was convinced he was my brother.* She remembered crying when her parents explained he wasn't.

"Now, Jim, don't lie to the lady," drawled Porter. "He's eighteen, sweetheart, and that's a fact."

Jim laughed, seemingly unfazed that Porter had called his bluff. "Oh fine, eighteen, then. I've had my license a year, but I've been flying since I was ten. You going to tell on me?" He leaned on the counter and flashed her a smile worthy of a Colgate commercial. "So where you want to go? Want to buzz up to Saipan? Great lagoons, beaches, and we could probably scare up some whales. How many in your group?"

"It's just me. Whales? Really?" She shook her head, feeling dizzy with nostalgia and almost forgetting why she was here to begin with. She slipped her hand into her pocket and wrapped her fingers around the paper inside to remind herself. "I mean—no! No, not Saipan. Look, I need to go to Skin Island."

The smile fell from Jim Julien's face. On the other side of the bar, Porter's hands froze on the glass he was drying. For a moment, the only sound in the bar was the tick and whirr of the metal fan beside Jim's elbow and the hum of the neon Budweiser sign above their heads.

"What?" she asked. "What is it?"

Jim's eyes darted from Porter to the men in the corner, then he took Sophie by the elbow. "Come with me."

"What? Stop it! Let go!"

He pulled her toward the door, shouldered it open, and then waved her through. Bewildered and irritated, she stepped outside and then whirled to face him as the door clanged shut.

"What's wrong with you? Why'd you drag me out like that?"

"Where'd you hear about Skin Island?" he asked.

"My mom works there. What's the big deal?"

Jim ran his fingers through his hair, which was thick, unruly, and in need of a trim, and looked around nervously. "You don't just *go* to Skin Island. Nobody goes to Skin Island, you—" He stopped dead. His eyes grew wide. "Wait, wait, wait. *What* did you say your name was?"

"Sophie. Sophie Crue."

"Sophie . . ." And then it must have hit him, because his mouth spread into a smile. "*Sophie Crue!* But—but I know you!"

She folded her arms, holding back a smile of her own. "So your brain finally catches up to you."

"But you're *Sophie Crue*! You're supposed to be this big!" He held his hand at hip height.

"And you're supposed to be running around shirtless," she retorted, then she flushed. "I mean—you know what I mean. You used to—"

"Always rip off my shirt and use it to haul the shells you insisted on collecting?" He grinned, apparently amused by her discomfiture. "I remember. And I remember *you* used to pick your nose."

She gaped at him. "I did *not!*"

"Oh, yeah you did. C'mon, you don't remember? We used to have contests to see who could—"

"Shut up!" she said, her face as hot as a sunburn. "Never mind. Look. We can catch up later, okay? Right now I just need to know if you can or can't take me to Skin Island. It's my mom, Jim. Remember her?"

His smile fell away and he paced around her, his boots crunching on the gravel parking lot. Sophie waited impatiently, biting her lip to keep herself from begging with every last breath she had. She wondered at everyone's reaction to the words *"Skin Island." It's not like I'm asking for a plane ride to Mordor*, she thought.

"She still works out there, huh?" he asked, his tone guarded.

"Always has. She moved there permanently when I was seven."

"Which is when you and your dad moved to the States."

"Yeah."

"I remember, but I can't take you to Skin Island. I'm sorry." He folded his arms and looked mildly embarrassed, but a wall of finality seemed to have risen between them.

"Fine," said Sophie, her ears burning. "Then at least tell me where it is—and where I can rent a boat. I'll go myself."

"What's going on with you?" he asked, unfolding his arms. "Why can't your mom help you out?"

"I don't know the details, but I know she needs me. She e-mailed me a few days ago and asked me to come, said it was an emergency." She took out the paper from her pocket and held it out. She already had the words memorized.

Sophie,

I need you. Please come at once. I'll look for you on Friday. Do not reply to this e-mail.

Emergency.

—Mom

It was the first time in Sophie's life that her mom had needed her, the first time she'd ever invited Sophie to the one place she'd never been allowed to go, the place that had stolen her mother from her and ended her parents' marriage. She couldn't go back to the U.S., not now. Not back to the stepmother who'd never loved her as much as her two natural children, not to the father with whom she'd argued to the point of tears. There was just one person in the world whom Sophie needed, and now at last, impossibly and wonderfully, that person needed her back.

Jim didn't look at the note. "You think you're just gonna sail yourself out to Skin Island?"

She pursed her lips and stared resolutely over his shoulder.

"You're crazy!" he said.

"Not crazy," she muttered. "Desperate."

He studied her, his eyes narrowed, as the wind ruffled his thick sun-streaked hair. Slowly, he shook his head. "If you were anyone else . . ." he murmured. "Sophie Crue. Who'd have thought? I'd almost forgotten all about you."

"Gee," she said. "Thanks."

He sighed. "I'll take you," he said, but before she could squeal with delight he held up a hand. "But I hope to God you know what you're getting into."

TWO

JIM

Jim pulled the chocks from the wheels of the faded old Cessna Caravan and tossed them into the grass on the side of the runway. The temperature seemed to be increasing exponentially, and his shirt was stuck to his skin. After shrugging off his faded bomber jacket, he pulled his bandanna from his back pocket, dark with grease and smelling of avgas, and wiped sweat from his neck and forehead. The heat in Guam was fairly mild, but the humidity could sap the energy out of him in a matter of hours, even after so many years.

There wasn't another soul in sight. The airstrip was almost completely abandoned, used only by a few locals like Jim and his dad. The airlines all went in and out of Won Pat, on the northern end of Guam. This little forgotten splash of pavement was much quieter, though he still had to deal with the larger airport's traffic control.

Two unpainted, narrow runways streaked toward the southern curve of the island, abruptly stopping just yards from the beach. The grass around them was tall and uncut, and a perpetual ocean breeze shuddered through it and curled beneath a loose flap of tin on the lone hangar, making it rattle and clap. Jim was so used to the sound he barely heard it, the same way he tuned out the steady hush of the surf and the throaty cries of the seagulls.

He ran his hands over the propeller of the plane, then along the familiar aluminum fuselage, feeling the smooth round rivets against his palm. It was warm to the touch from baking in the sun all day, and the green strip that ran from nose to tail was so faded it was nearly yellow. Dents and scratches marred the metal, each one telling a story of some landing or storm or parking mishap, and the floats beneath it had churned as much water as any boat. He knew each ding and dent by heart. Despite its age and appearance, Jim trusted N614JA more than the pavement beneath his feet. He fingered a scratch along the engine cowl that had come from a freak collision with a seagull during takeoff three years ago.

"Well, beauty, I guess we'd better get going," he said, slapping the edge of the wing as he ducked beneath it. When he came up on the other side, he found himself face-to-face with Sophie Crue. Her long blond hair and thin white cargo shirt fluttered in the salty breeze. *Little Sophie Jane, all grown up.*

"You made it," Jim said. He'd told her it would take a while to get the plane fueled and prepped, so she'd gone off in search of something to eat. That had given him an entire hour to reconsider the deal he'd made. On the one hand, this was Sophie Crue, who'd been his faithful follower for years, letting him drag her from one mild crime to the next, playing the sidekick to all his superhero shenanigans, covering for him when he set things on fire or broke valuable items. On the other, it *was* Skin Island he was flying to. The only aircraft flying in and out of Skin Island were black, expensive helicopters piloted by men in dark suits and sunglasses. They used the main airport, but never stopped to hobnob with the locals. He knew where the island was—all the other pilots did, because they had to avoid it—but he'd also heard the story about Nandu. The island had a whole canon of urban legends attached to it: boaters who sailed there and never returned, strange lights on the shorelines in the middle of the night, lab-created monsters that were half-man, half-beast. Jim didn't put much stock in most of the rumors that went around about the place, but he knew better than to test them himself. Now those stories cut through his thoughts like an emergency alert on the television, a warning he was tempted to heed.

He had vague memories of Sophie's parents, both doctors or scientists or something, who had worked on Guam but went out to Skin Island several times a week. When they did, Sophie stayed with him and Ginya, his Chamorro nanny. His mom had been a professor, and if he remembered it correctly, she met Sophie's parents at the labs in the university, which they used from time to time. Those days were a distant haze, another life. He thought of that time period as Before She Left, and it was a vault of memories he rarely opened. It only left him with a sucking hollowness in his chest. But Sophie Crue . . . She was a memory he didn't mind reliving, especially now that she was here in the flesh, nine years older than when he'd last seen her. *What can I do? Tell her no? Watch her walk away, disgusted with me?*

According to Nandu, the airstrip that serviced the island

was set on a smaller spit of land just off its north shore; he might not even need to set foot on Skin Island itself. He'd stay with the plane, let Sophie do her thing, not get involved. He ignored the voice in his head that pointed out that as many times as he'd sworn to stay out of other people's problems, it wasn't really his style, and interfering had gotten him in more trouble than he cared to add up. *Not this time, though.* He'd help Sophie, but he wanted nothing to do with Skin Island itself.

"Are you sure this thing is safe?" Sophie asked, giving his plane a dubious look.

Jim didn't deign to answer that. "You ready to go?"

"Sure."

She looked ragged, as if she hadn't slept in days, with shadows under her eyes and tangles in her hair. She was obviously going through some kind of hell, but was trying her best to just keep it together for a little while longer. He knew the feeling all too well.

"Not too much daylight left," he said. "You'll have one hour on the ground, two at the max. Got it? No delays. This trip—well, being Skin Island and all, I'll kind of be flying below the radar. Don't want to broadcast it to the whole world. They're touchy that way, these scientists."

"What do you know about them?" she asked sharply.

"Not much." Jim opened the passenger door. "You sure about this?"

"Why wouldn't I be?" She gripped the metal doorway and pulled herself into the cockpit, and he had to duck to avoid being slammed in the face by her backpack.

"You want to go to *Skin Island*."

"If it's so bad"—she leaned out of the doorway until her nose was inches from his, her turquoise eyes burning with a look that brought back an onslaught of memories, most of them involving their five-year-old selves running wild through the street markets—"why are you taking me there?"

Jim shut the door, making her sit back quickly to avoid getting caught in it. He grumbled to himself as he made one last walk around the plane, asking the same question. It came down to one, she was pretty and needed help, and that was a powerful combination, and two, simply for old times' sake. As he climbed into the pilot's seat and jammed his ancient headset over his ears, a third reason occurred to him: *I'm an idiot.*

Well. It was done now, and he wasn't one to go back on a promise. He checked to be sure Sophie's seat belt was strapped over all the right places and securely fastened—he was paranoid about seat belts ever since a Japanese tourist kid had left his off and gotten his head knocked on the ceiling during landing, resulting in a concussion that had severely damaged Jim's dad's finances (such as they were) in the resulting insurance fiasco.

Then he went though the preflight procedures, checking the throttle, flaps, instruments, brakes; on and on the list went. He set the altimeter, then pulled the headset over his ears and took a scratched pair of aviators from under the seat and slid them over his eyes. The plane rumbled and vibrated around him, making his heart beat faster. There was nothing more exhilarating than flying. When he was fifteen, and his mom finally gave up on him and his dad and returned to the States, Jim spent more time above the ground than on it, covering hundreds of miles of open sea and sky, trying to lose himself in the vast blue-white atmosphere. On the ground, he only ever felt half himself, an empty body going through practiced motions while his soul lingered in the clouds. Every time he went up, it was like slipping back into his real skin, like coming up for air after being too long underwater. Easy and natural and right.

Like going home.

The cramped, weathered plane felt more like home than the house he and his dad lived in. He thought of his dad, whom he'd found that morning passed out on their dilapidated porch, surrounded by empty bottles. Jim had dragged him inside and left him on the couch. It was becoming an all-too-common routine each morning.

He pulled an extra headset from the pocket behind Sophie's seat and dropped it in her lap. "Put that on." She pulled it over her ears, adjusted the arm of the mic, and then gave him a dazzling smile. He sighed and pushed her backpack over so he could reach the throttle.

Jim revved the engine and the plane jerked into a taxi. The Cessna roared up to speed, fighting to leap into the air, but Jim waited until he was nearly out of pavement before pulling back on the yoke. The climb was steep and swift, just how he liked it. Back when he'd bothered to care, Jim's dad had always criticized him for flying recklessly, but he himself was just as bad. He glanced at Sophie, wondering if she'd get sick from the rapid, rattling ascent, but she looked absorbed in her own thoughts as she stared out at the towering clouds rising around them like ghostly, vaporous skyscrapers. The smile was gone. He knew she must be worrying about her mom, and whatever emergency had called her to this godforsaken armpit of the universe.

When he reached six thousand feet, Jim leveled the plane and settled back for the short flight to Skin Island, hoping that in doing so, he wasn't making a terrible mistake.

THREE
SOPHIE

Sophie's heart beat as rapidly as the propeller of the plane, as if it might saw right through her ribs and burst from her chest. She didn't know which was stronger: her worry about her mother or her excitement to finally see the mysterious island that had stolen her mother from her. Her nails, which she'd had manicured just a week ago, were now bitten short, and she dug them into the denim of her jeans. As the plane clawed its way through the clouds, she had to force herself not to grind her teeth together, a habit various dentists had scolded her for on countless visits.

I'm going to Skin Island.

It hardly felt real.

But the plane around her certainly felt real; it jolted and shuddered worse than a subway train. When it bucked suddenly, throwing her against the seat belt, she reached out and grabbed Jim's arm, her stomach and heart tangled in her throat.

"You okay?" His voice was muffled in her ears, the headset transmitting so much static she winced.

"Fine." She let go of his arm, embarrassed by her jumpiness. He had only one hand on the yoke, and the other rested lightly on a knob on the center console. His amber eyes studied her sidelong from behind his dark aviators, and his lips quirked into a half smile.

"Scared of flying?" he asked. "We used to go up all the time with my dad, remember?"

"Not scared," she replied quickly. "It's just been a while since I was in such a small plane. I forgot how bumpy—ah!"

The Cessna tilted to the right, and she clamped her teeth onto her lower lip and slammed a hand into the window to steady herself. Jim laughed.

"You're doing great!" he shouted.

"I should have known you'd end up here," she said. "You loved this when we were kids."

He laughed again, and the knot of nerves in Sophie's stomach slowly relaxed. There was something soothing in his easy confidence, the way his eyes lit up as the plane gained altitude. Compared to this Jim, the one she'd spoken to on the ground had been half-asleep. She found herself staring at the line of his jaw, the way the corners of his lips continually twitched as if he were always on the verge of a smile. His thick, dark hair crested over his forehead in an unruly wave, and she wasn't sure whether she wanted to attack it with a pair of scissors or run her fingers through it. She was intrigued and a bit shy of this grown-up Jim, unsure of how much of the boy she'd once known still remained.

Realizing she was staring a bit too long, Sophie turned

away and looked through the windshield. Above them stretched a ceiling of clouds, bending away to the horizon. She felt a flutter of claustrophobia in her gut—*a strange feeling, considering I'm surrounded by the whole of the sky*—and to distract herself, she reached out and ran a finger over the yoke in front of her, wondering how it worked. She gripped it with both hands and tried to imagine what it would be like to fly the plane.

A string of white beads hung from the ceiling; they swayed with every movement of the plane. On each bead was carved a word in a language Sophie did not recognize. She reached up and took them in her fingers, running her thumb over the delicate letters. "What does it say?"

Jim glanced at the beads. For a moment he didn't reply, and she peeked behind his sunglasses to see his eyes had a faraway look. "It's a Chamorrita poem."

Chamorrita. The call-and-response poetry sung by the Chamorro people, who were Guam's original inhabitants. She remembered sitting on Ginya's lap as she sat on the porch with the other Chamorro women, braiding jewelry to sell to the tourists and singing intricate, clever verses back and forth, like freestyle rap, except sung by grandmothers. *I forgot how much I loved this place.*

"So what does it say?"

"It says, 'There is no brightness without darkness. There is no body without its shadow.'"

She let go of the beads, and they swung hypnotically, the sunlight flashing off them. "Some kind of good luck charm?"

He drummed his fingers on the yoke, and his tongue

darted across his lips. "So your mom moved out to Skin Island full-time, huh?"

"Yeah. I don't remember the details, and she doesn't talk about it, but I think she was promoted or something and had to move closer to the lab out there. That's when Dad and I moved to Boston. He teaches biology."

"Remarried?"

"Yeah. Her name's Karen. She has two kids, younger than me. What about your folks?"

"About the same as yours. Mom split three years ago, haven't seen her since."

Sophie stared at her hands in her lap. "Sucks."

"Yeah." He shifted in his seat, lifted a hand to massage the back of his neck. "Have you been to Skin Island before?"

"Never." *But not for lack of begging.* Sophie leaned her head against the glass window, then sat up again when the vibration made her teeth rattle. "I see my mom three times a year at least, and she e-mails and calls a lot. We've stayed close, considering." *Considering the distance. Considering how much my dad hates every moment I spend with her.* She'd never understood why her dad loathed her mom so much, or what had severed them apart all those years ago. Maybe Skin Island held the answers; it had certainly been a recurring topic of contention in their house when she was seven.

"We sure tore it up, didn't we?" Jim asked, lightening the mood with a grin. "Back when we were kids."

Sophie snorted and propped her elbow against the window, resting her head on her hand as she looked at him. "It's lucky I did move, or you might've landed me in jail."

"Nah. You were too cute to get in trouble. It was me they always blamed." He winked at her, and she rolled her eyes.

"You were the one that deserved it!" She studied him thoughtfully. "So how have you been, anyway?"

"Oh. You know." He shrugged. "Nothing changes here. Same old faces, same old drama."

"What about Ginya?"

"She left when I was about ten, to take care of her mom in Yigo. I'll see her every now and then. She hasn't changed a bit. You'd recognize her right off. She's like, ageless or something."

Sophie smiled, comforted by the idea that some people never changed, could always be depended on to be exactly the way they should.

"What about you?" he asked. "Boston, huh?"

"Ugh. It's cold and dirty. I miss here." She turned and looked down at the blue water below. "I miss the beaches and the never-ending summer."

He grimaced. "I'll trade you. You know I've *never* been to the States? I'm a U.S. citizen, but I've never once set foot on the continent of North America."

"You have a deal," she said. But it wasn't Guam she wanted, not really. It was Skin Island. This was the argument that had her and her dad at each other's throats lately. With her senior year approaching, Sophie was ready to make college plans, and her goal was to get through med school as fast as possible and then get a job with her mom. She couldn't imagine anything more worthwhile to do than find cures for the disorders and diseases of the world. Her mom was a hero, and all Sophie had ever wanted was to be by her side, helping her. But for reasons her dad never seemed able to articulate, he was dead set against her plan. *Well, if anyone can back me up, it'll be Mom.* If her mom was okay. Anxiety fluttered in her stomach like a wounded bird, and the note in her pocket weighed like a brick. Dozens of possible explanations came and went through her thoughts, from the mundane to the impossible. A broken limb? An incurable disease? The island was out of toilet paper? Was she being held hostage by a tribe of island cannibals out of a nineteenth-century adventure novel? Her imagination rampaged through a host of wild scenarios, and for the hundredth time she wished her mother's e-mail had been more specific. This wasn't 1860, when people sent messages by telegraph and had to pay by the letter.

She leaned her head back and stared up at the ceiling, which was covered with bumper stickers, most of them so old their colors were faded and their edges curled up. They blasted slogans like KEEP CALM AND FLY ON, I'D RATHER BE LUCKY THAN GOOD, and CAUTION: AVIATION MAY BE HAZARDOUS TO YOUR WEALTH. One depicted a Pegasus soaring through stylized clouds, but instead of feathery angel wings it had sleek airplane wings fixed to its shoulders. There were at least a dozen different AOPA stickers. She glanced behind her; the backseat was cramped and in some places, the cracks in the leather were covered with duct tape. It made her a bit nervous, as her mind couldn't help but imagine the engine being held together in a similar manner. Then she thought, *Can't go back now. Might as well make the most of it.*

Suddenly the plane burst out of the cloud and into another world. Sophie gasped. As a child, she'd flown in this same little plane, and she'd definitely seen the sky from above on the big Boeings, but she'd forgotten it could be like *this*. So close, so real, so *immense*. The clouds spread below and around them like some silent white city, with coiling spires and rivers and bulbous stacks, all made of the same pinkish white cloud. It was a dreamscape, a world that continually shifted and flowed, sparkling in the sun like ice cream. She felt the urge to open the window, reach out, and scoop the clouds into her hands as if they were foam in a bubble bath. It was dazzling and terrifying, and the more she stared the more impossible it seemed. The clouds seemed spun of silk the color of apricots, piled and folded and flung across the sky by an unseen hand. She had the strangest sensation that she was three years old, completely enraptured by childlike wonder, pressing her nose to the glass while Jim's dad laughed and wobbled the plane on purpose to scare them.

"Something, isn't it?" Jim's voice crackled through her headset.

"Very," she whispered, and she stole a look at Jim. Their eyes met and held, and he grinned. She found herself smiling in return, and feeling suddenly shy, she looked away.

They dipped back below the clouds, and Sophie fell into a trance, hypnotized by the endless wrinkling sea. It sparkled with a million winking lights, like a sheet of gray silk peppered with golden white glitter. She saw a few islands, dark green and bent into irregular shapes, pebbles dropped carelessly across the sea. They looked so small it seemed she could pick them up and slip them into her pocket.

Jim lifted one hand and pointed toward the east. "There she is."

Her reverie snapped in two. She leaned toward him and stared out his window as he took the plane lower.

Skin Island expanded as they approached, became brighter, more green, its mountains more pronounced. They steepled down the center of the island like satin green tents, their foothills crowded with dense forests of palms and pines. The shadows of their ravines were a deep purple, testifying to the range's steepness and height. A cloud cast a shadow over the southern rim of the larger island, where she thought she glimpsed something white—buildings, or perhaps just the beach. A smaller island graced the waters above the northern shore, like a dot over a fat, slightly bent lowercase *i*.

"The airstrip is on the smaller one." Jim's voice crackled through her headset. "I guess she's expecting you?"

"My mom? Yes. It's Friday, isn't it?" Her mind still felt a bit fuzzy whenever she tried to reckon out the time change, factoring in the international date line as well.

"It's Friday," Jim confirmed.

Sophie's eyes were fastened on the island. The whole situation didn't feel quite real. *Skin Island.* She had to keep reminding herself that this was it; there was the island rising up from the sea, the island that haunted her her entire life though she'd never seen it until now.

She'd lost count of how many times she had begged her mother to let her come to Skin Island, always to the same negative result—so why now? What had changed? She hadn't hesitated a moment when she saw the e-mail. It was if she'd been waiting an excuse to do this very thing, running off to Skin Island to see her mother in her element. She'd always wondered why she'd been sent to Boston with her dad, instead of here, with her mother. She didn't recall having ever been asked what *she* wanted to do. All she remembered was that one day, her mom kissed her on the forehead and said she'd see her at Christmas, and a month later Sophie and her dad were on a plane to the States. It was a whirl of dizzying changes that had assaulted her too quickly, too wildly for her seven-year-old mind to digest. She'd always resented her father for whisking her away to a new life and new family she'd never wanted, and always dreamed her mother would whisk her back. She'd just never imagined it would happen quite like this.

"They *are* expecting you, right?" Jim's voice crackled through her headset.

She blinked at him. Were they? A sudden, new scenario burst into her thoughts—what if the emergency had to do with the company her mother worked for? Sophie had never trusted the shadowy corporation and its penchant for secrets. What if they'd done something to Moira? "I . . . I don't know. I mean, my mom is, but—"

His fingers gripped the yoke tighter, making the veins stand out on the backs of his hands. "Look," he said, "I just want to stay out of it, okay?"

"What do you mean?" She slid him a confused sideways look.

"Just saying." He kept his eyes trained ahead, but she could see the tightness in the skin around them, even behind his glasses. "All I want is to fly in and fly out, okay? I don't know what your mom's got going on in that place, and I don't want to know."

She shrugged and turned back to her window. *That makes one of us.*

Jim tilted the yoke, and the plane sank through the air. Sophie's stomach rose and for a single moment she felt entirely weightless. Within seconds, she was looking straight ahead at the island instead of down at it; the plane seemed so close to the sea that she imagined she could reach down and drag her fingers through the water.

The plane began to jerk and shudder the lower they went, and Sophie gripped her seat and felt her stomach turn over, threatening to slosh up her breakfast. Jaw clamped tightly shut, Sophie trained her eyes on Jim, as if somehow she could will him to make the wind stop throwing itself against the plane.

He must have noticed her discomfort, because he gave her a lopsided grin. "Don't worry," he said, rolling his shoulders as if he was on a casual stroll down the beach. "I can handle this."

"Then shut up and start *handling it*," she said through her teeth.

Jim laughed. The plane tilted violently onto its side, and for a moment, she was certain they would roll over and slam into the ocean. The grin on Jim's lips slipped, and then she *really* began to feel nauseated.

"What's wrong?" she shouted, resisting the urge to grab onto his arm and hang on for dear life.

"We're fine!" he insisted.

The island rushed up to them. *Too fast too fast*, she thought, pressing into her seat with her eyes stretched wide and her heart pounding. Palms whipped past them, and suddenly there was a ribbon of tarmac unraveling below.

The plane slammed onto the ground, and Sophie was certain that was the end, it was over, she would die—but Jim was laughing and saying, "See? No problem! That was easy as—"

POP POP POP.

Something snapped, something Sophie knew was most likely *not* supposed to snap, and the plan went into a violent spin, skidding out of control across the pavement. She was thrown against the door, then against Jim, her seat belt cutting into her diaphragm and making it hard to breathe. Everything whirled around her as if she were caught in a giant blender, colors and shapes coalescing into a dizzying rush. An earsplitting screech sliced through her head, a thousand nails on a thousand chalkboards, or forks scraping china plates, so loud that she felt it vibrating in her teeth.

She felt Jim's arms around her, holding her tightly against him, and she pressed herself into him and was so seized with terror that she couldn't even manage a scream.

FOUR
JIM

Though it felt like the crash dragged on in slow motion, it lasted only a few seconds before the plane ground to a stop, propped on its wing and nosing slightly upward. The propeller still spun in front of them, clawing at a sky it could not reach.

For a long moment, Jim couldn't move. His arms were still locked around Sophie, who had her hands over her face. Her slim form trembled against him. She was utterly silent, and had been through the whole ordeal. He was dazed and shocked—the landing had been going perfectly, smooth as water over glass, and then . . . What? The runway was clear, but it felt as though they'd hit a boulder.

Carefully, Jim extricated himself from Sophie, keeping one hand on her shoulder. He gently pulled her hands away and found her staring blankly at nothing, her breath coming in short, ragged gasps. He shut off the plane and the propeller slowly wound down.

"Sophie?" He looked her in the eye, but sensed she couldn't see him. "Sophie, are you okay?"

Slowly, her gaze focused on his. She drew a deep, shuddering breath, and for a moment, he thought she might start hyperventilating. *Hell, what do I do?* He thought vaguely of a brown paper bag, but he didn't have one, and anyway, he didn't see how that would help.

Thankfully, she seemed to gather herself. She pulled away and looked around. They both seemed more shaken than the plane was, though Jim would have to climb out and inspect the exterior before he could know how bad the damage truly was.

"Are you hurt?" he asked.

"No," she said, her voice wavering. "I don't think so. You?"

"I'm fine. Come on, let's get out. Be careful."

She still seemed hazy, so he reached across her and opened her door, then clicked her seat belt off.

"If you wait, I'll come around and help you."

"No, I'm okay." She slid out of the plane, dragging her backpack with her.

After he was sure she could stand on her own, Jim jumped out his side and gave the Cessna a quick once-over. The undersides of the floats were streaked and smelled of burning metal from where they had scraped across the pavement, and the wheels lay in four deflated puddles on the runway.

Jim stepped back, ran his hands through his hair, and let out a long, deep groan. Sophie stood beside him and stared at the damage.

"Can you . . . fix it?" she asked tentatively.

"The landing gear is trashed. Look at that—tires blew

out, each one of them. No way." He rubbed at his face and winced, looking up the runway. Maybe the cracks in the pavement were worse that he'd thought. "But the floats are still intact." He dropped into a crouch to get a better look. The floats were dented and scraped and a bit loose, but if there were some way to get the plane into the water . . . *She could do it. Maybe.* He'd have to patch the holes in the floats and then do a complete engine check, to be sure there wasn't any internal damage. The only other option would be to ask for help from Sophie's mom, perhaps. There had to be a phone on the island, or some way he could contact his dad. He felt ill. *Of all the places to be stranded* . . . "Some holes in the floats. I'd have to patch it up."

"How? There isn't exactly an airplane shop around here." She swept her hand, indicating their isolation.

"Duct tape," he said.

Sophie raised one eyebrow. "Duct tape."

"Oh, yeah. I use it for everything, and it's never let me down." He climbed back into the cockpit, dug through a compartment in the back, and emerged with three rolls in each hand. "See? The stuff is practically made of miracles."

"Right." Her tone was flat and skeptical.

Jim sighed and studied the damage, knowing that even with the tape, it would take a real miracle to get the plane back into the air.

Sophie was edgy, looking around and pacing to and fro, wondering where her mom was, Jim guessed. He pulled his eyes away from his plane. "See her?" he asked.

She shook her head and mechanically shrugged her backpack onto her shoulders and then stood still. From where they were, Jim could see the entirety of the little islet. Unlike its much larger neighbor, this island was mostly flat, composed of a thin scattering of palms, a lot of sand, and the airstrip. Tall grasses shimmered around them, bent by the salty wind, and old coconuts littered the ground.

Skin Island looked closer than it really was, rising out of the sea into a series of green peaks. It was probably too mountainous for an airstrip, which is why they'd used the smaller island, Jim reckoned. He knew Skin Island had once been a posh resort in the seventies and eighties, but had shut down for several years and fallen into disrepair. Then a group of scientists moved in and set up camp. They never seemed to use the airstrip, at least from what he could tell; the helicopters landed elsewhere. He'd never known anyone to ask questions about what went on there; people seemed to sense that whatever it was, it was best left alone. It was one of the few things his neighbors actually didn't pry into. Jim had a running theory based on what he'd seen of the island communities in and around Guam—the smaller the island, the more time everyone spent in on another's business. Half his neighborhood had known about his parents' split before even he did. In fact, the morning his mom stormed out with all her belongings in two suitcases, there had been a crowd gathered to watch. They were all huddled in the neighbors' yards, trying to be surreptitious and failing miserably, and Jim had refused to speak to any of them for months.

But when it came to Skin Island, even the most notorious gossips he knew kept their lips sealed. When Nandu had returned from his ill-fated trip there, no one had asked questions. Skin Island was something of a local horror story, their equivalent to a haunted house—a haunted island.

"Jim?"

He shook himself and slowly stood up. Now that the initial shock had died down, the pain was setting in. His chest and stomach burned from the seat belt digging into him, and he knew the whiplash would only get worse in the next few hours. He stretched his arms, wincing a little as the movement sent a spasm of pain down his back. "Sorry, thinking. What is it?"

"There's someone coming."

He whirled to face the direction she was pointing. The ground slid downward from the airstrip, through a line of palms to a long, narrow beach that led to the channel between the two islands. A boy about their own age was strolling up the beach, his hands in his pockets, whistling to a flock of seagulls that screamed overhead.

Then the boy turned toward them, seemingly unsurprised to find them there. He began hiking up the slope in their direction, kicking aside the coconuts in his path. He had long dark hair that hung loose to his jaw and a sharp angularity to his features.

"Who are you?" Jim asked.

The boy pulled his hands from his pockets and let them hang loose at his sides, considering Jim with an odd look of amusement. "I'm Nicholas," he said, as if the fact were obvious.

"Did my mom send you?" asked Sophie, walking toward him. "Where is she? Is she okay?"

"Calm down, Sophie," Nicholas said, smiling. "Everything's fine."

She stopped short. "How do you know my name?"

Nicholas gave her a long, appraising look. Jim bristled at the way the boy's gaze lingered hungrily on her body. Jim stepped forward. "Hey, man," he said. "My plane . . . uh . . . had some trouble landing. . . ." The blood rushed to his face. "It wasn't my fault or anything—something must have come loose. Point is, I need a phone."

"Not one here you can use." He studied the plane, and shook his head. "Huh. They are *not* gonna be happy about this."

"Who?" Jim asked. "Why can't I just use the phone?"

But Nicholas was ignoring him. He'd gone back to ogling Sophie. "You came. You actually came."

"Of course I came! Where is she?"

Nicholas sighed. "Calm down, okay? I'll take you to her. You, pilot. You can't use the phone because there's only one on the island and it's locked up. Besides, they monitor the line, and the minute they find you're here they'll shoot you and dump you and your plane in the ocean."

"What?" Sophie's head flipped from one boy to the other. "Now, just wait a minute. Of course we can help him. My *mom* works on this island, and she'd never *shoot* anyone."

"Really?" He gave her a steady look. "And how well do you know your mother, Sophie Crue?"

She looked faintly blindsided by this. "Wh-what?"

"I've been rude. Forgive me. Welcome to Skin Island."

He held out a hand and she took it. He ran his thumb over her knuckles and drew her closer to him, Sophie looking uneasy but not pulling away. Jim's fingers curled into fists, and he thrust them into his pockets and kicked a loose scrap of metal that his plane had dropped.

"You'll take me to my mom?" she asked.

Nicholas nodded. "Don't worry. Everything's going just as it should."

"What does that mean?"

Jim looked from Sophie to Nicholas; they were inches apart, eyes locked on each other, ignoring him completely. He threw up his hands. "Okay, I'm done. Whatever trouble you're getting into, that's your problem and not mine." He turned and stalked back to the plane.

Sophie ran after him. "Jim! Come with us. I'm sure my mom can work things out."

"I'd rather not take my chances, thanks. From the sound of things, your mom's not in a position to help herself, much less me." He turned to see the look of distress on her face, and he sighed and shook his head. "Don't worry about me. I can manage this. Just go on." He glanced over her shoulder at Nicholas, who stood still, watching them with a mild expression. Jim leaned down and whispered, "I'll wait for you here."

"You don't have to do that. I'll be fine. If you can, you should just go back. I'll pay you for the trip."

"Nah," he said. "It was for old times' sake."

"You don't have to wait for me."

But he did. He couldn't just leave her in the middle of nowhere with the first random guy who waltzed up and flashed her a smile. "Go find your mom, and then let me know you're okay. Then I'll go."

"Fine," she said. "I'll come back in a few hours and let you know everything's kosher, okay?"

"Sure. I'll try to figure a way to get this thing into the water."

"The water?" Nicholas called, looking vaguely curious. "You can still fly that thing?"

"If I can get her to the water, I might be able to float her out," Jim said. He heaved a sigh and scrubbed at the back of his neck. "But it'll take a hell of a miracle."

Sophie took a step toward him, but he could tell from the way her eyes kept flickering to Nicholas that she was eager to move on and find her mom. He couldn't blame her. "Thanks, Jim," she said. "I'll see if my mom can't help. That is, if she's . . ." She stopped and bit her lip.

If she's alive? Jim wondered how she would have ended that thought. He shrugged. "Go on. I'll wait till dark."

"Thanks," she said. Their eyes met and held briefly, and Jim nodded. The look in her eyes as she turned away was fierce; he reckoned that if her mother was on Skin Island, Sophie would find her. She had a determination about her that wore him down, made him weary just to watch. Had she been this steely when they were kids? She seemed so much older now, in more than just her looks. He thought of all that had befallen them since those happy days, and how much it had altered them both.

Nicholas threw Jim a half salute, half wave, then took Sophie's hand and led her down the beach to where a small motorboat was anchored, out of Jim's sight until he took a few steps to his left. In minutes, they were speeding across the channel toward Skin Island, and Jim was left alone beneath the palms with his broken plane and a nagging feeling that something wasn't quite right.

FIVE
SOPHIE

She couldn't have said why she trusted him, and she wasn't entirely certain that she did, but for now Nicholas was her only guide and she had no choice but to follow him. After he anchored the boat in a small inlet and tied it to an overhanging pine, he led her up a wooded slope and into a grove of low-growing, heavy-leafed trees. Sunlight leaked through the canopy to dapple the sandy earth and Nicholas's skin. He walked slightly ahead of her, but kept glancing back every few moments, as if she might evaporate.

"Who are you?" she asked after several minutes of trekking in silence, listening only to the crunch of sand and leaves under their shoes and the fading rush and roar of the ocean. "I mean, I know your name—but what are you doing here? You seem young to be a doctor or scientist."

"Do I?" He held up a branch for her to pass underneath it. "Do you know *anything* about Skin Island?"

"Not much," she admitted, then added, "Well, nothing at all, really."

He nodded distractedly, letting go of the branch. It whacked her head from behind.

"Ouch! Hey!"

Nicholas stared at her as if seeing right through her, then he blinked and the look was gone, replaced by a sheepish smile. "Oh. Sorry."

He started forward again, but she caught his arm and held it tight. "Please," she said. "Just give me a straight answer. My mother, Moira Crue—where is she and *how* is she? She sent me a message, saying there was an emergency and that—"

He covered her hand with his. "Sophie. Sophie Crue. Everything is *fine*. Just relax. You're jumpier than a fish on a string."

She frowned and pulled her hand away. "Look. It's been a *really* long day for me, okay? I don't know who you are or what your connection to this place is, but I want you to tell me straight out—have you or anyone else harmed my mom? Because I *swear*—"

"Dr. Crue is waiting for you," he interrupted, and the smile came off his face. "She's fine. No one's hurt her. Now come *on*."

"Then why would she—"

He rounded on her, his vague demeanor suddenly sharpening into something intense and wild. His eyes were brown, not amber brown like Jim's, but gray brown, almost colorless, and oddly flat, as though someone had forgotten to add the flecks of green and black that should have been there. She was hypnotized by his gaze and did not move.

As if realizing his stare was unnerving her, he relaxed and gave her a shy smile, twisting his hands together. "You're very pretty," he said. "Prettier than I expected. Sorry, I'm not good with . . . with all the questions. We don't often get visitors, you know."

He stepped back, shrugging his shoulders apologetically. "You could say I'm not really a *people* person."

Slightly bewildered, Sophie brushed at her hair and watched him from beneath a furrowed brow. "It's okay," she said hesitantly. *He talks as if he's always been on this island.* If he had, she could understand his . . . eccentricities. "Just let's hurry, all right? I want to see her, to see for myself that she's okay."

He nodded crisply and charged on at a faster pace. Sophie hurried to keep up, but her mind was already miles ahead. If her mother was truly fine, as Nicholas insisted—why the message? What could her "emergency" possibly be that she would suddenly invite Sophie to the one place that had always been forbidden to her? It was true Sophie had always wanted to see Skin Island—but not under circumstances like this. Not because her mother was ill or dying. But was she? *Just what is going on here?*

She wondered what Skin Island had to hide, and what her mother had to do with it. For some reason, the usual explanation about medical research and Alzheimer's didn't seem to be measuring up to the level of dread Jim and the other pilots had about this place. She stuck close to Nicholas, weaving in and out of tall, swaying stalks of bamboo.

"How much further?" Sophie asked.

"Not far."

They came across a narrow path made of cracked pavement; at one time, it must have been smooth and flat, but now it looked like it was made of cobblestone, with grass shooting up between the cement plates. It led back toward the smaller island, winding through a grove of thick bamboo, and forward to, she hoped, her mother. She studied Nicholas as she followed him through the tall bamboo stalks. His hands were sunk deep into his pockets, and his chin maintained a perpetual upward tilt, so that he seemed always to be looking down on the world. He walked with the confidence of one well acquainted with his surroundings, and she wondered what his story was, why he was on this island—why he was *allowed* on the island when she was not.

"How long have you been here?" she asked softly.

He didn't turn or slow, but his head swiveled to the left, revealing the curve of his jaw and a hint of dark eyelash. "Too long," he said sepulchrally, then added in a brighter tone, "But not for much longer."

"Does your mom or dad work for Corpus too?"

He turned and walked backward, surveying her with, oddly, disdain. "No. Not exactly." He spun around, and a dozen more questions crowded her brain but she held them back. She wasn't here to get entangled in the affairs of some Corpus kid, however mystifying he was. Maybe he was older than he looked, and worked for them in some capacity. Maybe he was an intern. *Maybe it's none of my business, and anyway, we've been walking for ages. Shouldn't we have gotten somewhere by now?*

And at that moment, Nicholas stopped at a bend in the road, where the trees and bamboo opened to a sudden rocky cliff fringed with tall grass. "There it is," he said. "Halcyon Cove."

"Halcyon Cove?" She swatted at a cloud of gnats that hovered in front of her face and stared around him and across the shallow bay below, which glittered in a thousand shades of gold. The sun, just a hand's breadth above the horizon, burned red behind a cluster of buildings on the cliff opposite. They were sharp silhouettes against the sunset, black and harsh, the red light behind them making them look as if they were on fire.

"It was once a resort," Nicholas said. She glanced at him and saw that he was gazing at the buildings with smoldering intensity, as if they had wronged him in some unforgivable way. "But there's nothing of that left now except a bunch of buildings."

"My mom's over there?" She looked back at the buildings and had to hold a hand over her eyes to shield them from the sun's last rays.

He nodded. "Let's go. But . . . stay quiet. We might see people now, and if we do, it's best if they don't know you're here."

"Why?" Her heart clenched. "Did *they* do something to my mom?" She still wasn't sure who *they* were; she had a vague idea of white coated doctors like her mother, but after hearing the pilots' stories, she now imagined them holding assault rifles. "Nicholas, what do they do on this island? My mom's researching a cure for Alzheimer's, right?"

Nicholas studied her sidelong, his dark hair whipping around his face in the strong ocean wind. "Do you want to find out?" he asked.

Yes. "I want to find my mom." But she felt a tug of desire—desire to unmask the secrets that had been kept from her all her life. It went deeper than mere curiosity. Over the years, Skin Island and her mother had grown into a single amorphous entity. She felt that if she discovered one, she discovered the other.

Sophie stood on the bluff and stared at the place that had stolen her mother from her with the wind pulling greedily at her hair, as if trying to lure her over the cliff and to her death on the rocks below. She felt a sudden swelling of determination in her chest, a hardening of resolve. When she licked her lips, they tasted like the sea. She felt as if the island were laying a challenge before her: *If you can steal my secrets, you can have her back.*

She remembered something her dad had said to her, not long ago, when she'd first announced her plan to follow in her mother's footsteps: "She had her chance to be there for you, Sophie, and she gave it up. She chose her work. All these gifts, these lavish vacations"—he referenced the expensive dolls and toys her mother used to send her, which turned into electronics and cash cards as she grew older, the red Volkswagen on her sixteenth birthday, their trips together to Switzerland or Australia when her mother had vacation every few years—"they're just her way of trying make up for the time she chose not to spend with you. Why can't you see it?"

"You talk as if she's bribing me," Sophie had retorted, furious. "She's my mom! If you want to hate her, that's your problem—but why do you insist that I hate her too?"

"I don't want you to hate her," he said with a sigh. "I just want you to let her go."

But it was something Sophie could not do. Would not do. She loved her father, but when he said things like that, she hated him. As far as she was concerned, the day he dragged her across the ocean and forced her to restart her life, he lost all his right to interfere in her relationship with her mom. *We could have stayed on Guam at least. Or I could have had a choice.* Who knows? If she'd gone with her mom instead back when she was seven, she might have grown up with this Nicholas, maybe stayed friends with Jim. This Skin Island wouldn't be a strange, menacing place that filled her with anxiety—it would be home.

Despite the secrets it kept from her, from the moment she'd set foot on Skin Island, Sophie had been haunted with an inexplicable sense of familiarity, a kind of kinship with the palms and the sand and the sea. It had been calling to her for years and at last, she'd answered. "Take me to her," said Sophie.

Nicholas smiled.

SIX

JIM

Jim stood and stared perplexedly from the plane to the run-way to the beach. *If I could just get it to the edge of the concrete, it should slide down the beach. . . .*

He pushed. He pulled. He cursed. He slapped the mos-quitoes that hovered above his bare skin and snuck in a bite whenever he stood still. The plane, which had always felt light as a whisper in his hands when he was lost in the clouds, now felt as if it were weighted with a dozen tons of cement. He took the wheels off to see if there was some way to make use of them, but they couldn't have been in worse shape if he'd shot them with a machine gun. In frustration, he chucked the bolts and the rubber wheels as hard as he could into the ocean. Then he realized the material of the wheels might be useful for patches if he ran out of duct tape, and he had to strip down and dive into the water to find them again. When he emerged, dripping and still minus one wheel, he was ready to give up. He halfheartedly pulled on his jeans, then collapsed into the sand with one arm flung over his face to block out the sun.

"Damn, damn, *damn*." He propped himself on his elbows and stared across the channel to Skin Island. It had been over an hour, and he'd seen no sign of Sophie—or anyone else, for that matter.

I shouldn't have come here. But it seemed to be an all-too-familiar pattern for Jim: plunging into situations before he considered the consequences. There was the time he lost every penny of his once-substantial savings when he bet on his friend Manny to win the island's annual dragon boat race, and the time he and his friend Kong thought it would be a *great* idea to go cliff diving in the middle of the night, and Kong busted his arm and collarbone on the rocks and Jim had to jump in after him. Then the time he decided to go surfing just as a typhoon was sweeping in, and nearly drowned before his dad rescued him in their neighbor's canoe. In fact, now that he looked back, he realized his life was a study in "it seemed like a great idea at the time," going all the way back to the misadventures he dragged Sophie into when they were barely old enough to spell their names. Flying to Skin Island, however, could well be the worst of his great ideas yet.

But there wasn't any point in lying around feeling sorry for himself. He rolled onto his feet and trudged up the beach, carrying the wheel he'd managed to recover. Then he stood on the runway and stared for a long time at his plane, thinking.

He finally concocted a plan that he was fairly certain wouldn't work, but he knew he had to try. He dragged as many fallen palm trunks as he could onto the pavement, which amounted to three, since the last two he found were too heavy for him to carry. He laid them in front of the plane and then pushed the Cessna with all his strength. It crunched and scraped in protest, but finally caught on the first log and started, slowly, to roll forward. He almost thought he'd figured it out, but then the warped wheel chassis caught on the log and he had to wrangle with it for a half hour before it finally came off and he could roll the plane forward. It moved fairly easily over the last two logs, and he was feeling pretty good about himself, but then it slipped away from him. The logs rolled once, twice, but not fast enough, and the plane scraped nose first into the concrete. Hissing through his teeth, Jim raced to the front of the plane and twisted the propeller so it didn't get bent or snapped by the impact. If he lost the propeller, there'd be no hope at all. All the while, a pair of cormorants hopped a safe distance away, watching him with their heads cocked, and he could have sworn that their throaty cries were laughter at his efforts.

Confident his rolling-log method would at least get the plane into the water, he set about patching the holes on the undersides of the floats. He ripped open the rolls of duct tape and set to work, moving quickly to make the most of what daylight was left.

Once the holes were patched and all six rolls of tape had been used up, he started the entire process over again, dragging the logs around to the front of the plane and, more carefully this time, rolling the Cessna over them. His back and legs and arms all ached to the point of collapse, and he was drenched with sweat that stung his eyes and his chapped lips, but he kept going. Whenever he was tempted to take a break, he thought of old Nandu and his tale of guards with assault rifles, which was enough to spur him on, to pull on hidden reserves of strength he never knew he'd had. If he and Sophie needed a quick getaway, he would be sure they had one.

It was well after dark when he finally got the plane to the edge of the runway, facing a downhill slope to the sea. He collapsed onto the concrete, his back against the dented fuselage, and almost blacked out from exhaustion. The moon was nearly full and poured silver beams over the water; glimmering rivulets of moonlight rippled over the waves to stain the sand and Jim's skin pale blue.

Jim stared off to his left, across the channel—now at high tide—at Skin Island. The sky above was dark, but the mountains were darker still, black on deep blue, a vacuum that sucked in the light of the moon and stars. It had sucked Sophie in and held her still. She should have been back by now.

He'd ignored the warnings of the other pilots and his own sense in coming here. He hadn't even told his dad where he was going. Not that he would have expected Steve Julien to remember or even care where his only son was after he woke from his afternoon alcohol stupor, though he might notice something was wrong when Jim wasn't there to toss their TV dinners into the microwave. However unappetizing the frozen meals usually were, Jim wished he had one now—he was almost as hungry as he was tired.

"I've got to get out of here," Jim said aloud, his eyes fastened on the moon. The moon stared back, indifferent and cold. Jim sighed and rubbed his thumb at the corner of his eye, where a grain of sand had gotten trapped in his eyelash.

"Where are you, Sophie Crue?" Jim muttered. Maybe he

should have taken her offer of payment. The repairs to the plane would be costly, worth well more than what he'd have charged the average tourist for a trip like this. If he couldn't fly the plane properly, he couldn't make any income. Without income, he couldn't fix the plane. It was a vicious trap with no easy way out that he could see. It was highly unlikely that he could get insurance to cover anything, not when all the evidence pointed toward Jim as being the primary cause of the crash landing.

But that was the thing—he was *certain* that the landing had been smooth. The landing gear had been perfectly sound when they left Guam. The conditions had been ideal. There was no violent crosswind, no drastically uneven ground. But the way all four tires had blown at once . . .

Jim stood and walked back up the runway, past where he'd gathered all the pieces that had been torn away, to the spot where the plane had first touched down. Though it was dark, the concrete reflected the moonlight enough that he could see the cracks and stones on its surface. There were a few pebbles, but nothing nearly big enough to have caused that much damage. He combed the pavement, stooping at times to run his hand over a crack to see if it might account for the wreck.

Then he found it: two long, thin bamboo planks with nails driven through them, laid horizontally across the runway, the wood blending in with the concrete so it was nearly impossible to see.

The skin on his arms and shoulders prickled with goose bumps. This was no accident. Someone had meant for their plane to stay grounded—but who? Had the Corpus guards laid this out after Nandu's trip, to deter any future unwanted visitors? He studied the wood that held the nails in place. How long ago had Nandu been here? Six months? A year? The wood wasn't weathered or dirty, as it should be after a year of exposure. From what he could tell, it had been put down recently. Was it there to cripple just any planes—or whatever plane was supposed to bring Sophie to the island? If someone had discovered that Sophie's mom wrote to her, and wanted to prevent her from coming, wouldn't it have been easier to stop her *before* she reached the island? Or to just wait with guns ready for her to arrive? Why go to this length?

He swore and went back to the plane. The discovery had fueled his frustration and gave him the extra spurt of energy to push the plane down the beach, though it didn't slide as smoothly as he'd hoped and he had to keep using the logs to roll it along. Once he was up to his knees in the shallows, the floats finally took over, and all he had to do was tether the plane. He used the cord, looping it through the floats, and tied it around a bent palm that dipped low over the water. The plane bobbed on the surf, glinting in the moonlight. Jim pushed it as far out as he could so the waves wouldn't toss it onto the shore.

I'll give her a few more hours. Maybe she got held up.

He climbed wearily into the cockpit and settled into the cracked yellow leather of the seat, and in moments, the gentle roll of the waves rocked him into sleep.

SEVEN
SOPHIE

Sophie and Nicholas crept through a patch of spiky, palm-like plants, keeping low to the ground. Fifty yards ahead of them, across a swath of open grass, rose a two-story building with four long wings, crouched like a giant spider on the top of the high bluff. The windows all opened onto balconies drenched in morning glory vines, and Sophie remembered what Nicholas had told her about Skin Island's former life as a secluded resort. This building must have once been a hotel. Several windows glowed with warm yellow light, and intermittent floodlights lit the grass around the building. She didn't see anyone inside, but it looked as though all the windows had blinds on them, and some were even boarded up. Off to her left and down a narrow seashell path huddled a series of smaller buildings, and beyond those, she could just barely make out a line of tall, tile-roofed villas that marched away to the east. Faint starlight hung over the scene, staining the leaves around Sophie faint silver.

"Stay down," Nicholas whispered. "Guards are going by."

A pair of men in dark uniforms wandered by, rifles slung over their shoulders and caps pulled low over their eyes. They chatted in soft tones, their conversation lost to Sophie though she was only yards away. The foliage around her provided more than enough cover, especially in the dark, but she still shrank away from their approach. Her knee came down on a stick, and it snapped in half. The guards paused, glanced around, then continued on. They rounded the building and were out of sight.

"Why are we hiding?" she asked.

"They don't know you're here," he said.

"*Obviously.*"

"You're not supposed to be here."

"Why? What are they hiding?"

Now he looked her squarely in the eye, all emotion drained from his face. "Me."

Before she could ask what *that* meant, he jumped up and sprinted across the lawn, then pressed himself flat against the building. He looked right and left, then waved for her to join him. Sophie drew a deep breath, went into a runner's stance, and rocketed out of the bushes. She covered the stretch in a quick sprint. She reached the wall and leaned against it, startling several sphinx moths that had been crawling across the plaster.

"Now what?" she asked, her heart hammering as if she'd sprinted a mile instead of a mere fifty yards. "And what do you mean, they're hiding *you*?"

"Well," he said, "me and others like me. *Well.* Not really like *me*—I'm one of a kind." He smiled.

"There are more of you?"

He began inching along the wall, toward a metal, windowless door.

"Nicholas. Were you . . . *born* on this island?"

"In here," he said, opening the door.

"What? All this security and they just leave the door unlocked?"

"I jammed it open earlier. Now come on."

She followed him inside, and he softly shut the door behind her, then flicked the lock. "There," he said. "They'll never know."

"You've done this before," she commented, and again he flashed her a bright grin. She had to admit, this Nicholas had her intrigued with his sneaking around, his secrets, his infectious smile.

They stood in a narrow alcove that opened into a lit hallway. The air here was as moist and warm as it was outside; if the building had air-conditioning, it certainly wasn't on. The floor was apricot-colored tile laid in a swirling mosaic, and pale blue wallpaper patterned with seashells lined the walls. It immediately reminded Sophie of the condos her dad and stepmom rented each summer on the Florida gulf coast, all pastels and shells and beach tones. And yet there was a strong chemical scent to the air—formaldehyde and rubbing alcohol and latex. It smelled like her tenth-grade biology class, so much so that she almost expected hunchbacked Mrs. Forbes with her rubbery blue gloves and ancient bifocals to come limping around the corner, demanding to know why Sophie hadn't finished dissecting her frog yet.

"Where's my mom?" Sophie hissed.

"This way." He peered around the corner, then waved for her to follow as he slipped down the hallway.

Clam-shaped wall lamps lit their path. Sophie walked on the balls of her feet; the tile seemed to amplify her footsteps. She saw no one except Nicholas ahead of her. They passed door after door, most of them windowless with faded brass numbers tacked on them. 241, 242, 243 . . . Definitely an old hotel, then. It seemed like an odd place to put a research lab.

"Where are we going?" Sophie asked. Her nerves began to twist into knots. What if he wasn't taking her to her mother at all? What if this was some kind of trap?

"Don't worry," he whispered, without looking back. "I'll take care of you, Sophie Crue."

She had no reason to trust this Nicholas. For all she knew, he was the one who'd hurt her mother. Sophie began to slow a little, letting him put distance between them. When he turned to glance back, she waved and gave him a little smile, letting him know she was still following. When he turned back around, the smile dropped from her lips and she began looking for a way to lose him. They seemed to be working their way outward from the center hub of the building; from what she'd seen outside, the hotel's four wings connected in a central atrium. Nicholas was leading her away from that atrium, toward the end of the wing.

They passed a door that was slightly cracked. Sophie slowed and slipped her hand through the slit, pushing the door wide enough for her to peek through. The room was dark, but light spilled in from the hallway and illuminated a bed with a figure sleeping on it. A girl. She looked to be Sophie's own age, with a head of wild brown curls and a riot of freckles on her face. Sophie stared, her thoughts a jumble of questions and bewilderment.

Suddenly a hand grabbed her arm and yanked her away, and she had to bite her tongue to keep from squealing. Nicholas pressed a finger to his lips as he silently shut the door. "Do you *want* to get yourself shot?" he asked.

She turned her head to look him in the eye. "I want to see my mother. *Now.* Let go of me."

"All right! All right!" He released her and stepped back.

"What's your game?" she asked. "What are you after?"

"I'm trying to help you. Why won't you let me?"

"What did they do to you? And that girl in there—are you test subjects or something?"

"Or something. Do you want to see your mom or not?"

Sophie tried to read him, to get some idea of what he was and what he wasn't telling her. He made her head spin, with his constant verbal dodging, his hovering presence, his kinetic buzz. He reminded her of a racehorse at the gate, all nerves and energy and impatience, forced to walk when he wanted to burst into a run. His fingers constantly moved, tapping and twisting. Was he a druggie? Hyperactive? On some kind of medication? Maybe Skin Island was a rehab center, some kind of top secret therapeutic retreat for disturbed kids. But then, why the secrecy?

She finally nodded, and he rolled his eyes and went on. But wherever he was leading her, she never found out, because as soon as she saw an alcove that opened to an upward staircase, she darted into it and raced up, two steps at a time. She didn't pause to look back to see if he was following her. When she reached the top, she found a hallway identical to the one below, and cut right toward the center of the building.

There was still no sign of anyone. Maybe all these rooms were filled with sleeping people like the curly-haired girl. She ran as softly as she could, and when she reached the wide doorway opening to the atrium, she glanced back and saw Nicholas hurrying after her.

She raced around the wide balcony, which opened to a lobby below her, and above her stretched a dome of glass that gleamed silver white in the moonlight. There were few lights in the atrium, and no people. Three hallways plus the one she'd just come down branched away, two on her left and one on her right. She dashed toward the right one, then at the last minute whirled and climbed over the balcony, balancing on the outer ledge and staring down at the floor one story below. She was hovering just above a long marble receptionist counter.

Sophie heard Nicholas's footsteps above her, and she didn't hesitate, but let go of the balcony railing and dropped onto the desk, bending her knees and landing with surprising silence. Hazarding a look up, she saw Nicholas turn into the upper hallway; he hadn't noticed her go over the balcony. *Good.*

Sophie jumped to the floor and crouched behind the counter. Above her on the wall, a colorful mosaic depicted a mermaid on a beach. Across the lobby, double glass doors led outside, and a scattering of old wicker furniture occupied the floor space between.

The four lower hallways were all lit brightly. She ignored

the one she and Nicholas had entered first, and instead made her way around the perimeter of the room until she reached the next one.

I just want to have a look on my own. The island wasn't that big. She could find her mother herself, and if Nicholas really *was* just trying to help, she could make amends for running off later. Right now, she had only one goal: to find Moira Crue. If she had to scour every room in every building to find her, she'd do it.

She opened the first door she came to. It was a narrow closet, filled with chemicals, linens, and old microscopes. *So, it's a lab after all.*

The next room held four octagonal consoles set in the middle of the floor, with round gray towers rising out of them, as tall as she was. She walked around them curiously, unable to make sense of the numbers and letters stenciled on the gray exteriors. When she spotted a small lever on the side of one, she flipped it, and jumped back when the sides of the tower slid downward into the consoles, exposing an inner blue light and cold fog that rolled out and onto the floor. Inside was a series of glass shelves filled with small holes, and in the holes, tiny, apparently empty glass vials were suspended. An automatic arm lifted out of the console, a magnifying glass held in its grasp, and it lined up with one of the vials. Sophie leaned forward and peered through it to see an almost imperceptibly tiny sliver of metal floating in the vial in some sort of viscous substance. For some reason, it left her with a chill in her spine, and she hurriedly flipped the lever; the console closed itself, hiding the shelves and the fog and the little vials.

As she shut the door to the strange room, she heard voices. Her heart leaped into her throat, and Nicholas's voice haunted her mind: *Do you want to get yourself shot?*

She ducked back into supply closet and kept the door cracked just a hair—and she barely made it in time. A woman and a man strode past, voices low in conversation, clipboards cradled in their arms. The man was dressed in slacks and a white collared shirt; the woman wore a long white lab coat.

"Well, in my opinion, it's too soon," the woman was saying with a heavy French accent. "We need another four years at least."

"You know how it is, Laurent. We don't get opinions; we get orders."

"If it goes sour, it's not my fault."

"If it goes sour, it won't matter. This place has been balancing between success and failure for years. All it'll take is one mistake."

Sophie held her breath until they'd gone past, and waited another moment for their voices to fade before she crept out of the closet and tiptoed down the hall. Her senses were on high alert, listening and watching in case anyone else appeared.

She pressed her ear to the next door and heard no sound inside except the humming of a computer. Taking extra precaution after nearly being seen by the doctors, she peeked under the door to be certain the light was off. She was just about to turn the handle when she heard footsteps approaching from the atrium. Heart stalling, Sophie whipped open the door and slipped into the room, shutting the door softly behind her. Her muscles ached both from the crash landing and from the nerveracking business of sneaking around.

The room was lit with a soft blue glow, which came from the screen of the computer set against the far wall. She blinked as her eyes adjusted to the dim interior, and gradually made out a hospital gurney that stood in the center of the room. Several others were pushed against the wall to her right, but unlike them, the one in the middle held an occupant. She pressed a hand to her mouth and went stone still; if the person was awake, there was no way they wouldn't see her.

But the person didn't speak or even move. Sophie slowly crept across the room; if the person coming down the hallway opened the door, she'd be spotted immediately. She looked around frantically, but there weren't many places to hide except—*but it's so obvious*. Still, she was running out of time and options. The footsteps were getting closer. They were slowing down. She knew that in moments, the handle of the door would turn and she'd be caught.

Sophie ran to the gurney, intending to hide beneath it. As she did, she caught a glimpse of the sleeping figure's face in the pale blue light from the computer.

A cold chill ran down Sophie's spine.

She froze, her eyes locked on the face.

No. That's impossible.

Behind her, the door swung open and light from the corridor burst into the room and washed over the sleeping girl. Sophie's muscles seized, urging her to turn around, to run, to hide—but she couldn't move. Couldn't look away. Couldn't *understand* . . .

The girl on the gurney, her eyes shut and her skin pale and her breath so soft it was nearly imperceptible, was all too familiar to Sophie.

Because she was looking at herself.

Then she felt a shattering pain on the back of her head and she dropped into deep and all-consuming darkness.

EIGHT
JIM

Jim woke with a start, launching himself out of the seat only to slam his head into the roof of the cockpit. Sucking in a breath, he fumbled with the door. It swung open, and, caught off guard by a sudden pitch of the plane, he tumbled out of the cockpit and fell straight into the sea, where he swallowed a salty mouthful of water and startled a school of bright yellow fish.

Choking and now fully shocked to wakefulness, Jim dragged himself onto the beach and sat in the sand, blinking through the dripping hair that had fallen over his face. He shook his hair and coughed out seawater, then winced up at the sky. It was still dark, but now the moon was behind him, so he figured it was still a few hours until dawn. His back was stiff and sore, and his arms burned from hauling the logs and the plane around. The Cessna rocked on the waves, and a fallen coconut bobbed against one of the floats, clunking with each roll of the surf.

He climbed to his feet and looked around. There was no sign of Sophie or Nicholas or anyone at all.

Jim wandered up the beach and found his shirt where he'd left it the day before after diving in after the tires. He shook out the sand and pulled it over his head, then found his boots. His socks were damp, so he pulled the boots on without them. Then he stood staring across the channel. The tide was on its way out, slowly and reluctantly pulling away from the islands.

"Where are you?" Jim muttered, scanning the trees on the opposite island.

He swore and scrubbed at his hair, kicked the sand, started toward the plane, then turned around and came back. *This isn't your problem*, he told himself.

He could just go. He hadn't made any promises to Sophie Crue. Sure, they'd been friends once and all that, but he'd already gone out of his way to help her reach the island, had done as much as could be expected. *She probably found her mom, and they're catching up over coffee. Safe and sound.* He *told* her he wouldn't stay past nightfall. She knew he wasn't going to wait around. Maybe she thought he was already gone. Maybe he was waiting for someone who would never come. *She could have at least come back and said goodbye. For old times' sake.*

This was what he got for ignoring his own inner voice of alarm. He'd known better the moment he heard the words "Skin Island." He'd known things would get messy.

Jim stormed around the beach for a bit longer, deliberating and justifying, somehow always finding himself feeling guilty. But for what? He'd done what he said he would do and more—he ought to have gone home hours ago. *I don't owe her anything. In fact, it's the other way around.* He looked at his wrecked plane, wincing as the dollar signs began to pile up in the back of his mind.

"Hey!" he yelled across the channel. "That's it! I'm going, you hear? I'm counting to ten and then I'm outta here!"

Jim stalked back to the plane. He kicked off his boots, knotted the laces together, and slung them over his shoulders so he could wade out to it. Once he was back in the cockpit he tried the engine; it took a while, but it finally cranked. He was skipping nearly every point on his preflight checklist, but with the landing gear gone, it seemed to hardly matter. Already his mind ran through landing scenarios, trying to plan the best beach to put down at. Then he'd have to find a way to haul it to a mechanic. And *then* he'd have to find a way to pay the mechanic.

But try as he might to keep his mind occupied with these problems, his thoughts kept coming back to Sophie Crue. The initial surprise when he'd first realized who she was. Her constant nervous movement in the plane, toying with the instruments and with his mom's beads. And then that Nicholas, his hands on Sophie's, drawing her away, his eyes devouring her like a circling shark.

"Damn," Jim whispered, letting his head fall against the seat. He stared at the beads swinging from the ceiling. They glowed white, as if lit from within, and he could almost hear his mother's voice singing the poem: *Taya' mina'lak sin hinemhum, taya' tatauau sin anining . . .* She was the only American he'd ever known who could sit with the Chamorro women as they wove hats to sell to the tourists, and who could sing and compose verses out of thin air. She'd taken to Guam more quickly and deeply than Jim or his father ever had, but that hadn't stopped her from running away to the U.S. with the first stranger who gave her a second look.

Jim shut his eyes, let out a deep sigh, and then slipped out of the plane for the second time. He waded ashore, his boots over his shoulder, and walked through the shallows until he reached the point where the channel was narrowest. He twisted his torso back and forth, loosening his sore muscles as best he could, then plunged into the water.

The tide was low, but not so low that the current flowing between the islands was gone. It pulled at him, drawing him ever east, and he struggled with all his strength against it. The water had been rising instead of falling; the tide was coming in, not out, as he'd assumed. After over a decade of living on an island, he had the tide schedule fairly well memorized. It must have been later in the morning than he had thought. It took the last of his strength to make it to the opposite shore, and when he reached it, he collapsed in the sand and gasped for air, his body screaming with pain from the crash, hauling the logs and the plane, sleeping crunched up in the cockpit. *Should have gone home and left well enough alone.*

Well. It was too late now. He couldn't swim back, not until he'd rested and the tide had receded. Either he could sit here and wait or he could follow through on his harebrained plan of finding Sophie and making sure she was okay.

He rolled onto his back and groaned, then slowly rose to his feet. Water trickled down his face and his back and dripped from his hair. He had a nearly overwhelming thirst; what little water he'd brought with him he'd drunk the day before. To top that off, he was starving enough to catch a fish and eat it raw.

Maybe they'd have something to eat at the Corpus center. If he said he was with Sophie, maybe her mom could pull some strings, get him cleared, and just give him some food and a Coke and then they could all go their separate ways, no harm done.

He laughed aloud. *If only.* He doubted it would be as simple as that.

Jim pulled on his wet boots and began the trek across Skin Island.

When he reached the southern shore, dawn was already unfolding in the east, an origami masterpiece of scarlet and orange. The trees seemed kissed with fire, the edges of the leaves glowing with golden light. The beauty of the tropical sunrise was lost on Jim, who had seen it a thousand times already. His attention was divided between keeping a sharp eye on his surroundings and thinking of reasons why he should turn around and go home while he still had the chance.

He stood on a narrow beach at the foot of a high bluff, below the big hotel building that seemed to be the center of activity on Skin Island. He'd seen it on his approach, watched a few doctors and guards come and go. Then the bluff rose to hide it from sight, until he could only make out the roof from where he now stood. He climbed up the bluff, finding ample footholds where the water had eaten away the rock. The downside of this was that the rock was rough and left his hands scraped and bleeding. But he wasn't going to chance approaching the building from the north or east, through the trees, because he would be too easily spotted in the strengthening light.

When he reached the top of the bluff, he hauled himself

onto the grass and kept low; the hotel was about a football field's length away, and the space between was open except for the odd palm tree. Off to his right, on a grassy, flat patch of land, sat a dark helicopter. He recognized it as one of the only aircraft that ever left Guam for Skin Island.

He faced the double glass doors that led into the center of the building; they opened onto a covered veranda surrounded by hibiscus plants. A guard leaned on a sculpted column, smoking and reading a magazine. He didn't have a rifle, but Jim did see a handgun strapped to his side. Not very vigilant, but all the same, Jim couldn't just slip past him.

If Sophie was nearby, there was no sign of her. Maybe one of the other doors would be open, or a window. He could go around the side of the building, out of the guard's line of view, find another way in. Just as he was about to make a dash for cover, the doors opened and he froze. It was another guard; they must have been changing shifts. Jim took the opportunity to run across the edge of the bluff until the corner of the first wing came between him and the front doors. He waited ten seconds, then sprinted to the wall. The first three windows he passed were locked, and the first door. He started to go on, but suddenly the door swung open and he was sure he'd be seen. But he still flattened himself against the wall, by the hinged side of the door, so that as it opened it came between him and the person walking out. They shoved the door so wide that it nearly crushed him, and he had to suck in his breath to avoid being hit.

There was a tiny alcove to his right, where the building bent inward before branching out into the next wing. Jim slipped inside just as the person at the door emerged; it was a girl with a mass of curly brown hair, and she was followed by two other kids, both of them boys. They all looked to be sixteen or so, and were dressed in identical khakis and white polos, like a gospel choir.

"C'mon," said the girl. "Before they do the morning rounds."

"They'll go looking for us," said one of the boys, a ginger-haired, gangly fellow with a flashlight in his hand.

"Won't matter. We'll be clear across the island by then. Hurry, or we might lose him."

They walked right past Jim, but the morning was still dark enough that he was hidden by shadow.

"Think he's still hanging around?" asked the second boy. "What kind of idiot would come here?"

They're looking for me. The feeling of unease he'd had all night doubled. Had they seen his plane land? Had Sophie's mom sent them, or Sophie herself? He didn't think it would be on Sophie's behalf, to tell him she'd decided to stay on Skin Island and he could go home. They were taking too much care not to be seen by the guards; whatever their agenda was, it didn't seem to coincide with the doctors'.

And what were a bunch of teenagers doing here anyway? He knew the facility had to do with medical research or something like it. Were they patients? Test subjects?

The door was swinging shut. The trio was still in sight, heading away from the front of the building and toward the trees, but their backs were to Jim. He stepped out of the alcove and lunged at the door, managing to get the tips of his fingers on the handle before it shut. He glanced back, heart missing a beat, but they hadn't noticed him. Still, there was no time to relax in relief. He slipped into the building and softly shut the door. It locked behind him.

Well, now what? He couldn't very well wander up and down the halls, calling Sophie's name. At least it was still early enough that most everyone should be asleep, for another hour anyway. He hoped the three kids had been an exception, and that no one else on Skin Island was such an early riser. What if they made it to the airstrip and found his plane, but not him? Would they tell someone, launch a search? There were just too many variables, too much risk.

He did a harried and not very thorough search. The rooms here were all labs or storage, all of them empty and quiet, though the lights in the hall were still lit. He grew less cautious as time progressed, both because it seemed unlikely that there was anyone awake, and because he knew he was running out of time.

He reached the last door in the hall before it opened to the atrium, and told himself that if Sophie wasn't in it, then he'd leave. *I tried. That's good enough.*

He opened the door and found himself in a room lit with blue light, just bright enough to see the sleeping girl on the hospital bed. His heart stopped. *Sophie.*

He crossed the room in two strides and wrapped his hand around her wrist. Her pulse was very faint, but it was there. He breathed out in relief. For a moment, he'd thought she was dead, she lay so still.

"What did they do to you?" he murmured. He ran his fingers through her hair. "Sophie?"

She did not stir. There was a metal stand beside her, and on it hung a bag of clear liquid that pumped into her arm through a plastic tube. He looked around, frantic, as if there might be a nurse in the corner who could help him. But they were alone. He looked back at Sophie. She was hardly breathing. *I knew this was a bad idea. I knew it from the start.* Had she been hurt? Perhaps the IV was meant to help her—but if so, that meant someone here had to have been the one who hurt her. Nicholas? The scientists or the guards? He locked his hands on the back of his neck and stared from Sophie to the door in agitation, then made a snap decision.

He clamped his teeth together and pulled on the tube, and it snickered out of her arm. He felt ill, and his head spun—he had never been one for hospitals and needles. But he forced himself to stay steady as he scooped Sophie into his arms. She was astonishingly light, or else he was running on an extra surge of adrenaline. His heart beat so wildly that he was surprised she didn't feel it and wake up.

"I'm getting you out of here," he whispered. She was wearing a thin white hospital gown, and he could feel every curve of her body through it. Whatever drugs they'd given her, they must have been powerful. She seemed to be halfway into a coma.

Jim kicked open the door and burst into the hallway. Now his only ally was speed; there was no way he could sneak around with Sophie in his arms. If she would only wake up, she could walk and they might have a better chance, but even as he ran down the hallway she slept on, her head bouncing against his chest.

He went out the same door he'd come in by, though he had to pause to click the lock. Outside, it was full morning. The sky was blue, but the building still cast a long shadow over the bluff, giving them a modicum of cover should anyone glance their way. He couldn't run very well with her in his arms, but still he tried, and he made it to the cover of a wide patch of bamboo without being spotted.

"Hang in there, Crue," he whispered to Sophie. She groaned and flexed her fingers, and he waited to see if she'd open her eyes, but though her lashes fluttered they stayed sealed. "I'll get you out of here, I swear."

NINE
SOPHIE

Sophie wasn't entirely certain that she was awake; though she *felt* conscious, her eyes refused to open, as if her eyelids had been glued together. Light probed at them, red and white and painful. Her throat felt packed with cotton, and her tongue weighed like a brick. A strange sensation flooded her body, almost as if she were floating. Her head was heavy and immobile, but the rest of her felt light and airy as a dollop of whipped cream. Still, her body refused to obey her mental commands to move. It was as if someone had disconnected her brain, left a wire hanging loose somewhere. She was aware of herself but had no control.

Slowly, she realized there were people around her, talking in low tones. She wanted to call out, to ask for help, for a drink of water, but her tongue betrayed her and remained leaden.

". . . told Hashimoto to bring Lux upstairs. Where is she?"

"She has the morning off. Probably sleeping in."

A sigh from the first speaker. A woman, Sophie noted. Her thoughts were languid, struggling to keep up. "I'll speak with her later. Lucky we got here early. There's no time to waste, so let's get her upstairs and prep her for Andreyev."

It was like straining to understand a foreign language; every word took an extra moment to register in Sophie's brain. She vaguely remembered something happening, something before she blacked out . . . a room, a blue light, someone sleeping, someone impossible . . .

She felt movement. She was lying on a stretcher, and it was being rolled across uneven floor. Her body vibrated with every motion. She strained to open her eyes, but they stayed soldered shut. Light and shadow rolled over her. Low in her throat, she managed the smallest groan.

The stretcher came to an abrupt stop. "Did you hear that?" the woman asked. "I thought she —"

"She's been off the anesthestic for half an hour." The second voice was male, but high and a bit nasally.

"They don't usually wake this fast. Hand me the xenon. If she wakes up now we're all screwed—it's too soon."

Something plastic was pressed to Sophie's face, and she heard a faint hiss. *Oxygen mask*, she thought. She tried to groan again, but her voice seemed to have evaporated completely.

They were moving once more, and then she heard a metallic *ding*. The nature of the movement changed; the stretcher was still, but they were going up, in an elevator probably. It *dinged* again and then she was rolling.

The voices faded in and out; her consciousness was

flickering like a dying lightbulb. Sounds morphed into low, meaningless bursts of noise, like a tape put on slow motion.

". . . snuck out again," the man was murmuring. "Around dawn, they think."

"Let them go. It isn't as if they're going to actually *go* anywhere. They are teenagers and they will roam."

"Well. Not *exactly* teenagers, Moira."

Moira. Sophie's mind had been sinking deeper into a sea of mud, but at that name she lunged upward, grabbing hold of it like a lifeline. *Mom!*

"They're not harming anything, and anyway, maybe it's better they're out of the way when Strauss gets here. You know they like to cause trouble." It was her mother's voice. Why hadn't she noticed it before? *Mom, it's me! I'm here—why can't you see me?* She wanted to scream. It didn't make sense! Her mother was *right there*, so why wasn't she trying to help Sophie? Why—*oh.* The memory finally fell into place, the lost pieces of a jigsaw puzzle snapped together to form a complete picture. *The girl in the bed, the one who looked like me.* And not just like Sophie—*identical* to Sophie. Understanding flooded her thoughts. *They think I'm her. But why? How?* Just when she thought she'd figured it out, more questions followed. Where was the other Sophie? Surely when they saw that there were two of her, they'd realized something was up. Or were there a hundred girls like her on this island? What were they? *Why* were they? And her mother—Moira Crue sounded well and whole. She didn't seem to be dying or running for her life. *What is going on?*

"This had better work," said the man. "It's hard to believe

that two decades of research can come down to a single moment."

"We're ready for this."

"You say it with more confidence than I have."

"What can I say, Rogers? I'm an optimist."

"Corpus has been breathing down our neck for years. We only get one shot. This day will make or break us."

"Stop worrying. We need to keep our heads straight for this."

"I'm just saying. Hashimoto knows how important this is. She should have prepped Lux better. I mean, look at her." A finger brushed Sophie's shoulder, but she was so groggy she couldn't even flinch. "Is that a *bruise*? And here's another, on her cheek."

"It happens, when they're moved from one bed to another."

"Well, at least she had the decency to put a gown on her."

"Here we are," Moira said. "And look here. Everything's in place. Hashimoto isn't completely incompetent. She just forgot to bring Lux up. Still, I'm going to have a few words with her."

"Odd," the man muttered. "This IV looks used . . ."

Sophie heard a sudden crash, as if the door had been thrown open. Her mind was clouding over, and she fought to stay awake. Whatever gas they were feeding through the mask, it was working fast to shut down her brain.

"They're here!" a new voice shouted.

"Here? Strauss? *Now?*"

"Just landed."

"They're not supposed to arrive until nine!"

"Moira, it's eight thirty."

"What, already? Good Lord, don't just stand there! Laurent, stay with Lux. I'll go meet them."

No, Sophie thought. *Mom, come back, it's me, please see me, Mom!*

But she heard receding footsteps, then the door slammed shut, and she couldn't hold on to consciousness any longer.

TEN
JIM

He was growing more and more concerned for Sophie with every passing minute. She didn't wake; she didn't move. Several times he stopped to check for a pulse. Whatever they had done to her, he hoped it wasn't permanent. If he could just make it to the plane, he could get her to a hospital.

But that was the problem—getting to the plane. The island seemed twice as big as it had before. When he'd first lifted her, Sophie had felt light, but she grew heavier with every step he took. His physical exhaustion was catching up to him and had begun to wear on his mind as well, tempting him to stop, to give up, to leave her behind and save himself.

"No can do, compadre," he muttered. "We're both getting out of here."

A glinting dragonfly buzzed around his head, as if urging him to hurry, and a warm wind shivered through the bamboo around him; the leaves danced and cast shifting green-tinted light across Sophie's skin. She looked the opposite of everything Jim felt: peaceful, serene, even innocent. Her left arm was curled over her stomach, but the right one hung loose. He stopped and leaned against a tree so he could lift it and rest it on top of the other one; as he did, her fingers suddenly tightened on his.

He froze and stared intently at her face. "Sophie? Sophie, wake up. Please. Come on, kid, just open your eyes."

Her lashes fluttered, and his stomach tightened in anticipation, but she just sighed and seemed to sink deeper into her slumber.

Jim thought wildly of the old fairy tales, the ones where the sleeping princess would awaken only with a kiss. His eyes traveled inevitably to her lips, soft and pink. He shook his head. There was something . . . he couldn't place it exactly, but there was something too innocent about her. A kind of childlike purity to her repose that made the thought of kissing her seem vile. Which was strange, given that he'd fantasized at least five times about kissing her. But now, it just felt . . . wrong, somehow. She looked more like the Sophie he knew when he was seven than the one who was supposed to be seventeen, an odd mingling of child and woman.

He hurried on, though the thick bamboo made his going slow. It grew so close together that he felt stifled, almost as if he were underwater.

A few minutes later, he heard voices ahead, muffled and distant, but unmistakable. He dropped into a crouch, cradling Sophie to himself, and listened. *Those kids—the ones that went looking for me.* He'd almost forgotten about them. *Maybe Nicholas sent them to help*, he reasoned. *He knew I'd have trouble with the plane, so maybe Sophie convinced him to send them.*

But a part of him doubted it very much. If Sophie's mother trusted Nicholas enough to send him for her daughter, then surely Jim could trust him too. Yet he couldn't shake the feeling that there was something sinister moving beneath the surface, that Nicholas's sharp eyes hid purposes of his own.

He tried to tell if the voices were getting closer, but the trees and wind played with the sounds around him, twisting and morphing them. He'd thought they were ahead of him, but now they sounded as if they were off to his right, closer inland. He looked all around, flinching at every little noise. There wasn't much animal life on these islands, mostly just birds and insects, but as he listened even they began to sound more and more human.

Maybe the kids were only trying help, but still, he decided it would be best to avoid them.

The voices grew louder. Jim finally pinned down their direction—north, headed back from the airstrip, perhaps—and he hurried east, toward the center of the island, hoping they'd pass him by.

He was moving too slowly, encumbered by the girl in his arms. They were getting closer. If he was going to get away, he'd have to sacrifice either speed or silence. He went with silence, and began hurrying through the trees more quickly, his steps snapping branches and rattling the bamboo. Maybe he should have just ducked for cover, but it was too late now. If they'd heard him, they'd already be on his trail. He weaved through the tall green stalks and then burst out of the bamboo forest and onto higher ground, where the grass was as high as his waist and twisted and bristly pines rose out of the ground like bent old warriors. They didn't provide much cover, but he spotted a cluster of rocks at the crest of the slope, and he made for it.

The wind pushed at his back and slithered over the grass, which bent as if some giant invisible hand were running its palm over the hill. The grass hid the steepness of the incline, and he nearly lost his footing when it took a sharp upward ascent. Sophie jostled in his arms and made a sound halfway between a sigh and a groan.

He was nearly at the rocks when he chanced a backward look. He thought he could see someone moving in the bamboo, but it might have been a bird or the wind. Calling on the last of his energy, he broke into a run up the hill, his calves burning, and reached the rocks just as he heard a shout from the bottom. He spun and saw the three kids emerge from the bamboo, and he dove behind the rocks, unceremoniously dumping Sophie onto the ground. She moaned but lay still.

Jim gripped the rock with sweaty hands and watched the trio. The sun had finally risen over the trees to the east, its light washing over the hill like fire. But where his pursuers were, there was still shadow of the night, and he could not tell if they had spotted him or not.

He turned away and looked in the other direction. The land sloped downward into a narrow gulch before rising again into a green mountain supported by ribbonlike buttresses, their hollows purple shadows. There was no going back the way he'd come, so he scooped Sophie up and started down the gulch. The going was so steep that the grass couldn't grow there; it was bare dirt and loose rocks. He skidded and slid more than he walked, and it was all he could do to keep her in his arms. If he dropped her, she'd tumble and fall onto a bed of jumbled stones at the bottom of the gulch. *I won't drop her.* But his body protested every movement now, his muscles seizing and spasming mutinously.

I won't drop you.

He reached the bottom and stepped quickly but carefully from rock to rock, working his way ever north. If the trio had seen him, they would likely know where he was going and try to cut him off further along. Still, he had no choice. He couldn't go south; that only lead to the resort and now that he'd stolen Sophie back, they would know he was there and they would be looking for him. He felt like a fish in a net, slowly being drawn out of the water.

But he wouldn't give up, not yet.

The gulch emptied into a bowl-shaped meadow of flowers and golden grass. Halfway through it, he came upon a narrow, almost imperceptible path, likely left over from the resort's tourist days, some sort of nature trail. It led northeast, and he followed it.

Half a mile on, his legs gave out. He dropped to his knees and nearly dropped Sophie, but at the last minute managed to turn himself over so he fell onto his back with her on top of him. For a moment he lay there, gasping for air, his vision swirling with black spots. He was dehydrated, hungry, exhausted, and ready to give up.

Sophie stirred, her hand pawing vaguely at his chest. Her

eyes remained shut, but a long, high whimper slipped from her lips, a pitiful, animalistic sound. He winced and sat up, holding the back of her head with his hand.

"Sophie? Hey. Hey, look here. C'mon, just open your eyes."

"Over here!"

His head whipped up; it wasn't Sophie who'd spoken. She murmured wordlessly, but was still unconscious. Across the meadow, Jim saw them—and they saw him.

He was up and running before he even had a chance to wonder where he'd found the strength. Instead of carrying her in his arms, he had Sophie draped over his shoulder—not a comfortable position for either of them, but at least this way he could run a bit faster. Not faster than the ones pursuing them, however.

A quiet, exhausted voice in the back of his mind whispered, *You could just stop, you know. They don't have guns— they might be here to help you.*

But Jim's instincts told him otherwise. He actively ignored the fact that it had been his instincts, more often than not, that got him in trouble.

He pressed on, not bothering to turn from the path to hide. They were too close now. He was fairly certain he couldn't outrun them, either, but he was too stubborn to give up. *Trust all my bad points to come up at once,* he thought. *If things go wrong out here, I have only myself to blame.* But who was he kidding? *Things have gone about as wrong as they can go.*

Or maybe not.

The trail led directly into a steep ravine, its sides sheer rock faces to which only the most obdurate pines clung with spiderlike roots. An old rope bridge spanned the thirty-yard opening, and at the bottom of the ravine he could see a narrow but stony stream, about forty feet down. A fall at that height would more than likely break his neck.

He turned to see that he was trapped. The girl led the group, a thin smile slitting her face. Her curls bounced in the perpetual wind, giving her a Medusa-like quality.

"Hello," she said lightly. "I'm Mary. This is Jay"—she threw a thumb toward a boy with close-shaven brown hair, and then at the redhead—"and this is Wyatt."

"What do you want?" He took a step back, nearly stumbling when his foot came down on the edge of the cliff.

She scuffed a rock with her shoe. "Oh. You know. Just wanted to . . . chat."

He narrowed his eyes, glancing at Jay and Wyatt. They stared back with twin looks of amusement.

"Lovely," Jim said tonelessly. "But I really haven't got the time."

"The girl." Mary jerked her chin at Sophie. "What do you want with her?"

"Who, her?" He shrugged, then winced as the movement made Sophie's head knock against his back. "We're running away together. Gonna get married, buy a beach house, have a whole bunch of kids. So if you don't mind, I'm gonna go—preacher's waiting for us."

"Ha-ha." It was a statement, not a laugh, and unlike her friends, Mary didn't look the least bit amused. "We want to make sure you get a proper welcome."

He didn't like the sound of that. "Sweet of you. Really. But we're all good here, so just run on home, why don't you?"

"You should stay awhile. We *love* guests, don't we, boys?

But it's so hard to make new friends out here, in the middle of nowhere."

She was inching closer with every word, and Jim noticed each step. He felt behind him with his left foot, managing to get it onto the first rickety slat of the bridge.

"Next time, maybe," he said, maintaining a neutral evenness to his tone that might have won him a small fortune in a poker match. "I have a knack for finding myself in crap situations. I'm bound to turn up again."

He shifted his full weight onto the bridge. It swayed beneath him, but he kept his eyes fixed on Mary. She'd noticed the movement, and for a moment they locked gazes, each waiting for the other to make a move. Every muscle in Jim's body tensed, and she looked like a coiled cat about to spring at the moment the mouse twitched a whisker.

But it was Jay who made the first move, taking them both by surprise. "Get him!" he yelled.

Jim spun, nearly losing his hold on Sophie, and awkwardly crow hopped over the bridge, his feet moving faster than his mind, dancing over gaps where the slats had rotted away, his free hand clutching the rope rail while the other kept a desperate grip on his limp burden. The bridge shook and swayed like a dinghy at sea during a storm, and his stomach lurched with it.

They were coming after him, he knew. He could tell it from the way the bridge began to spasm beneath him. He heard a shocked cry and a snap of wood; one of the slats must have given way under them. With a vicious surge of satisfaction, he continued doggedly on. Had the bridge been only thirty yards across? It seemed to expand threefold, stretching an infinite length ahead. Sweat poured down his neck and trickled over his shoulder blades, as much from nerves as from the heat and exertion. He was surprised, from his dehydrated state, that he had anything left to sweat out.

At last, he reached the end of the bridge, but a long gap of open space was between him and solid ground. He glanced back; the trio was careening across the slats with wild looks in their eyes, but they were progressing no faster than he had. He turned back around, sucked in a deep swallow of salty air, and leaped.

He landed awkwardly, losing his grip on Sophie. She flew out of his arms and rolled across the ground to rest in a thicket of ferns.

There wasn't time to see if she was okay. He turned back to the bridge and began wrestling with the knots that held the rope in place around metal poles staked into the rock. The knots were practically congealed with time and wear, impossible to undo. So instead, he lifted a rock the size of his head and, with a grunt of effort, heaved it at the last few slats of wood. It crashed through them, widening the gap to an insurmountable distance, even if they took a running start. Any attempt to leap it, and they would drop into the ravine.

Mary froze, as did Jay and Wyatt behind her. Jim gripped the tops of the metal poles in either hand and flashed them a weary grin. "Oh, did I do that? Gosh, sorry. My dad always did say I had a knack for wrecking things." *Like his marriage.*

Mary glared at him, her curls snapping like vipers, her grip on the ropes so tight her knuckles were the color of paper. "There are other ways around, you know. We know every inch of this island. You can run, but we'll still catch you."

He tossed her a sarcastic salute. "Challenge accepted, sweetheart. I'm a pretty slippery guy."

Without waiting to hear her response, he gathered Sophie into his arms and charged off into the trees, moving with reckless abandon, not even bothering to steer himself. If he came across a bush, he bowled right through it. It was more from luck than skill that he avoided running headfirst into any trees.

At last, impossibly it seemed, he broke free of the tangle of palms and pines and shrubs and onto the shore. He could even see his plane, bobbing faithfully across the channel, waiting for him. His feet turned to lead; he churned a short distance down the beach, then fell to his knees. He crawled a few feet before his strength left him completely, and then he only barely managed to set Sophie down before he face-planted into the sand.

After a moment, when he finally couldn't hold his breath any longer, he rolled over and panted for air. His eyes were shut against the sun, and for a moment, he simply reveled in the fact that he was alive. And lying down. His body felt as though the bones had been sucked out of him, leaving him in a viscous state, like a puddle of jelly.

It seemed an eternity later, though in fact it was just a minute, that he opened his eyes and turned his head to look at Sophie.

Her eyes were open, and she was staring directly back at him.

ELEVEN
LUX

Suddenly, she *was.*
    Wasn't.
Was.
Just like that.
First there was light blinding burning stinging.
Then there was noise: static in her ears in her brain fuzzy and deafening.

hurts hurts hurts hurts hurts.

When she looked up, numbers ran across her vision, a dizzying stream of ones and zeros; when she blinked, they scurried away and were replaced by colors.

Her brain jolted; words came.

Blue and *sky* and *sun* and *light.*

There was a word for everything, too many of them, and they rushed through her.

Sand and *tree* and *stop* and *hurts.*

And *what what what what what* over and over, the loudest word of all.

Back, she thought, *want go back darkness hurts!*

Then came fear and panic.

She wanted—she wanted—the word burst to the top of her mind—*stop*! She wanted it to stop all of it *Hurts! Stop!*

She became aware of a new sensation, and with it came a flood of new words—*hands* and *sand* and *skin* and *arms*. Tingles in her fingers, the sense of weight.

What what what what?

Chaos and noise too much she was a void and the words and the sensations rioted within her she could not control them.

She didn't remember sitting up but suddenly she was she looked down and words bombarded her *legs* and *feet* and *knees* beyond them *sea* and *water* and *ocean*.

This was the world: sand and ocean legs and light.

She moved her eyes and every direction held new sights and words she couldn't stop them from coming *palm tree* and *rock* and *waves* and *clouds* and—

The words stopped.

The noise stopped.

The static in her brain stopped.

The numbers stopped.

Boy.

Her thoughts shivered scattered emptied and at last all was still and silent behind her eyes as she stared at him the world drew back waited.

Boy.

Then slowly the words crept in again they stacked and shuffled and rearranged.

Boy and *eyes* and *nose* and *mouth* and *hair* and *face.*

Her mind drew him in hid his image at its center folded over him the world slid into place the chaos ceased.

The words fell into line. She could *think* now. She could *breathe.* He gave shape to her thoughts and structure to her mind. She stared at him without blinking, memorizing the lines of his face and the colors in his hair. Her body relaxed.

She was at peace.

The boy was there, and the boy was everything.

"Sophie," he said. "Hey, you okay?"

His voice electrified her. Her brain rushed to process his words, to make sense of them. *Sophie.* A name, a girl's name. *Her* name?

Hey, you okay?

Before she could understand them, he spoke again. More words, more sounds. All in a rush. She struggled to keep up—*had* to understand him—but it was too much. She watched his lips. His teeth. The muscles in his throat.

"Say something," he said.

Say something say something say something.

"Mmm." A sound! From her own lips! She watched him anxiously, to see if he would approve. She *ached* for him to approve.

"Are you hurt?" he asked.

This was a word she knew. Hurt. Her tongue jerked into action, her lips parted—"*Hurt.*"

"What? You *are* hurt?"

A flutter of panic. A flurry of words. She spoke them as they came, desperate to speak. "No. Not . . . not hurt."

He spoke faster and faster, pouring words across the sand. She raced to pick them up and turn them over and interpret them, but he was too fast and she was too slow. She caught them at random, a word here and there: *boat* and *fly* and *away* and *remember* and *drug* and *Sophie* and *boat*.

She seized on that last one with desperation. "Boat." Ones and zeros crowded her mind; faded into an image of a boat on water.

"Hey," he said. "Hey, stay with me. It's me, it's Jim. Jim Julien?"

It's me, it's Jim.

Her heart jerked. She could understand this! He was Jim. The boy was Jim. She held the word close and the whole of her identity hung upon it: *Jim Jim Jim Jim Jim.*

"Jim," she said, delighting in the sound of it.

"Yeah, that's right." He followed with more words, but they rushed over her and evaporated before she could gather them in. That was okay. She had enough for now.

She had Jim.

And Jim was everything.

TWELVE
SOPHIE

The second time Sophie woke was like a sudden fall, an instant leap into full consciousness. Her eyes shot open, and the first thing she saw was an unfamiliar face. It was a man, somewhere in his fifties she guessed, with a receding silver hairline and oddly dainty lips, as if he were halfway into a kiss, but it was his eyes that transfixed her: stunningly blue and focused sharply on her, his pupils pinpoints of black. When her gaze met his, the skin around his eyes tightened, forming a network of wrinkles from their outer corners. She swallowed, half hypnotized, confused, waiting for her other senses to catch up. It was as if her brain had forgotten to alert her ears to the fact she was awake, because the sounds around her were murky. They slowly took shape, forming into voices, words—her mother was there.

Sophie blinked, and the spell was broken. The man leaned back, his eyes still on her but his features relaxing a bit. She licked her lips, which she found were dry and rough, and moaned.

"Is that it?" the man asked. He was seated in a plastic chair, facing her squarely. She herself was sitting in a metal chair that looked like something out of a dentist's office, slightly reclined, her hands perched on padded armrests.

Her mother stood behind the man, but a bright light was concentrated on Sophie and all else was in shadow. She could only see her mother's shoes and the hem of her lab coat, and beside her someone stood in a pair of white heels, a woman dressed in a white pantsuit, so bright she seemed to glow. But her face was also lost in shadow.

"That's it," her mother replied. Sophie heard the click of a pen; somewhere behind her, someone was scratching on paper.

"*Mmmom,*" Sophie moaned.

"What did she say?" The man turned around in his seat. He was wearing a silver suit that looked like it cost as much as Jim's plane.

"Nothing. She can't talk yet, of course. She's disoriented."

No, I'm not, she wanted to say, but she couldn't form the words. She'd never been so thirsty in her life.

"What do we do now?" asked the man, turning around again. He studied Sophie with his frigid eyes, his mouth pursing even further. He seemed wary of her, as if she might bite.

"We wait a little," Moira said. She finally stepped forward, into the light, and Sophie's heart jerked painfully in her chest. Her mother looked the same as she always had, as if she were agelessly frozen at thirty, with short, tight black curls and large blue eyes; she looked like one of the Victorian china dolls Sophie's stepsister Emily collected, minus all the lace.

Mom, look at me. It's me, Mom, please see!

But Moira was looking at the man, not Sophie, and she remembered that her mother still thought she was the other Sophie. What was her name? The memory was vague, difficult to catch. She'd heard them talking earlier, when she'd started to wake up . . . *Lux.* That's what they'd called her.

"It will take about twenty-four hours for her to acclimate," Moira was saying. "Walking, talking, basic motor functions—it comes pretty quickly in the newer models, but still, it isn't instant. She's imprinted on you, Mr. Andreyev, and that's the important thing."

"Please," he replied, a soft Russian accent curling around the edges of his speech, "call me Constantin. Or Connie."

A tight smile danced across Moira's face. "Thank you, Connie. Now, do you have any questions for us?"

"I have a question," said the woman in white. She also stepped forward. Her brown hair was trimmed boyishly short, but that did nothing to soften the angularity of her features. Hers was a face you could cut yourself on. She regarded Sophie through half-lidded eyes, as if she were bored or dismally unimpressed.

"Of course, Victoria." Moira's voice came out soft and ended in a whisper.

Sophie looked curiously at her mother. *She's afraid of this woman.* She could feel her strength returning, and sensed that if she were to speak up, her voice wouldn't betray her again. But she didn't. Instead, she stayed still and silent, watching to see what would happen.

The first thing, the most important thing—her mother seemed entirely well and whole. Whatever her emergency was or had been, it didn't seem to affect her physically, not, at least, in any way that Sophie could tell. She didn't seem to be held against her will. She seemed . . . fine. Perfectly fine.

Sophie felt as if she'd been punched in the gut. *I don't know the whole story*, she thought. *I have to give her the benefit of the doubt.* But she felt used. Betrayed. Bewildered. It didn't make sense, none of it. *Why am I here? What is this about?* Looking at her mother standing so composed, she almost sensed that Moira Crue had no idea that her daughter was on the island.

Had Nicholas told her?

Where *was* Nicholas?

And who had hit her on the head?

She had a feeling she knew the answer, and it only made her more nauseated. *He tricked me.* It had to be true. There was no other explanation. Somehow, Nicholas had known she was coming. He'd met her at the airstrip and lied about being sent by Moira when he'd probably had no intention of taking Sophie to her mother at all. But . . . *why?* What was his game? How did he factor into all this?

She needed to know what Skin Island was, certain that that would answer half her questions at least. Her mother's life's work, Nicholas's part in it, the mysterious emergency, the other Sophie . . . it all came down to the secrets in this room. *I can play along a little longer.* She had no idea what this Lux was supposed to be or why she looked like Sophie, but apparently she couldn't talk. Or walk. That was pretty simple to stick to. *Just shut up and listen*, Sophie told herself. *They're bound to spill a few answers.*

She'd been so lost in her own head that she'd missed what

the woman—Victoria—had to say, and she struggled to catch up while trying to look as uninterested as possible. Her mother was speaking.

"The bond won't be evident until she's able to speak and function. But we've never had a case in which the imprinting failed."

"If she has only just, for all intents and purposes, been born—how is it that within a day she will be able to speak and walk?" asked Andreyev.

"To answer that, I must back up a little. I'll start at the beginning, though I'm sure you read all of this in the dossier Victoria gave you. Still, it's a lot to take in, and I want to be sure we're clear." She drew a deep breath. "The Vitros are the result of a groundbreaking neurotechnology we call the Imprima Code, and the chip on which it is contained." She held up a vial, and Sophie recognized it as one of the vials she'd seen in the freezer consoles the night before.

Moira went on. "We take embryos left over from in vitro procedures—there are millions of them all over the world, tiny cellular clusters of potential—and we raise them, well, in vitro—in glass—and plant the computer chip at just the right moment of embryonic brain growth. The brain grows over and around it, and we monitor it very closely every day. Once the subject reaches nine months of gestation, we can begin transferring data to the chip. Then, when we wake the subject—"

"They already know their ABCs and 123s," Andreyev finished.

"Oh, much more than that. Basic motor functions, a rudimentary knowledge of math and history. The chip is brilliant, an extremely valuable technology in and of itself. Why, the opportunities afforded us by the chip, even without the imprint technology, is enough to—"

"Yes, yes," interrupted Victoria. "Explain to Mr. Andreyev the imprint technology. That is, after all, what he is here to see." She extended a tight smile to the Russian that made her face look as if it were made of Saran wrap.

"Yes," Moira said, a bit faintly. "Of course. The imprint technology is what makes the Vitros so . . . interesting. I developed it myself."

"And we are very pleased with your work," said Victoria, and her and Moira's eyes met in a glacial lock. They looked like rival cheerleaders vying for the spot at the top of the pyramid, only instead of lipstick and pom-poms these cheerleaders had P.h.D.'s and secret laboratories to play with.

"How long has she been sleeping?" Andreyev steepled his index fingers and pressed them to his lips as he leaned back in his chair, regarding Sophie from beneath a low brow.

"Seventeen years," said Moira. "That's the only way this works. We can't wake them until we are ready for them to bond with someone. You have to be the very first person they see, and then they'll never imprint on anyone else. This is Lux's first impression of the world, and because *you* are the first one she has seen, you have become the center of her world."

"Well," said Andreyev, his frown deepening. "But *why*? How does it work?"

Victoria's eyes flitted to Moira.

"Ah," said Sophie's mother patiently. "Many species of

animals are born with the instinct to imprint. Ducks are a prime example. A newly hatched duckling imprints on the first thing it sees, whether that's its mother, a human being, or in some cases even an inanimate object like a shoe or a duck decoy. It will follow that first impression—the imprintee—in order to learn how to function. How to forage for food, how to court, how to migrate. Even humans have this instinct to a lesser extent. It's the reason a baby can identify its mother apart from other people." She stepped toward Sophie and slowly ran her fingers over a lock of her hair; it was all Sophie could do not to flinch. "The chip isolates this imprinting instinct in the brain and amplifies it exponentially. In essence, it creates a deep, psychological need in the subject, a need to imprint, to mold itself around the mind and will of another. It creates a hole in the subject's psyche that is filled by the first person that the subject sees upon waking for the first time." She fell silent for a moment, her eyes studying Sophie with a slight tension around their corners. Then she turned to Andreyev. "The moment Lux awoke, her chip activated, and all that information—the ABCs and 123s, as you call them, as well as her motor functions, her memory, every cognitive process in her brain—it all clicked into place with you at its center."

Andreyev swallowed. "I did read the files, of course. I didn't think . . ." He stopped and cleared his throat, looking very unsettled. "I didn't realize . . ."

"It's a lot to take in," Victoria said crisply. "We know that."

"Yes." His voice was hoarse. He looked as if he wanted to be as far from Sophie—Lux—as possible.

"Her will is bound to yours. She will obey any command

you give her," Moira went on, a bit vengefully. "She *has* no will of her own, no sense of self. Her identity is wholly formed around yours."

"I understand." Andreyev's eyes shifted around the room. His left hand, which rested on his knee, opened and closed convulsively. "It's just . . . she looks so young, so innocent."

"Of course, that's part of the charm of the Vitros," Victoria said, too brightly, as if she were trying to counter the somber depression that had settled over the room, gathering like shadows in the corners. "They are aesthetically pleasing, as well. Surely you see the possibilities? And you read the section about the various classes, I hope?"

"Yes. . . . Well, parts of it."

"Moira?"

Moira gave a grunt of affirmation. "The classes, yes. By specially designing the code on each Vitro's chip, we have been able to create a diverse range of specializations. Lux, for example, is what we call a Class Three Bodyguard. She may not look the part, but that is by design. Her chip is supplied with the kinetic and mental resources that will keep her on constant defensive mode. If you are ever threatened, she will intervene on your behalf to defend you against all threats. The only thing that would stop her from protecting you would be a command given by you."

"And the other classes," said Andreyev. "They all exist?"

"Of course. We have a prototype Vitro for each category. Lux is, of course, the eighth successfully imprinted Vitro to be born on Skin Island."

"Only the eighth?" He frowned. "I thought there were more than that."

"Well. There are four others—early subjects. They didn't . . . They weren't successful. However, of the eight—any of whom we can demonstrate for you—we have another bodyguard. We have three domestics, programmed in cooking, housekeeping, and such duties. We have three intelligence models, who specialize in research, memory, translation, and information processing."

"And of course, these are only the classes we have already produced," Victoria added. "But the possibilities are limitless: soldiers, nannies, pilots; whatever you can think of, we can manufacture."

"It's a limitless new world," said Moira softly, her gaze traveling to Sophie but not quite meeting her eyes. "And we are only just beginning to explore it."

Sophie felt bile rise in her throat. So this was Skin Island. This was the Great Secret Thing that had lurked between her and her mother for so long. Her blood pounded angrily through her veins; she had never felt such deep, total revulsion. *It's a hideous new world. And you are its architect.*

THIRTEEN

JIM

"Sophie?" Jim scrambled to his knees and crawled to her. "Hey, you okay?"

Her eyes were stretched wide and fastened on him. She said nothing, only looked at him with such intensity that the hair on his neck rose on end. The sea was reflected in her turquoise eyes.

"Hey," he said, softer, "what happened to you, huh?"

She sat with her legs bent to one side, her hands clutching the sand. Her feet and legs were bare; the hospital gown she wore fluttered in the wind, hugging her slim frame. He hesitantly reached out, cupped her shoulders in his palms, and studied her face. The relief he'd felt when she'd opened her eyes was fading away, back into concern.

"Did you find your mom? Did Nicholas do this to you? Sophie?" He hadn't forgotten that the other kids were still hunting for them, and he scanned the beach and the trees for any sign of them. "We have to get out of here. We have to swim . . ." But as he said it, he realized it was impossible. The tide was at its highest, and he could almost see the current between the islands ripping the water. They would never be able to cross it, especially not with Sophie in this condition.

He turned back to her, trying to hide his panic. "Okay. Okay, listen. When you left with Nicholas, he had a boat. Do you remember where he left it?"

She simply gazed at him, silent and still, her long pale hair coiling and uncoiling in the wind. The palm branches rustling overhead cast a dancing lattice of shadows over her skin. There was none of her spark, none of her drive. She seemed . . . emptier, somehow. Blank. Had they brainwashed her or something? His skin prickled; he looked at her, really looked at her, searching for clues to explain her bizarre condition. And he noticed things he'd missed before: her skin was pale—*too* pale. Sophie had had a very light peppering of freckles on her cheeks. This Sophie had none. Her hair was longer, her nails were longer—he remembered distinctly that Sophie's nails had been bitten short. It was something he always noticed about people, whether or not they bit their nails, because it was a habit he always looked for in his dad. His dad chewed his nails when he was drunk, for no discernible reason, but it was always Jim's first clue that his father was wasted.

"You . . ." He stood up and stumbled back, his mind filled with thoughts exploding like fireworks. "If you're not Sophie . . . who are you? And where is *she?*"

Whoever this girl was, she seemed either to not know, or was incapable of telling him. He looked around in complete bafflement. Should he go back, look for the real Sophie? Take this one on to a hospital? *Oh, God, what if she was hurt and they were helping her—and now I've gone and made her worse by dragging her across the island.* He grimaced as he thought of the IV he'd pulled out of her arm.

"Hey. Hey, can you talk?" He lifted his hands and held them on either side of her face. "Just talk to me, okay? Say something."

"Mmm."

Well. It was *something*, anyway. At least she seemed to be able to understand him. "Are you hurt?"

Her lips moved, as if she were trying to speak but couldn't summon her voice, and her eyes fixed on his mouth.

"*Hurt*," she whispered.

"What? You *are* hurt?"

Awkwardly, as if not quite in control of her limbs, she touched the tips of her fingers to his lips. "No. Not . . . not hurt."

"Well, can you stand up, then? We have to get to the plane—I'm not even sure if it will fly—but we've got to get away from here. Do you remember what happened? What they did to you? Look, I think they knocked you out, gave you some kind of drug. I can get us out of here, but I need your help—you gotta get up. There's a boat around here somewhere. . . ." He took her hands in his, wrapping his fingers around hers. "They're coming after us, and they took my friend. I can help you both if we just get out of here."

"Boat." She must have been more drugged than he thought. She didn't show any sign of urgency, just maintained that hungry look.

"Hey. Hey, stay with me. My name's Jim. Jim Julien."

"Jim."

"Yeah, that's right." He heard a crack from the trees and threw an arm across her, his eyes darting from one shadow to the next, watching for Mary and her friends. He didn't see anyone, but they could easily be hiding in the thick ferns and pines.

When he turned to face her, she was smiling a vacuous, contented smile. "Jim."

Genuinely concerned now that something was very wrong with this not-Sophie, he took her hands in his and stood up. "Can you walk? Come on. We can look around. Get up."

The smile transformed into a frown of concentration as she tried to stand. It was like watching a newborn colt struggle to find its legs. She wobbled, swayed, and trembled, and would have collapsed if Jim weren't holding her. When she finally did reach her feet, she looked down at her legs as if surprised to see them there. A little blue butterfly landed lightly on her toes, and her face brightened with childish delight.

"That's it," Jim murmured, watching her warily. "Now. Let's take a look around. The boat has to be here somewhere."

He kept an eye on the trees as he walked across the sand, one hand holding the girl's. She moved slowly, uncertainly, as if each step was only managed with great concentration. With every passing second, Jim's apprehensiveness grew.

The girl looked around her with open wonder lighting her eyes. The trees, the sand, and the sea all seemed to fascinate her as if she'd never seen them before. They passed a depression in the beach where the waves had left a deposit of shells, pastel clamshells and gray sand dollars and broken pieces of conch. She stopped, pulled her hand from his, and bent to inspect the collection. An ambitious wave swept up the sand, and water poured into the hollow and swirled around the shells. She made a high-pitched squeal and gripped the hem of her gown in alarm, then hesitantly extended one finger to poke at the water.

Jim watched in mute horror. *It's like she's two years old, like they rewound her brain fifteen years. What is she?* Sophie didn't have a twin sister—he'd have remembered something like that. Was she a clone? Some kind of copy?

She began touching each shell, fascinated by the textures and shapes, completely absorbed in her little world. Jim watched the tree line nervously, wondering what he would do if Mary and the others appeared. It would help if he knew what they wanted and who had sent them. When he looked back down at the girl, she had shells clutched in both her hands, and she smiled up at him and held them toward him, as if showing off a treasure.

"Ah . . ." He cleared his throat. "Very—um—very nice."

"Jim," she said happily, and she picked up more shells.

"Just . . . just put them down, will you?" he said, his voice snapping from his lips, too sharply.

She stopped smiling. Her hands shot open and the shells clattered back into the pile.

"I'm sorry." Jim sighed. "I didn't mean to yell. Just let's keep looking for the boat, okay?"

This was beyond him. He hadn't signed up for this. Even if he did get her back to Guam—what then? What if she didn't snap out of this trance or whatever it was? Could he just drop her off at the hospital, tell them some story about finding her on the beach? But no. The other pilots and the bartender all knew he'd gone to Skin Island with Sophie Crue, and if anyone started asking questions, the truth was bound to come out. And then what would stop the powers behind Skin Island from coming after him? From finding this girl and finishing whatever vile experiment they'd started on her? What if the authorities thought *this* was Sophie and that he'd done this to her?

You could leave her, a voice hissed in the back of his mind. *You don't owe her anything. She's not Sophie.*

He ground his teeth together. *Too late for that,* he thought. He couldn't leave her in this state, barely capable of speech and movement. It'd be like leaving a baby to fend for itself.

He saw no sign of the boat. Nicholas had motored it out of his sight when he'd taken Sophie across the channel, and all Jim knew was that they'd gone east. *We'll have to come across it eventually.* It wasn't as if Nicholas could have dragged it into the trees to hide it. There had to be a dock or a bay somewhere.

He felt a tug on his hand, and turned to find the girl enthralled with a puff of sea foam left on the sand. She nudged it with her toe, her lips rounded into a perfect O of wonder.

"Come on," he said for what seemed the hundredth time. It was like trying to hold the attention of a toddler. "Let's keep going."

She instantly snapped to attention and followed him, her gait growing more even and steady, her limbs starting to coordinate. She was constantly on alert, her eyes fastening on every movement as if she were determined not to miss a single thing, but always they returned to Jim. He wondered if she expected him to run off or disappear.

"You know this place, right?" he said, after they'd gone another fifty yards without seeing so much as a spare oar from the boat. "If you know where the boat is, please just tell me." He stopped walking so that he could look her squarely in the eye.

Her brow furrowed; she seemed almost in pain. "Boat?"

"Yes, boat boat *boat*—where is it?"

"I . . ." She bit her lip, her hands curling into fists. "I do not know. I do not know *boat*." She said the words with great effort, and then beamed at him as if she'd just won a spelling bee.

For a moment, all he could do was gaze at her in exasperation. Then he turned away, gripped his hair in his hands, and kicked savagely at the sand. The plane was out of sight. There was no sign of the boat or, thankfully, Mary and company, though they were no doubt closing in. What they intended to do, Jim had no idea, but he was certain he didn't want to find out.

"Jim?" the girl asked softly, uncertainly.

"What?" He rounded on her, his pulse pounding in his ears. "What is it? Do you remember where it is now? I'm trying to get you out of here, I really am, but you're making it *so difficult*! I just—if I could get to the plane—"

"I . . . I am sorry."

"Sorry! Ha! Well, if you're sorry, then why don't you just swim across the channel and bring the plane over here?"

Immediately he felt regret for lashing out at her, when obviously she was in no position to be blamed, but before he could apologize he realized he'd just hit upon the only possible solution. He took a few steps past her and stared toward the smaller island, just visible to the west. If he could swim the channel and get to the plane, he could taxi across the water to the main island and pick the girl up, and then they'd be on their way. He knew he could do it. All his life, he'd grown up swimming in the Pacific, cliff diving into the sea, snorkeling and scuba diving and exploring underwater caves with his friends. He knew the sea and he knew his own strength. *I could do it*, he thought. *I have to do it—there's no other choice.*

"Listen, I have an idea." He turned around, but she was gone. "Hey! Where are you?"

He scanned the beach, but there was no sign of her. Had Mary snatched her? Impossible. His back hadn't been turned *that* long. He spotted her footprints in the wet sand and followed them. They meandered down the beach, toward the water, and disappeared into the ravenous surf.

Dread unfolding in his stomach, Jim ran into the surf. She was yards ahead of him, floundering in the water. From the looks of it, she couldn't swim. He caught one glimpse of her pale hand reaching for the sky before she slipped beneath the surface and didn't reappear.

"Hey!" he yelled as he plunged after her, arcing into a shallow dive that took him under the choppy waves. He swam along the bottom, sending up clouds of sand that blocked his view. When he resurfaced for air, there was no sign of her. Jim treaded water and spun this way and that, desperate for a glimpse of her, but he saw not a single golden hair.

He dove again and scoured the murky water. The floor dropped away beneath him, turning in an instant from clear turquoise to unfathomable dark blue. He finally spotted her, floating listlessly beneath the water, her hair a golden flower blossoming around her face. His lungs screamed for air and his skull burned from the pressure, but he couldn't go up until he had her. With a few strong strokes he reached her and looped an arm around her middle. Then he bent his knees and planted his feet on the sand and launched them both upward. It seemed to take an eternity to finally break through the surface, and when he did, he gasped in a mixture of air and sea spray, then began stroking toward the shore.

The waves pushed him along, finally dumping them both onto the sand. He pulled her out of the surf while coughing up seawater from his own lungs, then fell immediately into CPR, recalling the lifeguard lessons he'd taken years before.

It took only three pumps on her chest for her to spit out the water she'd swallowed, and she fell into a coughing fit that racked her entire body. He held her as she choked and stroked the hair from her face, murmuring assurances.

At last, she leaned against him, shuddering a little, and he realized the water on her face wasn't entirely from the sea.

"Hey. Hey, why are you crying? It's okay, you're safe now."

"S-sorry," she stammered.

"What? Why?"

"Tried . . . to swim . . . get plane for Jim . . ."

"What?" Holding her face in his hands, he gave her a look of bewilderment. "But I didn't mean for you to actually swim across! Are you crazy? Hey, look here. Don't cry."

She gulped and blinked furiously until her tears were gone. Jim's hands slid down to her shoulders, then her hands, and he gazed at her in astonished confusion. "What did they do to you? Why are you doing this?"

She just stared mournfully at the ground.

"Oh, hey now. Put your chin up. We'll get out of here."

She jerked her face upward, tilting her chin to the sky.

An uneasy feeling nibbled at the edges of his thoughts. "Hey . . . stop that. Put your head down."

She tilted her face downward again. Jim's skin prickled.

"Um. Clap your hands."

She started clapping, smiling vacantly all the while.

"Okay, stop."

Her hands fell into her lap.

Jim stood up and turned away, cracking his knuckles in agitation. *The hell is this?* He watched the jungle for a moment, his attention divided between the girl—or whatever she was—and the fear that Mary and the others would catch up to them. When he turned around again, she was digging her fingers into the sand.

"Look here," he said softly, bending down to crouch in front of her. "Why are you doing that? Why are you . . . playing this game, huh? Some kind of Simon Says?"

She blinked at him, as if he'd lost her.

"Why are you doing everything I say?"

A particularly ambitious wave swept up the sand and licked her toes. Her brow drew together; she looked almost in pain from thinking. "You . . . You are . . ."

"What?"

Her face contorted as if she'd eaten something very sour, her cheeks growing red and tears forming in her eyes. Jim grabbed her shoulders. "Hey, calm down. It's okay. Never mind."

He sat beside her on the sand as the island seemed to close in around him and the horizon pulled away. Despite the damp, warm air that clung to his skin he felt as if he'd caught a chill he couldn't shake.

FOURTEEN
SOPHIE

After another doctor escorted Constantin Andreyev away, to get him settled in his room, Sophie was left alone with her mother and Victoria Strauss.

She'd learned more truths about her mother in the ten minutes she'd pretended to be her own doppelgänger than she'd learned in seventeen years of being herself, and the irony of this left a bitter taste on her tongue. She felt betrayed, lied to, marginalized more than ever before.

Though she'd learned much about her mother's reprehensible research, there were still questions left lingering, and above them all, the question of why her mother had summoned her to Skin Island in the first place. Sophie had a hard time holding on to the concern she'd had for Moira Crue in the past few days. She instead found herself questioning everything she thought she knew about her mother.

All her life, Moira Crue had been a paragon of intelligence and self-sacrifice, and Sophie had worshipped the

ground beneath her. Well, except for that brief stage of rebel-
lion when she'd been in middle school, when she'd spent the
majority of her time sulking and avoiding her mother's phone
calls. But that hadn't lasted for long. When she had imagined
her mother on Skin Island, she'd imagined her curing demen-
tia and developing vaccines for third world countries, saving
the human race with cutting-edge science, Mother Teresa in
a lab coat and latex gloves. She'd known, of course, that there
had to be more to it, that there was a reason for the secrets
her mother kept—but she'd never dreamed it was because her
work involved manufacturing human *slaves*.

She gripped the armrests of the chair and looked at her
mother now as if seeing her for the first time. She felt frozen
to her seat, her body unable to react.

"Well," Moira said as the door shut behind Andreyev,
"how do you think that went?"

Victoria Strauss sat in the chair the Russian had previously
occupied and crossed one leg over the other. Her heels were
three inches long. Sophie wondered how in the world she
managed not to break her neck every time she took a step.
"Not as well as I'd hoped."

Moira's eyebrows rose, disappearing beneath her side-
swept bangs. "Oh? I thought he was intrigued."

"I need him to be more than *intrigued*, Moira. I need him
to invest, and now. I don't think you realize how precarious
your position is."

Moira's lips pinched together, and her nostrils flared in a
way Sophie recognized as dangerous, evidence that her mother
was holding back harsh words. "I understand perfectly."

"The Vitro Project has been going on for eighteen years,"

Strauss sighed. "And with no return. You know how it works. Corpus is not a charity. We can't support a project that can't attract its own investors. You need this funding. Constantin Andreyev is your last chance, Moira, so don't screw it up."

"The Vitros are ready to be marketed. I'm not worried. Your . . . what is he anyway? Arms dealer? Politician?"

"Mr. Andreyev, if you must know, is a businessman of exceptionally substantial means, and more importantly, he is discreet. That is all that you should concern yourself with."

"Well, your Mr. Andreyev is getting everything he ordered in Lux, and more."

"Mm." Strauss's eyes slid over Sophie, her half-lidded gaze giving her a reptilian quality that made Sophie's skin crawl. "We'll see, I suppose. She hasn't done much but sit there so far."

"You've seen them wake before. You know it takes a little time. Tomorrow she'll be functioning as well as you or me."

"God, I hope not. She's meant to take orders, not give them."

Moira opened her mouth, then clamped it shut again, as if thinking better of what she'd been about to say. She took a moment to inhale, then said, "Have you given any thought to the proposal I sent you?"

"Which one? Oh, yes. I remember. About the chip."

"Now that the Vitro Project is successfully completed, I really think we should begin considering what I believe to be the chip's true value. The diagnostic possibilities could—"

"Moira, please. Stop."

Moira's lips pursed together as she reached behind Sophie

to pick up a glass of water, which she held to Sophie's lips and softly urged her to drink as Strauss continued.

"The Vitro Project is only just *beginning*. Even if you win Andreyev over and he puts in an order for fifty of them, you'll still have work to do here. They may be ready, but they're not perfect."

Moira said nothing. She set down the glass and lowered an arm extension bolted to the back of the chair Sophie was sitting in. It was some kind of metal dome, almost like a modified hair-dryer dome. She pressed a button and the chair hummed slightly.

Strauss kept talking, but Sophie had stopped listening. She watched her mother instead, trying to read her, trying to tell herself that what she'd just heard couldn't possibly be the truth. Moira's eyes were fixed on a computer behind Sophie; whatever the dome was doing, she must have been reading its results. Sophie tensed—what if she didn't pass whatever test this was? Was she checking for the chip thing, the one she'd apparently implanted in the brains of a bunch of helpless babies? As Strauss droned on, Moira's eyes flickered down to Sophie. Her brows drew together, creasing her forehead, and she started to say something when there came a knock at the door.

Moira shut off the computer and jerked the door open. A young doctor stood there, her black hair bound into a bun with a pencil and her narrow glasses perched low on her nose. "I'm here for Lux's therapy," she squeaked.

"Oh, Hashimoto, come in." Moira stepped aside to let her through. "She's ready to go."

Strauss watched with disinterest as Moira and Dr. Hashimoto took Sophie's arms and stood her up. She wasn't sure how to keep up the act; as long as the others were talking around her, she'd seemed to get by just by staying quiet.

"She'll be a bit unsteady, so keep a hand on her," said Moira, but she looked at Sophie as she said it, frowning.

Sophie let her legs go a little limp. It wasn't hard to do. Whatever drug had knocked her out still seemed to be running through her body, making her muscles wobbly. She wished she could stay near her mother, to hear more secrets, but it seemed Moira was staying behind to continue her conversation with Strauss. Dr. Hashimoto, her hand securely around Sophie's upper arm, led her out of the room. Sophie made sure to go slowly and awkwardly, trying to live up to what they apparently expected from Lux.

When the door shut and she was sealed off from Moira, she considered bolting and running back to Jim—if he was still waiting, which she doubted. A part of her wanted to wash her hands of Skin Island, Corpus, and her mother altogether—but the other part said, *Wait. You might be missing something.*

Despite everything, Sophie found herself still wanting to believe the best about her mother. *She's creating slaves*, she told herself as she limped along with Dr. Hashimoto. *She steals their wills from them and binds them to people who would use them and throw them away.* Skin Island was a slave hatchery, a factory that churned out custom-designed, entirely controllable minions. Bodyguards, Moira had said, and domestic servants. Translators and nannies and soldiers. To think that her own mother was involved in creating helpless victims who didn't even have the ability to say no filled her with revulsion. *I hate her. I do, I hate her with every bone in my body.*

And to top it off, she was dealing with and catering to criminals. *Businessman,* Strauss had called Andreyev. Sophie doubted it—or at least doubted that his kind of *business* was legal. He had the look of a mobster, Sophie thought, not that she knew much about mobsters. But to even be here, to even consider purchasing a human bound helplessly to his will, with no ability to think or choose for herself, was proof to Sophie that he was more soulless than the slaves he hoped to buy. *This is an island of monsters.* She suppressed a shudder.

Where does Nicholas fit in? she wondered. He certainly didn't seem imprinted, as they called it. Or maybe he was. Maybe he was working for someone on the island, Moira or another doctor, and in running away from him Sophie had spoiled whatever plan he'd been ordered to carry out with her.

Dr. Hashimoto led her through the atrium, and they approached another doctor as they entered the opposite hall. He was a small, balding man, carrying an armful of paperwork, and he was trailed by a boy Sophie's age—not Nicholas. The boy had a vacant look in his eye and a vapid smile on his lips.

Dr. Hashimoto stopped and nodded to the man.

He glanced at Sophie. "Andreyev's girl?"

"Yes. I'm taking her into therapy now."

The man nodded, looking Sophie up and down. "Caleb, hold this." He dumped the paperwork into the hands of the boy, who took it with a softly murmured, "Yes, sir."

The doctor took Sophie's face in his hands and squinted at her, his gaze inspecting her face as if looking for a flaw.

"There's something off about this one," he said to Dr. Hashimoto.

"She only just woke up. And she's one of the first batch, so she's been sleeping for seventeen years."

"Hm. It's not that. Her eyes—look at them. They see more than they should. If I were Moira, I'd take a closer look at this one. Wouldn't want our prize Vitro to go bad, would we, not while Andreyev's around to see it."

"We haven't had a Vitro 'go bad' since Jay," said Dr. Hashimoto, batting his hands away. "We fixed that little problem, remember?"

"We?" He snorted. "You weren't even around. You're practically still an intern, Hana, so don't presume too much."

Dr. Hashimoto's eyes flashed. "That may be so, but Lux is my responsibility, not yours. Good day, Dr. Michalski."

"I'm just saying," he said as Dr. Hashimoto took Sophie's hand and stormed on down the hall. "We don't want another Nicholas running around this place! Should have put that one down years ago. But what do I know? No one ever listens to me around here."

Dr. Hashimoto muttered under breath, and then Sophie heard a crash behind her. For a moment she forgot herself, and she whirled around. The boy, Caleb, had dropped the papers all over the floor.

"Stupid!" Dr. Michalski hissed. "Pick them up!"

"Sorry, sir," the boy said. He dropped to his knees and grabbed up the papers.

"Faster, Caleb!"

Caleb's hands moved in a blur, snatching papers and stuffing them into a messy pile in his arm. "Sorry," he said again.

When he had them all up, he stood and gave the doctor a bland smile, his expression glazed.

Sophie was struck with horror. She couldn't look away. But then she felt Dr. Hashimoto tugging on her arm, and she forced herself to turn around. The young doctor was frowning at her.

"Perhaps Michalski was right," she said thoughtfully, regarding Sophie through slitted eyes. "There is something . . . *off* about you."

Sophie said nothing, but her heart pounded on her ribs so violently that she was certain Dr. Hashimoto would hear it. It was too soon to lose her cover; she still had too many questions, and it seemed Lux had access to the answers Sophie had never been able to find. Thankfully, the doctor shrugged and shook her head.

"I'll mention it to Moira later. Come on."

She took Sophie into a large room that looked like a cross between a gym and a lounge. Several pieces of exercise equipment cluttered one end of the room, while the other was taken up with couches and a wide-screen television. Andreyev was sitting on one of the couches, nursing a cup of coffee while attended by a pair of doctors and yet another teen, this one a slightly chubby boy with golden curls and glassy blue eyes.

Dr. Hashimoto led Sophie to a pair of horizontal bars and instructed her to place her hands on either one, then to walk down the middle.

"You're doing surprisingly well for a newborn," she said. "But still. Got to work on those legs. Hm . . . that's strange. Your muscle development is remarkable." Sophie froze, sure her cover would be blown by something as stupid as her calf muscles, but then the young doctor shrugged. "Perhaps the somatropin doses they gave you were too high. You are pretty small for your age."

Holding back a sigh of relief, Sophie made a show of tripping and finding her feet, all the while keeping an eye on Andreyev, who was also keeping an eye on her. One of the doctors, whose voice Sophie recognized—he'd been the one who helped her mother roll her upstairs that morning— seemed to be doing some sort of demonstration for Andreyev. *Rogers*, she remembered.

"He's a bodyguard model, just like yours," said Dr. Rogers. "Watch. Gary?"

The other man—who, Sophie realized from his clothes and the gun at his hip, wasn't actually a doctor but a guard— pushed a table aside to make room in the center of the floor. Then Dr. Rogers sat casually beside Andreyev, leaned back, and folded his arms.

"Now," he murmured. "Gary here is going to try his best to hit me. But Clive won't let that happen, will you, Clive?"

The golden-haired boy shook his head with a smile.

Dr. Rogers picked at his nails. "Clive, don't let him get past you. Go ahead, Gary."

The guard rushed at Clive, and Sophie's breath caught in her throat, certain he'd clobber the boy. But Clive moved with the grace and speed of a tiger, spinning aside and catching Gary's ankle with his foot, at the same time delivering a sharp chop to the back of his neck. The guard fell heavily onto the floor, with a grunt of resignation.

"*Lux*," Dr. Hashimoto hissed, and Sophie jumped. The doctor must have said her name twice before Sophie remembered that *she* was supposed to be Lux. She pulled her eyes away from the strange tableau and found she'd reached the end of the bars. Dr. Hashimoto watched her sharply, and Sophie forced herself to focus on maintaining her charade. The thought ran through her mind again—*If I'm here being Lux, then where is Lux?*

She couldn't account for it, but she would hold on to this farce for as long as it took to answer all her questions. It had paid off so far.

She could hear the fight continuing on the other end of the room. It seemed a very mismatched pairing—the guard was no match for pudgy Clive with his cherubic curls. *It's part of the act,* she thought. *They're pulling the same thing with Lux. No one suspects a pretty little teenager to be capable of taking down an armed man.* She could see how someone like Andreyev, who likely needed body guarding from time to time, would find that attractive. It made Sophie want to retch.

"Enough," a voice said abruptly, and everyone in the room froze and looked at Andreyev. He drained his coffee. "I can see that he is more than capable," he said, glancing at Clive. "Thank you for the demonstration."

Dr. Rogers seemed disappointed that Andreyev wasn't more impressed. He glanced at Lux. "Of course, Clive isn't who you came to see, is he? Maybe you'd like to see Lux demonstrate *her* abilities."

Dr. Hashimoto cleared her throat. "Ah, Rogers, Lux is only just learning to access her motor functions. She isn't up to—"

"Bring her over."

"I really don't think—"

"Hana, who is the senior research partner here, you or me? I said bring her over."

"It's really not necessary," Andreyev said, looking a bit pale.

"No, it's fine," Dr. Rogers said, waving a hand. "Just watch."

Dr. Hashimoto looked cornered, and turned to Gary for help. He shrugged as if to say, *Don't involve me in this.* Clive just smiled and stood beside Dr. Rogers. Sophie realized he must be imprinted on the doctor, and that the boy in the hallway must have been imprinted on Dr. Michalski.

"Oh, come on," Dr. Rogers said impatiently. "We don't expect her to be Bruce Lee—not yet, anyway. We just want a little demonstration. For our esteemed *investor*."

"Fine," sighed Dr. Hashimoto. She muttered so that only Sophie heard her, "Anything to please the investors."

"Gary," said Dr. Rogers, his eyes following Sophie's progression across the room. She tried to keep her steps as clumsy as she could without falling onto her face, hoping that if she proved to them she was barely capable of standing he might let up. "See how you fare against Mr. Andreyev's Vitro."

Andreyev's eyes slipped to the door, as if he were trying to gauge how quickly he could reach it. *Odd,* Sophie thought. *For someone investing in these Vitros, he doesn't seem to want much to do with them.*

Dr. Hashimoto left her standing in the middle of the room, and Sophie, feeling abandoned and in way over her head, faced Gary uncertainly, her back to Andreyev. Dr. Hashimoto slipped out of the room, muttering some vague excuse, and Sophie hoped she was going to get Moira and Strauss. *Check that. Just get Mom.* Strauss seemed even more bloodthirsty than Dr. Rogers, and Sophie wasn't at all sure she could count on her to intervene.

"Well, get on with it," said Dr. Rogers, waving a hand impatiently.

Sophie couldn't hold her vacant expression. She stared at Gary with open desperation. The guard was thickset and tall, with an Italian complexion and brooding eyebrows that gave him a permanent scowl. He seemed unsure what to make of her, whether to expect a female version of Clive or a helpless wisp of a girl who'd been "born" just an hour ago. Sophie didn't know which part to play. *This was a bad idea*, she thought. *A really bad idea. I should have run when we were in the hallway. I should have told my mom who I was the minute I saw her. I should have—*

She didn't have time to add to her regret, because Gary lunged at her. His swing was halfhearted, but it still caught Sophie in the stomach with all the force of a brick. She dropped to her knees, doubled over and gasping. There was no acting about it. The air had been punched from her lungs, and she saw stars.

"Stop this!" Andreyev said, stepping back with a stricken look. "It's insanity!"

Dr. Rogers was suddenly in front of her, crouching down to meet her eyes. "Get up, Lux."

"Uhn . . ." she moaned.

"*Get up.*" His eyes flickered to Andreyev. "You tell her, sir; she has to listen to you."

Give it up, Sophie told herself. *Before you get yourself killed.*

"I think not," said Andreyev, his voice suddenly taking a sharp tone. "That is quite enough, Dr. Rogers. Let her be."

A look of uncertainty crackled over Dr. Roger's features, as if he regretted what he'd done. Sophie couldn't bear it any longer. She had to tell them the truth, and then trust her mother to back her up.

"I—" She winced. Speaking made her chest hurt. "I'm not—"

The door slammed open and Moira burst into the room. "What's going on here?"

Sophie groaned and climbed unsteadily to her feet as Moira rushed toward her. Her mother held her tightly and glared around at the others, waiting for an explanation.

"It was my idea," Dr. Rogers said tightly.

"Well, it was a foolish one," Moira snapped, and she looked as if she wished they were alone so she could unleash stronger vocabulary on Dr. Rogers. "She needs to be monitored and fed, not *punched*." She turned a withering glare on Gary, who looked as if he wanted to crawl under the couch.

Moira helped Sophie across the room, and Sophie cast a curious look back at Andreyev before her mother pulled her into the hallway and slammed the door shut, leaving them alone. Then she turned to Sophie and ran her hands over her hair, her eyes brimming with wrath.

"Sophie Jane Crue," she hissed. "What the *hell* do you think you're doing?"

FIFTEEN
LUX

"Where is she?" he asked.

And she had no answer.

"Who are you?" he asked.

And she had no answer.

It pained her that she could not tell him the things he wanted to know. Why didn't she know the answers? What was wrong with her?

Even when she tried to obey him, to swim across and get the plane, she did it wrong. She fell under the water and couldn't get up again. She felt *angry* that she couldn't do what he asked.

There was just so much happening. The words were like the waves, sucking her down and overwhelming her until she couldn't breathe. She wanted to understand him, but he moved so fast that trying to keep up with him was like drowning. She felt the same way when he asked her questions she could not answer: suffocating, choking, falling beneath the water. . . .

When the feelings of inadequacy surged through her, her brain served up only the words *I am sorry I am sorry I am sorry* but they weren't enough weren't nearly enough to release what she felt she would bust if she couldn't give him the answers!

But then he moved on, talking and walking and looking all around and she could only watch and struggle to follow. He walked up and down and she walked behind him, stepping where he stepped, matching her footprints in his.

The world tugged at her. So much to take in, too much to see. Shells and birds and leaves and rocks and water and sand, and she wanted to touch it all, smell it, understand it. The things that had terrified her at first now fascinated her. She wanted to hold it all in her hands, but when she tried she only dropped things, the shells and the rocks and the little white crab she found in a little sand hole.

But more fascinating than sand and shells and crabs was Jim: how he moved and talked, how he turned and ran his fingers through his hair, how his face changed and his voice rose and fell like the water, how his shadow slid across the sand. She watched him and she learned. She did what he did, stepped where he stepped. When he scratched his ear so did she. When he stopped and looked up at the sky so did she. When he spoke she moved her lips.

Every time he looked at her she felt brighter inside, and she yearned to keep his attention, to hold his gaze.

This was her world, her world of sand and sea and the boy named Jim, and she was content.

SIXTEEN
JIM

He decided to go for the police. Or possibly even the navy. This was beyond him, well and above his reach, and he hadn't the slightest clue what else he could do. At the least, he could find some way to reach Mr. Crue, to let him know Sophie could be in trouble.

He muttered to himself and kicked the sand up as he walked, and his hands worried at his hair and his face in agitation. The girl copied him, her hands matching his movements with eerie exactness. It made him so uncomfortable that he forced himself to keep his hands at his sides.

Whatever she was, this not-Sophie, it seemed that he'd stolen her. They would notice she was missing, and they would come after him. Mary and her friends already *were* after him. He couldn't fend them all off, and he doubted he'd be able to go back for Sophie. Her look-alike was no help at all. She seemed to know nothing about the island, the doctors, Sophie, Nicholas, any of it. His questions only got him traumatized looks, as if she *wanted* to give him answers but simply couldn't. She was a conflict of appearances and behavior. A child in a nearly full-grown body. She might have looked identical to Sophie on the outward, but she wasn't *like* Sophie at all, unless, perhaps, he compared her to Sophie as he'd known her a decade ago.

At least he could take comfort in the hope that if it wasn't Sophie with him now, maybe the real Sophie was okay after all. Perhaps she'd found her mother and all was well and it was just Jim who was in a mess.

I could go back, he thought. *Tell them I'm sorry, I made a mistake.*

But he couldn't get past the fact that Sophie had gone into Corpus's arms and hadn't returned. And if Sophie *was* all right, she would have let him know. It followed, then, that she wasn't and that the island really was hostile and the whole situation needed to be taken to the authorities.

That only brought him to another obstacle—reaching the plane. The tide wasn't going out any time soon, and if Mary was going to make good on her promise, he couldn't afford to wait.

"Okay." He stopped walking and pressed his hands together and then touched his fingertips to his chin, staring at the girl, whose name even she didn't seem to know. "Here's what we'll do. I'll swim the channel and see if I can break through the current. Don't know how but don't know what else to do. In the unlikely event that I *don't* drown, I'll get to my plane, taxi it over here, and pick you up. And then . . ." His voice trailed off. *And then we fly by the seat of our pants.* "Stay here," he told her. "Don't wander off. I'll be back for you. Maybe. If I don't drown first."

He tugged off his shoes and his shirt and left them on the sand. Then he stood in the surf and inhaled slowly, trying to psych himself up for the swim. The water rushed at him and threw itself against him in taunting waves. He cracked his neck and rolled his shoulders, and then dove underwater.

For a bit, all seemed to be going well. His hopes even rose; perhaps by some lucky chance he'd picked a time of day when the current was weaker than it looked. He stroked along, clawing his way through the water at a steady pace. Salt stung his eyes and lips, but he was used to that. He'd grown up on the beaches of Guam, and the sea was as familiar to him as the sky. Sea and sky and sand; they were his school, his home, his world. *I can do this*, he told himself. *This is my turf as much as it is theirs.*

His mother had loved to swim, but she'd hated flying. She'd hated it when *he* flew. His dad had begun teaching him how to pilot when he was just ten years old, and some of his bitterest memories were of his parents arguing over his flying. It was in those arguments that the differences between his parents were most obvious. His mother liked order. Her life was a series of annotated planners and drawers of neatly sorted silverware. Nothing put her out of sorts quite like spontaneity. She couldn't handle it. Either she shut down and retreated to her work as a professor at the University of Guam, or she lashed out at Jim's father. Steve Julien was the yang to Elaina's yin, but instead of coming together in a cohesive whole, they clashed like fire and water. Steve was laid-back, hated schedules, and acted entirely on whim. He lived on impulse, and Jim was very much like him. Father and son rolled like water, always changing and following the tide; his mother was an immovable island whose edges they slowly eroded. And eventually, they wore her too thin, and she flew off to the mainland with a naval officer named Lance.

The current caught Jim completely by surprise, slamming into him like a wall of rock, sweeping him eastward into open sea. He was as powerless as a leaf on the wind. The water sucked him under, and he fought against it until his lifeguard training took over, and he remembered that it was better to go with a current than fight it. So he relaxed and let it take him, and he resurfaced long enough to gasp for air and get his bearings. He'd been swept wide of both islands and was quickly being borne even further out to sea. He could see not-Sophie on the beach watching him but not moving. He couldn't expect aid from her, nor did he want it. She'd already proven she couldn't swim.

He knew he had to do something quickly or he'd be carried so far out that he'd never make it back, but he had to wait until the current weakened. It was a rip current; it couldn't go on forever. Fighting it would only wear him out, and he'd drown for sure.

Eventually he started to slow down, and that was his sign that it was time to get out. He started to swim north, toward the airstrip, but when he glanced back, his blood turned cold, and it had nothing to do with the temperature of the water.

Mary and her two friends were walking out of the woods, and they'd spotted the Sophie look-alike. She sat with her gaze still fixed on Jim, unaware of their approach behind her.

He hesitated, and the current, though weak, dragged him ever outward. He had to make a decision fast. Once he was out of the current, he wouldn't be able to swim across it again.

Gritting his teeth together, Jim thrust his arms through the water with all his strength. It wasn't easy; the current was still strong, and for a moment it seemed he was standing still. But then he broke out of the stream as quickly as he'd entered it, and then he began churning water as fast as he could. He timed his strokes with the onrushing waves in an attempt to speed himself along. But they'd already reached her, and Mary gripped the girl's hair and was pulling. He was a good distance away, but he could still hear her scream in pain.

"Stop!" he yelled, expending precious energy. Either they didn't hear him or they didn't care. They watched him swim in with impatient expressions, as if they couldn't wait to pounce on him. When he was close enough, the two boys charged into the surf and grabbed his arms, dragging him onto the sand. He was entirely spent, helpless in their hands. His body trembled with exhaustion, and he felt sick. He coughed up salt water, and that made him fall into a fit of retching. Then, abdomen aching, he collapsed and let them drag him onto the dry sand where Mary was waiting, her hands still entwined in not-Sophie's hair.

"Tsk," she clucked when they dumped him at her feet. Her brown curls snapped in the wind. "Naughty little pilot, stealing our precious Lux away from us."

He was gasping and choking still, but managed to croak, "So she *does* have a name."

"What are you doing on our island?"

"Hunting for pirate treasure."

Her eyes flashed at the boy on his left—Jay—and Jay delivered a kick to Jim's side that sent him cringing into a fetal position.

"Where's Sophie?" he gasped. "What happened to her?"

"I'm the one asking questions. Not that I particularly care why you're here. I don't."

He groaned and pushed himself onto his knees. Trying in vain to ignore the pain in his side, he cracked her a crooked smile. "You're cute when you're mad. Want to go out sometime?"

She dropped Lux's hair, and Lux, whimpering, drew her knees up to her chest and gazed at Jim with round, pleading eyes. Her look sent a wave of guilt through him. He didn't like that. He didn't want to feel responsible for her—he had nothing to do with her.

Mary noticed their exchanged glances and scowled. "Do you know what you've done? What she is?"

"Please," he said. "Enlighten me."

"She's a Vitro, you ass. We all are, really, but *we're* not like *her*. Let me guess," Mary sighed. "She does whatever you tell her, to the letter. She grovels at your feet." She crouched beside Lux and pinched her cheek, speaking through pouty lips as if speaking to a puppy or a baby. "She just tries *so hard* to please her precious master."

"What?"

Her eyes crackled at him. "She's a pathetic puppet, like all the others. But you've made a mess. Oh, quite a mess. The investor came today, you know, to see *her*." She wrapped an arm around Lux and stroked her cheek. "And now there's no doll to put on display for him—ah! I wish I was there to see it. Strauss must be murderous."

Jim had no idea what she was talking about. He narrowed his eyes. "What do you want? Who sent you after me?"

She groaned. "I'm bored. You're awfully boring, did you know that? Jay, Wyatt, just beat him up a bit. That'll keep him put."

"You just want to keep me put? That's it? Well, all you had to do was ask. I'd do anything for a pretty girl like you, Mary." His voice grew frantic as Jay and Wyatt pulled him to his feet.

Mary rolled her eyes. "I always have to clean up Nicholas's messes. Didn't I say the nails were a dumbass idea? Go on. Hit him until he's unconscious. I want to get back to the Vitro building to see what's going on. They're probably stirred up like sharks over blood with Lux going missing."

"Wait! Let's just talk about this for a—"

They didn't wait. One of them—he never saw who— cracked a fist into Jim's jaw, and his vision went spotty. He reeled backward and slammed into the sand, tasting blood in his mouth.

Then he heard a shout of surprise, and though he braced himself for a second blow, none came. He blinked away the black spots in his eyes and gaped.

Lux had sprung up like a cat. She whirled and kicked, catching Jay in the stomach. He doubled over. In an instant, she was on Wyatt. Her movements were clumsy, uncoordinated, but effective. Her hair flared in the wind like a silken cape. A punch, a kick, and a head butt, and Wyatt was laid on his back, gasping. Mary's eyes went wide, and she held up her hands, but Lux swiped her feet out from under her and then pounced like a tiger, her hands around Mary's throat.

"Lux!" Jim scrambled to her. Her eyes were flat, dead, unseeing, and her grip tightened around Mary's slender throat. Mary's eyes grew wide, and her cheeks turned a sickening shade of blue. "Lux, stop!" he yelled.

And just like that, she let go.

Mary threw Lux off of her and crawled backward across the sand, choking for air.

"Go," she whispered to her friends. "She's a bodyguard model like Clive!"

"What?" Jay winced, his arms still around his middle. "I didn't know that. But she's a newborn!"

"Doesn't matter," said Mary. "Let's go."

The three of them started running up the beach, but Mary paused at the tree line and yelled back, "You won't leave this island alive, either of you! It's too late."

"What are you talking about?" He was still trying to swallow his astonishment at Lux. "If you know where Sophie is—"

"I don't know where your girlfriend is, but if Corpus has her"—Mary smiled, a thin, cruel smile—"I wouldn't count on seeing her again."

SEVENTEEN
SOPHIE

Sophie was caught completely off guard. She froze to the spot, speechless, unable to look away from her mother's eyes. Moira Crue's face was a thundercloud.

"What are you *doing* here?" she whispered, her lips tight.

"I—your e-mail," Sophie stammered. "You asked me to come."

Now it was Moira who looked blindsided. "E-mail? What e-mail? I never sent you an e-mail, Sophie. What is going on? Where's your father?"

Her stomach twisted. "He's home. In Boston. He doesn't know—*you* e-mailed me! I have it here—oh." The copy of the e-mail had been in the pocket of her jeans. She realized, with a shudder of horror, that whoever had hit her on the head must have also undressed her and put her in the gown she now wore. She wrapped her arms around herself, clamping her teeth shut to keep them from chattering. She felt violated, afraid, and suddenly all she wanted was for her mother to put her arms around her and tell her everything was going to be okay.

But Moira didn't. Instead, she wrapped her fingers around Sophie's wrist and pulled her down the hallway, walking at a pace that had Sophie jogging to keep up. They were the only ones in the hall, but her mother glanced around anxiously, as if expecting someone to jump out at any moment.

"Ouch, Mom, you're hurting me!"

Moira didn't loosen her grip. "Stop talking. Do what you were doing before."

"What?"

Moira stopped and whirled, going nose to nose with Sophie. Her blue eyes bore into Sophie, making the space between her eyes tingle. "It's not safe here. Keep impersonating Lux. We'll talk in private. Come on."

Sophie swallowed and nodded.

Moira took her to a small office tucked at the end of the hallway where Sophie had woken to Andreyev and Strauss. The office was cluttered and worn; she could tell that her mother spent a lot of time here. Filing cabinets were crammed along one wall, and opposite them rose a massive floor-to-ceiling, wall-to-wall bookshelf overflowing with books, binders, and lab equipment. A whiteboard hung on the wall behind the desk, scribbled over with formulas Sophie didn't understand; the multicolored ink was so old the reds were faded to pinks. Small photographs were taped to the frame of the board— children, all of them. They looked like younger versions of some of the kids she'd seen in the building already. There was a cherubic boy who had to be Clive, and the girl with the brown curls, and Nicholas, his hair short but his eyes holding the same odd expression that was a mingle of boredom and epiphany.

There was something missing, and it took Sophie a moment to realize what it was: there were no photographs of her. Not one. *Maybe this is someone else's office, and not my mom's.* But Moira sat in the chair behind the desk and folded her hands on top of the papers strewn before her with a familiar ease that told Sophie this was indeed her mother's office, and that for reasons unknown to her, she was not allowed here. Not in photographs, not in the flesh. This room seemed to Sophie to be the heart of Moira's life, the room that was the center of her world—and Sophie was very obviously not in it.

"Tell me everything," Moira said. She nodded at a chair in the corner, and Sophie carefully set aside the coffeemaker on it and took a seat.

"You didn't send me an e-mail telling me there was an emergency and that you needed me?" she asked flatly.

"No." Moira kept glancing at the door, as if afraid they'd be discovered.

"Well, *someone* did." Sophie's face was growing very warm. That was one question answered, at least. There was no emergency. Her mother had never wanted her here, and that hadn't changed. "All it said was that you needed me and that I should come, so I did. It was signed by you and sent from your e-mail address."

Moira leaned back in her chair, regarding Sophie thoughtfully. "Someone on the island, then. They couldn't access the servers from anywhere else."

"Mom."

"How did you even *get* here?"

"A pilot." *Better she doesn't know which one.* "It doesn't matter. He's come and gone." At least, she hoped he'd left. She was sorry she'd roped him into her plans to begin with. If anything happened to him . . . *I can't think about that. Anyway, I'm sure he's long gone by now.* He'd been itching to leave since the moment they'd landed, and she imagined Jim had taken her continued absence as an excuse to clear out—that is, if he'd gotten the plane repaired. She uneasily forced her thoughts away from the pilot. She had enough to handle here in this room.

Sophie leaned forward on her elbows. "I heard everything. About the Vitros. And Lux."

Moira's face was expressionless. "I'm aware."

Sophie jumped out of her seat and slammed her hands onto the desk, sending loose papers flying. "How can you just sit there? How can you be so calm? You're making *slaves*."

"It's not what you think," Moira said softly.

"Not what I think? I heard every word in there!" She pointed toward the hallway. "How could you?" she whispered. She lowered her arm and curled her fingers into a fist. "It's sick and it's wrong."

"Do not presume to lecture me, young lady." Moira's voice was low and dangerous, and she looked up at Sophie from beneath a rigid brow. "Sit down and tell me how you got here."

Sophie sat, her back straight and her shoulders high with tension. "Does it matter? You're going to send me back to Dad, anyway. Well, fine. Try it. But I'm not going back there. Dad doesn't get me, doesn't want to let me make my own decisions." She drew a breath, pausing on the edge of the words, and then she jumped. "I wanted to work with you," she said, all in a rush. "I wanted to be part of this"—she gestured at the walls around her—"and I argued with Dad about it for months. Now . . . now I don't know what to think. Now that I've seen what you *really* do it's like I don't know you at all. And if I go back . . ." *I'll have to admit he was right all along, that you are untrustworthy and deceitful. All those years I defended you, and in the end, I was defending someone who didn't exist.* The only thing that outweighed the shame she felt for having to admit her father had been right was the hollow and shocked disappointment she felt when she looked at her mother.

Moira opened her mouth, then thought better of it and sighed, steepling her fingers under her chin. "This is bad. You were never supposed to be here."

"At least now I know why you've been hiding the truth from me. You knew I'd hate you for it."

"*Sophie.* You don't hate me."

She wanted to, and she thought she was very close to it, but when she tried to say it the words caught in her throat. "Whatever. How is this place even legal?"

"How long were you unconscious down there?" Moira's brows drew together inquisitively. "Just when, exactly, did you arrive?"

"Yesterday. Someone knocked me out and put me in *this.*" She fingered the thin gown. "Next thing I know, I'm staring at that Russian guy. *Kids*, Mom? Really? You grow and sell *kids*? I saw the others—Caleb and Clive. They're nothing but puppets. And Nicholas—what's he got to do with it?"

Moira stiffened. "You met Nicholas? When?"

"Just tell me *why*," Sophie whispered. "Why would you do something like this? Something so horrible? And what about Lux? Why is she . . . what is she to *me*?"

For once, Moira dropped her gaze and Sophie was certain there was a flicker of shame in her eyes. Her mother stared at an empty mug on her desk and absently fingered the tea bag tag that draped over the side. "Sophie . . . I'm sorry you saw this. Your father . . ." Her voice dwindled to a whisper, and she pressed the heel of her hand to her forehead. "Your father was right about me." She lifted her eyes, and they were filled with regret. Whether the regret was from her own guilt or just that she regretted that Sophie knew about her work, Sophie could not tell. Moira gave a short sigh and lifted her chin. "If Strauss knows you're here, she'll forbid you to leave. You'll be stuck here for good. You've simply seen too much."

"Strauss is a monster. I ought to tell her so, to her face."

"No!" Moira rose to her feet, and her nostrils flared as she exhaled in indignation. "You will not throw your life away. I won't let you. This place—you've seen what it is. What it stands for. I won't let you be a part of it."

"*You're* a part of it."

"Strauss will never know you were here, and that is the end of this discussion. Now." Moira put her hands on her hips. "Where is Lux?"

"I don't know."

"She isn't downstairs with the other Vitros. I already looked."

"Other Vitros?"

"There are twenty more of them who are still asleep. I found you this morning, when I was looking for Lux. You were lying unconscious in an empty room, arranged as if you'd been there—where *she* had been—all along. We need to find out who's behind that. Few people have access to the sleeping Vitros. And speaking of Lux, she isn't among them. So where is she?"

"I told you, I don't know! I saw her last night, when I first got here. She was in that room, the same one I was in when I woke up and saw you and that Russian guy, and she was sleeping. That's when someone hit me from behind."

Moira pressed her hand to her mouth, her index finger tapping rapidly, as if she were hyped on too much coffee. "It doesn't make sense. Why would anyone want to switch you girls?"

"Mom." Sophie moved from her chair to the desk, and leaned across it so she could take her mother's hands in hers. She looked Moira in the eye and felt her tears gathering. "Why are you doing this?" Her voice barely left her lips, a thin, pleading whisper.

Moira met her gaze for a moment, then broke it, turned her head aside, and hid her expression. "It wasn't supposed to be this. Not at first. But I lost control, Sophie. The Vitro Project slipped through my fingers and Strauss . . . no, not just Strauss, but *Corpus* . . . They changed it, made it what it is. Because that's what they do." She turned her head back, her eyes steely. "They consume you and bleed you dry, and when they've exhausted you, they spit you out. You can't win against them, because sooner or later you will always come to a line, a line you aren't willing to cross—but they will. That's how they win, every time. That's why we can't let them know you're here. Corpus will swallow you whole, Sophie, and you'll find yourself doing things you swore you'd never do." She stared at her hands, still cupped in Sophie's. "I came here to create. Instead, they've made me destroy. It's not too late for you. Go home; forget about this place. Forget about me, if you must."

Sophie pulled her hands away. The biggest questions of all still remained. "Why does Lux look like me? Is she a clone?"

"A clone? No, of course not. None of the Vitros are." Moira twisted her fingers together, still staring at her hands. "She's your twin sister."

"Your own daughter." Sophie felt cold all over. "How could you do that to your own child? Raise her in a tank? Strip away her will and sell her to a criminal who will just use and abuse her?"

"I . . ." Moira paused, then licked her lower lip. "It's not like that. When I . . . when I was pregnant . . . Lux was dying, Sophie. She was too weak and wasn't going to survive. We almost lost her altogether, so we decided to give her the only chance she had—we made her a Vitro. We gave her life, at a cost, yes, but we gave it to her the only way we could. Anyway. That's all in the past. You should forget about her."

"How can I?" Sophie's voice mounted in volume. She felt the urge to knock things off shelves, so she folded her arms tightly across her chest. "She's my *sister*, apparently. Forget about her? Impossible!"

"We don't even know where she is." Moira groaned and planted her face in her hands. "Who am I kidding? It's over anyway. Andreyev will find out that everything's gone wrong, and he'll pull out. We'll lose what little funding Corpus gave us. It's over."

"Is that a bad thing?" It seemed to Sophie that she'd arrived just in time. If by replacing Lux she'd thrown a wrench into Corpus's plans to make and market mindless slaves, perhaps her coming to Skin Island wasn't going entirely awry after all.

"Sophie." Her mother gave her a grave look. "If they cut the Vitro Project, they cut the Vitros."

At first, she didn't get it. Then the reality of her mom's words slammed into her brain, and she felt sick. "You mean—"

"No loose ends." Moira stood and turned around, and her fingers brushed over the photos on the whiteboard. "I know you see them as mindless. But Sophie. I've seen these children grow up. I was there when each of them opened their eyes for the first time. Maybe they're damaged; maybe they'd have even been better off never being born. But they were. And I'm responsible for them." When she turned back around, Sophie expected, from the catch in her voice, that there would be tears in her eyes. But Moira's gaze was smooth as glass. "I will do whatever I must to save them."

Sophie nodded once. "I understand, but . . ."

Her mother folded her arms on the back of her chair. "I know. You're still judging me for what the Vitros are, and I don't blame you. But you have to understand—it's out of my control. I help them as much as I can, but in the end, I'm powerless."

Sophie didn't believe her. She thought that if it was *her* in Moira's place, she'd fight tooth and nail to stop what was going on. The essential wrongness of Skin Island was noxious to her, but it seemed Moira had already given up without a fight.

"Dad walked away, didn't he?" she asked softly.

Moira nodded, her gaze going distant. "He was stronger than I was."

"That's why you two split." For years Sophie's mind had

struggled to untie the knots of the past, and all at once the knots came undone, unraveling in her hands. "So . . . what? You compromised on me and Lux? I went with Dad, you kept Lux?"

"You don't belong on Skin Island. You never have. It was right for you to go with your father. He is . . . he has always been the better parent."

Sophie always thought her father was the weaker one, the one who gave up and quit and went home while her mother stayed to continue what Sophie had thought was noble work for the good of humanity. *I got it all backward. Mom was the weak one, the one who left us, and Dad is the one who was strong.* Had he hidden the truth from Sophie because he knew how much she adored Moira and he didn't want to break her heart? Had he wanted her to come to the truth herself? Suddenly all the warnings her father had given her made sense. *He was protecting me.* Did she wish he'd just been truthful? Did she resent his secrets? At first she thought she did, that she should be as angry with him as she was with her mom. But then she wasn't so sure. *If I had known the truth, I would never have known my mom at all.* Perhaps the happy memories she had of her mother were tinged with lies, but if she'd known what her mother's work truly was then she'd have no happy memories at all.

She looked long and hard at her mother, a woman whom she was only just beginning to truly know, and she hoped—desperately—that she could find some way to redeem her.

They both jumped when a knock rattled the door. Moira froze, whispered "Be Lux!" and then snatched a clipboard off the desk as she called out, "Who's that?"

The door burst open and Strauss strode in, her eyes suspicious. "There you are! What are you doing?"

Immediately Sophie let herself glaze over. Her mother was perched on the edge of the desk as if she'd been there all along. She gave Strauss an irritated look. "I'm going over a quick psych evaluation with Lux. What's wrong?"

"I heard there was an incident with Andreyev."

"I already settled that," Moira said calmly, scrawling with great concentration what Sophie could see were meaningless loops on her clipboard.

Strauss looked more closely at Sophie. "Why are you in here? Shouldn't she be in physical therapy?"

"She should be in here, taking her psych eval!" Moira retorted. "And now you're distressing her."

Sophie blinked at her mother, then winced and tightened her hands around the armrests, trying to look distressed.

"Well, don't take all day about it," Strauss said, still studying Sophie through narrow eyes. "I can only keep Andreyev entertained for so long."

When she'd left, Sophie let out a long relieved sigh. Moira shook her head grimly and set down the clipboard. "She's not stupid." She gave Sophie a solemn look. "It's only a matter of time before she figures out who you really are."

"So what if she does?"

"Sophie. If she does—she may take it in her head that you're more of a liability than you're worth."

It took Sophie a moment to interpret what that meant.

Her spine tingled as if ice had been dropped down the back of her shirt. "She wouldn't!"

"Never underestimate her, Sophie." Moira's eyes went distant, as if she were looking backward into the past. "You wouldn't be the first threat Strauss has had eliminated."

EIGHTEEN
LUX

Lux sat in a tangle of limbs and stared at the horizon with wide, unblinking eyes. Outwardly, she was still as stone, but inwardly she trembled.

The moment the boys hit Jim, something terrible and powerful had snapped inside of her, and she lost all control. She did not understand it and she did not like it but she could not stop it. It was as if the entire world stopped existing except for one all-consuming command roaring inside her head: *Protect Jim.*

Then her body took over and left her behind: It whirled and danced and moved with a speed that made her thoughts spin.

Protect.

The words took over, pushing her aside and moving her hands, her feet.

Kick. And her body followed. She spun and threw out a

leg and her foot slammed into the stomach of the one who had hit Jim.

Punch the other one. Her fist plowed into his jaw.

Still not down. Kick him. A sharp upward kick between his legs. He gasped and doubled over, but still remained on his feet.

Bring him down. She snapped her head against his, and he fell at last, groaning and writhing.

Now the girl. The girl was the leader. She had to be stopped. Lux dropped onto her hands as her legs swung in a wide arc, knocking the girl's feet from under her.

Now eliminate the threat.

Lux leaped forward, barely registering what she was even doing. She looked down and saw her hands around the girl's throat. The girl's eyes were wide. She was trying to breathe but Lux would not let her. She tightened her grip. *Eliminate the threat.*

But . . . Deep, deep in her mind, Lux whimpered. *I am hurting her.*

Yes! Eliminate the threat!

She could not stop. The words were too powerful. There was a voice inside her brain that was not her own, and it commanded her body. She watched as her hands tightened, tightened, tightened. The girl twisted. Struggled. Made raspy throat noises.

"Lux!"

Jim's voice was dim and distant.

Her eyes fixed on the girl. She felt a throbbing in her temples and in her wrists. Suddenly she wanted it to stop—all of it—the hurting and the struggling and the voice in her head that kept saying *Eliminate the threat eliminate the threat eliminate the threat* but she could not turn it off.

"Lux, stop!" Jim yelled.

And she let go.

The voice, the words, *eliminate the threat*: They shut off and disappeared, and the girl threw her aside.

Lux lay in the sand in a sprawl and trembled. Jim was talking to the others; they were running away. She hardly noticed. She stared at her hands and rocked back and forth. *Hurts hurts hurts hurts*, which did not compute because there was no pain. Then why did she hurt? Her heart hurt and her head hurt and her hands.

What am I?

The thought punched her mind the way her fist had punched the boys, leaving her gasping.

What am I?

I am Vitro beta model—

No. That was not the answer she wanted. She wanted *more.* She wanted—she *wanted*—there was no word for it. Her mind was blank. She was missing something so very important, but she did not know what it was. She had found that the longer she stared at something, the more she knew about it. She could stare at a tree and know more and more about how it worked—*roots below the ground* and *sunlight on the leaves* and *it begins with a seed.* The ocean held *fish* and *dolphins* and *microorganisms* and it covered *71 percent of the earth's surface.* But when she stared at herself, at her hands, at her sandy legs, at the ends of her hair, nothing came into her mind. She was blank, a wordless being. She could look anywhere around her and *know* what she saw, but when it came to herself . . . She was a hole in the universe.

Suddenly she felt as if there were hands around *her* throat, and she reached up—but there was nothing there. Yet still she felt a panic in her throat, in her chest. She bent over, pressed her forehead against her knees, wrapped her arms around her legs, and held them tight.

What am I?

This time, her brain made no reply at all. She sat silent and empty. Listening for words that never came, for an explanation that did not exist. *I am I am I am I am* . . . Blank.

Hollow.

Empty.

Then at last, slowly, softly, a word bubbled up from the bottom of her mind.

Afraid.

I am afraid.

NINETEEN
SOPHIE

Sophie paced the length of her small room with all the restless energy of a cat in a box. She'd been locked up since morning while her mother made excuses for her, telling the others that she was working with Lux one on one, that everything was fine, not to worry. The only person she had seen since was Dr. Hashimoto, who had brought her a light lunch consisting of a sickeningly bland sort of oatmeal that tasted like Elmer's glue. Was this standard Vitro fare, Sophie wondered—or just some special recipe reserved for those newly awoken from years of slumber? With the exception of Dr. Hashimoto's lunch delivery, Sophie was under strict orders not to open the door to anyone except Moira, who was off trying to discover what had become of the real Lux.

The room was small and simple, like any number of hotel rooms, with a twin bed and a flimsy dresser. Impersonal prints of seashells and beach scenes hung on the wall, perhaps left over from Halcyon Cove's resort days. It was on a hall of similarly furnished bedrooms occupied by, she reckoned, the Vitros. She heard them and the doctors throughout the day, walking past and talking in low voices. After digging through the dresser, she found a pair of khaki shorts, underclothes, and a white tank top that fit her perfectly. They must have been put there in anticipation of Lux. She couldn't find any socks, but the small closet produced a pair of brand-new white Keds, the sort she'd worn in first grade and which, she remembered with a start, Jim had stolen once and doodled all over with a Sharpie.

She was certain now that he must have left. If the plane were still grounded, wouldn't he have turned up at some point, looking for a phone or for Sophie? She was surprised at the disappointment she felt at the thought. Though she was glad he was gone and safe, something inside her stretched out its hand, seeking to stop him, bring him back, but it was too late.

When she was tired of pacing, Sophie flopped onto the bed or stared at the ceiling or hovered at the window. It looked out over a span of grass that ended abruptly in a steep bluff; beyond it lay the endless sea. She was gazing out the window when she heard voices from the hall. These were different than the ones she had been hearing all day—louder, angrier, and younger.

She crept to the door and pressed her ear to it. The voices were unfamiliar. She reached for the doorknob, her fingers hovering over it indecisively. She wanted to see who it was, but she didn't want to give herself away. So she bit her lip and tried to overhear the conversation.

"We're not telling Nicky anything," a girl said. "I can handle it. He's not in charge of us! He thinks he is but he's not."

"I'm just saying," a boy replied, "that he's gonna want to know what we saw."

"And what, exactly, *did* you see?" That was Nicholas. He must have surprised them, because Sophie heard a moment of silence from the others. "Mary, Mary, so contrary," Nicholas sang. "What don't you want me to know?"

"We found the pilot," Mary grumbled.

Sophie pressed a hand to her mouth as her stomach tightened. *He's still on the island?* What joy she might have felt at the knowledge that Jim was still nearby paled in comparison to the twinge of alarm in her gut. *Why is he still here? What happened?*

"And?" Nicholas asked, his voice so low that Sophie barely caught it.

"He has Lux."

A moment of silence, then, "You don't say? Well, that explains a lot. Did she wake up?"

"Look at Wyatt's eye and you tell me."

"God! She did that? Already?"

"He got the plane into the water somehow. Anyway, he's stuck until the tide goes down, unless he finds the boat."

"He won't find it."

"Where have you been, Nicky? We looked everywhere for you."

"Oh, you know. Around. Go on, get out of here. I'll let you know when I need you."

"You're not our boss."

"Shut up, Mary. Whose plan is this? Whose idea was it? Go."

Shuffling footsteps told Sophie that they'd gone, but just when she started to move away from the door, the knob began to turn. She sprang back as the door opened and Nicholas walked in.

"There you are," he said cheerily, shutting the door behind him. "Been looking for you."

She backed up until she was pressed against the wall beside the window, watching him through slitted eyes. "What are you doing?" she asked.

"Your pilot's made a mess," Nicholas said with a grimace. He shook his hair back from his face, then tucked it behind his ears, which gave him an elfin look. "Don't pretend you don't know it. You heard us out there."

She folded her arms and glared. "I know it was you who hit me last night. Why?"

He looked offended. "It wasn't me!"

"It had to be you! Anyone else would have reported me to Strauss or my mom."

"Anyone except *Mary*."

"The girl in the hallway?" She pointed at the door.

"Yes," he sighed. "She's crazy. In fact . . ." He stepped closer and lowered his voice. "She and her friends, Jay and Wyatt, they're all psychopaths, you know. Certifiable. They're the Vitros who went *wrong*. The experiments that went bad."

Sophie digested this, then narrowed her eyes. "Mary hit me on the head?"

"I found her standing over you. She'd used an old Bunsen burner. Must have hurt. Oh, sit down, Sophie. You're all cagey and mean. It doesn't help your looks."

Smoldering, Sophie sat on the edge of the bed, her arms still folded. "Why did she knock me out?"

"I told you. She's a psychopath."

"And what are you?"

He met her gaze steadily, his face serious. He hooked a foot around the chair by the dresser and slid it in front of the door, then sat, his fingers dancing on his knees. "I'm the first Vitro. The oldest one. That's the truth. That's who I am. When I found Mary standing over you I sent her away and made her swear to say nothing about you. You wouldn't wake up, and I didn't know what to do, so I hid you with the other Vitros, thought they'd never look there, that you'd blend in. But then Lux went missing and they went searching and then they found you and . . . it all spun out of control."

So he *had* been the one to put her in the gown. She reddened and folded her arms over her stomach, suddenly wishing he would just go away. "But it was more than just a bump on the head. I was drugged—I know I was. I felt it. When I tried to wake up I just fell back under, as if you wanted me to *stay* asleep. And where are my clothes?"

"Ugh. Details. *Boring.*" He leaned forward, his feet bouncing and his eyes bright. "So what do you think of Skin Island? The Vitros? Your mother? Come on, tell me—I'm dying to hear your impression."

She felt as if she were playing tennis without a racket, and his words ricocheted around her and bounced back to him without her ever managing to get a handle on the conversation. He made her dizzy. "*Nicholas.* Why did you send me that e-mail? I know it was you—it had to be you. You knew to meet me at the airstrip yesterday, and you knew the message was supposedly from my mom. But *why?* Why do you want me here?"

His face darkened and he leaned back, crossing his left

ankle over his right knee, his foot still bouncing. "I wanted your help."

"My *help*?" She hadn't expected that. She uncrossed her arms. "To do what?"

He leaped from the chair to the bed in one swift move, sitting beside her before she could get away. He took her hands in his and met her eyes steadily, his gaze suddenly desperate. "I think you know."

She tilted her head, studying him as if he were an optical illusion presenting one image until she blinked, and suddenly he was something else. "You're not like the other Vitros. They're all . . . puppets, weak and mindless. But not you. Why is that?"

"Does it matter? I'm not imprinted on anyone, thank *God*." He turned over, propped on one elbow. He picked at a loose thread on the comforter. "I've been trapped on this island my entire life, and I spend my days cleaning up after the doctors, scrubbing toilets, mopping floors, reorganizing their sock drawers if they ask. It's not a life, Sophie. I just . . ." He bent over, his hands knotted over the back of his head so that his hair hung like a black curtain around his face. "You have no idea what it's like to be trapped your whole life, to be looked at as if you're a monster even when you've done nothing wrong. The only escape I've had is in my mind. Every time this place closed in on me, when I felt like I was suffocating, I thought about you, about how free you were and what you must be doing."

"What do you want from me?" she asked softly.

"Moira talked about you, you know. Ever since I was little, you were this image in my head. . . ." His fingers strayed to hers, then stopped as if he were afraid to touch her. "You were my escape."

She stared at him, her chest suddenly hurting, trying to imagine what his life was like. She turned around fully, her legs bent beneath her, to gauge from his expression whether or not he was telling the truth. He looked at her, more earnest than she'd seen him yet.

"I need your help," he said.

He stood up. "Please, Sophie."

"By helping you escape? Then why did you go through all the trouble of lying to me, bringing me all the way here? Jim could have flown off by then and you'd have missed your chance."

He shrugged and rolled onto his back. "I saw how he looked at you. He wasn't going anywhere, not without you."

Sophie reddened. "So . . . what? You were going to give me a tour of the place and then try to convince Jim to fly you away into the sunset?"

"Something like that," he said. "But then Jim, brilliant Jim, steals Lux thinking she was you, and now Moira's on alert and soon the others will be too, once they discover that you're a fake and Lux has imprinted on a no-account idiot—*bleh*." He grimaced in disgust. "Messy. So here we are."

"How many of you are there? Non-imprinted Vitros, I mean?"

"Oh, just us four. But that's not important now. What *is* important is that we hurry and leave the island, before Strauss finds out you're here."

"And how do you propose we do that?"

"The Corpus helicopter is parked on the other side of this building. We don't know if your pilot's plane will fly—not after he mangled it up. All we need is a chopper pilot."

"Jim?"

"Lux."

"What?"

"She's a bodyguard model," he said patiently. "All the bodyguard models come preprogrammed with the ability to operate every vehicle under the sun. I'd say let's take Clive, but this way you'll have an extra incentive—you get to save both me *and* your twin."

"My twin," Sophie echoed in a hollow tone.

"Yes, your twin. What did you think we all were? Clones?" He shook his head and looked at her as if she'd suggested he was an alien.

"I don't trust you," she whispered, her gaze caught in his as if hypnotized. He was close enough to kiss. He could dominate a room and make her head spin, and his sudden vulnerability confused her. *I barely know this boy.* She had to remind herself of that when he ran his fingers down her arms, leaving goose bumps in his wake.

"But I'm trusting you," he said softly, as serious as she'd ever seen him. "Your mother did this to me, Sophie. Made me what I am, trapped me on this island, stole every chance I might have had at a normal life. She took the world from me. Will you give it back? You have a chance to make things right. To stand where she fell and atone for her mistake. Please." His voice broke suddenly, and he looked down, drawing a deep, trembling breath. "I need you." He brushed the backs of his fingers over her cheek, and as much as she wanted to pull away, she froze. Guilt crept over her like a shadow, laying its heavy cloak around her shoulders.

"Jim has to come too," she said. "I won't leave him behind."

He sighed and dropped his hand. "Fine."

"What do we do first?"

"I'll go lift the chopper keys off the Corpus pilot, then find Jim and Lux. Meet me out front. And stay low."

She didn't like it, but she had to consider that this might be her only chance to escape. If Jim hadn't been able to fix the plane, and if Corpus really was as dangerous as everyone seemed to think, she might regret not taking this opportunity.

"This better work," she warned.

"Sophie, Sophie." He grinned. "It couldn't possibly go wrong."

Nicholas left first, telling her to wait an hour before meeting him so that he'd have a chance to get the helicopter key, as well as Lux and Jim. She waited in a state of nerves, pacing the room, wondering if she should have insisted on going with him. When a knock sounded on the door, she jumped nearly out of her skin, then froze and stared at the door as if it had grown teeth. Then, tentatively, she crossed the room and cracked it open.

"Sophie, it's me," whispered her mother, and Sophie let her in, her pulse hammering.

"I can't find Lux anywhere. You're going to have to keep acting the part," said Moira. Her face was damp with perspiration, making a few curls cling to her forehead and neck.

She looked as stressed as Sophie felt. "I can't keep making excuses, and Strauss is eager for you to spend more time with Andreyev."

"But . . . but I don't know enough. I was lucky to make this far."

"I'll be right beside you. I'll distract them as much as I can."

Sophie grappled for a way to get out of this. If she was stuck in a room with Strauss and Andreyev all day, there was no way she could meet Nicholas, Jim, and Lux at the helicopter.

She ground her teeth together. *Should I tell her?* Her mind raced. Would Moira help them escape? She seemed to want Sophie off the island—but would she let her take Lux? A day ago, Sophie would have thought that surely Moira would help her, but after what she had seen, she no longer knew what to expect from her mother. If she told her where Lux was, maybe her mom would be distracted enough in going after her that Sophie could slip away . . . or maybe, just maybe, she *would* help them. *How can I know if she's still trustworthy if I don't have at least a little faith in her?* she thought, trying to swallow her rising panic. *This isn't a plan—it's a swan dive into shallow water.* "I know where she is," she said, watching Moira closely, trying to gauge from her reaction whether or not she could trust her with their plan.

"What?" Moira's eyes shot wide. "Where?"

"She's with Jim."

"Jim?"

Sophie sighed, letting this truth slip through her fingers. "Jim Julien. Remember him?"

Moira's brow crinkled. "Steve and Elaina's boy?"

"He's the pilot who brought me here."

"Little James Julien . . ." Her mother's eyes narrowed to slits. "You told me he dropped you off and then left."

Sophie grimaced. She had mentioned that, because she'd thought it was true. "Well . . . he didn't. He's still here. Nicholas saw him with Lux."

"Nicky's a part of all this?" Moira pinched the bridge of her nose and groaned. "Not good. Not good at *all*."

"I told you I'd met him."

"Yes, well, I've been looking for him too, but it's impossible to find that boy when he doesn't want to be found. Where is the Julien boy? And how in God's name did he come to acquire Lux? Oh." The blood drained from her face. "Did she wake up? Sophie, did she imprint?" Her nails dug into Sophie's shoulders.

"Ow! Mom! I don't know—I guess so!"

Moira dropped her hands. "I have to find her. But still, we can fix this." She pounded a fist into her open palm repeatedly, as if trying to drum an idea out of her skin. "I can use one of the other unwoken Vitros to imprint on Andreyev after you're safely out of the way. And Jim! We can blame all of this on Jim, say he landed here accidentally and wandered into the building . . . yes. He woke Lux and tried to leave, but she followed him. You never need come into this. Of course, if Jim's brought into this he'll tell them about you, so it's better if he's . . . ah"—she glanced at Sophie—"not in a position to tell them."

"You'd kill him," Sophie said disbelievingly.

Her mother squared her shoulders defiantly. "I'm trying to protect you."

"Well, screw that. Maybe I don't want your kind of *protection*."

"Sophie! I'm your *mother*. At this point I'm more worried about keeping you safe and getting you off this island. The best way to do that is to keep Strauss mollified for a few more hours to give me time to sort this mess out."

Because she could think of no other way to avoid it, Sophie acceded. She followed Moira through the building, her eyes watching every exit wistfully as she contemplated simply making a run for it. But unless Nicholas, Jim, and Lux were waiting at the helicopter and ready to go, her dash would be in vain. Her mother might let her go, but she doubted Strauss would simply stand by and wave them off.

They found Strauss in some kind of break room with a counter cluttered with coffeemakers and packets of sugar and upholstered chairs arranged around a central table. One wall was a mural depicting a mosaic sunset, and Strauss sat framed by red and orange rays of asymmetrical tiles, like a model in a Mucha painting. Dr. Michalski and Dr. Rogers sat on either side of her, both of them leaning toward her; from the look of things, the three of them had been in conversation. Dr. Hashimoto was cleaning the coffeepot in a sink, and when she saw Moira and Sophie in the doorway her cheeks turned red.

"Victoria," said Moira evenly, "I brought her, as you asked. Where is Andreyev?"

"I sent him outside to play for a bit," Strauss replied, her voice oil over glass.

Moira's gaze flickered to the doctors on either side of Strauss; Dr. Michalski was looking away, his lips pursed, while

Dr. Rogers returned her gaze challengingly. "What's going on here?" she asked.

"Funny," Strauss replied, "I was going to ask you the same question."

Moira's hand flinched, as if she were going to take Sophie's hand, but then she thrust it into her pocket. Her pale face belied her steady tone. "What on earth do you mean?"

"What I mean, Moira, is that your associates here have been informing me of some . . . what did you call them, Dr. Rogers?"

He cleared his throat. "Irregularities."

"Ah. Of course. Apparently there have been some irregularities with your Vitro." Her gaze shifted to Sophie, who could feel the coldness of it on her skin. "Irregularities of which you have failed to apprise me. Please, Dr. Michalski, will you tell Moira the interesting theory which you just told me?"

Dr. Michalski looked as if he'd rather wrestle a shark, but he swallowed and nodded. "It's just that . . . her muscle development, her complexion, even her fingernails . . ."

"What about them?" Moira said lightly. Too lightly.

It was Dr. Rogers who answered, rolling his eyes at his hesitant colleague. "This isn't Lux, is it, Moira? Which means she can only be—"

"All right!" This time, Moira did grab Sophie's hand. Her voice hissed through her teeth. "I can explain."

Very slowly, Strauss unwound a tea bag from her finger and dropped it into a trash receptacle. She then set her mug on the counter, matched up the fingertips of her hands, and finally lifted her eyes to Sophie. *You wouldn't be the first threat*

Strauss has had eliminated, her mother's voice echoed in her head. Sophie swallowed, her throat suddenly dry.

"Michalski, Rogers," Strauss said evenly, and though her voice betrayed no emotion, it nonetheless made the hairs on Sophie's arms stand on end. "Leave us." They scrambled out, followed by Dr. Hashimoto.

"Victoria, let me —" Moira began, but Strauss cut her off with a flick of her hand.

"I'm speaking with the girl. Sophie, is it?" Strauss said, not even looking at Moira. "Tell me everything."

Sophie felt as if she were filled with helium she was so light-headed. She looked at Moira, who nodded. "I wanted to see my mom, so I paid someone to fly me here. I was curious about Skin Island and wanted to see it for myself. I . . . I fell asleep in one of the rooms, and I guess someone mistook me for Lux. When I woke up and saw all of you, I just went along with it."

"Hm." Strauss pulled out a chair and sat, her hands perched primly on the edge of the table. "Why are you lying to me, Sophie?"

"What? I'm not!" She heard Moira make a soft sound behind her, like a strangled warning, but she shook her head stubbornly. "That's the whole story. I swear."

"Who brought you here?"

"Just a pilot. But he's gone now, back to Guam." Her mother glanced at her, her lips twitching, but she said nothing.

Strauss sniffed. "Dobbs, take your men and head north to the airstrip." Sophie turned; she hadn't even heard the guards arrive. One of the doctors must have gone to alert them. "If you find a plane, it means the pilot is here somewhere. Find him and kill him."

"No!" Sophie cried. "Please—he isn't part of this!"

The guards ran off, their boots squeaking on the tile. Strauss's calmness was deadly. "Moira, where is Lux? The *real* Lux?"

Her mother stepped forward. "I'm working on that. She's on the island; I know that much. Nicholas might be able to help us, if I can just find him."

"Your incompetence astounds me. *You* are the one who should be outraged right now, not me. This project was conceived by my father—I just inherited it. I'll do what I must to make it successful, but if it fails, the failure is yours and not mine."

"We can fix this. Yes, Sophie is here, but no irreparable damage has been done. We have other Vitros we can show Andreyev."

"Ah. Andreyev." Strauss leaned back. "He will not be amused by this, Moira. If he withdraws his support—"

"He won't," Moira snapped. "This is just a misunderstanding. The Vitros are no less viable than they were yesterday. He'll see that."

"For your sake," said Strauss, "I should hope so. Take this girl and hold her somewhere. I want her locked away until this is cleared up."

"She's no threat to us. She's my daughter."

Strauss tilted her head forward; her glare could cut diamond. "*Now*, Moira."

Moira stiffened, then reached out and took Sophie by the arm. "I'll take care of it."

Strauss nodded and gave Sophie a brief, disdainful look. "If I find out any part of your story is false, or that you've left out anything, I'll have you shot. Are we clear?"

"I understand," Sophie whispered, and her mother marched her away.

TWENTY

JIM

There was no chance of swimming the channel now. He didn't have the strength. Nor could he risk trekking back to the resort, at least not until nightfall, when the darkness could compensate for his lack of energy to run away. The morning had left him exhausted and ravenous. From the sun's glaring position overhead, he judged he'd already missed both breakfast and lunch. When he asked Lux if she was hungry, she just gave him a confused look, as if she didn't know.

He decided to wait out the day and make one final attempt to rescue Sophie. After what Mary had said, he couldn't pretend that Sophie was all right.

He trudged into the palms, looking for a shady spot to sit. "I'm an idiot, Lux. What do you want to follow an idiot for?"

But follow him she did, with unwavering doggedness. He watched her warily, his mind replaying what he'd seen: Lux spinning into action with almost cartoonlike speed, laying all three of Jim's attackers out without breaking a sweat. She'd seemed perfectly at ease, unsurprised at her own skill, as if she were peeling a banana instead of channeling some kind of ninja warrior. And yet she still moved unsteadily, her body at odds with itself, though he noticed she was gradually getting more stable, like someone adjusting to solid land after spending a week on a boat in rough seas.

Mary had called her a "bodyguard model" after Lux had gone all Chuck Norris on them. He imagined, for some reason, a conveyor belt transporting boxes of girls identical to Lux, like giant Barbies, with *Bodyguard Model!* stamped on them in swooshy pink letters. He shook his head and grunted, disturbed by the image.

He found a flat space of sand between three tall palms and made a kind of mat out of dried fronds, within view of the beach but obscured by a thicket of low-growing, broad-leaved shrubs, so that anyone searching for them from the shore wouldn't spot them unless they stumbled upon their exact location. Then he gathered an armful of coconuts and hunted for a rock to open them with. He found a nicely sized boulder deeper into the trees, and, with Lux looking on, he smacked the first coconut against the rock. It split neatly in half. He grinned and extended a half to Lux.

"Learned that from a bum named Nico," he said. "He lived off coconuts and shellfish he pried off the docks. Guy was crazy as a bag of cats, but he knew how to crack a coconut."

Lux blinked at him, then looked down at the coconut.

He held up his half. "You *do* know how to eat a coconut, right?" He slurped up the milk, then used his nails to scrape out the white meat. It curled up easily, the smell making his mouth water and reminding him of the Chamorro women in his neighborhood back home when they gathered during fiestas with their special coconut-grating benches to make fresh coconut shavings. He and Sophie used to sit at their feet and catch shavings in their hands; he remembered that he used to pretend the soft curls of coconut were snow, which he still had never seen with his own eyes. Like an echo from across the sea, he could still hear the rhythmic scraping as the women shaved the coconut meat, and their husky, soothing voices as they sang and gossiped.

"There, see?" He stuffed a handful of coconut into his mouth. Lux stared at her coconut for a moment, then began to mimic his actions.

"Lux," he said, and her head swiveled and her aquamarine gaze locked on him. "What are you?"

She tilted her head, like a puppy trying to hear better. "I am Vitro beta model 2.1."

Despite his feast of coconuts, his mouth went dry. "Are you . . . human?" His voice cracked as he said it, because he couldn't believe he *was* saying it. It was too weird, too inconceivable that this was actually happening. It wasn't a question he ever thought he would hear himself ask.

"Yes," she said, after a moment's hesitation.

"Are you . . . a clone or something?"

She looked down at her hands, her brows lowered in thought, then back up at him. "The answer cannot be found," she said cryptically.

He worked very hard to keep his expression blank. "Um. Okay. So, how old are you?"

Again she hesitated, then said, "Four hours, twelve minutes, fifty-seven seconds." A pause, then, "Fifty-eight seconds . . . fifty-nine seconds . . ."

"Okay, I get it!" He waved his hand to stop her, though in truth, he didn't get it at all. *Well, that's not true, is it?* He understood what she was saying—in theory—but it was impossible. He sighed and leaned back, his head clunking against the trunk. "The answer cannot be found," he muttered. "That should be my new life motto. You're saying you woke for the first time just four hours ago."

"Yes."

He thought back to the moment he had found her lying unconscious, of her sleep so deep that his mad run across the island, over hills and rocks, with her in his arms had not woken her.

A gust of wind snapped a dead palm frond high above their heads, and it smashed to the ground off to Jim's right. Lux flinched.

"Do you think those three will be back any time soon?" Jim asked, not expecting an answer. "Or maybe we have time to nap . . ."

He relaxed against the tree; he hadn't realized how much tension had been knotted in his muscles until he couldn't hold it any longer and it seeped out of him and into the sand. . . .

Jim woke with a start, and the first thing he saw was Lux watching him, eternally patient. He was lying on his side; he must have dropped off and then literally dropped to the ground, too exhausted to even wake. The side of his face was crusted with sand.

Jim sat up and stretched with a groan. He'd been lying on

half of a drained coconut, and now there was a stinging pain in his hip where it had left a deep indent in his skin. "How long was I sleeping?" he croaked, his throat dry.

"Six hours, nine minutes, four seconds," said Lux.

"You counted?"

"Yes."

Jim exhaled noisily and climbed to his feet. He was still sore, but the nap had taken the edge off his exhaustion. "Any sign of Mary and the gang?"

Lux looked around, inspecting every direction before answering. "No."

The sun had crossed the sky while he slept and now sank in the west, but they were still several hours from night. He roved the vicinity restlessly, wondering if he should go ahead and strike out for the resort now or wait until full dark. He didn't think they'd run into anyone if they rounded the eastern side of the island, keeping the mountains between them and the path that led to the resort, and then when he approached the buildings he'd come from the east, where they might not be looking for him. If Mary had told the guards about him, they'd have already converged on him and Lux by now.

There was one aspect of Lux that continued to disconcert him, and the more he dwelled on it, the more disquiet stirred inside him. She obeyed everything he said without hesitation, without question, without resentment. All the thoughtless commands he didn't even realize he was dropping—*Stop that* and *Come here* and *Try this* and *Look over there*—she responded to with alacrity. It wasn't just congeniality; it was deeper, instinctive. Mary had known. *She just tries so hard to please her precious master*, she'd said. And it seemed all too accurate a description.

Jim asked Lux again, "Why do you do everything I tell you?"

This time, she replied, "I must."

"Why?"

"You are Jim." She smiled, as if that explained everything.

"That doesn't mean anything," he said. "Can't you *dis*obey? If I tell you to go climb that tree, and you don't want to—you can say *no*, Lux."

This seemed to distress her. Her face twisted into a grimace. "I do not . . . The answer cannot be found."

"Fine. Listen. Lux, you don't have to obey me."

She cocked her head, her eyes troubled.

"Now, go climb that tree," he said.

She ran to the tree and threw herself at it, but it was a branchless palm and she could get no purchase on its trunk. He ran after her and saw her knees were bloody and scraped from trying to attempt the climb, but even so, she kept clawing at the bark, trying to find a way up.

"Lux!" he shouted. "Lux, *stop!*"

She went still, her hands at her sides, breathing heavily. Her hair hung in damp, bedraggled strings over her shoulders and a trickle of blood ran down over ankle. Jim watched her in mute horror, guilt souring his tongue. She stared at him, and it seemed to him that there was a little less bright spark in her eye and little more blankness.

"I'm sorry, I'm sorry, Lux," he said, his face hot. "Come on, let's clean that up."

She followed him to the water and stood silently as he washed the blood from her knees, though he knew the salt water had to sting the cuts.

When he was done, he was left with a deep sense of dread and guilt. He stared at her in helpless stupefaction, and she stared back unsmiling.

"I've decided," he announced. "We'll leave now for the other end of the island so we can look around, maybe see some sign of Sophie before we go in after her."

He said *we* because it gave him a slight sense of confidence, as if he weren't going into this alone. But he wasn't fooled; Lux was more of a liability, even if she could take out three people bigger than her without breaking a sweat. Maybe she was better at handling herself than Jim was, but she was so childlike that he couldn't even imagine entangling her in his mess. He would tell her to stay put while he went after Sophie, and then the three of them could escape together. That was his best-case scenario; he was fairly certain things wouldn't go that smoothly.

"Okay, kid, let's move out." He held a hand to Lux, and she stared at it blankly. "Take my hand," he added. "I'll help you up."

She did, and he pulled her to her feet.

They trekked along the eastern shore, walking just within the tree line where the ground was firmer and they were concealed from anyone on the beach.

Jim's stomach grumbled at him as they walked; the coconut had taken the edge off his hunger but it had not entirely appeased it. He found himself fantasizing about cheese fries for the majority of the walk. He asked Lux if she'd ever had cheese fries, and she said no, and once again he was reminded that she wasn't the average seventeen-year-old girl.

She grew tired long before he did. Her gait had improved, but her muscles were still weak; if she'd been sleeping for seventeen years he wasn't surprised that she'd be suffering from atrophy on some level. They must have had some way to stretch and exercise her limbs while she slept or she'd be a stick figure, incapable of standing up.

Finally they came to a bend in the shore, and he realized they'd reached the southern edge of the island. When he looked around, he saw buildings obscured by overgrown trees and vines; this part of the resort had been completely abandoned and was well reclaimed by the island. With Lux a quiet shadow behind him, he slipped between two-story villas and dilapidated shops, following a path made of cemented seashells. Grass poured up through cracks in the sidewalk; he felt as if he were walking through a ghost town. Empty, gaping windows stared malevolently as they passed, and he startled when the wind clacked beneath a broken shutter. It sounded like a gunshot, and his heart jumped onto his tongue.

Gradually the villas began to look less abused by the elements and more kept, and he started seeing signs of habitation: a laundry line draped with men's clothing, a wind chime on a balcony tinkling like a mad fairy, a garden that actually had flowers in it instead of weeds. These must have been the villas the doctors and guards lived in. On the porch of one of the villas he spotted a row of women's shoes. He snagged a pair of bright blue Nikes and put them on Lux's feet; they were a bit large so he pulled the laces as tight as they would go and knotted them securely. When he asked her how they felt, she just smiled.

He found the door to the villa unlocked, and, proceeding on pins and needles, he slipped inside. The villa seemed to be inhabited by one person, a woman judging by the coat hung next to the door and the shoes he'd found on the porch. He made for the small galley kitchen off to the left, only to find the cupboards maddeningly empty. When he searched all the drawers, he found a pack of granola bars—no telling how old—which he shared with Lux. She took it with great care, nibbling tiny pieces, the expressions on her face spanning from awe to terror as she ate. In the end, she had half a bar to Jim's four, and when she seemed content, he didn't press her to eat more, not wanting to abuse her odd capacity for obedience. He was glad to leave the place; no matter who these people were, rifling through their kitchens made him feel like a criminal.

Eventually the path turned and ran uphill, past a gymnasium and an open-air restaurant with a thatched roof. Though most of the tables were dusty and unused, a handful were wiped clean and had chairs set around them; they must have used the restaurant for meals from time to time. The roof was supported by tall thick poles, and airy curtains served as walls. They fluttered in the breeze. Beside the restaurant sat an old excavator; with its huge arm and claw bending out the front, it looked like a giant, silent scorpion. A crater in the hillside was evidence of recent work, though a lot of dirt had fallen back down into the hole.

Jim crept around the restaurant and found himself looking

up the hill at the building where he had found Lux. Guards stood in front of it, looking more alert than they had that morning. Three doctors were walking briskly up the hill toward them, talking animatedly. Something was up. They all looked riled and excited—had it anything to do with him or Sophie? He had to assume it did, and that they were right now hunting for him. A dark helicopter crouched on the grassy clearing between the building and the bluff; that was new. He was certain it hadn't been there that morning.

There was no sign of Sophie, though he knew it wouldn't be that easy. He waved to Lux, unnecessarily since she seemed bound to follow him anyway, even if he walked off the edge of the cliff beside them, and he moved north, using fences, shrubs, and palms for cover. There was no way, with this kind of activity going on, that he'd have a chance of getting inside while any light lasted. Not that darkness would be much help; light posts dotted the perimeter of the building, and floodlights were fixed over every door. He could hardly expect to slip in the way he had that morning by sneaking through a door opened from the inside.

"Okay, here's the plan. We'll wait here until—"

Jim froze, then dropped to the ground, motioning for Lux to do the same. A triplet of armed guards walked by, toting rifles and moving with haste, as if on the hunt. Jim's pulse quickened; he was certain now that they were onto him. On the bright side, if they all ran off to look for him, he'd have a better chance of sneaking in to find Sophie. On the not so bright side, if they knew about him they probably knew about Sophie, which meant she could be locked up and guarded . . . or worse.

The guards had almost passed them by when the wind caught the black ball cap on the third man's head and whisked it off. He turned to grab it, and it blew into the bush behind which Jim and Lux were crouched. Jim had milliseconds to make a move; he could stay put and hope the man didn't spot them, or he could start running now in hopes of putting as much space between them and the guards before they could start firing.

He hesitated too long. The guard plucked his hat from the branches and then shouted when he saw Jim.

"RUN!" Jim bellowed to Lux. He grabbed her hand and sprinted into the trees, away from the guards and the resort.

The thickness of the foliage made running difficult; he kept snagging his foot on vines and rocks and barely avoided smashing face-first into the palms. He glanced back and saw the guards following; they zigzagged through the trees, which, at least, prevented them from getting a shot at either Jim or Lux. He wondered if they would risk shooting her; he got his answer when he heard the crack of a gunshot. He glanced at Lux to be sure she wasn't hit.

They emerged from the trees and onto an old putting green that was flooded with an inch of muddy water. Water splashed up his legs and filled his boots, but he didn't dare slow down. Lux tripped when they reached a sand pit, the soggy crater catching her by surprise. He helped her up and pulled her along. They vaulted up the opposite bank and found themselves in even denser undergrowth. The trees and ferns and shrubs tangled together in a mess of leaves and vines, like a giant trap intent on snaring them.

Looking back, he saw that they had gained a short lead on

the guards, but if they stopped for a moment the men would have no trouble firing at them. By weaving back and forth, he was able to avoid giving them a direct shot, but as the ground began to incline, their pace slowed.

Ahead of them was a mountain, a short but steep pyramid of rocks and greenery, devoid of trees. He knew he had to avoid the open area; it would only give the guards that much more of an advantage if they began firing. So he cut to the left, rounding the foot of the mountain and heading directly toward the declining sun, Lux a half step behind, her hand clenched in his. Light beamed at them from around the tree trunks; he felt as if he were running into some kind of otherworldly portal. The leaves glowed around them, dewdrops catching and reflecting light like a million tiny prisms. Behind him, he could hear the guards thrashing and yelling, calling for them to stop.

A bullet pounded into a tree to his right, and his heart jumped into his throat. He ran doubled over, trying to make himself a smaller target, and he began weaving between the trees like a drunk, careening this way and that. He dropped back a step so that he was between Lux and the guns.

More shots whistled around them, and he had the feeling the guards weren't taking much time to aim properly. Maybe they were just hoping a bullet would happen to bring him down, or maybe they were trying to intimidate him into stopping.

Suddenly the ground dropped off in what at first looked like a sinkhole, but when he looked down he saw it was a kind of hidden lagoon. Bright blue green water shimmered at the bottom; he couldn't tell how deep it was. There was no way around, and it was just wide enough that they couldn't jump over it. Jim looked back to see that the guards were gaining on them.

"Lux, listen to me," he said, taking her shoulders and looking her dead in the eye. "Don't fight them. They have guns and they'll shoot you, understand? Don't try to fight them off."

"Yes, Jim," she said amiably.

She wasn't scared, he realized. She had no idea how much danger they were in. Her naïveté filled him with a sudden wave of frustration, and he nearly shook her to try to make her understand. Instead, he pulled his hands away and clenched them into fists. *We'll just have to try to reason with them,* he thought, his stomach heavy with dread. Reasoning with people wasn't one of his stronger skills.

He turned to face the guards, who had reached them and were slowing down. They spread out, cutting off what few avenues of escape Jim had.

"Hey," Jim said casually, as if they'd just met in line at the gas station instead of in the middle of a hostile island. "How's it going?"

"The girl," one said to another, as if Jim had never spoken. "What do we do with her?"

"Strauss didn't say anything about her," the other said. "I guess . . . shoot him and take the girl."

Jim swallowed. Hard. "Uh . . . guys? Come on, guys. Isn't that a bit . . . hasty? Let's just take a step back and—"

The guards raised their rifles, each one aimed at his chest, and instinctively he stepped backward—and the ground disappeared and Jim found himself free-falling. So sudden was the fall that he couldn't even shout; his stomach twisted as he dropped, air streaming around him. Then, with an enormous splash, he plunged underwater. He immediately began swimming, reaching for the surface. The water was deep and freezing cold and, he noticed with surprise, it was fresh.

Lungs burning, Jim clawed desperately at the water, blinded by bubbles. When he finally surfaced, he sucked in a deep breath and looked around. He'd fallen into the inland lagoon at the bottom of a tall cylinder of rock hung with ferns and vines. The water around him sparkled cerulean, and looking up, he saw the canopy of palms, their fronds golden in the light of evening. There was no way up; the walls around the lagoon were at least thirty feet high, and any possible handholds were obscured by thick, heart-shaped leaves that rolled in a wave over the ground above to pour down the sides of the rock. If he'd had time, he might have used the ropy vines that hung straight down into the water to pull himself up, but time was definitely not a commodity he could afford. The guards appeared above him. Lux's face was among them; one of them was holding her tightly by the arm and, true to Jim's orders, she wasn't lifting so much as a finger to fight them. He had to remind himself that that was a good thing, that if she did try to fight them they'd kill her *and* him. At least this way one of them would survive.

When they saw him trapped like a frog in a bucket, they began angling their guns at him.

Jim looked around, more desperate than ever. He was treading water, and the effort was quickly wearing him out. Then he noticed something he hadn't seen before—a light under the water. He gulped down a deep breath and sank beneath the surface, swimming toward the light as bullets zinged through the water around him, leaving spiraling columns of bubbles in their trails. The light came from an underwater tunnel made of rock, and after a moment's hesitation, he wiggled into it and pulled himself along. He was barely small enough to fit through. His shirt snagged on a root, and he thrashed and pulled until it ripped and he was free.

When he emerged on the other side, body aching for air, he pushed off the rock with both feet and shot out of the water, sobbing for oxygen. He was in a deep, narrow stream with high leafy banks on either side. The water rushed along, carrying him with it, and he let the current sweep him away. Looking back, he saw the spot where the stream poured out of the lagoon, with the land above it stretching upward. Jim started to relax, spreading his arms and legs so he could simply float to safety. He could feel his pulse in every limb, pounding frantically through his veins. His arms and legs ached intensely from running and swimming and pulling himself through the narrow tunnel. He agonized over Lux, wondering what they would do, if they'd change their minds and shoot her anyway. He heard no gunshot, but it didn't assuage his anxiety.

The river coursed like a winding road, and he sensed it was slowing. Soon, it widened and grew shallow, and he was able to stand up and walk. Around him, the land had become flat and covered in tall grasses and short, twisting pines. The sky had turned from blue to scarlet as the sun set behind the island. He sloshed toward the sea, soaked and weary, and when he reached a long white beach he collapsed into the sand and lay on his back, eyes shut, breathing deeply of the briny air. The stream broke into a dozen narrow rivulets that cut through the sand and drained into the sea.

Jim lay there for ten minutes without opening his eyes, feeling his muscles relax and his heart rate gradually fall. His mind reeled at how close he'd come to death, hunted through the trees like a wild animal, like a deer chased by a pack of bloodthirsty hounds. He was alive, but he was no closer to rescuing Sophie and now he'd lost Lux as well.

TWENTY-ONE
LUX

She watched mournfully as Jim disappeared beneath the water. She wanted to follow him, but the man holding her was too strong. Recalling how she'd fought the boys and girl on the beach, she knew she could get free if she tried, but Jim had said *Don't fight them.*

Her heart throbbed painfully in her chest, and she watched the water to see if he would reappear the way he had when he swam in the ocean, but he was gone.

Gone.

Panic and fear twisted in her stomach she could not see him but she needed him without him she was losing control was falling apart.

The men dragged her away away from Jim and she could not stop them because *don't fight them don't fight them.*

"What's wrong with her?" someone said. "Is she having a panic attack?"

"Let's get her back inside. Call Chad's group; tell them to search this area. He won't get far."

"Think he drowned down there?"

"I'm not gonna find out. We'll go down later and check, with the right equipment, see if he's there."

They marched through the trees and Lux marched with them, but she twisted and turned, trying to look back, trying to find him, but he was nowhere. *Drowned drowned drowned* the man had said, and Lux exploded inside couldn't bear it couldn't *breathe.*

"The hell's the matter with her?"

"Separation anxiety, looks like. I've seen it before with the new ones. Sorry creatures can't handle the stress of being separated from their, well, whatever you call them. Masters? Owners?"

Their conversation wandered out of Lux's grasp, and she gave up trying to listen. Her heart pounded in her ears. Without Jim to balance her, the world moved too quickly and confusingly, sucking her down and crashing against her like the waves.

Soon they reached a building on an open hill, and Lux gazed at it in wonder. It was huge and black against the setting sun. She didn't want to go inside. She wanted to run back into the trees to find Jim. But the men dragged her along even when she dug her feet into the ground, and then she had to relent and go with them because *don't fight them.*

Inside she found a strange new world, a world of walls and too-bright lights and solid floors that squeaked beneath the shoes Jim had put on her feet. Strange floor, hard and smooth beneath her feet. She stared at it and fought down the panic that battered at her brain.

"You found her!" cried a voice, and Lux looked up. A woman rushed toward her, a woman with tight black curls and blue eyes and a big white coat. She reached out and took Lux's face in her hands, then studied her all over. The men let go of her arms, and she stood trembling as the woman turned her around, and looked at her hands, at her feet, her scraped knees.

"Poor thing, she's been all over the island in this state?"

"Found her with the pilot, but he got away."

"Come with me, Lux. I'll get you cleaned up. Thanks, Thornton, I'll take her from here."

The men left and Lux was glad to see them go. The woman held her hand and led her into a room. She looked around in a daze, taking it all in, trying to make sense of the strange new objects and sounds and sensations.

"Sit here," the woman said, patting a thing Lux suddenly knew was *chair*.

She sat.

"Let me take care of those hands and knees." The woman moved around, picking things up, and opening drawers and jars. She pressed a wet cloth to Lux's cuts. "I'm Dr. Moira Crue," the woman said. "I'm going to take care of you, dear."

"Where is Jim?" Lux asked.

"You've had a very stressful awakening," Dr. Moira Crue said. "I know you must be very frightened and confused, but just trust me, all right? You're safe here. I won't let anyone hurt you."

"I want Jim."

"I know." The woman's eyes pinched at the corners. "I know."

She took a thing from her pocket—*flashlight*—and shone it in Lux's eyes. Lux winced and tried to turn away, but Dr. Moira Crue held her chin and murmured that it was okay, she wasn't going to be hurt, but Lux didn't care about hurting she just wanted Jim where was he why did he not come why did he leave her—

"Lux!"

She blinked, her thoughts grinding to a halt.

"Lux, you're panicking. You need to breathe. Breathe in. Breathe out."

I do not want to breathe I want Jim I want Jim where is he where is he—

Lux yelped as pain pricked her arm. She looked down to see the woman sliding a needle into her skin.

"I'm sorry, Lux, but you're having an anxiety attack. It's common among newborns, but Jim isn't here to calm you down, so I'm giving you some medicine. Do you understand?"

"Hurts . . ." Lux whispered, but then a warm, soft feeling washed over her, and she swayed.

"There. See? Everything's fine." The woman held her up. "I only gave you a little bit. Can you walk?"

"Walk," Lux echoed dreamily.

"Come on. Try."

Lux locked eyes with the woman. "What am I?" she whispered.

Dr. Moira Crue's eyes widened, then narrowed. "What?"

"What am I?" Lux gazed at her in anguish.

"Lux . . . you're a Vitro. A girl. A . . . a human being—what a strange question." She tilted her head, studying Lux closely. "Why would you ask that?"

Lux sighed deeply. The woman gave her answers, but none of them were right. There was still something missing. Something big, something so, so important . . .

TWENTY-TWO
SOPHIE

The cell in which Sophie's mother had deposited her was in a lower basement level that had no windows and none of the upper floors' outdated resort chic. The room was small, ten feet by ten feet at most, with the floor, walls, and even ceiling covered with stark white pads. She sat curled in the far corner, facing the door, outwardly silent but inwardly screaming.

If Jim was murdered, his blood would be on her hands. There was no way around it. Her pulse pounded in her ears, beating out a steady rhythm by which she could mark time's passage.

The room was lit by a fluorescent bulb high above her; it was covered by a grate wrapped in foam. The light flickered every few seconds, with a faint metallic click. Other than that, no sounds issued from the hall. She was, as far as she could tell, the only person on the entire basement floor.

Her mother had been silent as she led Sophie away. At

first, Sophie had thought her mom might let her go. When they were out of Strauss's hearing, Sophie had suggested they run for it. They could find Jim and Lux and Nicholas and flee the island together. She thought surely after Strauss's display of power and menace that Moira would see reason, would understand that this was no place for either of them.

Moira had only given her a look, a look that said *stop talking now before you get in worse trouble*, and Sophie said no more on the matter. Her heart had sunk lower and lower, until she felt as if she were dragging it behind her on a string, and now it lay pathetically at her feet like a despondent pet.

She'd been silent as her mother opened the door to the padded cell, silent as the door shut behind her, silent as Moira's footsteps faded down the hall. Hours had passed, as best as she could judge, and she hadn't made a sound. She drifted in and out of sleep, but her dreams were filled with a chaos of voices and images that left her feeling less rested than she had before she shut her eyes. She wondered what time it was. By the ache in her stomach, she'd missed several meals.

When the door finally opened, she lifted her head just enough to see who it was. Moira was there, and Strauss, and Dr. Hashimoto, peeking over their shoulders.

And there was someone else. She stood in front of Moira like a ghost, like a reflection in a pool: Lux.

Again Sophie was left breathless as if punched in the gut. But this time it wasn't the physical resemblance between herself and Lux that had her reeling; it was the look in Lux's eye: deep, hollow sadness, as if her heart had been carved out of her with an ice cream scoop.

If they had Lux, that meant they must have found Jim too.

"Well," she said coldly, looking past Lux and her mother, to Strauss. "Did you shoot him?"

"Get up," Strauss replied.

"We have to tell Andreyev," Moira explained, her gaze vacant.

Sophie recalled what the consequences would be if Andreyev withdrew his funding of the Vitro Project: her mother deposed, the Vitros either exterminated or sold off. Sophie wasn't sure which she would choose in their place. It seemed to her that living without control of your own will was hardly a step above not living at all. She would rather be shot than become an empty, voiceless vessel existing only as an extension of someone else. *But that's not a choice I can make for them*, she thought. She knew, deep in her heart, that if the Vitros were killed by Corpus, written off as failures, some of the blame would fall on her. *I never wanted any of this.* She'd been played the whole time, led by the nose by Nicholas. But she couldn't well shift blame on him—he was only trying to break free of the people who'd controlled and used him his entire life. She'd have done the same in his position.

Sophie stood and went to the door, her eyes drawn to Lux. Her mother handed her a sandwich wrapped in a paper towel, which she ate in five giant bites. They walked down the hall, toward the staircase leading up, and all the while Sophie summed up her twin, comparing herself to Lux from head to toe. *Why you?* She halted at the doorway to the stairs, letting Lux go first. *Why did she keep you and not me?*

She churned with a conflict of envy and relief. Lux was the daughter Moira had kept, while Sophie was the one she'd abandoned. On the other hand, Lux was the one she'd turned into a listless doll; at least Sophie had a will of her own even if, at times, it landed her in trouble. She knew she'd drawn the long straw between them.

They found Andreyev outside, where the afternoon was fading to evening—she'd been in the cell for nearly twenty-four hours, she realized with a shock; he was being looked after by two of his personal bodyguards and was hitting golf balls off the bluff and into the sea with a heavy driver. Several of his balls went wide and only narrowly missed smashing into the Corpus helicopter crouched off to the right; his bodyguards flinched whenever this happened. Dressed in a striped polo, khaki shorts, and an argyle tam, he looked like a harmless middle-aged tourist on vacation. But when he turned around and saw Sophie and Lux standing side by side and Moira's and Strauss's grim expressions, a dark look fell over his face that banished any such illusion.

"Let me explain," said Strauss, but then she gave a short, bitter laugh. "Rather, let Moira explain."

Moira did, succinctly. Andreyev listened without expression, looking down at his driver, which he swung absently at the grass. When Moira finished, Andreyev swung the club and Sophie flinched, thinking he was going to hit her mother with it, but he just propped it against his shoulder and turned a narrow eye on them all.

"A strange mess," he said. "So my Lux has imprinted on this pilot instead of me. And where is he?"

Strauss cleared her throat. "He's on the island. He has nowhere to run, so it's only a matter of time before we bring him in."

Sophie let out a small, relieved breath. He was alive, at least. *For now.*

Andreyev nodded as if only half listening.

"We have other Vitros," said Moira. "In just a few hours we can—"

"Is this atrocious disorganization indicative of all your projects, Victoria?" Andreyev asked, cutting Moira short as if she'd never spoken. "Or am I to lay all the blame on Dr. Crue here?"

Strauss and Moira exchanged challenging looks, as if each wanted the other to take the blame.

"Why don't we go inside?" said Strauss. "We can discuss reparations in private."

"Is there anything we can get you?" Moira asked. "Dinner? Coffee?"

Andreyev sighed and handed the club to one of the bodyguards. "Don't try to coddle my goodwill, Dr. Crue. I am about finished with Skin Island and all of you."

Strauss shot Moira a dark look. Sophie couldn't take it anymore; she stepped forward. "It's my fault!" she said. "Stop blaming them—*I* was the one who got in the way. My mom has nothing to do with it."

"Come inside, Sophie," said her mother. "You're not helping."

"Mom, you have to see how wrong this is," Sophie said, begging. She searched Moira's eyes for some sign of regret, but Moira seemed more concerned with hushing her up than contemplating her life decisions. Strauss looked wrathful and Andreyev tired; Lux's eyes were lowered, hidden behind the fringe of her pale lashes. Her brief flare of righteous anger fizzled into smoke, and Sophie let herself be led inside.

Her mother, Strauss, and Andreyev closeted themselves together in Moira's cramped office while Lux and Sophie were put into Lux's room. The door was locked from the outside, and a guard took up station in the hallway. The girls would be left alone with each other until, Sophie guessed, the adults worked out what was to be done about them. If Lux was useless to them, having imprinted on Jim, would they let her live? If they killed Jim, would her bond with him be broken? Would she be free, or would she just imprint on someone else?

Sophie threw herself into a small wooden chair by the window, hooking one leg over the armrest. Lux perched delicately on the edge of the bed and stared at her hands. Sophie watched her closely, wondering how deeply beneath the skin their similarities ran. If Lux was just a day old, she doubted they had much in common beyond appearance.

It was inappropriate and made no sense at all, but a small pang of jealousy struck Sophie in the chest when she looked at her twin. Of course she would never have wanted to be in Lux's place, but at the same time . . . Was it because of Lux that Moira moved to Skin Island and gave up Sophie and her dad? It seemed a valid explanation. Her father must have rejected the idea of using Lux as a Vitro, and that's why he left. If it hadn't been for Lux, would her mother have left with them?

Sophie sensed there was something she was missing, some final, hidden stroke that would paint the complete picture of her life. Why did Moira Crue stay on Skin Island—and why did she allow such a terrible fate as imprinting to befall her own daughter, even if it was to save her life, as she'd claimed? No sooner did Sophie think she'd found all the answers than yet another question arose and shattered her illusion of truth.

"So." Sophie dug her finger into a chip in the back panel of the chair. "You've imprinted on Jim, so you have to do whatever he says." She looked at Lux sidelong. "When he tells you something, do you *want* to do it?"

"Yes," Lux said.

Sophie didn't want to believe her. There had to be a way around the chip. She couldn't accept that Lux, or any of the Vitros, truly had no single independent thought, no preference as to the direction their life took. "Even if he told you to jump off a cliff?"

"Yes."

"Even if he told you to push *him* off a cliff?"

Lux looked up then, her brows knitted together and her eyes pained. "I . . . If he said . . . but he *didn't* say. The answer cannot be found. I do not understand."

In time, if she were given her autonomy, would she become more like Sophie? She wondered how much of herself was locked away inside Lux, or if there was a whole different girl in there, trapped inside the metal chip in her brain, forbidden her freedom.

Sophie sighed. "Look at you. Your gown is torn and dirty and those shoes are too big. Here."

She went to the dresser and pulled out a clean pair of underwear, a white shirt, a sports bra, and a pair of athletic shorts, which she tossed to Lux. "Put these on. And there are shoes in the closet."

Lux held the clothes and looked at them uncertainly. She tugged at the gown, only getting herself tangled up in it. With another sigh, Sophie helped her out of the gown and into the clothes. It was awkward and frustrating; Lux seemed at odds with her limbs and clearly had never put on a shirt before. But when she was dressed she stood in front of the mirror hung behind the door and stared at herself for a long while. Sophie sat on the bed, her legs folded beneath her and her arms hugging a pillow to her chest, watching Lux watch herself.

"You've never seen your own reflection, have you?"

Lux put out a hand and pressed it against her image. "This is me?"

"Yes."

"I look like you."

"That's because we're sisters. Or something."

Lux turned around and looked at Sophie as if seeing her for the first time. "Sisters."

"You know what it means?"

"Many meanings," she said softly. "Many words."

"Well, in this case, it means we have the same parents. The same mom and dad. Moira you've met. Our dad's name is Foster. He's a doctor too—or he was once. Now he's a biology teacher and he's . . ." She shut her eyes, picturing her dad, tall, lanky, his hair never brushed, his glasses always slightly askew. She saw him sitting at his desk in the family den, grading papers, one hand always in his hair. She saw him when they argued, when he'd snatch off his glasses and wave them around, his face red and his shoulders hunched with tension. "He's a good dad," she finished, and she echoed it with regret, wishing she had said goodbye before charging off on this mad venture, wishing they had been on better terms, wishing she had given his warnings about her mother and Skin Island more credence, wishing he had told her the whole truth from the beginning. She opened her eyes and looked at Lux, wondering if her sister would ever have the chance to know him for herself.

Sophie was seized with a sudden affection. "We'll get out of here," she said fiercely. "We'll go back to the States and you can meet Dad and he'll take care of you. I can find a way to free you from the chip. They have to let me take you, Lux. You're no good to them now, not after you imprinted on Jim."

"Jim," Lux echoed sadly.

"Forget him. He can fly us out of here, but after that, it'll be you and me. I'll be eighteen—uh, *we'll* be eighteen—in three months. We can go wherever we want." She tossed the pillow aside and walked to Lux, standing behind her and looking over her shoulder into the mirror. The resemblance was dizzying; she was seeing double. "We'll be real sisters, Lux." She hesitated, then put her arms around her sister, holding her tight, releasing the small seed of envy that had been wedged inside her and feeling lighter for it. "Would you like that?"

Lux seemed unmoved by Sophie's affection. "I want Jim," she said.

Sophie released her. "He's not your boss, Lux! He's not your master. You can be your own person. I can help you. Please—let me help you be free."

"I want Jim."

"Jim isn't here! I am!"

"He is."

"What?"

"He *is* here."

Lux pointed at the window. Jim was there, waving frantically, and when he saw them looking, he hurled a rock at the glass and it shattered across the floor.

TWENTY-THREE
JIM

"Don't just stand there!" Jim said. "Come on!"

The girls shot into action. They ran to the window, and there was a moment of confusion as they tried to sort out who would go first. Jim took the hands of one and pulled her through, realizing with dizzy shock that he didn't know which one it was—Lux or Sophie. Lux was no longer wearing her wispy hospital gown, and now he couldn't tell one from the other. But there was no time to exchange names; there were guards crawling over the island looking for him, and he knew they had to move fast.

"You're lucky I looked in and saw you," he said to whichever twin he was now helping through the window. "I was about to give up."

Circling the building had been extremely tricky. Guards roamed the perimeter, and he was only saved from being seen by the tall grass that grew along the walls. When he saw a guard he would dive into the grass and lie flat until they passed. He was covered in dirt, scratches, and sandburs and he didn't think the day could possibly get much worse.

Once both girls were out and standing on the grass, he glanced each one over, trying to tell them apart. They were both scratched from the broken window and their hair was mussed. His eyes fell to their hands, one with nails bitten short and the other with nails long and delicate, and he finally identified them.

"Sophie," he said, "we have to get to the plane."

"Wait," she said. "Where's Nicholas?"

"Nicholas?"

"Didn't he find you?"

"Was he supposed to?" Jim shook his head. "There isn't time. There are guards everywhere! Let's go." He started to take off, but she grabbed his arm.

"But I promised him I'd help him escape. He was the one who sent that e-mail, not my mom! He's behind everything because he just wants to be free." Her eyes entreated him. "I promised I'd help him."

"He did this?" Jim barked a laugh. "Well. Screw him, then."

"Jim, no! You've seen what they do to people." She glanced meaningfully at Lux. "He's not my favorite person, either, but—all of this is my mom's doing. I can't help but feel guilty. If I can save him and Lux . . ." She bit her lip. "Maybe I can undo some of her wrong."

"Sophie." He took her shoulders in his hands. "It's not your job to atone for your mother's crimes."

"But I have to do *something*." She tilted her chin upward, her gaze unflinching.

"We can leave now and send help. We'll tell someone what we've seen and let the government or somebody handle it. They'd do a better job than us, anyway. Leave Nicholas."

She faltered; he could see his argument swaying her. Finally, she gave a curt, resentful nod, and he sighed in relief. "Let's go," he said gently.

He led them along the wall, ducking when they passed open windows. If a guard walked around the corner now, they'd have no chance of hiding. The grass was tall, but there were three of them, and he knew he was running out of what miserable luck he had left.

"Just a bit further," he said. "Once we reach the trees we can run."

To their left the land dropped away to the sea; there was no beach below, only rocks. The span of grass grew narrower between the bluff and the building, until they had to walk single file.

When Jim turned the corner, he came face-to-face with an armed guard. The man looked as stunned as Jim felt, and for a moment they stood and blinked at each other. Then the guard reached for the Beretta on his hip.

"Go back!" Jim yelled, turning and pushing the girls the other way, keeping himself between them and the gun. "*Run!*"

Would the guard fire on all three of them?

He got his answer when a loud crack sounded, and at first he thought it was something else, like a tree falling. But then he saw Sophie stumble and fall, and he felt his heart implode. Blood rushing in his ears, drowning out the shouts of the guard, he bent, snaked his arm around her middle and helped her up, and ran as fast as Sophie could manage. He saw Lux glance back, and he yelled through gritted teeth for her to keep running.

Sophie was conscious but groggy. The shot had only winged her, nicking her left shoulder. Still, blood stained her shirt and dripped down his arm, hot and crimson. She mumbled something, her face white with shock, and he told her to hush.

His gallant rescue was crumbling around him. More guards appeared ahead of them, their rifles raised warningly. There was nowhere to run, unless he jumped off the cliff and threw himself onto the rocks below. For a moment, he did consider it. At least with the rocks he might have a slim chance.

Jim slowed, dropped clumsily to his knees, and set Sophie on the grass. Lux stood beside him, her hand resting lightly on his shoulder.

"I'm sorry," he whispered to them both.

Sophie's eyes rolled and then shut. She had fainted, probably from shock.

A group of people rushed across the grass toward them—a woman in a white pantsuit, several doctors in white coats, and a man in golf attire flanked by two suited bodyguards.

"James Julien?" said a small woman with dark hair and blue eyes. *Moira Crue.* She'd changed little since he'd last seen her a decade ago. She saw Sophie and let out a small cry. "What happened?" She looked up to the guard approaching them from behind. "You *shot* her, Dobbs?"

"'Shoot on sight,' that was the order," Dobbs replied gruffly.

"The *pilot*, not my daughter!"

Jim wondered if he should be surprised that the mother of his childhood friend had tried to have him killed, but it seemed his threshold for astonishment had reached astronomical limits lately.

"Michalski, help me!" Moira said, and one of the doctors came forward and picked up Sophie. She moaned in his arms, her bleeding shoulder immediately staining his shoulder.

"It just nicked her," Jim said wearily. "She passed out from shock."

"*I* am the doctor here, Jim," Moira said with a withering glare. "I'll make the diagnoses, thank you."

Jim lifted his hands in surrender. "So what now? You going to shoot me?"

"This is Victoria Strauss," Moira said as the pantsuit came forward. "You'll be turned over to her." She faltered, wincing slightly as she whispered, "I'm sorry, Jim. But you shouldn't have come here."

"Take him to the cliff," the woman said, "and shoot him. He's just in the way. Then get rid of his plane; scatter some pieces of it offshore. His death will be credited to a crash."

Jim's heart froze over. He felt the blood drain from his face and he leaned forward, grabbing fistfuls of grass, on the verge of vomiting. It was so quick, so final. She spoke the words as if she were instructing someone to clean up spilled milk. He fought to control his breathing, his mind stalling when he tried to think of something to say that would get him out of this.

Two guards grabbed his arms, hauled him to his feet, and marched him toward the cliff. When they reached the edge, they shoved him back onto his knees and he stared down at the rocks below, barely comprehending what he saw. His ears were filled with the rush of blood and surf and wind, and he felt himself detach from his body, as if his soul were abandoning ship.

One image consumed his mind, and it surprised him: not his mom's back as she walked out the front door the final time, not his father in one of his rare sober moments when they could have an actual conversation—but Sophie's eyes as they rose above the clouds; the sun staining her hair gold.

He was shaking all over, and he hated himself for being such a coward. But he couldn't deny the truth: He didn't want to die. Especially not like this, not balancing on the edge of a cliff on a godforsaken island with a bullet drilled through his brain.

He braced himself, trying to focus on the cool wind against his face, on the distant sparkling horizon, on the memory of flight, the pristine sky.

I've never even seen real snow.

The sounds around him were vague and distorted in his ears, as if he were hearing them through a long tube: a word, a shout, a thump, a blast of the gun. He toppled forward, thrown off balance by a sudden weight against his back, and desperately he threw out a hand and snagged a tuft of grass. He dangled over the cliff by one hand, and he felt the roots of the grass beginning to give way. Sand and dirt rained down on him, blinding his eyes, but he grappled with his free hand for something to hold on to.

Suddenly the grass broke loose and he began to fall, his stomach rising up his throat; then a hand closed around his wrist—Lux. She wasn't strong enough to hold him, but he managed to grab the grass and pull himself up, and just in time. The two guards who'd been about to execute him were lying unconscious, but three more were charging at Lux. Everyone was shouting and running around.

Lux dispatched the first guard with a graceful arcing kick to his jaw that snapped his head back. He collapsed noiselessly. Jim noticed she'd improved in her movements by half since the tussle with the Vitros that morning. The next two came at her with their rifles raised, calling for her to stand down, and Jim tried to yell at her to stop but he was so shaken by his near death that his voice came out as a whisper. Lux spun, avoiding the guns, and collared each with a chop to the throat. When they doubled over, dropping their guns to clutch at their windpipes, she struck at the back of their heads, dropping them cold.

Lux didn't stop there. She went after Strauss with silent purpose, streaking past Moira and Sophie. The man in the golf clothes fell back, his bodyguards glued to his sides. Strauss called for more guards, but Jim knew they were probably still scattered across the island looking for him.

His mind leaped into overdrive, his senses heightened, perhaps, by his near extinction. He stumbled to his feet and ran to Moira; before she could react, he snatched Sophie from her arms. The woman may have been Sophie's mother, but she didn't seem to be doing Sophie any good. She wouldn't bleed out, not with the graze the bullet had made, so he had no qualms about getting her off the island. As far as he was concerned, this was their one shot at escaping; Lux was distracting Corpus, and he wasn't one to let an opportunity go to waste.

On a mad whim, he made for the small yellow excavator parked down the slope by the restaurant. He had no way of knowing if the keys were still in it, but he had to try. He couldn't carry Sophie across the island, not fast enough anyway.

He reached the excavator just as a triplet of guards came running out of the jungle; they must have heard the shots. He recognized them as the same ones who had chased him and Lux across the island. They saw him and began shooting without hesitation. Jim dumped Sophie into the cab of the excavator and jumped in behind her; bullets pinged off the heavy metal exterior and ricocheted in every direction.

"Lux!" he yelled, but she wasn't in sight. Had they gone inside? Had they taken Lux? He looked everywhere but there was no sign of her. Sophie stirred beside him; she blinked her eyes open and tried to sit up.

"No, no, stay down," he murmured. "Bullets."

She looked disoriented, but she nodded vaguely and lay still. Jim fumbled at the ignition; there were no keys. His heart pulsing faster, he searched the cab frantically, running his hands over the dash, along the seat, even on the floor. *Damn.* The guards were now approaching the excavator with their rifles raised. All they would have to do was open the door and shoot him where he sat, and Sophie too. He slammed his head into the steering wheel in frustration.

Sophie groaned and rolled over. "This what you're looking for?" She held up a set of keys she'd been lying on.

With a wordless growl, Jim grabbed them and began shoving key after key into the ignition. Finally one fit, and he cranked it and stomped on the gas at the same time. The engine rattled and roared like a waking dragon, and they began to roll laboriously forward. The guards had to leap out of the way to avoid being crushed, and their bullets pounded harmlessly off the dozer. One of them jumped onto the side and tried to wrest open the door; Jim helped him out by shoving it open—right into the guy's face. The guard fell backward, his mouth open in a shout that Jim couldn't hear over the engine.

He flinched when he heard a thump from the opposite window, expecting to see another guard. But it was Nicholas who was pounding on the glass, yelling to be let in.

"Take me with you!" he cried.

"Let him in," said Sophie. "Please, Jim."

"There isn't room!"

"Let him *in*!"

He growled and held his door open long enough for Nicholas to scramble around and crawl in, awkwardly lunging across Jim to wedge himself between Sophie and the window. He was carrying an old blue JanSport backpack, which he held gingerly in one hand. She had to half sit on his lap for all three to fit. The little cabin was really only meant for one person.

He looked around for Lux, but she was still nowhere in sight. Feeling like the worst kind of traitor but left with no other options, Jim floored the gas pedal and drove the excavator over everything in its path; it crushed flower beds and sidewalks and wore deep tracks into the freshly clipped grass. Soon the *ping* of bullets faded and stopped. Either they had outdistanced the guns or the guards had given up on penetrating the metal plates that covered the vehicle.

"They'll come after us in their trucks," Nicholas warned.

"Not if I can help it," Jim murmured as he headed for the road that led to the northern end of the island. When he reached it, he drove a hundred feet and then pulled randomly at the controls to the giant claw hanging in front of him. When he found the lever that lowered the arms, he yanked it all the way down and the heavy metal claw crashed into the concrete. A network of cracks spread out from the point of impact. He raised the claw and then smashed it down again until the pavement was reduced to rubble. No truck short of an off-roader could navigate across the chunks and piles of cement, and the loose sand and trees on either side of the road allowed no means of passage around it. Jim sent the excavator rumbling over the broken road. It roared appreciatively.

"Well," said Nicholas drily, "suppose that should do it."

Sophie laboriously sat up and pressed a hand to her wounded shoulder. "We can't leave Lux," she rasped.

"We don't have a choice," Jim snapped, immediately regretting the edge in his tone when Sophie's face fell. "I'm sorry," he said more gently, "but the only help we can give Lux now is for us to get away. We'll come back with someone who can actually put a stop to this place."

She said nothing, just stared out the window with her jaw clenched, partly from pain, he guessed, and partly with anger at him. He reached over and covered her left hand, which she had pressed into the seat. "We'll come back, Sophie."

She refused to look at him.

TWENTY-FOUR
LUX

This time, she held nothing back.

They were going to shoot Jim. Her brain churned with words and images, things she'd never seen but were in her mind anyway: *Guns have bullets and bullets kill. Kill means dead—they will make Jim dead.*

Dead.

Dead.

Dead.

This was intolerable.

Her blood roared in her veins. She trembled with anger, with fury at the ones who would make her Jim dead, who would *dare* hurt him.

This time, she let her body do all the thinking.

And she became *powerful.*

She moved with speed and grace she'd never felt before. Heady with her own strength, she marveled at how *easy* it was to make them fall, to drop them one by one.

JESSICA KHOURY

Chop.
Kick.
Duck.
Sprint.

Her brain picked out target points: this chin, that stomach, this chest. Her body followed through with deadly precision. She melted from one attack to the next, flowing across the grass, her muscles hardening into steel at the right moments, then relaxing so she could spin away and pursue the next target.

Eliminate the threat.

And there were so many threats.

She kept an eye on Jim. He and Sophie were running away—good. *Go,* she thought. *Get away.*

She'd identified the leader: the woman in white. Much like the girl Mary on the beach, this one gave orders. She was the most important threat, and Lux had to eliminate her.

She sprinted across the grass, and leaped for the woman's throat.

But then the woman was gone. Lux hit the ground hard and rolled, landing in a crouch. The woman was quick; she had stepped aside just in time to avoid having her throat punched. Lux tightened her fist and tensed, but before she could spring again, she felt a sharp jab of pain in her neck: Moira Crue and her needle.

Immediately a warm sensation spread up her neck and enveloped her skull. She shook her head, trying to clear her thoughts, but her vision blurred and darkened. She lurched forward blindly, reaching for the woman in white, but she was helpless and weak. Her strength melted away, abandoning her; she landed in a crumple on the grass, tried to crawl, couldn't find the strength.

As she lay there, fading from the world, one last thought managed to surface and swirl across her mind before she lost her grip on consciousness:

Jim said don't fight them.

But I fought them anyway.

0111011101101000011000010111010000001101000010 10 Drowning water all around no air cannot breathe Jim where are you help me please oh what what what am I? What is happening to me please stop stop stop! Falling darkness must protect must protect011101110110I must protect1000011000010 111010000100000I must011000010110110100100000001001 001 . . .

When she woke, she was lying on her back, on something soft, and she was soaked with sweat. She jerked upward, only to find her hands and feet were stuck.

Groggily, she blinked away the static in her eyes and looked around. She was inside. In one of the *rooms*. The light above her hummed; it was too bright, scalding her.

She groaned, her voice sludge in her throat.

Her head was a riot of numbers and words, nothing making sense, all scrambled up, all jumbled out of order. And it *hurt*. Her skull throbbed, her eyes throbbed, and she felt a swirling in her stomach that kept surging into her throat.

"Lux," said a voice.

Moira Crue's face appeared, flickering and out of focus.

"It's okay, Lux. You're safe."

"*Jmmm.*"

"He's okay. You did your job. You protected him."

"Moira . . ." A different voice. Lux rolled her head to see who it was: another woman with dark hair, dark eyes, white coat.

"Her primary concern is protecting her imprintee," Moira said. "She needs to know he is safe or she'll go into shock. I've seen it happen before, when we were testing Clive."

"She looks like she's going to throw up."

"It's a combination of stress, sedatives, and overstimulation. She's been exposed to too much too soon. They normally need several days just to acclimate to their own bodies. Lux has been forced into a maelstrom of completely new experiences and sensations. Remember, everything she is seeing and hearing, she's seeing and hearing for the very first time, with nothing but her chip's limited data to interpret for her. If she'd been awoken properly, she'd have plenty of time and therapy to help her along. As it is, she's had to largely fend for herself."

"If Strauss catches that pilot and—"

"Sh. You'll spark another anxiety attack in her. If they catch Jim—the pilot—and . . . if *that* happens, we'll have only two choices. Put her in an induced coma until we can find a way to reverse the imprinting, or . . ."

Silence fell. They both stared down at her.

Then Moira Crue said, "Let her sleep. She'll fade in and out the next few hours. It's best we give her time to process."

Their faces disappeared, and for a long time, the room was silent.

Lux didn't like being alone. To occupy herself, she replayed Moira Crue's words in her mind, searching for answers, for understanding. There was so much, so many words that slipped through her fingers and evaporated before she knew their meaning. It was too much, all too much. She floated on a dreamy wave of warmth, her muscles limp, her mind sluggish. Eventually, she gave up on thinking and shut her eyes, losing herself in darkness.

TWENTY-FIVE
SOPHIE

Sophie's shoulder, chest, and arm ached with pain that made her head swim, but she forced herself to keep moving and stay alert. When they'd reached the end of the road at the top of the north beach, Jim had used the keys to tear a strip of cloth from the bottom of Sophie's shirt, since his was too dirty to use as a bandage. He wound it around her shoulder and under her arm to help stop the bleeding.

They left the excavator on the side of the road. Head spinning and her body protesting every step, she trudged along as Nicholas led them to the motorboat in the narrow inlet on the northwest bend of the island. The tide was low now, and they had to half drag the boat into the water; luckily it was a small outboard and floated easily in the shallows.

Nicholas steered recklessly across the channel and ran the boat aground without slowing, and the impact sent Sophie sprawling on the bottom of the boat.

"Sorry," he muttered as he helped Sophie out. She gritted her teeth as a wave of pain washed through her.

"We could take off and let them think we're gone," she said, "then we can sneak back and get Lux."

Jim shook his head as he climbed out of the boat. "Too dangerous."

She started to protest, but bit her tongue. What right did she have to ask Jim to risk his life anymore for her sake, or even Lux's? He had nothing to do with any of this. He looked as terrible as she felt, and she realized she had little idea what he'd been through in the past twenty-four hours.

"Come on," he said. "The plane's that way."

The sky ahead of them blazed scarlet, but the sun had already fallen beneath the horizon, and the light it left behind was quickly fading. Behind them, a few stars glimmered, flecks of white against a deep blue wash. The temperature had dropped to a comfortable, balmy degree that took Sophie back ten years, to the nights when she and her parents would camp on the beaches and build little fires out of driftwood.

"Why does she listen to me?" Jim asked when his story had concluded with him losing Lux and then launching his only partially successful rescue plan. "She follows me like a puppy."

"It's how she's programmed," said Nicholas.

"What—like a robot?"

Nicholas gave a short laugh. "What an idiotic thing to say."

Jim bristled and shoved his hands in his pockets, and Sophie briefed him on what she'd learned about Lux and the other Vitros. "I promised Nicholas I'd help him escape. It's the least I can do, after what my mom has done."

Nicholas smiled at her.

"Doesn't make him your problem," said Jim.

"Will you two just be nice?" she asked, exasperated. The last thing she wanted to deal with right now was their competing egos. Jim and Nicholas exchanged hostile looks, and then Jim took her arm and whispered that he wanted a private word.

"I don't trust him," Jim said, when he'd taken her aside.

"Nicholas? Why?"

"I think he's the one who sabotaged my plane."

"What? Why would he do that?"

"It's something Mary said when she was chasing me and Lux. Something about keeping me put, and she implied Nicholas had something to do with the nails."

"He didn't want you taking off without him. And understandably so!"

Jim shook his head. "You're not getting it! If he put down the nails before we landed, that means he wanted me—well, *you*, really—stuck here from the beginning. See?"

She frowned. "I don't know. . . . I mean, you don't know it was him who sabotaged the plane. Maybe he just meant to keep you here *after* you'd landed. Why would he sabotage his chance of escape?"

"I don't know. All I know is that I don't trust him."

"Well." She was getting angrier with him by the moment. First he didn't want to go back for Lux, and now he wanted to leave Nicholas behind too? "Why don't we ask him, then?"

"Ask him?"

"If it was him who sabotaged the plane."

"As if he'd admit to it!"

She looked at Nicholas. He was scuffing the sand with his shoe and watching them, his hands in his pockets. He didn't look dangerous or untrustworthy. He looked . . . lost. Alone. Desperate.

"Just . . ." Jim stopped, ruffled his hair, and started over. "Come with me. Just you."

"Jim! I have to help them!"

"And you can help them, I promise! But *after* we leave this place."

She ran her teeth over her lower lip as she stared at him, his eyes wild and imploring, then nodded slowly, swayed by his intensity.

He looked relieved. "Thank you. You tell him. I'll get the plane ready."

When she walked back to Nicholas and told him, her eyes downcast, that she and Jim were going without him, he went very still and his eyes flickered to Jim. "Oh?" he said simply, his hand tightening on his backpack.

"I'm sorry. I am. But I'll come back soon, I swear, with help."

"And who will help us?" he asked. "Who will care?"

"I don't know," she admitted. "But I'll find someone."

"Don't go," said Nicholas suddenly. He grabbed her hand. "Stay with me. We'll take the chopper. You and me and Lux. We'll go back and get her and fly out of here."

"Nicholas . . ." She watched Jim, who was prepping the plane for takeoff.

"Sophie, please." He shifted so that he interrupted her view of Jim, his eyes wide and his brows drawn together. "Please help me. I need you. All these years, it was you who kept me going. It was the thought of you, out there, that made me believe escape was possible. That another *life* was possible. You came all this way to what? Just leave? Just walk out on us?"

She wanted to yell in frustration. Decisions warred one another in her mind, the voices of Jim and Nicholas and Moira all clashing together, pulling her in different directions, until she felt she would snap into three separate pieces.

"I . . ."

"Sophie!" Jim called. He was wading ashore, the spray of the surf drenching him and plastering his hair to his forehead. "We're ready!"

She turned to Nicholas, biting her lip. "I have to . . . I just . . ."

She turned and ran, clutching her arm painfully, toward Jim. A wave of dizziness swept over her, and she nearly fell headfirst into the sand, but he caught her and steadied her.

"You okay?"

"Yeah."

"Plane's waiting."

The Cessna bobbed on the surf, tethered by a long cord to a nearly horizontal palm. The beach bowed inward, creating a small, shallow bay; Sophie could see bright yellow-and-blue schools of fish darting in complex patterns over the white sand, and further out, a cluster of pink-and-white coral formed a kind of underwater city, bristling with anemones and long, stringy seaweed. The water cast pale, undulating reflections on the trunks of the palms and across her and Jim's skin, giving the impression that they too were underwater.

"We'll have to swim out," he said apologetically. "I checked her over, ran the engines. She should fly, but there's no guarantee."

"Right."

He looked at her sharply, his amber eyes filled with concern. "You look a little pale."

"I'm fine."

"Yeah? Because you lost a lot of blood."

"I'm okay!"

"Geez. All right." He backed away.

Sophie felt bad for snapping at him after all the trouble he'd gone to in helping her, but her thoughts were racing and she was having difficulty focusing on what he was saying.

"Sophie, come on!" He'd gone several steps ahead, but she remained fixed in one place, her feet sinking into the sand.

Slowly, she shook her head. "You go. I'm going back."

"What?" He gripped his hair, a gesture she was beginning to understand was his token expression of exasperation. "But—no! I can't let you! It's too dangerous."

"Since when do you *let me* do anything, Jim Julien?" she replied hotly. "Lux is my sister and Dr. Crue is my mom. If I run away now when they need me the most—what does that say about me?"

"If this is about trying to fix the mess your mom made—"

"Yes, it *is* about that! But it's also about doing what is right! It's about family, Jim." She forced herself to relax a little, and unclenched her fists. "I know you don't want to get involved here, and I don't want you to. Go home, Jim. Send someone to help. But I can't do that. I can't walk away. Because when you love someone, that's what you do—you get involved. You get so involved that *their* pain becomes *your* pain. You get involved to the point where there's no getting *un*involved because that's what love *is*, and that's what family is. Don't you get that? Can't you understand it? The Jim I knew ten years ago would have understood!"

"Look, I *did* get involved, Sophie, the moment I decided to go back for you. I risked my neck to save yours, and now you just want to go throw all of that away. Well, *fine*. If I'm just the guy you paid for a service, if that's all I am—then *fine*."

"Jim!"

"Go on. Go back. Try to save your sister and your mom and get yourself shot or whatever. I don't care. I'm just the pilot, and you're just another client."

"I didn't—" She groaned in frustration; she didn't want him to be angry at her. She didn't want to part like this. He had risked his life for hers, and she felt like an ungrateful jerk for blowing him off, but she realized she couldn't have it both ways—she couldn't have Jim and save her family. She'd have to just let him think she didn't care, or he'd never let her go. "You're right," she whispered. "That's all this is. Sure, we had fun a long time ago, but now . . . I paid you to do your job, no more than that, and now I—I'm done with you. Go home and don't try to stop me."

"Is this about *him*?" Jim asked, pointing at Nicholas.

"Hey, buddy," said Nicholas, "if you've got a problem with me—"

"Maybe I do! It was you who put the nails down on the runway, wasn't it?"

"Jim—" Sophie started, but he ignored her and stepped toward Nicholas, who took a step back.

"What's your game, man?" Jim asked, spreading his arms. "What do you *really* want with her?"

"Hey. Come on. I don't want trouble." Nicholas brushed his hair behind his ears and swallowed, his eyes darting about nervously.

"Did you do it? Answer me straight! Did you sabotage my plane?"

"Jim, *stop!*" Sophie yelled. "Leave him alone! This isn't about him! I made my decision, now just *go!*"

He turned, his wet hair flinging droplets of water, and for a moment they glared at each other. Then the fight went out of him and his shoulders dropped. "Fine. Whatever. Goodbye, Sophie."

He turned and walked toward the surf. Sophie stared after him, the anger melting from her eyes as she realized their fight had left a hollow ache in her chest. She didn't want him to go. She needed him, more than she'd realized. But she also couldn't let him get hurt, and she knew that letting him go was the right thing to do. She looked away, forcing herself to stay strong and not beg him to turn around. She caught Nicholas staring at her, his eyes hard.

"Hey," said Nicholas, calling to Jim. "Wait up." He dropped to his knees, zipped open his backpack, and fiddled with its contents. Then he ran down the beach, making Jim flinch when he drew close. "Easy. I just—here. Take this. It's mostly food and stuff, but there are some documents that might help you convince someone out there that this place is real. Information on the project, Corpus, you know." He shrugged. "Just take it."

Jim glanced at Sophie, who nodded, and he grabbed the backpack without a word, then turned and stalked away. Sophie realized she was shaking, and drew a deep breath to calm herself. She watched as he swam out to the plane, then turned and headed back to the boat with Nicholas, her arm throbbing.

The outboard whined as she and Nicholas sped across the channel. Her face burned with shame for debasing Jim the way she had, but she didn't know of any other way to convince him to go on without her. *It's not like we're friends anymore,* she thought. *It's like I said. That was a long time ago. We've both changed.* But it didn't feel that way. She felt as if the ten years they'd been separated had never happened. Sure, at first she'd felt awkward, unsure what to make of this nearly adult version of her old Jim, but that had quickly passed. His friendship was so easy and natural, and gave her a warmth under her skin that she suspected, with some degree of surprise and wonder, went even beyond mere friendship. She *did* care about Jim—perhaps more deeply than she'd even realized. She wanted to tell him that. She wanted to rearrange reality, make it so that Skin Island and Lux and Nicholas and all this had never happened, so that she could rediscover Jim properly, focusing all her attention on him and who he had become, somehow making up for the years they had lost.

But now she'd ruined the relationship they had, and likely all potential they'd had of deepening it.

Just let him go, she told herself. *You didn't come here for him.* She had to help Nicholas and Lux, and maybe even her mother, if she could.

When Nicholas slid the boat onto the sand and helped her out, Jim was beginning to start up the plane. She could hear the engine cough and then growl to life, even over the surf. The prop begin to spin, faster and faster until it was a blur. She stood on the beach and watched as the lights on the tail and the wingtips blinked on, red and white, and then the plane turned and began taxiing across the water like a Jet Ski. Then it lifted in a white spray of water and climbed into the sky. She felt a sense of relief; there had been a possibility it wouldn't fly after their rough landing.

"*Finally.*" Nicholas's voice rose above the surf, and she turned to see him rolling his shoulders as if he'd just finished running a race.

"What?"

"I mean that idiot of a pilot is finally out of the way. *God,* he was grating on my nerves."

She frowned. "Out of the way? Out of whose way?"

A change swept across Nicholas's features, a change so uncannily physical that she blinked to see if her eyes were being tricked. All the imploring, the desperation, the pitifulness drained away like a mask of smoke, and in its place spread a look so smug and crafty that he didn't even look like the same person he'd been ten seconds earlier. A smile, thin and leonine, squirmed across his lips as if drawn with a fine-point pen.

"On Skin Island," said Nicholas, "there is only one way. And it's *mine.*"

"What?"

He pointed at the plane, his index finger extended and

thumb vertical in the shape of a gun. He shut one eye, as if aiming at the Cessna, and then clicked his tongue and lowered his thumb.

Jim's plane burst into a ball of flame, lighting the sky like a thousand fireworks. Blazing debris shot in every direction, fireballs trailing sparks to land, hissing in the ocean. Like a horrible burning flower the explosion continued to blossom, getting bigger and brighter, casting red light over the palms and the water, the flames reflecting on the undulating surface of the ocean.

Sophie heard a violent scream and realized it came from her own throat. She was on her knees, her hands digging into the sand. "NO!"

Nicholas stood over her, his hands still in his pockets, his eyes glinting orange with the explosion as if the fire burned inside him. And he laughed, a low chuckle of delight, and he all but rubbed his hands together in glee.

"*You did this?*" she howled, and she lunged at him nails first, going after his eyes, but he caught her wrists and held her off. She screamed wordlessly, kicking and writhing, but he pushed her into the sand onto her back and pinned her down.

"Sh," he said soothingly. "It's better this way. You'll see. Things are simpler now. Hush. Stop that!"

She struggled beneath him, her rage mingling with horror. The explosion faded from the sky, but the image of the plane bursting apart was still burned to the undersides of her eyelids. When she closed her eyes she saw the flames. She saw the pain in Jim's eyes as he turned away, cut to the heart by her cold dismissal.

Nicholas kept shushing her until she lay quiet, her heart

pounding, her lips crusted with sand. When she was too exhausted to fight anymore, he relaxed his grip on her wrists. He was straddling her, his weight too much for her to throw him off.

"What was in that backpack?" she howled. "What did you give him?"

He snorted. "Well, it wasn't Twinkies and *documents*, I'll tell you that much. It's amazing, you know, the chemicals you can find in the average laboratory. Put them together in just the right way, toss in an alarm clock . . . *Kapow!* It was supposed to go in the Vitro building. I had it timed beautifully too. It would've been the perfect distraction while we took the chopper—but oh, Jim. Stupid Jim had to run off with you—well, I couldn't have that, could I? And now I don't have my lovely little bomb anymore. Still, it was worth it." He looked up at the sky, at the dissipating cloud of smoke that was all that remained of Jim Julien and his plane. Turning back to her, he sighed, then smiled. "Well. I can always come up with something."

"What is *wrong* with you?" she asked, her voice a low croak.

"Don't you know?" he asked.

She couldn't focus on him, could barely comprehend what he had done. Her mind was filled with Jim, seven-year-old Jim and eighteen-year-old Jim blurring together until they disolved into a red miasma of pain and shock.

"I never imprinted, Sophie, remember? The chip damaged the part of my brain responsible for forming that kind of bond. Or *any* kind of bond."

"You're a psychopath," she whispered. "Like Mary. Like the others."

He leaned down as if they were lovers entwined in each other's embrace, making her shiver, and whispered in her ear, "I am a certifiable psychopath, Sophie. We're *all* psychopaths. The experiments that went bad." He chuckled and kissed her, briefly and cruelly, before she could turn her head away. "They just never knew *how* bad."

TWENTY-SIX
JIM

The worst part was, she never apologized.

He never understood why it bothered him so much. She'd never been the apologizing sort. She was proud and stubborn, and had to always, always be right. She never said she was sorry, and that was the part that hurt the most.

"Son," she'd said, her patience infuriating him, "sometimes people fall apart."

Sometimes people fall apart.

What kind of a lame excuse was that? As if her cheating on his dad was some kind of accident, some kind of unfortunate twist of nature, as if their "falling apart" was no different than rain at a picnic.

If people could fall apart, why couldn't they fall back together?

But he didn't ask; he just nodded. His fury was the numbing kind, the kind that froze rather than burned. He couldn't talk, couldn't argue with her. He just nodded, like a useless idiot, and let her excuses wash over him.

"You can come with me," she'd said. Come with her to the mainland—well, with her and Lance, the navy guy she'd been sleeping with for two years behind his dad's back.

But going with her meant leaving Dad. Meant cheating on him the way she had. He wasn't a cheater. He couldn't betray the only parent who hadn't betrayed him. She didn't like it when he refused. That was the moment she cut him off. He saw it in her eyes, a kind of closing door, a burning bridge. "Fine," she snapped, and suddenly she stopped caring. He never understood how she did it, how she could turn people off, cut the ties between them as effectively as if she'd slammed a coffin shut over their dead bodies. She'd done it before, to his uncle, to his grandfather, to her friend Bettina when Bettina finally confessed to Jim's dad that his wife was cheating on him. And she'd done it to her husband years before, only Jim had been too stupid to see it at the time.

Once she cut someone loose, she never looked back.

You say people fall apart, Jim thought, but it's you who does all the falling.

He remembered it was the shouting that woke him that morning. His dad, his dreamer of a dad, still hoping, never giving up on her, chasing her down the hallway and trying to take her bag from her hand. She'd wrenched it away, and the key chain on it—the one with the beads with the Chamorrita poem engraved on them—had come loose in his hand, breaking off its metal ring. He was shouting, pleading, begging her not to go, and she yelled at him to lay off, and that was what woke Jim. He stood in the doorway of his room in a pair of sweatpants *and an Atari T-shirt, confused and disoriented as she swept past him. She paused, just a half step, just long enough to glance at him and say, "The lemon tree needs watering twice a week."*

Not "I'm sorry." Not "goodbye." Not even "I love you." The last thing his mother had said to him was about the stupid lemon tree. She'd raised it from a seedling; she didn't have any way to transport it to California when she left.

He'd watered the lemon tree twice a week, never missing a day, until exactly one year later on the anniversary of her infamous departure. That day, he calmly carried the tree into the yard, set it on the driveway, and lit it on fire. It had two small lemons on it. He never forgot the way they smelled, those burning lemons.

Jim's eyes shot open, and he stopped himself from inhaling just in time. He was underwater, and if he breathed in then his lungs would fill and he would drown.

He couldn't tell how deep he was. It was too dark. There were no lights in any direction, just inky water, as if he'd fallen into a sea of black paint. For a moment, he couldn't even tell which way was up. What if he swam in the wrong direction? What if instead of going toward the surface he only went deeper, deeper to a watery death?

After a few seconds he oriented himself and began swimming what he was fairly sure was upward. When he broke out of the water, it was on his last stroke, his head screaming with pain and his lungs flaming. He gasped in air and then fell back underwater, thrashing and struggling. For several minutes his life hung by a thread, balancing on the outcome of his battle with the sea. Every time he found the air a wave pushed him down again, as if the ocean was determined to have him.

But he fought back with all his strength until at last he found a length of aluminum bobbing on the water and he threw himself over it. Then, exhausted and panting, he drifted aimlessly for a long while as the stars grew brighter and the moon rose higher. It felt like hours, but barely thirty minutes had passed when he finally lifted his head and looked around. He was extremely disoriented, having no idea where he was or what had happened, and the memories trickled slowly through his thoughts.

The aluminum.

He looked down, then pulled away as if he'd found himself clutching a dead body. It was a piece of the wing of his plane. Bile surged in his throat, and he had to grab the wing to hold himself up when he retched, half from horror, half from being tossed by the waves.

The plane had exploded, and him nearly with it.

The only thing that had saved him had been his growling stomach. With one hand on the yoke, he'd used the other to open Nicholas's backpack, curious to see what snacks the Vitro had packed. Instead he'd found an alarm clock bound to large vials of clear liquid, and he didn't need to look twice to know what it was, or to see that the timer on the clock was within seconds of hitting zero.

He threw open the door to the plane and jumped, hitting the water feetfirst and feeling as if he'd dropped into a sheet of concrete. The pain had shattered up his body, and he blacked out. How long had he been sinking before he awoke? How much longer did he have before his air ran out and he drowned?

He stopped thinking about it. He was alive and that was

all that mattered, though his situation was still pretty dire. The darkness cloaked the island, and he turned in a circle, scanning the horizon for any sign of land.

It was hard to concentrate with his mind pulling in the other direction. *Nicholas tried to kill me. He literally handed me a ticking bomb, and like an idiot, I took it.* And now Nicholas had Sophie. Whatever he wanted her for, after what Jim had just witnessed, he knew it couldn't be good.

Well, whatever was happening on Skin Island, all he could do now was swim for his life and hope Sophie could take care of herself for a while. He could wait till morning, conserving his energy, and then hope to spot the island in the daylight. But then he would risk drifting out of sight entirely. He knew this area from the thousand times he'd flown over it; Skin Island was a lonely strip of land in a wide empty sea. Most of the other islands were miles and miles away, too far to offer him any chances. It was Skin Island or it was the ocean. Only one held a chance of survival, however slim.

The longer he stared at the darkness, the better his vision became, as long as he didn't look directly at the moon. He was shivering; the water was warm enough, but his mind was a riot of memories: the pain as he hit the water, the image of his mother dragging her suitcase down the hall, the sound of his plane exploding above him, the smell of burning lemons.

"You could have said you were sorry," he whispered. "You could have at least apologized."

Only the stars were there to listen, and they maintained glittery silence.

Jim dropped his head onto the wing with a clunk. The metal smelled burnt, like used gunpowder. He'd loved that plane, loved it more than anything else he owned, though technically it was his dad's. It was the Cessna that had taken him above the world when the world had no place for him. Lost in the noise of the engine and the haze of clouds, he could almost forget. It was his one haven, his last sanctuary, and now it was scattered across the Pacific in a million burning bits.

It just wasn't *fair*. Jim pounded a fist against the aluminum. If he'd just stuck to his own advice and stayed out of Sophie's business, he'd be home by now. But no. Oh, no. He just *had* to entangle himself in problems that had nothing to do with him. *Getting involved means getting hurt.* He'd tried to mend things between his parents, been naive enough to believe he could fix everything as if they were living some cheesy, feel-good Hallmark Channel flick. And what did he get in return? His mother shut him out, and shortly after, his dad might as well have. He lost himself in drinking and Jim lost himself in the sky.

"You get involved to the point where there's no getting *un*involved," Sophie had said. "Because that's what love is."

Well, then love was stupid. He had no place for it. Love was treacherous and it cheated and it blocked other people out. It burned bridges that could never be rebuilt. Love was just an excuse people used to get what they wanted. It was the all-powerful so-called virtue that people threw around like an overused trump card, a trick ace played to win the pot and beggar the competition. What good was love if it was so easily abused? What good was love if it could be turned into a weapon?

He should have known better. He should have told Sophie no the moment he saw her.

But now Jim was involved to the point where he couldn't be uninvolved, just as Sophie had said, though it wasn't for love. It was because his plane was in more pieces than a LEGO kit and his only chance of getting home now *was* Sophie. He had to find her and her mom and hope he could work out some kind of deal. There was always Lux. . . . No. He wouldn't go there. He couldn't abuse his power over her that way—it was sick. Anyway, what could she really do to help him? She was hardly capable of walking on two legs.

None of this would matter if he didn't find the island. He forced all his attention on finding it, and after consulting the few star patterns he could remember to orient himself, finally settled on a slightly darker smudge of black to the southeast.

Jim began to wearily kick his legs, propelling himself and the wing in the general direction of the shadow he hoped was the island. The waves tossed against him, rolled him along, pushing and pulling. He seemed to be getting nowhere, but he swam anyway, though his limbs were weak and wobbly and about as much good as spaghetti noodles.

Oddly, he kept thinking of some stupid poem he'd had to study in his tenth-grade lit class. He couldn't remember the title, just something about an albatross around a guy's neck, dragging him down, and one rhythmic line that pounded through his brain in time with his pulse: *Water, water, every-where, nor any drop to drink.* . . . He found himself mouthing the line as he swam, like an escaped lunatic.

Water, water, everywhere, and nor any drop to drink. . . .

TWENTY-SEVEN

SOPHIE

"Keep up!" Nicholas called, yanking the cord that he'd wrapped around Sophie's ankles. Her hands were free, but she couldn't attempt to run or he'd just jerk the cord and bring her crashing to the ground. The knots around her ankles were just loose enough to allow her to walk, but running was out of the question.

She gritted her teeth and said nothing, waddling awkwardly behind him. They wove through thick, rolling groves of bamboo, heading south. Sophie stumbled blindly, too overwhelmed with shock and grief to put up much of a fight. Every time she closed her eyes she saw Jim's plane breaking apart, shattering in the sky in a ball of hungry flames.

"What do you *want* with me?" she mumbled. She was still trying to wrap her mind around the fact that the boy she'd pitied, the boy she'd gone out of her way to help, had turned out to be a conscienceless, homicidal psychopath who had played her like a piano. "Why are you doing this?"

He stopped and looked back at her, at the bloody bandage on her shoulder and her skinned knees and her pale cheeks, and he sighed. "We'll stop for a few minutes."

They were at the highest point in the bamboo forest. The land dipped on either side of them, though any view of the island below was obscured by darkness. But to the west, the rising moon gave view of the infinite sea. When Sophie looked at it, she felt a cold knot rise in her throat, and she dropped to her knees and vomited bile over the edge of the bluff.

"It's my fault," she gasped. "You killed him but I'm just as guilty."

"Good God, will you stop *whining*?" He sat on a half-buried rock and crossed his legs, looking intensely bored.

She looked at him over her shoulder, burning with hate. "I was almost in that plane. I would have died with him. If you want me dead so badly, why don't you just push me off this cliff now and be done with it? Why all of *this*?" Her voice turned to a snarl, and she yanked the cord between them.

"Because," he said calmly, "I don't want you dead. Why do you think I begged you to stay? The bomb was meant for him, not you. The pilot did a thing very few people can do— he made me angry, so I had to eliminate him. But you—*you* and I have plans."

"You're delusional." She eyed the drop below; the cliff plunged into rocks and violent waves. If he were just a yard closer she could grab him and throw them both off the cliff. It would almost be worth it; they both deserved to pay for what had happened to Jim.

Nicholas sighed and rubbed his thumb over the cord in his hands. "So they say. So they say. Enough resting. Let's go."

"Wait." She paused and licked her lips, wincing at the memory of his harsh kiss. If she could stall him from executing whatever plan he had in mind, maybe the guards or doctors would find them first. She'd rather be in their hands than his. They had to be out scouring the island; had they seen the explosion?

She turned away from the cliff, abandoning her mad inspiration of tossing Nicholas and herself over it, and instead scanned the trees for any sign of possible aid. But she had to keep Nicholas sitting still for as long as possible.

"Why do you need me?" she asked. "Do you really believe I'll still help you, after what you just did?"

He studied her flatly, then rose and held out a hand. "You're trying to stall me. Well, it won't work. The guards won't find us, not in this bamboo. Still, it was a nice try."

She ignored his proffered hand and stood on her own, her face burning.

"Come on," he said. "I want to show you something."

He led her inland, through a grove of dense jungle and then a clearing riddled with rocks, all of them covered in moss and leaning at crazy angles, their shadows deep purple pockets of cool air that made her shiver when she passed through them. After that, more bamboo, and a narrow, lively stream filled with smooth, round stones. Moments later they stepped out of the jungle and onto an old concrete pathway that must have led back to the resort. It had been overgrown with vines and grasses, and a rotting fence ran along its length, large portions of it having crumbled away altogether. They went some distance down the path until they began passing buildings lurking in the vegetation: a spa, its windows shattered inward by some past storm, a restaurant with a giant wooden lobster on its roof. More than ever Sophie sensed the ghosts of this place.

"We're here," Nicholas finally announced, and pointed at a one-story stucco building with a sagging front porch and terra-cotta tiles on the roof. Many of the tiles had slipped off and were smashed on the ground around the building.

"What is this place?" she asked.

"Old salon," he said. "For the ladies to get their hair done."

What do you know about salons? she wanted to ask, but she bit her tongue.

"Well?" he said. "Do you want a haircut?" He bounced the light over the wooden steps leading to the door, which had once been made of glass, but she could see shattered fragments of it littering the porch.

Sophie frowned. "Why are we here?"

"Come in and find out." He regarded her with sudden gravity. "Don't you want to know the truth, Sophie Crue? The whole truth?"

She studied Nicholas very carefully, trying to imagine what went on inside his head. "What truth?" she asked carefully.

"The one you know is still out there. The piece you know you're still missing."

She drew a deep breath and stared through the gaping doorway. It was dark inside. "Do I have a choice?"

He laughed. "Of course not."

Heart frantically pounding, as if trying to push her in the other direction, Sophie carefully climbed the steps. They creaked and bowed under her feet, but held. The broken glass crunched as she crossed the porch and stepped through the gap it had once filled. Nicholas followed close behind, still keeping a hold of the cord. Inside, Sophie found cobwebbed walls and moldy carpet patterned with faded roses. The building smelled strongly of damp must and mildew. A curling poster on the wall showed a woman with long outdated clothing and a huge perm.

The poster alone attested to the years of disuse this place had seen, as if the dust, wallpaper, and bowed ceiling weren't testimony enough. With a chill, Sophie wondered what Nicholas planned to do to her in this creepy ruin. She was prepared to fight him tooth and nail. When she found herself contemplating how to wrap the cord around his neck and strangle him from behind, she swallowed a rush of nausea. *What am I becoming?* He'd not only revealed the evil in himself; he was also revealing the evil in Sophie.

"Through there," he said, directing her to a doorway at the end of the hall. She went toward it, feeling as though her body temperature were dropping by a degree with each step. The room inside was windowless and completely dark. She froze and nearly retreated. She'd never been scared of the dark before, but was beginning to suspect Skin Island would change that.

"Scared?" Nicholas said. He closed in on her from behind, standing so close she could feel his breath. "Tell me, what does it feel like to be scared, Sophie Crue? I have always wondered."

"Everyone gets scared," she breathed.

"Not me." His hand reached around her, and for a moment she thought he was going to grab her, but he only flicked a light switch on the wall. A glass globe in the middle of the ceiling blinked on with a high whine. She felt a flash of terror, as if expecting to see a dead body or some nightmarish monster, but it was just a small studio with three chairs facing three mirrors and a row of hair-drying seats. The huge dome dryers were polished clean, which surprised her. As her eyes adjusted to the light, she saw the room had been recently cleaned and redecorated. Rows of pictures hung on the wall. Unlike the posters in the hallway, they were untouched by humidity and age. They looked like magazine clippings and all showed different shots of New York City. On the floor sat half-used candles, playing cards, a croquet mallet, and boxes of crackers. Nicholas opened a small refrigerator in the corner and took out two grape sodas. He tossed one to Sophie, cracked his open, and fell into one of the dryer seats, taking up the slack in the cord by wrapping it around his wrist.

"That's New York City," he said, nodding at the pictures on the wall. "Corpus is based there. We'll go there, when we leave this place."

She looked around the room. It looked like a hideout. Maybe this was where Nicholas snuck away to with Mary and the others.

"You didn't have to kill him," she said. "We were trying to help you. He was going back to Guam to get help, you know." She leaned against the wall and stared unseeingly at the calendar from 1994 hanging opposite her with a picture of a half-dressed cowgirl seductively draped over a John Deere tractor. Her eyes slipped shut, releasing the first tears. "Jim was . . . he was my—"

"Jim, Jim, *Jim*—shut up!" He jumped to his feet and rushed toward her. She pressed against the wall and held her breath, heart lurching, as he stood over her and gripped his soda can so hard the metal dented. "I'm *sick* of hearing about Jim! You hear me? *Sick*. He's gone! Forget about him!"

Nicholas stepped back, drained his soda, and tossed the can into the corner. He drew a deep breath, let it out with a sigh, and then smiled. It wasn't a cruel smile, but a charming, slightly mischievous one. Sophie didn't know what to think. It was like looking at a completely different person. He moved from emotion to emotion as if he were changing hats, as if the expressions were mere masks.

"Look," he said, "I'm not really angry. See?" He spread his hands wide and bowed.

He's insane, Sophie thought.

"C'mon, Sophie. Sit down. I'm just messing with you, you know. That's all. Sit down and I'll tell you about yourself." But he didn't let her sit. He kept her pinned to the wall with his body, and as he tilted his face down to look into hers, his hair fell forward, creating a kind of curtain around their conversation. She felt as if he'd sucked her into his own small, dark world.

"I know everything about this island," he said. "Every room, every key, every secret. I know when the tides come and go and where to find the seagulls' nests and how many steps it is from north to south—and I know everything about you. I know that you think you're special, because you're Moira Crue's daughter. You think you're better than us. But you're not. You're not as special as you think, Sophie Crue."

Suddenly he kissed her, hard and rough and greedily, and she pressed her hands against his chest and shoved him away. He stumbled backward, dropping the cord, and Sophie leaped forward. But he caught her by her hair, pulling her backward, and she screamed and dropped the soda she'd been holding. His arm snaked around her waist, and she grabbed it and bit it. With a shriek, he let go of her hair and she darted forward again. This time she scooped up her soda can, whirled, and smashed it into the side of his head. Grape soda sprayed all over the room, splattering the mirrors and staining the carpet. He hissed and dropped to his knees, his hands pressed to his temple. Before she could make a dash for it, he grabbed the cord and pulled her feet from under her. She fell heavily to her knees.

He shook his head as he stood up and gave her a pity-ing smile. "Look at you. You're pathetic," he said. "Now look at me." He spread his hands wide; Sophie had never known anyone else who could strut while standing still, but Nicholas pulled it off. "They *say* psychopathy is a 'condition,' a handi-cap, a thing to be cured and treated. But it's so much more than that, Sophie. It's a gift! It's ultimate freedom—freedom from the stupid conventions of conscience and guilt. It's the true ticket to happiness, you know. I mean, *look* at me! I can blow up your sad little boyfriend—*pow!*—just like that and not think twice about it! I can do anything!"

She stood up and slapped him, leaving a cherry red mark on his cheek. He froze, then laughed.

"You can't make me mad," he said. "I don't get upset. I don't cry. I don't *care*, Sophie. That's what it all comes down to. I don't care about your pilot being blown apart into a mil-lion tiny pieces of skin and hair and bone and scattered all over the ocean for the fish to eat. I don't care that you hate me for it. I don't care if you think it's wrong or evil."

"You're twisted," she hissed.

"It's so liberating." Nicholas's tone took a dreamy timbre. "You don't get held back by feelings. You can do whatever you want and never feel bad about it. It doesn't make sense to me, you know? How people like you can hurt someone and think, *Oh, man, I shouldn't have done that. It makes me feel so bad. So wrong . . .* What's it like, Sophie? Is it like wearing a collar all the time, having some invisible moral hand yanking you around, dragging you away from the things you really want?

"You know what I think?" Nicholas went on. *Does he never shut up?* Sophie wondered. "*I* think you people aren't as good as you say you are. Okay, okay, stop." He held up his hands. "I know. I have an idea. Close your eyes."

She glared at him.

"Oh, come *on*, just do it! Just close your eyes." When she still refused, he pushed her roughly into one of the dryer seats and wrapped a hand around her throat, choking her just enough to make her panic a little. "*Close your eyes,*" he insisted.

She closed her eyes.

"Good! Now, just imagine, just think about this: Have you ever wanted to lash out at someone but you knew you couldn't because you'd get in trouble? Or maybe you wanted to just *take* something from someone because you knew they didn't deserve it? Ever want to just cut out all the crap and the fakery and the shallow politeness and just *be* who you want to be?"

She refused to let him into her mind, and instead pictured herself somewhere else; on the soccer field, pouring all her strength into strikes on goal and cheering with her team the way they had after they won regionals. The fantasy was strong, but it didn't block out his voice, not enough.

He released his grip on her throat, and she opened her eyes. "See," he said softly, contemplatively, "I don't buy this whole *conscience* thing. At least, I think it's a kind of last defense. Like, you already want to do something terrible, and you probably think about how you'd do it and how you'd get away with it. But then your conscience steps in and is all, '*Oh, Sophie, you can't do that, that's wrong.*' And so you don't. Or even if you do, you feel bad about it. Your conscience beats you for it for days, right? But, see, what if committing that terrible thing in your mind is the *real* crime? Maybe there's not such a difference between you and me. Maybe the only difference is that I have the guts to do what you'll only *think* about."

He dropped to a whisper and ran his hand over her hair and her cheek, studying her with consuming intensity. "Are you really so noble? So good? The urge is in you to do terrible, unspeakable things. It's in everyone. It's part of us, like a monster in our heads. Are you really so different from me?"

"You are completely obsessed with yourself," she said, narrowing her eyes in frank, horrified fascination. "You really are. You think you're some kind of enlightened messiah, don't you? Unlocking the secrets of the universe, discerning the core of the human psyche. But you're just a delusional, lonely little boy inside who throws a tantrum when he doesn't get his way."

Nicholas stepped back as if she'd slapped him again, and he scowled. "You're the child, Sophie Crue! Not me."

"Really? What do you honestly know about the world? You grew up on this island, isolated from real society. What, do you watch movies? Read books? You must have some kind of Internet access to have sent me that e-mail. Do you really think you know what people are like, when you can count the number of people you know on two hands? Oh, the other Vitros don't count—they're just shadows of people."

"I'm going to leave this island," said Nicholas, "and I'm going to take whatever I want."

"If you're trying to impress me, the only thing I'm impressed by is how ridiculously stupid and narcissistic you are."

His hand rose to slap her, but she blocked him and raised her knee, driving it into his groin. Nicholas gasped and doubled over, and she jumped out of the chair, but he tackled her from behind, cursing and hissing threats. He flipped her over and grabbed her hair, yanking her head back and then covering her mouth with his other hand when she started to scream.

"Enough," he whispered in her ear. "You want to know why I brought you to this island?"

She twisted, trying to throw him off, but he was sitting on her stomach and when she moved he just pulled her hair; her eyes flooded with tears of pain, and she could only moan.

"I watched you grow up, Sophie Crue," he said. "Oh yes. You've been watched your entire life. Photos, videos, medical records, even artwork and school reports you sent to your mom. She keeps it all in a little room behind her office, and I am the only person who knows about it. *I* found a way in. I know every corner of this island, down to the forgotten rooms and the spaces inside the walls themselves. I know every secret on Skin Island, and you are the best-kept one of all. I know everything about you."

He smiled. Her skin crawled; even if he was lying, just the thought of him stalking her from the other side of the planet was enough to chill her to the bone.

"I know you hate your stepmother," he murmured. "I know you broke your arm when you were ten by trying to run away, and they put you on medication to keep you from trying it again. I know you had a yellow parakeet named Popcorn, but your stepbrother strangled it with dental floss when you were twelve and hung the body over your bed, and when you tried to tell his parents about it he said it was you who'd done it, and they put you back on the meds."

Sophie froze from head to toe, her heart icing over. "Mmph," she groaned, but he didn't stop.

"I know that when you were thirteen, your stepsister Emily stole your journal and read it aloud to all her friends, and when they laughed at you, you hit Emily so hard you broke her nose. They said there was something wrong with you, didn't they?" He chuckled. "They said you weren't normal. They even whispered things like *antisocial*, didn't they? Funny." Nicholas's grin widened. "That's just almost like saying you're a *psychopath*."

She stared at him, transfixed with horror. He knew everything, every dark secret she'd buried deep in her memory. Every part of herself she kept most hidden he dragged out and pinned to the wall. She felt as if he were vivisecting her right thereon the ground.

"*Mmm,*" she groaned, and he finally let go of her mouth.

"I'm not a psychopath!" she shouted. "It wasn't me—none of that was me! Yeah, I hit Em, but she deserved it, and it *was* Noah who killed Popcorn! *You* are the psycho, not me. Get off of me!"

"Don't you think they knew that?" he asked. "According to *this*, they did." He rose up and hooked his foot under a drawer in one of the dressing tables, pulling it open. Then, keeping an eye on her all the while, he lifted out a thick binder packed with papers.

"What is that?" she whispered.

He turned it so she could read the label on the folder: *Sophie Jane Crue.*

Her blood froze over.

"This folder," he said slowly, crouching beside her and rubbing his hands over it, "contains the story of your life." He opened it, pulled out a photo, and showed it to her: It was her and her mother, kneeling side by side as they did a tea ceremony at a restaurant in Osaka. Sophie had been ten on that trip. It was still one of her favorite memories, but pinched between Nicholas's fingers, it suddenly sickened in her mind, like a leaf turning brown and ugly before dropping away.

"What—what is this?" she asked. "My mom will kill you for—"

"Oh, come on!" He gave her a disgusted look. "You don't need her to defend you! Why can't you stand up for yourself? Is this what you've been your entire life—a whiny, needy brat who blames all her problems on her absent mom? Look. There's just one rule, just one basic law that everyone lives under: Take control or be controlled. That's what it comes down to, Sophie Crue. You've been controlled your entire life, haven't you? By your mom, by Corpus, by your fake family." He shook his head and gave her a pitying look. "They tried to control me, too. But not anymore. *I'm* taking control now. Why won't you? The first step toward being free is recognizing that you're *not*."

"She loves me."

"Oh, oh, yes she does, I'm sure. And guess what? She loves me too, in her own way—because she created me. I'm her project; she doesn't love me, but the reflection of herself in me."

He crumpled the photo in his fist and dropped the folder, making it fall open. Photographs, every one of them a memory Sophie held dear, scattered across the floor. Sophie at twelve, smiling from horseback in one of the expensive riding lessons her mother had paid for. Sophie at fourteen, holding up a third-place trophy from some soccer tournament. One photo caught her eye in particular and cut her like a knife: her fifth birthday, a photo of her blowing out the candles on her Little Mermaid cake—and a tiny, freckled Jim Julien behind her, holding up bunny ears over her head and grinning impishly. She stared at it with wide, unblinking eyes, a crescendo of grief roaring in her head, searching for a way out.

"What is this?" she said hoarsely. "Where did you get these?"

"You should be more like me, Sophie," Nicholas said. "You *should* be that person they said you were. If you were—if you just stopped following their idiot rules—you'd realize how stupid they all are. How fake, how shallow. You'd be free like me. You'd finally be in control of your own life—isn't that what you want?"

"I don't want to be anything like you." She couldn't tear her eyes away from the photo.

"We'll see." He stood up and hauled her to her feet by her hair. She blinked away tears, biting her lip so hard she drew blood. "It's all about the *control*, Sophie. You don't even know what you are."

"What do you mean? What do you want from me, Nicholas?" Exasperated and bewildered, she could only stand helplessly lest he wrench her hair out by its roots.

"I want *you*," he said, his smile dropping, replaced by solemn steadiness. "You think I don't know anything about the world, but I know one thing—I know *you*. And I have dreamed of this day for years." He pulled her close, his one hand still tangled in her hair but the other pressed against the curve of her lower back, thrusting her against him. When he spoke, his breath was a hot cloud against her forehead and the tips of his long hair brushed against her eyelashes. "*You* are my window to the world, Sophie. Everything I know about what lies beyond this island, I learned from you. And now we're going to leave together. We'll take the world together. You'll be mine as you've always been mine, only now you know it."

"*Creep!*" Sophie choked. "You're insane!"

"Maybe." He shrugged, unperturbed.

"I'll never go anywhere with you!"

"What else are you going to do? Go back to your stepfamily? Stay here with your so-called *mom*, who's been lying to you your entire life? Run off with your pilot boyfriend— Oh. Wait." He smirked. "That's right—I killed him."

She roared like a wild animal and began beating at him with her fists, managing to knock his jaw and his temple before he caught her wrists and wrestled her into submission again. This time he drew more cord from his pocket and twined it around her wrists, so tightly that it bit into her skin and red welts began to show. She twisted and fought, but he was too strong for her, and she only succeeded in wrenching her hurt shoulder and doubling her pain.

"You don't even know what you are," he said again. He almost looked genuinely sorry for her, though she knew it was all an act, every bit of it. He could change emotions as if they were masks he carried in his pocket. "Poor little Sophie. You're a very special girl, you know."

"What do you mean?" she asked, though when he said it, she suddenly felt as if she had always known the truth, that it had been hidden inside her from the start.

He reached for the folder and drew out a photograph. Before she showed it to her, he studied it closely, his head tilted to the right. Then he turned it around, a slow smile spreading over his face. It showed a wide-eyed baby with light blond curls that Sophie recognized as herself, held tightly by a much younger Moira Crue—who was standing in the same lab in which Sophie had first seen Lux. Nicholas ran his thumb over the baby's face and stared intently at her.

"You're a Vitro, Sophie. Skin Island's own special, very first Vitro."

TWENTY-EIGHT
SOPHIE

She shook her head and shut her eyes, denying it with every fiber of her mind.

"Oh, come *on*," said Nicholas above her. "You seriously never saw it? Never suspected? Never wondered?"

How could she? She hadn't known the Vitros existed until yesterday.

"You're pathetic, Sophie. Now get up."

She heard him, but only distantly. Her brain moved as if she'd left the emergency brake on: haltingly, agonizingly. *I'm a Vitro.*

"Get *up*." He hauled her up by her collar and kept a firm grip on her neck to keep her from sinking down again. She slipped on the glossy photographs of her past. "Get control of yourself, will you? There's still so much to do!"

"You can't make me!" she spat.

"Oh?" He seemed amused by her vehemence.

"I'll fight you with every ounce of strength I have, you bastard."

"Not after you've imprinted on me," he whispered in her ear. "Now let's move."

Nicholas led her through the resort and smuggled her up the hill to the Vitro building, where he took her through a side door using a key he carried in his pocket, on a ring stuffed with them.

"You steal all of those?" she asked hollowly.

He rolled his eyes and pushed the door open.

The hallway was deserted, but she heard loud voices from the atrium—her mother, Strauss, Andreyev, among others. They were arguing intensely, from the sound of it. Nicholas led her in the opposite direction, to a small door that led to a downward staircase, and into a long hallway. They passed rooms with padded walls, and Sophie recognized the one in which she'd been kept after she'd blurted out her identity to Strauss. For a moment, she thought Nicholas was going to lock her back inside, and she panicked and jerked away, nearly tripping when the cord went taut and caught her ankles.

"Relax," he said. "I'm not going to lock you up."

"What do you think you're going to do?" she said. "Make me imprint on you, really? That's impossible. It's not like I'm a baby you can start hardwiring, like the rest of them."

"You'd be surprised at what I can do." He pulled her further along, past the padded cells. Her borrowed sneakers squeaked on the tile.

She felt raw inside, worked over like a lump of used

chewing gum. He knew everything about her, all her darkest memories. Had her mother been whispering the secrets of Sophie's life into his ear? Was she just a source of gossip for the people on Skin Island to laugh over? *The control, it's all about the control.* His laughter echoed in her ear, and she looked up abruptly, but his face was solemn and the laughter was only in her head. *Skin Island's own special, very first Vitro.*

She couldn't process. Couldn't breathe. A lifetime of lies. A mother who was not her mother. A father who was not her father. A sister she never knew existed. *Lux is all I have—my only true family. And I don't really have her at all.* Her sister was an echo of another person, without a will or identity of her own. She felt as if she'd toppled off a high wall and was falling still, wind rushing in her ears, her stomach in her throat and her heart in her mouth.

She felt hollow with the loss of Jim and the baring of her soul to the person she now hated most in the world, more than her stepmother, more than Strauss. She didn't know how many more blows she could take before she *would* deserve one of those padded rooms. She felt as if the layers of her life were being stripped away one by one; she was being whittled down, smaller and smaller, until she was nothing but a tiny speck on the face of the planet, a pebble, a scrap, a nothing.

Nicholas opened a door, and the room behind it glowed with faint blue light. It was completely empty.

No, wait . . . There was something odd about the walls. They were lined from floor to ceiling with panels made of filmy glass, and the blue light was shining from behind the panels. Trailing the cord between them, Sophie walked to one wall and pressed her hands to the panel; it was warm. She squinted at the glass, at the shadowy figure behind it.

Horrified, she pulled away, looking at Nicholas in sudden comprehension.

"The rest of the Vitros," she whispered. "The ones that haven't been woken yet."

He nodded, a slight, intent smile on his lips.

She turned back to the panels, her eyes moving from one to another; she had to stare at the glass for a moment before she could make out the sleeping Vitro behind it. There were at least two dozen of them.

In vitro, she thought. *In glass. They're literally raised in glass boxes.* She shivered, correcting herself. *We*, she thought. *We are raised in glass boxes.*

The place made her feel dirty, creepy, as if she were watching a stranger shower. These sleeping people were intensely vulnerable, and she felt as if she'd broken into a private sanctuary.

Nicholas, however, seemed to feel no such compunction. He walked around the room, pressing buttons beside the panels. One by one, they hissed and slid open with a rush of white gas.

"What are you *doing*?"

"Sh." Nicholas pressed a finger to his lips as he popped open a smaller panel in the wall that revealed a handheld instrument inside. "I'm creating a diversion. And also getting a little revenge. And also just creating general chaos. I'm very good at it, you know."

"Very good at which one?"

He paused, then grinned. "All three." He pulled out what looked like half a hair straightener; it was a thick baton with a plastic grip on one end and a thin metal plate screwed to the other.

"What's that?" asked Sophie.

"This is a . . . well, we don't really have a fancy name for it. We just call it the wand. It activates the Vitros' chips. Wakes them up."

He walked back to the first glass panel, which was so low on the wall he had to get on his knees to look inside. The boy lying within—Sophie could see that they were all the same age, around sixteen—was pale, thin, and groggy. Nicholas pressed a button on the wand and held it over the boy's head. After a moment, it beeped three times, and the boy's eyes opened.

"Stop!" Sophie cried. "You can't do this! They're helpless—leave them alone!"

He looked up at her. "You want to do it instead?"

"You're evil."

"Oh, *seriously*," he sighed, standing to wake the next Vitro. "You shouldn't see the world in such black-and-white terms. It's very naive of you."

"I won't let you!" she yelled, and she charged at him, intending to beat him over the head if she could.

But he still held the other end of the cord, and he pulled it quickly, bringing her crashing down. Her head hit the floor and stars exploded in her eyes; foggily she grappled with the knots around her ankles, but they were too tight, too complicated. Her skull aching, she tried to crawl toward Nicholas to pull his feet out from under him, but he just sneered and dragged her to the door, where he tied the cord to the handle, taking up all the slack in the line so her hands were forced up over her head. Her fingers tingled from the tight knots that hindered her circulation, and her shoulder screamed; if she'd been hit directly she was sure she'd have died of sheer pain by now. She felt as if she'd been mauled by a mountain lion—what would a real bullet wound feel like? She couldn't imagine anything worse than what she was already feeling.

"And it's no use shouting," he said. "They're all outside hunting for you, so they won't hear. But still. If you *do* make a sound, I'll stuff your mouth."

She could only watch in horror as he woke the Vitros one by one, taking the time to look each in the eyes, giving them a chance to imprint on him.

"I've wanted to do this for years," he said amiably. "But I had to wait for the right time."

"Why? What part do they play in your delusions?"

"I *told* you," he replied, impatiently. "Don't you listen to a word I say? I'm creating a distraction."

"So you can imprint *me*," Sophie said flatly.

"Now you're getting it." He was halfway around the room now, smiling encouragingly as a black-haired Asian girl blinked her eyes open for the first time and locked gazes with him.

"But you still haven't said how you plan to do that."

"And I'm not going to. I'd much rather show you."

She twisted her hands against the cord; she thought the knots might be coming loose, but it was hard to tell. A thin trickle of blood ran down her arm from where the cord had cut her, and she bit her lip, holding back whimpers of pain as she worked at the bonds. Whenever he turned her way she froze, hoping he wouldn't notice.

After he'd woken all the Vitros, he began helping them out, making them stand on wobbly legs. They stumbled and swayed as if they were made of paper; if a kitten had rubbed against their legs they would have fallen over. They clumsily clustered around Nicholas, making no sound but the shuffling of their bare feet. Each one wore a plain white gown that hung loose on their shoulders and fell to their knees. Some still bore white patches that clung to their faces and arms, where tubes had run into their veins until Nicholas had pulled them out. Their nails were inches long on their fingers and toes, and their skin had a saggy, sallow look that made Sophie's stomach turn. They looked almost like cadavers. Had Lux looked that way, before the doctors brought her out of this place and cleaned her up to present her to Andreyev?

When they were all awake and on their feet, Nicholas stood in their midst like a god, touching their faces and shoulders as if he were blessing them. They reached out to grab his hair and his clothes, to press their fingers to his lips, their eyes wide with adoration.

Sophie resisted the urge to vomit. Everything about the scene was eerie and perverse; she felt nauseated just from watching.

"Come," Nicholas murmured to his acolytes. "Follow me."

He led his stumbling, disoriented crowd of newborn Vitros out the door, slowly and with much awkward shuffling. They could hardly stand, let alone walk, but he helped the ones who fell and led them by the hand. Sophie tried to trip him when he went by, but he just laughed and hopped over her.

"What will you do with them?" she asked when the last Vitro was in the hall.

"Set them free."

"How?"

"I really don't see why you should care. Soon, you'll be one of them." His Vitros waited in the hall, staring at him vapidly and blinking in the harsh fluorescent lights while he knelt and brushed her hair behind her ears. She jerked away but only succeeded in hitting her head against the door. "Wait here," he murmured, then chuckled. "As if you had a choice."

He returned to the Vitros and began leading them away down the hall. She heard the ding of the elevator; he likely didn't trust them to handle the stairs. By scooting along the floor, Sophie could swing the door shut, which put her outside the room and in the hallway, her hands still tethered to the handle. She caught a glimpse of the last Vitro disappearing into the elevator before the doors slid shut.

Hollow silence fell across the basement hall. Sophie took the chance to wrestle at her bonds, pulling against them with all her weight. She twisted and bucked, then forced herself to stop and think. She couldn't see the knots very well because her hands were bound behind her back, and though she was pretty limber, she couldn't get herself turned around without pulling her shoulders out of their sockets. So she began feeling with her fingertips for any loose coils, but found none.

Her wrists were red and raw by the time Nicholas returned, not five minutes later. He glanced at her hands and raised a single eyebrow. "Get anywhere, did you? Maybe if you broke your wrists?"

She snarled at him like a trapped raccoon, but he ignored her and untied the knots himself, loosing her from the door but keeping her wrists bound. Then he dragged her down the hall to the next room and shouldered the door open.

"The Vitro prep room," he said cheerfully as he pushed her onto a large, padded metal bench. "You've been here before, though you wouldn't recognize it."

"This is where you hid me after . . . wait. It wasn't Mary, was it? If was *you* who knocked me out."

He shrugged. "You shouldn't have run off. I really didn't think they'd find you here, I must admit. But I never planned on your pilot making off with Lux, or I'd have stashed you somewhere better. Ah, well, everything's worked out in the end."

The room resembled an exam room in a clinic, with a counter, a sink, and cabinets, and assorted mystery equipment hung on the wall. The only thing missing was thin tissue paper to cover the bench. Nicholas flicked on a light that hung directly above Sophie; the bulb's conical shade directed the glare in a kind of spotlight, illuminating her in yellow pool but leaving the corners of the room in shadows, like the room in which she'd awoken to Moira, Strauss, and Andreyev.

"This is where they usually wake the Vitros," he said. "I've seen it several times. I'm not just the botched experiment they keep like a pet, you know. I help them." He waited, perhaps to see if she'd be impressed, but she wasn't. He shrugged and went on. "Granted, mostly they have me cleaning things, sorting their crap, changing sheets, and filling out dull paperwork they don't want to deal with. But it lets me see everything. *Everything*. When you're just standing in the corner wiping off scalpels, no one pays attention to you, especially when they think they *know* you." He shut the door and locked it. The *click* of the lock gave Sophie a chill; the hair on her neck rose on end.

"What are you doing?" she demanded.

He pulled the wand from his back pocket. "I'm activating your chip, Sophie."

Her heart clenched. "How?" she whispered, her mouth suddenly dry. "I'm not a newborn like those others."

"God, you never shut up."

"I swear, Nicholas, if you don't—"

"*Sh!*" He pressed a finger to her lips. "Just listen . . . wait for it . . . *wait for it . . .*"

An echoing blast shattered Sophie's eardrums, but it didn't come from the wand.

TWENTY-NINE

JIM

When he reached the shoreline, he didn't recognize it. It was Skin Island, not the smaller airstrip island, but that was all he knew. The shore was a thin line of sand that quickly gave way to a short bluff overhung with roots and twisting pines. He rested for a while, exhausted from kicking his way through the water and then battling the surf to reach land. He'd let the wing go when he reached the shallows, and felt a pang of sorrow as it drifted away. It was the last piece of the Cessna he'd had, and letting it go was like relinquishing everything he loved about the sky. But he couldn't very well lug the thing around on land.

Once he could stand again without his knees wobbling beneath him, he began trekking south, knowing that sooner or later he'd come across the Vitro building. Would Sophie have made it there by now? How long had he been in the water? It was difficult to judge; the moon seemed substantially higher by now, but it was still obscured by the trees.

He was tired. Tired of trekking back and forth across the island, tired of being nearly killed, tired of dancing one step out of disaster's reach, tired of *trying*. His exhaustion began deep in his mind and spread outward like a disease, like a leech sapping his strength from within, but he planted one foot ahead of the other with dogged persistence. He let his muscles think for him, lost himself in the monotony of walking, and let his mind run on low, barely floating on the surface of consciousness.

The beach ran along the foot of a high cliff; he recognized it from his first ill-fated attempt to rescue Sophie.

He pressed a hand against the rocky cliff to help himself along, finding handholds in ledges that were covered in dried gull droppings. High above him, the birds nested and watched him with glittering black eyes. Every now and then one would call out, harsh and sudden, startling him. The sea nibbled at his soggy boots then fell away, back and forth like a relentless terrier. There were places where the beach dissolved and he had to feel his way across rocks beneath the water. He went slowly, cautiously. He half hoped a wave would just wash up, grab him, and pull him out to sea so he could have a good reason to just give up, but no such wave obliged.

The shore gradually bent eastward, and by keeping an eye on the stars, he was able to determine when he'd reached the south shoreline. There had to be a way up to the buildings. He saw no ladder, no stair—*no, wait*.

Ahead of him, a narrow stair was cut into the cliff and lined with rickety metal railings. It zigzagged twice before reaching the top and was barely visible in the darkness. He reached the foot of the stair and began to slowly climb, keeping one hand on the cliff face and the other on the rail, though it wobbled at his touch.

Hardy tufts of grass clung to the sides of the stairs and brushed against his legs. The wind picked up as he went higher, and he pressed himself against the face of the cliff to keep from being blown off balance. Each step was worn at the middle, evidence that they'd been here long before Corpus, back when the place truly was a resort. He imagined men and women in retro swimsuits running up and down these stairs, clutching sun hats to keep them from blowing away, laughing, enjoying their vacation, like models in a vintage Coke ad. They had no idea what this place would become when they had gone. No idea that their paradise could turn so dark.

He tried not to look down. He wasn't afraid of heights, but he couldn't help remembering the dizzying view from the top, when he'd been on his knees in front of the Corpus guards, certain that the rocky beach below would become his grave.

When he finally reached the top of the cliff, he ducked several stairs down, out of sight. The area surrounding the Vitro building was ablaze with light and voices. There was a lot of shouting, a lot of commotion. They were still in a riot over Jim and Sophie's destructive escape, it seemed. He felt a pang of worry for Lux; was she all right? Would they have shot her the way they were going to shoot him? He felt wretched for bringing her into the middle of it all. If he hadn't blundered in and lugged her out of that building, she'd have been fine—maybe they all would have been fine. Maybe he'd be home by now, sleeping in the plane as he sometimes did when he and his dad had been arguing.

"Catch him!" someone shouted, so close to Jim that he flinched and nearly hurtled down the stairs. But it wasn't him they meant; he looked up and saw a blond-haired boy his own age—another Vitro, perhaps—standing on the edge of the cliff. The boy was dressed in a thin white gown that was too small for his nearly six-foot frame. He looked ridiculous, but Jim found no humor in the way the boy's vacant eyes rolled disinterestedly over Jim and on to the rocks below.

What's he doing? Jim wondered.

The boy leaned slightly forward, shifting his weight from his heels to his toes.

"Grab him!" a voice screamed.

A hand reached out and made a grab for the boy's neck, but it was too late. He didn't jump, didn't shout, just fell forward. Jim had to press himself as flat as he could to avoid colliding with him. He nearly reached out to try to catch the boy, but he wasn't quick enough.

The boy's gown fluttered around him as he fell, and to Jim it seemed he was dead before he even hit the rocks. He didn't scream or wave his arms or even *look* afraid; he just fell as if he were empty, didn't care, had no sense of self-preservation whatsoever. The crunch his body made as it slammed into the rocks made Jim's blood curdle.

His stomach heaving, Jim forced himself to stay utterly still as a doctor looked over the edge above him, down at the boy's still, pale form, at his arms and head twisted into unnatural angles. Bile rose in Jim's throat, but he dared not move or the doctor would spot him. The only thing concealing him was shadow, and if the doctor shifted his eyes even an inch lower, he would see Jim. Then, all it would take was a kick, and the doctor could send him hurtling to join the broken Vitro below.

"He's gone," the doctor called, and he turned away in a hurry. "There goes another! Quickly, someone—stop her!" His footsteps pounded off, out of Jim's hearing.

Jim let out a soft, relieved sigh. His heart was turning somersaults in his chest, and he knew if he stopped to think about what he'd just seen he'd be sick, so he turned his mind to what lay ahead, and not below.

He chanced a quick look over the edge of the cliff. There were Vitros everywhere, all of them dressed in white gowns. They wandered with the same awkward clumsiness Lux had had when she first woke, as if they couldn't tell foot from hand and knee from elbow. They looked like broken robots shuffling around in the grass, or very ineffective, disinterested zombies. And all of them were trying to head for the edge of the cliff. The doctors rushed around in a fervor, but all the guards must have still been out scouting for Jim and Sophie, because they were outnumbered by the Vitros. Jim watched as one by one, the Vitros reached the cliff and tried to throw themselves off of it, with the doctors hastening to pull them back in time. They were trying to herd the Vitros into the building, but every time they did, another made it to the cliff. It was like trying to dig a hole in the sand; the more they grabbed, more broke free.

Most of the activity seemed to be off to his right, where the floodlights were concentrated. To the left, the grass was more shadowy. He had a sudden inspiration—sneak inside, use the Vitros' distraction as an opportunity to find a telephone, and call his dad or the police or the U.S. Navy.

He waited until he was certain everyone's attention was averted from his general area, then slithered over the edge into the grass and took off at an awkward run, bent double in an attempt to make himself less recognizable. Maybe if someone did see him, they would mistake him for another Vitro.

He reached a lone palm between the cliff and the building and slipped behind it, heart hammering. A cautious look around the trunk revealed that he'd not been spotted. He slumped a little, relieved; the dash to the building would be easier, for the darkness was thicker ahead of him.

On the count of three. His legs tensed, ready to spring out like a runner from the line. *One, two*—

He stopped as a Vitro meandered past him, a slim Asian girl, with prim features and a dark curtain of hair that hung to her waist. She stumbled by as if sleepwalking. Jim looked around to see if someone was chasing her, but it seemed as if she'd wandered away from the pack and no one had noticed.

Conflicted, Jim looked again at the building. He was so *close*—and he could even see an open door on the side of the atrium, left ajar in some doctor's haste, no doubt. He could be inside in seconds without being seen.

He whipped his head around to look at the girl. She walked in a clumsy, wavering line, but she was undoubtedly heading for the edge of the cliff. With her white gown and long hair fluttering in the wind, she looked like a broken, forlorn ghost.

Ah, screw it. He sprinted after the girl.

She reached the edge before he could reach her.

"No!" he yelled. "Stop!"

She teetered, leaned forward, her arms spread wide, her hair billowing behind her like a dark cloak.

"*Stop!*" Jim lunged at her, wrapped both arms around her waist, and for a moment they both swayed dangerously on the tip of the cliff; his heels were on the grass but his toes hung over empty space. His heart shot up his throat, and for a moment, all of time froze around him, as if the world were waiting breathlessly to see if they would fall. He could have sworn this was the exact spot in which the guards had nearly executed him.

With one last effort, Jim threw his weight backward and crashed to the ground, landing hard with the girl's head knocking against his chest, driving the breath from his lungs. Wheezing, he blinked up at the stars and tried to steady his wheeling vision, but then the girl lunged upward—surprisingly spry—and crawled toward the cliff on her hands and knees.

"No . . . you . . . *don't!*" Jim grabbed her ankle and dragged her roughly backward. "I'm trying to save your life!"

He sensed movement to his right; another Vitro, this one a skinny boy with a shaggy Afro, was within inches of plunging to his death. Jim threw out his free hand and grabbed the boy's calf. The Vitro looked down, blinked as if unsure what to make of Jim's hand, then tugged his leg in an attempt to break free.

With one struggling Vitro in each hand, Jim wriggled backward, dragging them both with him. "Hey!" he yelled. "A little help over here!"

He managed to wrap his arm around the girl's waist, and he held her tightly and struggled for a better grip on the boy. He reached up, yanked the hem of the boy's hospital gown, and slammed him onto the ground. Under other circumstances he might have felt guilty for hurting them, but at the moment he was burning with anger. He'd been shot at, shoved around, almost blown to bits, nearly drowned, nearly lost at sea, and now he was giving up his last chance at escaping to save the lives of two miserable kids who didn't want his help in the first place. He cursed at them beneath his breath and held on doggedly, despite their struggles. The girl waved her arms as if they were swords, and she caught him hard across his nose.

Suddenly the doctors were there, two of them. They grabbed the Vitros and held them tight, whispering soothingly to them though it seemed to do zero good.

Jim scrambled up, and his eyes darted to the trees behind the building; he could make a run for it—but where would he go?

He never got to find out, because Strauss ran toward them with a pistol in her hand.

"On your knees!" she shouted to Jim. "Now!"

THIRTY

SOPHIE

Crack!

The gunshot echoed around the room.

Nicholas yelped as the wand flew out of his hand and crashed against the far wall, its metal plate severely dented by the bullet Moira Crue had fired at it. She stood framed in the doorway, her gun leveled at Nicholas.

Sophie bolted upright and started to call out *Mom*—but then she remembered, and the word stuck in her throat.

"Back away, Nicky," said Moira. "*Now.*"

He didn't move. His face hardly registered surprise as he said, "Did you like my little present?"

"Do you realize what you've done?" Moira said softly, her eyes fixed on Nicholas as if he were a snake about to strike. "Nicky, they won't forgive you. They won't tolerate you. You've given Strauss and Corpus every reason to end you."

He shrugged. "We'll see. I've got a few more cards to play."

Moira looked sorrowful. "No. I'm afraid this ends now.

You've gone too far, Nicky. Why did you do it? Everything was going so well. You had a life here, which is more than you would ever have had without this place."

"Oh, don't *lie*, Moira," he snarled. "You hate me. You all do. Since the day I was born all I have been to you is a failure, a reminder that you're not God."

"That's not true." She lowered the gun slowly, straightening with a gentle sigh. "We raised you kids as if you were our own."

Sophie sat frozen on the bench, her ears roaring. She watched Moira through hard eyes.

"Sophie," Moira said, walking toward her but keeping an eye on Nicholas. She held out her free hand. "Are you all right? Your shoulder—"

"Don't—" Her voice came out as a barely audible rasp. "Don't touch me."

Moira drew back, her eyes widening. "What did he tell you?"

"The truth," Nicholas interrupted, a bit sulkily. "Which is more than *you* ever told her."

"We'll talk," Moira said to Sophie. "When this is all over, we'll talk about this."

Sophie said nothing. She stared at the wall behind Moira , eyes wide and unblinking, refusing to look at the woman who had let her live a lie for her entire life.

"What are you trying to do, Nicky? Are you trying to *imprint* her?"

"She's a Vitro." He shrugged and leaned against the bench, inspected his nails. "Don't you want her to live up to her full potential?"

"Yes, *Dr. Crue*, I'm a Vitro. Didn't you hear?" Sophie's voice was black and bitter. She still didn't look Moira, but rather at the spot just over her shoulder. She wasn't sure she could look her in the eye without crumbling.

"Nicholas, get out of here. *Now.* The Vitros are imprinted on you—you have to stop them. What you did . . ." She stopped, then swallowed. "This is evil, Nicholas, even for you. You went too far. Get your butt up there and help the doctors."

He gave her an elaborate bow, then sidled out of the room. Then Moira turned to Sophie.

"No, Sophie, I'm not your mother," Moira replied, looking impatient, as if she couldn't be bothered to have this conversation right now. "I don't even know who your mother is, though I'm sure we could track down her information in our records."

"The thing you told me about Lux, about her almost dying and your making her a Vitro to save her—that was a lie. You lied through your teeth. All my life! You lied that you were my mother!"

"Yes. Yes, I did, but I had to—I needed you to believe me. Lux *is* your sister, because eighteen years ago we split a zygote into two embryos and thus created a pair of identical twins that would become you girls. That's what all the Vitros are— leftover clusters of potential, frozen embryos locked in freezers in the basements of fertility clinics all over the world. We take them because no one else wants them, and we put them in ectogenetic tanks and raise them. We give them life when they had no hope of life, Sophie—is that wrong? If it wasn't for me you'd still be nothing but a microscopic, frozen bunch of cells."

"It's not you I've been trying to get to all my life," Sophie whispered, more to herself than to Moira. "It's this island. This is my home. This is where I was born."

"Nine months after we thawed you out," said Moira. "You're a Vitro, yes. The very first Vitro. Older than Nicholas by a week and a half. You're a control, Sophie."

Sophie held up a hand, shaking. "Wait. A control? Not *the* control?"

Moira fingered the buttons on her coat, her eyes slightly averted. "There are ten of them, ten sets of identical twins created in glass vials. Half of them are here, and the other half are out in the world, living normal lives. You were the first. I suspect Nicky's known about you for years, though he hid his knowledge from me—but he can't have known about the others. Their records are kept in another facility in . . . well, that doesn't matter."

Sophie fell silent a moment, imagining nine others like herself, all ignorant of their origins, living lives built on lies. "Did I ever know them? Were they on Guam too?" she asked softly.

"No. They were all placed in homes through private adoptions, long ago. We've monitored them in secret, at a distance. They have no inkling Corpus even exists, and they never will."

Sophie forced herself to meet Moira's eyes. "Then why not me? Why am I different?"

"You weren't . . . you weren't supposed to be." A shade of weariness fell over Moira's features, dragging the corners of her mouth down and settling on her brow in the form of a deep crease between her eyes. "You were to be adopted out like the others. But your father and I . . . well, Foster and I, we were young and we'd always thought we didn't want children.

But we saw you, just a baby, just a tiny, blue-eyed baby with a smile that split our hearts, and we . . . we bent the rules a bit."

When she felt the corners of her eyes begin to sting, Sophie stretched them wide open, refusing to cry.

Moira went on. "We couldn't keep them all, of course—all those baby Controls, with their twins still encased in glass. But you captivated us from the start. You must believe me. Choosing you, convincing Corpus to let us have you—it had nothing to do with the project or with our research. It was pure enchantment. We adored you from the start, don't you see? We both did. We fell in love with you, darling, and we couldn't stop ourselves." Her voice gained momentum, as if tumbling downhill, her words getting away from her in a rush. "We took you and raised you as our own, and I have never regretted a moment of that."

Sophie sucked in a breath and held it, felt it burning in her lungs as she glared at Moira. "Well, obviously that's not true."

Moira bit her lip, looked down at the floor. "Our separation had nothing to do with you. Nothing in the least. My greatest regret in life is letting you go—but don't you see? It had to happen. You couldn't have stayed in Guam. You were too close. Sooner or later you'd make your way here, and all the work we put into shielding you from this place would have gone to ruin. Though," she laughed bitterly, "here we are, I suppose, so what good did it do? But what came between your father and I had nothing to do with you. There was so much more to it."

"Do I have a chip?" Sophie asked, her voice hollow.

"No, of course not."

"But . . . it beeped. That wand thing."

"Nicholas was trying to intimidate you, make you fear him. He's a psychopath."

"Yes," said Sophie, going monotone. "So I've heard." *He killed Jim. He killed Jim.* The words chased themselves around her head, making her dizzy. It still didn't feel real.

"His stunt with the wand . . . It's a classic psychopathic move, a kind of display of power. Put it out of your mind. The only abnormal thing about you is that you were created in a glass box. Well. That, and your remarkable aptitude for stubbornness." She sighed. "As for the Controls. Having never raised a fetus through ectogenesis—artificial gestation, being born from a machine instead of a mother—we needed to be able to measure ectogenic children uninfluenced by a chip against those who were. None of you have chips."

"Proper scientific method, eh? Never change more than one variable at a time. You needed me and the other Controls to live a normal life—huh, well, as normal as could be, considering. So you posed as my mother. Watched me grow up. *Measured* me, as you say. Go on, then. Give it to me straight. No more lies."

Moira exhaled slowly, then nodded. "Your father may have left the project here, but no one can ever fully escape Corpus. He's held up his end, keeping me updated on you. Written reports, sound files, videos. I've watched you grow up, Sophie, even after you moved to the States. You are a remarkable young woman. So brilliant, so motivated, so strong."

You think you're better than us, but you're not. You're not as special as you think, Sophie Crue. Nicholas's laughter pierced her thoughts, and her skin prickled as if he were standing right behind her. *The very first Vitro.* And her own so-called father, spying on her for Corpus, never telling her the full truth. She had been able to forgive him for not telling her the truth about Skin Island—but could she forgive him for not telling her the truth about herself? She didn't know. She needed time, time to think, to evaluate from this new perspective. She wanted to go back, pull out scrapbooks, memories, home videos, to review every moment of her past with clear eyes, unsullied by the lies that had tainted her years. *Who am I really? What has my life truly meant?* She could never look back at her days spent running wild on the beaches with Jim the same way. Her rough acclimation to New England, the exotic vacations around the world with Moira, every conversation, every look, every moment with her father was different now, with new meanings and undercurrents brought to light that she'd never even suspected were there.

She wasn't even a Crue. She was just Sophie. Sophie Nothing.

She let out a long, slow breath as a peculiar feeling came over her: buoyant, exhilarating lightness, as if she'd swallowed a lungful of helium. She felt as though a thousand-pound pack had been lifted from her shoulders, and she could suddenly fly.

"Sophie?" Moira asked uncertainly. "Let me look at your shoulder. Please. That bandage is done all wrong."

Sophie sat very still as Moira unwrapped the cloth Jim had hastily tied and then bit her tongue to keep from whimpering as Moira's fingers probed the wound. When she shut her eyes, she saw an explosion of red on the inside of her eyelids, and she felt a rising surge of panic and grief that she struggled to keep down, packing it away. She could deal with only so much at once, and she decided to deal with the easier trauma first, feeling cowardly for doing so, feeling as if she were betraying Jim by putting off the internalization of his death.

"It only clipped you," Moira said, sounding relieved. "Let me take care of it." She found some gauze in a drawer, and a cool cream that she gently applied before wrapping the shoulder in a quick, effective bandage. As she tied it off, she whispered, "I know you must be devastated. But I do love you."

She loves me too, in her own way—because she created me, Nicholas had said. *I'm her project; she doesn't love me, but the reflection of herself in me.*

"You have a home here, Sophie," Moira went on. "If you want it. The reason I said no before—you must believe me that I wanted you to have a life of freedom. Yes, Corpus has been watching you your entire life, but you didn't know that. You felt free—and so you were. But now that you know the truth, I guess it doesn't matter. We needed you to feel that freedom, to grow up as ordinary a girl as you could be, so that we could measure the differences between you and Lux. As with all the Vitros and their Controls, we needed to know *how* different Lux would have been compared to a perfectly normal version of herself."

I wasn't even created to be Sophie—but a version of Lux. An alternative Lux leading a fake life. But even that thought didn't weigh down the burgeoning sense of weightlessness in Sophie's chest—and that astonished her. *Why am I not angrier? Why am I not crying or yelling or demanding to know why?*

"Do you hear what I'm saying, Sophie? You can stay here. There's no point now in your going back, if you don't want to."

"No point."

"No." Moira reached out, rested her fingertips on Sophie's knee.

Sophie drew away. "No *point*?"

"Sophie, what's wrong? Talk to me, sweetheart?"

"No." Sophie stood up, keeping the bench between them. "No," she repeated, her voice calm. "Don't you see?" she said, spreading her hands. "Don't you see what this means? I can go, Mom—no, *Dr. Crue*. I can stop trying to impress the mother I never had. I can stop living my entire life around you, stop packing myself into little boxes just to live up to your standards. The meds they make me take, all those times Dad told me I was crazy for still loving you—I *hated* it. I hated myself. I thought the reason you left me was because I was broken." Now she was crying, and she dashed the tears away angrily. "I thought that if I could just prove to you I was okay that you'd come back for me. But I've lived my entire life to please a *lie*." Sophie pressed her hands to her temples, her breath coming in deep, heady drafts. "But not anymore. No, I won't stay on Skin Island. I may have not known you were there, but you were pulling strings the whole time. Well, I won't be controlled anymore." She turned around again. "The first step toward being free is recognizing that you're not. I've done that. I won't go back now, not to what I was."

"You can't run. It's not that simple. Your father can't protect or hide you."

"It doesn't matter." She wasn't *happy*, no. Nor sad nor angry. There would be time for that, she suspected, days when she would cry and days when she would want to scream and break things. But right now there was only an overwhelming sense of freedom, of possibility. She could be anyone, do anything at all.

"All the meds, the shrinks, the exams—you guys thought I was like Nicholas, didn't you? You thought I was a psychopath."

"We didn't know *what* you were, or what you'd become," Moira replied. "And I'm certain now that you're perfectly fine. But we had to keep an eye on you, just in case. Ectogenesis was—still is, really—a very new and relatively untested technology. We didn't know what the psychological side effects would be, so we had to monitor you closely."

"All these years I thought I was messed up, that that's why you stayed here and left Dad. Do you realize what that's done to me?" She slammed her hand onto the bench, making Moira jump. "I thought I couldn't have friends. I stayed away from people. Jim Julien was the best and last friend I ever had, did you know that? I couldn't bear to have anyone around me after we left Guam—I thought I was a freak! And as it turns out, I was right. I may not be a psychopath like Nicholas, but I'm not normal."

"But you *are*. I didn't want to screw that up for you, Sophie, which is why I never told you. I wanted you to have a chance at a real life."

"No, you didn't! At least you didn't do it for my sake. You did it because I was a better control if I was ignorant, if I lived thinking I was normal. Isn't that it? Well, isn't it?"

"Sophie!" But Moira's eyes told her all she needed to know. She'd been given as normal a life as they could grant her, but it had never been for her. It all came back to Corpus.

"It doesn't matter," said Moira. "None of this matters anymore. After what happened today, I'll be fired. Corpus will exterminate all the Vitros Nicholas woke, and they'll likely kill him too. There's nothing I can do. Nothing." She looked drained, as if she could barely hold her head up. She slid down the wall and sat with her knees drawn up, her hands kneading her hair. "It wasn't supposed to end like this," she whispered. Gun still clutched in her hand, she pressed the heels of her palms into her eyes. "Nicky may have woken them, but I destroyed them."

Sophie thought of the bleary-eyed newborn Vitros, of their nightmarish introduction to the world. "Is there a way to reset them? Can you erase their memories or something, put them back to normal?" She didn't want any part of it; she wanted to walk away now and never look back, to forget this woman, this place, all of it. But she was haunted by those empty faces, and she knew she would never stop hating herself if she didn't try to help them.

"It doesn't work that way," said Moira. "There's no cure. This is what they are. This is what I made them to be."

"What about Nicholas?" Sophie threw out. "What makes him immune to imprinting? What's the difference between him and those miserable kids out there?"

Moira looked up through a mess of hair and fingers. "I told you. He's a psychopath. Him and Mary, Jay, and Wyatt."

"Yes, but *why*? Why didn't they imprint like all the others?"

"It was . . . there were complications."

"That's it? That's all you can say—that there were *complications*?"

Moira made no reply.

"Fine. Whatever. Keep your secrets for now." She began

pacing the length of the wall, one arm crossed over her stomach and her other hand cupping her chin. "Think, Mom—Dr. Crue. Whatever. Can't you save them? Reverse it somehow? If they're imprinted on Nicholas, then they're useless to Corpus, I get that. But if they *stopped* being useless—don't you see? We've got to make them nonexpendable. We've got to make them *necessary*."

Moira turned the gun over in her hands, her brow knitted in thought. "We can't undo it. Once imprinted, imprinted for life. It even extends beyond death." Her hands froze, the gun pointed at the ceiling. "Philip Wolf—one of the doctors—he had a stroke, and there was nothing we could do to save him. But one of the Vitros, a girl named Clarissa—" Her voice choked out; she shook her head. "She was imprinted on him. It was like she just . . . crumpled. Couldn't take it. Couldn't stand for him to be gone. She went crazy, breaking things, trying to dig up his grave . . . We had to put her down, in the end."

"*Put her down*," echoed Sophie, pausing to stare at her. "Like she was a dog."

"You weren't there. You didn't see how bad off she was. We tried everything else—erasing her chip, medication, even electrotherapy. Nothing worked. Her world ended when his did. So it's no good shooting Nicky—might as well shoot them all. Do you know what he *did?*" Moira's hands trembled with anger. "He told them to jump off the cliff. He'd murder them, just to get back at me."

Sophie's mouth opened in horror. *That sick, twisted bastard.*

"Is there *no* way to save them?" She was thinking of Lux now as much as she was of the other Vitros. *She's the only family I have now. If there's any chance of saving her—*

"The other doctors are trying to deal with them. I came down to see if there were any left sleeping, but he got to them all. They won't give up trying to carry out Nicholas's orders unless he tells them to."

"Yes—but I mean isn't there a way to save them permanently? To un-imprint them?"

"It all comes down to the code," said Moira, shaking her head. "The computer code on the chips—we call it the Imprima Code. We can manipulate it, but we can't erase it—the chip is too integrated with the brain. Even if we took all the data off of it, the information would be stored in their cerebral cortex. We'd have to insert a new code, something to override it." She shook her head. "But there's not time. And there's no way of knowing what that code would be. It's like trying to invent the bicycle before the wheel. Like trying to paint something you can't see."

"What I don't understand, what I've been *trying* to understand all this time—is why would you even do this to begin with?" Now Sophie was ranting, spitting out words simply because she was tired of holding them back. "How could you be so heartless as to give people life only to strip away their identities? What's in it for you?"

"It wasn't supposed to be like this!" Moira rose quickly to her feet, her eyes burning defiantly. She slipped her gun into the deep pocket of her coat. "It wasn't about imprinting in the beginning. That was an accident, a sort of side effect. You should have seen this place back then, when we were first getting started. Your dad and me and the others—we were so full of hope and excitement about the future. We were working to save the world, not . . . not *this*. The chip technology was originally intended to be a new form of psychotherapy. This technology is *huge*, Sophie—it's world changing. We can influence the human mind by speaking to it through computer code. We've achieved a human-machine hybrid technology whose full ramifications we're only just beginning to realize. At the beginning, the chip was meant to be a cure. We knew that if we could manipulate the psyche with the aid of the chip to translate computer code into human thought, affecting the brain in the same way you'd download a program onto your computer, we could cure almost any mental disorder and, in time, even physical ones. We could cure Alzheimer's and bipolarity and schizophrenia and . . . and psychopathy."

Sophie stared at Moira, her mind hardening around a new realization. "So you created test subjects. You created psychopaths so that you could try to cure them."

"Yes," Moira whispered, not returning her gaze. "We performed a kind of advanced lobotomy on Nicky and the other three, creating an induced psychopathy, and then we tried to cure them. But for Nicky, Mary, the other two, it was too late. By the time we administered the reversal code, they were too old, their personalities too cemented. The worst part was that we knew what they *should* have been like—thanks to their Controls. We'd created little monsters we couldn't cure, and their twins are out living normal lives and reminding us every day of what we destroyed.

"We had to improvise and experiment; eventually we

learned that for the cure to work, the subject had to remain unconscious throughout the entire chip procedure. If they woke, even for a moment, we'd lose them and they'd become just like the first four Vitros. So we did it all at once, without them ever gaining consciousness. And then, after the first few successful Vitros were born and Corpus decided to shift the focus of the project to simply creating more Vitros, we found we didn't need to induce psychopathy at all—we just needed the cure."

"The cure that became their curse," Sophie said darkly.

"It reversed the psychopathy in the most dramatic possible way," Moira admitted. "Psychopathy, sociopathy—they're nearly interchangeable terms—stem from one's inability to relate, to feel empathy, to connect with another person. When we tried to reverse it with the chip, it resulted in the subjects' psyches overreacting, going to the other extreme—they fixated on the first person they saw, over-connecting, forming an unbreakable bond. When we realized what we'd done, it was too late—Corpus threw out all our plans of cures and therapies and instead focused on creating Vitros, and on developing the Imprima Code, which enhanced their imprinting instincts a thousandfold. Moldable, perfectly obedient workers. The code originally intended to heal people was instead turned to programming bodyguards and servants, equipping them with the skills needed to serve their masters."

"And you just went along with it, even though Dad refused."

"He refused to take part, threatened to out Corpus and the project to the media. I admired him for it, Sophie, and I always have, but I couldn't break away like he did. I was too

entrenched here, and I had so much still to accomplish. . . .
Foster did what most of us here only dream of doing, and certainly speak of—he walked away. He turned his back on Skin
Island even though it meant they might have killed him for it.
But it wasn't just out of his sense of morality—it was because
of you. Before you came along, I think he might have stayed
on, but you changed him. You changed us both, really, but
him most of all." Her eyes seized on Sophie's. "You mustn't
blame him. He loves you so very deeply, and he risked everything for your sake when he left the project. Corpus let him
go, but not entirely—they never let go entirely. They watch
him as much as they watch me and you, and you must never
think he is free of their influence. He was careful in his break
with the Vitro Project. He went through all the right channels, appealed to all the right people, and in the end, he won
himself more freedom than most of us here will ever know.
He lied to you because he knew that he'd stretched Corpus's
mercy as far as it would go, and that if he broke away for even
a second, they would have him in custody or killed within
hours. He lied to you so that he could live and protect you.
If you must blame anyone, blame me, blame Corpus. Your
father . . ." She shut her eyes. "He was and is all of the good
things I never found in myself, and the only thing I regret as
much as I regret losing you is the day I lost him."

"You could have walked away with us." Sophie spoke in a
rasp, her breath squeezing around the knot in her throat. "If
he could do it, so could you."

"I did what I thought I had to do, and even now, I'm not
sure I'd have chosen any differently. It didn't matter if I refused
and walked away—they'd have kept on without me, as they

kept on without Foster. At least by staying, I could help the Vitros as much as possible. I could be sure they weren't abused to an even greater extent. At least, that's what I thought. But then I just . . . I lost control." Moira spoke in a hush, her eyes distant, unfocused. "It was slow, and I didn't even know it was happening until it was too late. But my power over this project was usurped by the teaspoon until one day, it was gone. I'd lost control."

Don't we all, thought Sophie. She remembered what Nicholas had said to her in the salon: *Take control or be controlled.*

Corpus had played them all for fools.

Sophie drew a deep breath. "Then take it back."

Moira gave her a puzzled look.

"You lost control—so get it back."

"It's not that simple."

"Isn't it, though? From what I can tell, this Vitro plan has crashed and burned, thanks to Nicholas. You set out to do something good, to *save* people, as you said." Sophie planted her hands on the bench and leaned forward, her eyes intent on Moira. "So do that. Get this train back on the right track. It isn't too late until you give up."

Moira was staring at her searchingly, as if Sophie were a map she could not read. "Why are you so concerned about this? Why don't you just walk away?"

The question was already in Sophie's mind. All her life, she thought she knew who she was. *I thought I was your daughter. I thought if I could only reach you, make you see me, that all the pieces of my life that didn't make sense would magically fall together.* Well, in a way that had happened, but not how she'd expected. She had found herself, but she was not who she thought she was. All her life, she'd lived in Moira's shadow, but now the ties between them had been cut and Sophie felt almost buoyant. *I don't need her approval anymore. I can be whoever I want to be, do whatever I want to do.*

She didn't want her first deed in her new life to be a betrayal of her own. "Because Lux is my sister," she said. "And I won't give up on her. And I won't let you give up on her." She swallowed, then crossed the floor between them and stood in front of the woman who had been her mother. "Please." She met Moira's eyes and willed herself to stay strong, not to break, not yet. "Help me. Take back Skin Island."

Moira said nothing for a long moment. She stood very still and did not look away. Sophie saw the torture in her eyes; how long had she been aching to do just that? How long had she chafed under Strauss's and Corpus's rule, hating what they made her do but lacking the courage to defy them? Sophie gazed at her intently, wishing she could channel her strength into Moira, but knowing she barely had enough for herself.

"If you ever loved me, even in the smallest way," said Sophie softly, "if you have any love for Lux or Dad or the other Vitros, if there is a shred of love left in your body—do this. Do this for me. For Lux. For all of us, all the ones you've wronged. Please, Mom." Her voice faltered on the word. "You're the only mom I ever had. You gave me life as surely as if you'd given birth to me yourself. So *be* my mom—you owe me this. You owe all of us, so get out there, take back your island, and save us."

Sophie held her gaze as tears came into Moira's eyes. Moira pressed the back of her hand to her lips and drew in a deep, shaky breath. She shook her head, lowering her gaze for a moment to the floor. Then, at last, Moira looked up and tipped her chin in the smallest indication of assent. "I can't face her on my own—I don't have the resources. For Strauss, it always comes down to numbers—costs and overhead and profit. Without financial backing, none of this matters. Sophie, it's no use. I . . . I have to go. I've been down here far too long. I have to help the others."

She reached out, awkward and shy, her eyes averted, and brushed her fingers along Sophie's cheek. Sophie could feel her trembling; her skin burned where Moira touched her. Then her mother turned and fled out the door, her coat whipping behind her. It brushed a tray of clear glass vials on the counter and sent them spinning across the floor. Some of them rolled, bouncing and skittering into the shadows, but the rest shattered into a million glittering shards.

THIRTY-ONE
JIM

Jim dropped to his knees, slowly putting his hands behind his head. He wasn't an idiot; he could tell when he'd been beaten. The Vitro girl made a clumsy dash for the cliff, but a silver-haired doctor snagged her before she could get three steps and held her tight.

He looked around and saw that all the Vitros had been rounded up. They were all sitting or lying on the grass, watched by a few doctors but relatively listless; they must have been sedated. Sure enough, the doctors slipped needles into the necks of the two Jim had saved, and in seconds, their eyes glazed over and they slumped to the ground.

"Where's Dr. Crue?" Strauss asked.

The silver-haired doctor replied as she gently lowered the Vitro girl to the ground, "She went down to the vault, to see if there were any left."

"Can someone please explain what the *hell* this is?"

"Someone woke them up. And, apparently, gave them one order—to march off the cliff."

"Yes, *obviously*. But who?"

"It wasn't any of us," the doctor replied sharply.

"Someone give me some answers!"

"Can I buy a vowel?" Jim piped up before he could stop himself.

"*You*," Strauss hissed, and she crossed the ground between them and pressed the barrel of her pistol against his forehead. She narrowed her eyes. "You did this, didn't you?"

He did his best to look offended. "Uh . . . Kidnap your science project? Check. Steal your bulldozer? Check. But wake all those kids and tell them to jump to their deaths?" He shook his head. "What kind of sick bastard do you think I am? Oh, and speaking of sick bastards, has anyone seen Nicholas lately? Or how about Scary Mary? No? I didn't think so. Maybe you should start questioning *them*."

Strauss kept her eyes on him as she turned her head to shout to the doctors. "Where's Nicholas? And all the other little psychopaths you keep as pets?"

Psychopaths? Well, Jim couldn't say he was surprised. Of *course* they were psychopaths. Murderous teenagers, explosions, plane crashes, crazy women with guns, a girl who obeyed his every word—it seemed only a matter of time before psychopaths got thrown into the mix.

"I'll go search for them," said a tired-looking young doctor, and she sighed and headed into the building.

"Hey, buddy," said Jim, in as reasonable a tone as he could muster with a gun pressed against his head. "You don't *have* to kill me. I have money, lots of it—I can pay you. And I've got family that'll notice, and they won't give up looking for me. They'll hire detectives and everything." He wasn't sure which was the bigger lie, but he was pulling out every card in his pocket, down to the jokers. If he could bluff his way out of this, he would, and the consequences be damned.

"Just *stop talking*," said Strauss. She ran her free hand through her hair, and he realized she looked as exhausted as he felt. Well. Almost. He doubted *she* had been doing much leaping from exploding planes or swimming across half the Pacific. He felt as if he'd been taking part in an Olympic decathlon, one that involved running, swimming, jumping, dodging bullets, and carrying unconscious hundred-and-thirty pound girls up and down mountains.

Strauss had pulled a radio from her pocket and was calling the guards who were still out scouring the island, letting them know she had Jim. Then she paused, her finger hovering over the talk button. "The girl—Sophie—where is she? When you left she was with you."

"She was hit by a bullet," he said. "She's dead."

"You're lying."

"I am *not*. You people think I'm some kind of monster! Murdering your kids, *lying* to you." He tried to look offended, but he ended up just grimacing. He told himself he needed to stop provoking her; he always seemed to react to trouble by piling more trouble on top of it.

"Michalski!" She snapped her fingers at a nearby doctor, a small man with round spectacles and a drastically receded hairline.

"Yes, Miss Strauss?" He jogged over and stood fidgeting nervously with his glasses.

"Have you questioned them?"

"Yes, Miss Strauss."

"Well?"

"Ah." He winced and scratched his scalp. "It would seem Nicholas woke them and had them imprint on him. Then he, ah, gave them one order."

"To march off the cliff."

"Yes, ah, yes ma'am," Dr. Michalski mumbled to his shoes, as if *he* were the guilty one.

Strauss shut her eyes and pressed the gun to her forehead. Jim estimated the distance between him and the edge of the cliff; he might make it if—

Too late. Strauss opened her eyes and waved the gun at him. "Stand up," she said. "Dr. Michalski. Dr. Laurent." The woman holding the Vitro girl nodded and waited. "Tell everyone to take the Vitros inside." She drew a deep breath and let it out in a rush. "I'm pulling the plug."

"Victoria—" Dr. Laurent began, but Strauss spoke right over her.

"I thought this situation couldn't be any more screwed up, but I was wrong. I told Moira years ago that Nicholas and the other failed Vitros should have been put aside, but she wouldn't listen."

"If you'll just wait a few minutes," Dr. Laurent said, her matronly face crinkling with distress, "I can get Moira. We can discuss—"

At that moment, Moira Crue burst onto the scene. "What's the status here?" she demanded. "Victoria, have they all been rounded up?" She began counting the Vitros, her eyes flickering over Jim for a brief moment.

Jim started to call out to her, to ask if she'd seen Sophie or Lux, but at that moment Strauss set two guards on her. They took Moira by surprise, wrestling her to the ground before she had a chance to realize what was happening.

"Victoria!" Moira yelled. "What the *hell*?"

"No more discussion, Moira," said Strauss primly. "No more excuses, no more empty promises. You are fired. You're no longer in charge of so much as kitchen duty. I want you gone. You two," she said to the guards, "take her inside and hold her until I'm ready to deal with her. Dr. Michalski, you're in charge for now."

"Ah." He prodded at his glasses and looked as if *he* wanted to take a dive off the cliff.

Moira's cries were muffled as the doors of the building swung shut behind her and the guards escorting her, and Jim lost sight of her as they dragged her away.

"Take them inside." Strauss prodded the sedated Vitro girl with her foot, her expression a mingle of disgust and disappointment. "I want them put down. You do have a facility prepared for this, do you not?"

Dr. Laurent, who'd been staring in horror as Moira was manhandled off the scene, turned to Strauss and blanched. "That seems a rather hasty decision!"

"Hasty!" Strauss laughed, swinging her gun around in a way that had Jim twitching. "Hasty, Dr. Laurent? I think not. This place had one last chance, one last shot at proving its worth. I'd hoped you would pull through—really, I did. But the risk is too great and the return too little. The Vitros are finished. They *will* be exterminated, and I want it done quickly. I'm supposed to be in South America by the end of the week, and I don't plan on being delayed."

She paused, looking around at the horrified faces of the doctors. "Well? *Get to it!*"

They snapped into action, passing word to the others. One by one, the doctors turned nauseated looks to Strauss, who thoroughly ignored them. She waved her gun at Jim.

"You. Get up."

He rose warily, his throat dry. "Might be a bad time to bother you—but I was just wondering . . . what exactly do you mean by *exterminate?*"

"Exactly what you think I mean, young man. Now move."

"Where to?"

"Inside," she said acidly. "With the rest of them."

"With the Vitros?" He tried to swallow, but his mouth felt packed with sand. "To—to be exterminated? Ah . . . I'd rather not, but thanks. Not my kind of party."

"*Move,*" she said, and he jumped.

Prodded by her gun, which remained trained on the spot between his shoulder blades, Jim followed the gray-faced doctors and the groggy Vitros into the building. Each doctor had two Vitros in hand; they had to all but carry them, both because of the sedatives and because those Vitros still lucid enough to think were making vague, clumsy dashes for the door. Somehow the doctors kept them in check, and they made their way laboriously through the atrium and down a stairwell into the basement.

Jim's skin prickled as they walked. He waited for an

opportunity to escape, but none presented itself. *This is so many kinds of bad . . .*

Strauss was going to murder them all. That was the plain, short truth of it, and he could see no way out. *At least Sophie isn't here right now.* But her chances of doing any better seemed slim.

Strauss was sending off some of the doctors now, telling them to round up the rest of the "failed" Vitros: Nicholas, Mary and company, and Lux. He wanted to say something to persuade them to stop, but he couldn't think of what. He could only stand and watch helplessly as they departed.

He and the Vitros were shepherded down a long hall, past many closed doors, to the very last room. His scalp tingled as he passed through the doorway, and he knew exactly what this room was without having to ask.

It looked like a large community shower, akin to the ones in the gym locker rooms in his school back on Guam: tiled floor, a drain in the middle, and vents along the top of the wall. But there were no faucets, no towel racks, no benches. The room smelled of chemicals—had they used it before? He felt dizzy and sick to his stomach; he had to lean against the wall to keep from falling over.

Dr. Michalski stood in the doorway, his eyes averted, keeping the Vitros from wandering out. Most of them were too dazed by the sedatives to make an escape attempt and slouched against the wall or sat on the floor. The rest wandered around, disoriented perhaps, their eyes a little wild. He wondered what they'd do if they were kept from fulfilling Nicholas's command indefinitely. Go mad? Forget what he'd told them?

But who am I kidding? We're not going to find out, are we?

Strauss stood further off down the hall, muttering into her radio. Jim sidled up to the door and summed Dr. Michalski up.

"Hey," he whispered, and the doctor looked up, startled. Maybe he'd forgotten Jim was among the Vitros and hadn't expected any of them to realize what was going on and fight back. "You aren't honestly going to let her do this, are you?" he asked.

"Stay back," Dr. Michalski said, his voice cracking. He glanced at Strauss, and Jim took the hint.

"Easy, man. You don't need to bother her. Just listen, will you?" He took a step closer, until he was looking down at the nervous doctor, who was several inches shorter than him. "This is mass murder, Doctor. I know you realize that. You look like a smart guy. So tell me—what do you think a judge and jury would say about shoving twenty kids into a gas chamber?"

"There is no law out here but Corpus," Dr. Michalski said. "I'm sorry."

"*Sorry*," Jim echoed in disgust. "Sorry or spineless?"

"Jim!" a new voice cried.

He looked down the hall to see several guards dragging Mary, Jay, Wyatt—and Lux. She'd spotted him and was smiling bright enough to light a room.

"Lux!" *No, no, no.* It was just getting worse. "Lux, *fight!*" Her smile turned into a confused frown.

"Lux—they're going to—just *fight!* Run! Get out of here!" If anyone could escape, it would be her. He felt the barest flush of shame for exercising his control over her. He didn't want to inspire in Lux the wild-eyed, dogged obedience Nicholas's

Vitros had shown, but if it saved her life, he would gladly swallow any moral qualms.

She snapped into motion, driving her elbows into the sternums of the guards on either side of her. But before she twitch another finger, Strauss clubbed her on the back of the head with the butt of her pistol, and Lux crumpled.

"I *told* you to sedate her," Strauss growled. "Put them inside. Where's Nicholas?"

"No sign of him," a doctor replied.

Panic ran rampant on Mary's face. She clawed at her escorts, trying to gouge their eyes. They held her tight and propelled her along; behind her, Jay and Wyatt fought just as fiercely. Their wild yelling bounced off the narrow corridor and tiled walls of the chamber, magnified to a deafening chaos of noise.

"Just sedate them all!" Strauss ordered, a little wild-eyed herself; she had the look of someone who was driving without brakes but refused to take her foot off the gas. Even the guards looked uneasy as they held down Mary and the two boys for the doctors to sedate them.

Jim caught Lux as she was pushed through the doorway. She was barely conscious; her eyelashes fluttered and she groaned, but all the fight had been knocked out of her. He began to panic. The hallway was clogged with doctors and guards and guns and Strauss. He could never bull his way through them all. There were no windows, no stairs, not even so much as a ventilation shaft, except for the narrow ones set in the tiled walls around him—and even if he could fit through one, he'd only end up crawling toward his death.

"Stop!" he yelled, opting for begging—it was the only card

he had left. "Don't do this. Just listen to me—please!" Holding Lux with one hand, he reached out with the other and grabbed Dr. Michalski's lapel. "They're kids. They're not even kids—they're like toddlers! This is murder, man, can't you see it? Look me in the eye and tell me this isn't mass murder!"

But Dr. Michalski just wrenched Jim's hand away and stepped back, his eyes unblinking and his face green. He looked to Strauss for support, and she stepped in with her handgun, which she pressed against Jim's chest. She pushed him back with it, until she was standing in the doorway of the chamber.

"Look at them," he whispered, his heart drumming a tattoo against his ribs. "They don't deserve this."

She met his eyes and he searched her for a trace of pity, of hesitation, but found none. *Nicholas isn't the only psychopath on this island*, Jim thought.

"They're not kids," she said softly. "Look at them. They're mindless, soulless. They're just things we made, machines of skin and bone perhaps, but their every thought is ignited by a mechanical code."

The Vitros weren't people to Strauss. They were merchandise. It made him ill.

"Dr. Michalski," she said, without looking away from Jim. The doctor lifted his head. "Ready the chamber."

"Yes, ma'am," he mumbled, and he turned around and opened a panel on the wall, began to flip switches and punch buttons.

Jim shook his head, slowly at first, then harder. "No. No, you can't do this."

"I can," she said, her voice calm. She backed away, reached

for the door, and hesitated one moment. "You should never have come here," she said. "If you like, I can have them sedate you. It will make it easier."

He tightened his arm around Lux and realized he was trembling. "No," he whispered. He wouldn't spend his last moments in a senseless fog. And he still wasn't giving up. *There has to be something, some way out . . .*

She shrugged, and the mask of indifference slipped back over her features. She slammed the door shut.

Almost immediately, pale white gas began filtering from the vents above their heads. A small window in the door gave Jim a view of Strauss's grim face before she turned away. *You'll kill us all, but you don't have the balls to watch.*

The Vitros began to choke and cough. Only Mary, Wyatt, and Jay could possibly know what was happening, but they were so drugged Jim wasn't sure they even knew their own names at the moment.

He crouched low and pulled Lux down with him. She was coming to slightly; he wished he'd asked for a sedative for her, but it was too late now. He hardly knew her, but she'd already become important to him. He'd never felt responsible for anyone in his life other than himself, and he'd never wanted to be. Lux had come out of nowhere, a sudden, unexpected shadow. He'd never realized how much someone needing him would make him need them in return. That being important to someone else suddenly made them important to you.

She finally opened her eyes and mumbled his name.

"Keep low," he whispered. "It's okay."

Her gaze settled on him and she smiled; she trusted him when he said it, believed him with an innocence that made him rage inwardly. It wasn't *fair*. He could accept that his own stupidity and ill luck had landed him in this room, though he was far from content with it, but Lux didn't deserve this, and neither did her Vitro brothers and sisters.

The room was quickly filling with the toxic gas, and still it poured from the vents. Jim lay flat on his stomach and told Lux to do the same. He drew a deep breath and held it. Around him, body after body began to collapse. The sound of coughing and gasping roared in his ears; several of the Vitros were drooling and convulsing. He heard a thump behind him, and turned his head to see Mary lying on her side, twitching, her eyes rolling back in her head. Time dragged past. He could see now why Strauss had offered him a sedative; this was no quick, easy death. No, death took its time in this room. It hovered in the corners, lingering awhile, a spectator looking on and biding its time, seeing how long it could dance just out of reach.

"Lux," Jim croaked. He shook her. Her eyes were shut, and he couldn't tell if she was breathing. He rolled her over and pinched her nose, drawing once more on his lifeguard training as he placed his mouth over hers and breathed into her. The gas was making him light-headed and a bit delirious. Instead of choking, he heard waves rushing up and down a beach. Instead of the groans he heard his lifeguard instructor Cate, who lounged lazily on a beach towel giving half-hearted instructions to her class of young, overeager male students. Like most of them, Jim had signed up for the class only because Cate was the hottest senior in high school and every underclassman, including himself, was crushing on her.

But no, it wasn't Cate on the towel, spreading sunscreen

on her legs. It was Sophie, and she was snapping at him to get up, to save someone—but who? Oh. It was Lux. She was drowning out in the surf, but Jim had been too mesmerized by Sophie's sunscreen application to notice. He had to get to Lux in time. He floundered into the waves, but they just pushed him back and pulled her further out. The water was too strong; it shoved him ashore and sucked Lux under.

"No!" he yelled, and he dove again and again only to land on the sand instead of in the water. "Lux!"

It was too late. She was gone.

He choked on the water; salt stung his eyes. This time when he dove, the water took him and dragged him down, down, down into darkness.

THIRTY-TWO
LUX

She had found him again. Peace flooded her, a calm that had nothing to do with Moira Crue's needles. This peace began at her center, with Jim, and spread outward, intoxicating, warm, wonderful.

She had found him and all was well.

She was in his arms and he was looking down at her, saying "It's okay," and she believed him. All the anxiety, the panic, the chaos fell away, and at last she could breathe.

Jim shifted, told her to lie down. He stretched out on his stomach and she did the same beside him. Now that he was here and she was still, she could look around. They were in a small room with a lot of people, strange new faces. It was very noisy here, and she didn't understand why they couldn't go back to the beach, where it was quiet and open and beautiful, but if this was where Jim wanted to be, she wanted to be here too.

She became aware of a hissing all around them; it came from the walls. It looked as if clouds were pouring into the room—pretty, but it made her cough. She laid her cheek on the cold, slick floor and locked gazes with Jim.

He was coughing too. That wasn't good. She frowned, tried to say his name, but she only fell into a fit of coughs. Her throat burned; her eyes burned. What was happening? Why couldn't she speak?

They were all coughing, all the people around her, the boys and girls. She reached toward Jim. He covered her hand with his and squeezed it tight. When she tried to breathe in, nothing happened. Her lungs were on fire. Her muscles spasmed painfully as she struggled for breath, but none came.

She fell into darkness and terror.

Something was horribly, horribly wrong, but she didn't know what it was. She had no name for it, no word, just a feeling, a terrible, sick, trembling feeling.

She felt Jim, heard him call her name, and she tried to answer but there was no breath in her lungs. *I am here*, she wanted to say. *Jim, I am here. Help me!*

She was sinking; she could feel herself growing smaller, weaker. She fought against it, but she was so lost in the darkness that she couldn't find her way back.

Cold and dark and scared and lost and alone, she screamed in her mind but no sound left her lips.

Then: air.

She felt her chest expand, felt her mind clear a little. She could breathe again.

She opened her eyes, barely opened them, and saw Jim lying beside her, so very, very still that her body seized with terror and her mind screamed *NO!* She pressed a hand to his chest, over his heart. *Check for a pulse*, said her brain.

Was he dead?

Was he gone?

She crawled to him. *Protect protect protect.* She followed her instincts, followed the commands her brain fed to her: Open his mouth, breathe into him, give him her air, make him live, *protect protect protect.*

His chest rose. Her heart soared.

Again. Again. Again.

She had very little breath, but what she had, she gave it all to him. And every time his heart beat against her palm she smiled.

She was smiling still when she gave him her last breath, and smiling when her head hit the floor and her eyes slid shut.

THIRTY-THREE
SOPHIE

Sophie leaned against the wall until a wave of dizziness passed. She'd intended to follow Moira out, to help recover the lost Vitros, but the more she moved, the more her arm pained her, until it was all she could do to keep from passing out. When she finally reached the atrium, she spied activity through the glass doors—doctors running around, Vitros lying still or stumbling across the grass. She thought she heard her mother cry out, off to her left and down the first hallway, but when she looked that way she saw nothing and supposed it was a trick of her mind, the walls of the place bending sound in strange ways. She started toward the exit when a movement down one of the other hallways caught her eye. *Nicholas!* He was supposed to be helping outside. What was he up to, then? She looked from the glass doors to the hallway uncertainly, then drew a deep breath and went after Nicholas.

She'd caught only a glimpse of him as he disappeared through a doorway, and she wasn't even sure which door it was. This hallway was between the one with the Vitros' bedrooms and the one she'd just been on, and it seemed to be mostly offices. She passed one wide doorway and glanced in to see it opened to a cafeteria, a large, tiled room with carved columns and a glass wall overlooking the island's interior. Constantin Andreyev was inside with his two bodyguards, who were wearing sunglasses even indoors at night. They stood with their hands folded in front of them while Andreyev sat at a table and ignored the food Dr Hashimoto was plying him with. Behind them, a long buffet sat dark and dusty; most of the tables were pushed against the walls, between towering stacks of chairs. Only a few tables were left on the floor, all of them deserted except for Andreyev's. All the lights except those over the tables in use were out. The room was a disharmonious blend of past and present; stepping out of the shadows into the circle of light was like moving across four decades all in one moment.

They looked and saw Sophie standing in the doorway. She froze, uncertain whether to go on or not. Nicholas didn't seem to be in the room.

She flinched when Andreyev called her name. "Sophie Crue! My little imposter. What are you up to? What is going on out there that these doctors are trying to hide from me, eh?"

"Uh . . ."

"Mr. Andreyev," said Dr. Hashimoto, putting forth an admirably calm front, "everything is fine, I assure you! Isn't everything *fine*, Sophie?" The smile she turned on Sophie was strained, and her eyes practically shouted for Sophie to go along with the act.

"I am tired of being *babysat* while you people sweep up

more of your messes, trying to act as if everything is normal. I know it is not!" cried Andreyev, rising to his feet.

"No one is insulting your intelligence, Mr. Andreyev."

"Then speak." He seemed to rein himself in a bit, and he sat down and folded his hands on the table. "What is Strauss trying to hide from me now? What is she doing to those poor sorry bastards she calls Vitros, eh?"

It was the way he said it, the softening of his voice, the concern in his eyes, that sparked the idea in Sophie. She straightened and pushed the fog of pain from her mind with a mighty inhale of air. "Dr. Hashimoto! My mother—Moira—she said you ought to go help the others outside. She said . . . she said they needed more sedatives." She was pulling words out of thin air, crossing bridges as fast as she could build them.

"What?" Shaking her head in confusion, Dr. Hashimoto crossed the space between them. "What are you talking about? Strauss told me to—"

"They're waiting!" cried Sophie. "Go on. Don't worry. I'm sure Mr. Andreyev can hold his own fork and knife."

Andreyev's laugh bounced off the walls. "That I can. Go. Let my little imposter look after me, eh?"

Dr. Hashimoto went, though she looked far from convinced, and the moment she was out of sight Sophie wobbled across the floor and fell into the chair opposite Andreyev. His bodyguards flinched, their hands straying inside their coats at her sudden movement. Sophie didn't spare a moment. She leaned across the table on her unhurt elbow, nearly nose to nose with the Russian investor.

"You want to know what's going on?" she asked.

His eyes glimmered. He carefully placed his silverware on

the table, pushed aside the plate of untouched mashed potatoes and filet mignon, and folded his hands on the tabletop. "Go on," he said softly, locking gazes with her.

"Nicholas—you've met him I believe, one of the first Vitros?"

"Long hair, sneery look."

"Yes. He woke all of the remaining Vitros who were lying in stasis, and they imprinted on him. He's ordered them to jump from the cliff outside, and Strauss and the doctors are trying to stop them. I think he means for it to be a distraction so he can escape the island, but I'm not totally sure. He's a hard one to predict."

Andreyev blinked. Sophie wondered if he'd been expecting such a blunt, straightforward answer, but he seemed appreciative because he nodded slowly and leaned back. "You are a bold one," he said. "I like you, Sophie Crue."

She felt a surge of hope lift her heart. Her last-minute hunch about Andreyev had been little more than that—a whim, a vague, unreliable feeling—but perhaps she'd been right.

"We need your help," she blurted out.

He arched his eyebrows. "Oh?"

"What I mean is . . . um . . . that I have a proposition for you."

Andreyev folded his arms and slipped into a poker face, neither encouraging or discouraging. "You know that after what I have seen here, you are being extraordinarily presumptuous in making any proposal to me at all."

"I understand."

"You realize I owe you and this project nothing."

"I just want you to hear me out."

He stared at her with such searching intensity that she felt her face redden, but she met him without flinching. Then he nodded slightly. "I am listening."

Sophie drew a deep breath and then told him everything that Moira had told her of Skin Island's bright beginnings, of the creation of the psychopathic Nicholas and the failure to treat him, of the accidental creation of the Vitros, of Corpus's revised plan for the project in making Vitros instead of pursuing the remedial properties of the chip. She even told him about her father's decision to risk everything by leaving the project, and how she had only just discovered her own true origin on Skin Island. All the while, Sophie watched Andreyev carefully, but his expressionless mask never once slipped. He listened impassively, but closely.

"The Vitros *are* successful," Sophie admitted. "But not in the way they were originally intended. They've been warped to fit a new vision, one my mother did not create, and . . ." She drew a breath, knowing she was taking a gamble, knowing she had to at least try, then dived ahead. "And I don't think you like it. I saw you in the room with Clive. Something in you *knows* this is wrong, that it can't be allowed to continue. You know that it won't end here."

Sophie tried to gauge his reaction, inwardly cursing his stoicism. "This ability to control people will never be contained once the world knows about it. It'll be more than just Vitros—it will be entire populations. Escorts, workers, armies, nations—where does it end? In the wrong hands, this technology could enslave millions of people. It's in the wrong hands *now*, and look what damage has already been done!"

She stood up and leaned forward on her hands, never once breaking eye contact with the Russian. "But more than that, it destroys the foundation of a person's humanity—it strips away their free will. The Imprima Code eradicates choice, thought, and identity. Mr. Andreyev, please. My mom—" She faltered on the word again, but plunged on. "She can turn this around before it is too late. She can build something good here, but she needs your help to do it. Something good, and something profitable. You're a businessman, right? I'm asking you to believe in the potential the chip has to heal and not destroy. Because you know what I think? I think everyone out there"— she pointed in the general direction of every place that wasn't Skin Island—"would agree with me on this. Maybe a hundred years from now you could convince them to buy into the idea of brainless slaves, but not now, not today, not in *my* world. In my world, people will pay a whole lot more for life. So." She seemed to be running out of words to say, and sank back into her chair, swaying a little from exhaustion. "So I think any *smart* businessman would bet on life, and on developing a technology like the one my mom can make, that gives life and doesn't take it away."

Her eyes solemn, she leaned back and let out a soft sigh; everything was in Andreyev's hands now. Sophie crossed her fingers beneath the table and hoped her gamble wouldn't break them all.

"You have no results," Andreyev said slowly. "You have no proof that this plan of yours will work. In fact, all you have to show me is your surrogate mother's failure to cure a problem she created, in Nicholas. And yet you ask me to risk a fortune on this plan of yours."

"Well . . . yes," Sophie said, reddening a little. "But she never had the chance to—"

"Do you think I became the wealthiest man in Eurasia because I went about listening to little girls cry or wasting money on charities?"

Sophie's face burned. *This was a mistake. I should have known he was just like the rest of them.* "I'm sorry I bothered you," she said through clenched teeth.

Andreyev sniffed and turned back to his dinner. She started to rise to her feet, her blood boiling, when the door to the cafeteria burst open with bang, and both of them jumped—but not, Sophie noticed, the statuesque bodyguards, who merely slipped their hands back into their jackets, presumably to whatever firearms they had stashed in there.

Dr. Hashimoto ran into the room, looking stricken.

Andreyev rose to his feet. "What's wrong?"

Dr. Hashimoto doubled over, her hands on her knees, panting for breath. "It's—it's Strauss."

"What has she done?"

"They sedated all the Vitros . . . got Jay and Mary and Wyatt too . . . They're in the—the—" Dr. Hashimoto's eyes flooded with tears; she was choking on her own voice. "Moira tried to stop her, but Strauss had the guards take her."

"Where is Moira?" Andreyev snapped.

"Follow me!"

Her heart pounding in her ears, Sophie followed Andreyev, his guards, and Dr. Hashimoto down the hall and into the first hall, the one Sophie thought she'd heard her mother in. Dr. Hashimoto gestured frantically at a door, and without waiting for the others, Sophie charged in.

She found her mother tied and gagged in a chair in some sort of small laboratory, guarded by two men who jumped to attention and drew their rifles at Sophie's loud entrance. She froze, and so did they, as Moira called out unintelligibly from behind her gag. Andreyev and Dr. Hashimoto stopped on either side of her, the bodyguards behind them.

The guards moved first, grabbing Sophie and Dr. Hashimoto, spinning them around to face Andreyev and holding them tightly. They looked flustered and confused, but shouted for Andreyev's bodyguards to drop their weapons and leave the room.

"This doesn't concern you, Mr. Andreyev," said one of them. "But Strauss will want this girl and this doctor for questioning, for helping Dr. Crue. Go on now, gently."

"Go," said Sophie coldly to Andreyev. "Find Strauss!"

He gave her a steady stare, then nodded once and turned to usher his bodyguards out. When the door shut, the guards relaxed their grips on Sophie and Dr. Hashimoto. They stepped away and whispered severely to each other, presumably about what they were to do with these two new prisoners. Moira struggled at her bonds and stared wildly around, but Sophie stopped to gather her thoughts and take stock of the situation.

"Dr. Hashimoto," she whispered, and the doctor gave her a wild-eyed look. "Did you get those sedatives I told you to get?"

Her hand strayed to a set of syringes in her lab coat pocket. Sophie nodded slowly. "Good. Hand them here."

"Mmmph!" cried Moira, but Sophie ignored her. In the briefest of seconds before she could let her better judgment catch up to her, she took the syringes, slipped the caps off the needles, and lunged at the guards and slammed the needles into the backs of their necks, her thumbs pressing the plungers as hard as they could. She gritted her teeth against the pain that shot up her arm. The guards didn't even have a chance to turn around. They wobbled, blinked owlishly, then slid to the floor, their rifles clattering.

When Sophie turned around, her hands shaking and her heart still paused in midbeat, Dr. Hashimoto was already untying Moira. The moment the gag slipped free Sophie's mother burst out, "The Vitros! Strauss has them in the gas room!"

"Mom!" Sophie yelled, as her mother leaped out of the chair, vaulted over the guards, and went barreling down the hallway, Sophie and Dr. Hashimoto hurrying to keep up. "What is it? What's wrong?"

"She's killing them! We have to hurry!"

With those words, they passed Andreyev and his guards in the hallway, who turned astonished looks on them as they ran by, and then Andreyev slid smoothly into motion, staying right on Sophie's heels. Moira skidded to a halt in front of the elevator and punched the button repeatedly until the door slid open. "Strauss has taken the Vitros downstairs. She's pulling the plug on Skin Island! There's a—a room in the basement. A gas chamber."

Sophie's stomach somersaulted. *"What?"*

Moira stepped into the elevator, and the others squeezed in beside her, but the door slid shut before Andreyev's harried bodyguards could get in.

"It was a precautionary measure," Moira said, tapping

her foot impatiently as the elevator lowered. "It was Corpus's idea. They wanted a way to contain the Vitros if they ever . . . Well."

"Revolted?" Sophie asked. "If they ever broke the Imprima bond and turned against you?"

"Yes," Moira admitted.

The door dinged and slid open, and Moira darted out, Sophie on her heels. Andreyev followed at a more measured pace. A door in front of Sophie popped open suddenly, and his bodyguards spilled out, nearly crashing into her. For once, they looked flustered, until they spotted Andreyev and caught up to him. Sophie could hear them muttering about Andreyev always running off, as if he were a naughty child in the grocery store.

The hallway was lined with silent doctors. They were slumped against the walls, seated in soggy, teary clusters on the floor. When they saw Moira coming, they rose and flocked to her, all talking at once. She pushed her way through them, and Sophie and Andreyev followed in her wake.

At the end of the hall Strauss stood with a gun clutched so tightly in her hand that her knuckles were white. Next to her, Dr. Michalski stood with his eyes as wide and round as his glasses.

"Moira." Strauss lifted her gun. "Enough. You're relieved of your duties on Skin Island and are ordered to return to Corpus headquarters with me."

"Turn it off, Ed!" Moira ignored Strauss as completely as if she were a smudge on the wall. "Turn it off, *now!*"

He looked at Strauss uncertainly.

"You listen to *me*, Ed, not her!" Moira snapped.

"Dr. Michalski listens to the one who writes his checks, not his *former* colleague, Moira. I said you're relieved—"

"Shut up, Victoria. Ed, *turn it off*. They're dying in there!"

The door behind Strauss was shut, and the small window in it hazy with fog. Sophie's blood turned to ice when she realized the fog must have been poisonous fumes, choking all the newborn Vitros to death. She glanced at the wall, where the exposed panel displayed numbers and lines she didn't understand. A small light blinked red above a metal lever marked with numbered increments.

She didn't wait for permission. Before Strauss could react, she darted past her and grabbed the lever, slamming it downward. She heard a loud hissing from within the walls around them, then silence where the panel had been humming earlier.

"It's too late," Strauss said. "I'm cleaning up your mess, Moira. It had to be done."

"Don't open it!" Dr. Michalski warned. "It has to be properly ventilated and cleaned before—"

Moira and Sophie wrenched the door open together. Sophie yelped as three bodies fell forward with the door: all Vitros. Gas poured out of the room and spread through the hall; doctors began yelling and scrambling away to escape the noxious fumes. Strauss fled with them, crowding into the elevator and sending the slower runners on to the stairs when it was full. Following her mother's example, Sophie held her shirt over her mouth to avoid breathing in too much of the stuff, though already she could feel her eyes and throat burning.

Dr. Hashimoto appeared at her side, along with Andreyev,

which surprised her a little. Together they hauled the Vit-ros out. Their bodies were limp, their lips blue. Sophie's heart pounded so hard she felt her pulse in her temples and wrists, surging with adrenaline and horror. After a moment, Andreyev's bodyguards wordlessly pitched in.

Despite their makeshift masks, they had to wait a few moments before they could enter the room. Moira worked the controls on the panel in the wall, then froze.

"What?" Sophie asked. "What's wrong?"

"It's broken," she whispered.

"What's broken?" Andreyev asked.

"The vents to leech the gas from the chamber." She turned a dial. "And the valve to shut off the gas." She looked up, her face white. "There's no way to turn it off."

"How is that even possible?" Sophie asked.

"Someone would have had to manually cut the line."

"Sabotage?"

Moira slammed her hand against the panel, her shoulders heaving as she breathed in and out. "This whole building is filling up with hydrogen cyanide. We have to get everyone out now. Hana, go tell the others to bring stretchers!" Moira yelled. "And the kids will need oxygen, fast! We have to get them out of there *now*."

Andreyev turned to his bodyguards "Find those cowardly doctors and drag them back by their hair if you must."

His men looked sour at leaving him alone, but they went. Sophie had to give the Russian credit; he didn't need a com-puter chip to inspire obedience. He had an air of authority that made Strauss look like a fourth-grade bully.

Moira pointed at a door down the hall. "Sophie, open that

supply closet. There should be towels inside. Take them out and tie one around your face."

She obeyed with alacrity, tossing a towel to Moira and Dr. Hashimoto. With the cloths secured over their mouths and noses, they plunged in and began carrying out the rest of the bodies. Sophie hoped they weren't carrying corpses, but it was difficult to tell. Andreyev tied an apron he'd found over his face and worked alongside them, carrying Vitros out of the poisonous room and into the relatively clearer hallway, though Sophie could see the gas escaping to fill the basement. She worked feverishly; she was too small to carry anyone, so she took them by the arms and dragged them instead. Nearly all the Vitros had been evacuated when Sophie reached the last two figures slumped against the wall.

Her mind turned inside out. Her lungs went flat as her breath rushed from her lips.

Jim.

THIRTY-FOUR
SOPHIE

She sucked in a breath, which only sent her head spinning, then knelt and reached out to gently pry Jim's arms from Lux's limp form. He was sitting with his back propped against the wall, his head fallen forward onto Lux's. She was curled against his chest like a child, her hands knotted in his shirt. Neither moved when Sophie touched them. She felt tears sting the corners of her eyes. Her mind reeled at finding him there; he should have been ashes in the sky. She'd seen the plane explode with her own eyes—but she wasn't about to question whatever miracles were dropped in her lap, not when she needed one so desperately. She could feel herself unraveling from the inside out, and willed herself to hold it together long enough to get them to safety.

"Jim . . . Jim, wake up. It's me. It's Sophie."

Moira crouched beside her and covered her mouth with her hand, her eyes pinched with sorrow. "Oh no. Oh, Sophie . . ."

"He's okay!" Sophie said fiercely. "Both of them. They'll be fine. Won't they?"

"Let's get them out of here."

With Andreyev's and Dr. Hashimoto's help, they carried Jim and Lux out of the room and laid them in the hallway with the Vitros.

Sophie dropped to her knees beside Jim, and finally let loose the tension that had been exploding in her chest since the moment she'd seen him slumped in the chamber. She couldn't help it; she burst into sobs, tears of relief mingling with tears of fear, that she had found him only to lose him again. "I'm sorry," she whispered, leaning over him and pressing her forehead to his, whispering into his hair. "I'm sorry for the things I said. I didn't mean it, I didn't mean it at all. Jim, Jim, please wake up. *Please.*"

All the horror she'd felt when she'd seen his plane burst into flames rushed back to her now at double strength, a tidal wave that overpowered her and sucked her into a maelstrom of terror and savage desperation. She cradled his face in her hands and willed him back to life, willed her own life into him, had to stop herself from digging her nails into his skin.

"JIM!" She screamed his name, feeling herself lose all control. It was too much too fast too soon without a moment to breathe and she was drowning in panic. Someone was pulling at her, trying to release her grip on Jim, saying words she did not understand.

"Sophie. *Sophie!*"

It was her mother, her not-mother, her lie of a mother.

"No!" she said, and she pressed her hands to his chest and began pumping. "He's not dead—he's *not*! I won't let it happen! You hear me, Jim Julien? *I won't let you!*"

"Come *on*," Sophie said, over and over with each press of Jim's sternum. "C'mon, c'mon."

"Sophie." Moira's eyes were deep wells of pain. "Sophie, stop. He's gone."

"No. No, he isn't. If I just—"

"Sophie, *stop*. We have to go. It's getting too dangerous down here." She coughed. The air was getting thicker with hydrogen cyanide. Before long, the entire basement level would be a gas chamber.

But Sophie couldn't leave him. Losing him twice in one day would kill her. Her heart felt like it would burst into pieces it was pounding so hard, her pulse a hammer against her skull.

"He's Jim," Sophie sobbed. "*My* Jim!"

"I know. I know, baby."

"I'm not your *baby*." Sophie pulled away and shoved Moira backward. "You're not my mom and I'm *not* your baby!"

"You're right!" Moira held up her hands. "I'm not. I didn't give birth to you. My genes are not your genes. But Sophie. I *do* love you."

It was Andreyev who finally wrestled her away and put her in Moira's arms. Her mother held her tight while the Russian felt for a pulse. The grim set of his lips brought a dry heave to Sophie's chest. She doubled over, gasping for breath. Maybe the gas had gotten to her. Maybe she was dying. Maybe she would wake up and all of this would be a nightmare she could forget.

Down the hall, a few of the Vitros began to cough. Sophie's heart leaped. *Maybe it's not too late.*

"I must save him," Sophie heard someone whisper. She looked over. It was Lux. She began to crawl toward Jim like a broken windup toy.

"Lux, no." Moira took two strides and pulled her away, held her in one arm and Sophie in the other, the girls cradled against her as if they were four years old. Their hair curled together into an indistinguishable tangle on Moira's chest.

"Connie, go down the hall. Third door on the left—there should be some oxygen tanks and masks in the closet. He needs oxygen *fast*."

He nodded and stepped around the bodies on the floor to reach it. With a wild twist of her body, Sophie broke free of Moira and ran after him, because she couldn't bear standing still, watching Jim, hoping for a sign of life. She needed to help, needed to move, needed to *do* something. She scrubbed the tears from her eyes with her shirt and gritted her teeth, channeling the pressure inside of her into movement.

Andreyev found the tanks and handed two of them to her. It took another minute to locate the masks, which she draped around her neck. Then, feeling like an astronaut preparing to dive into space, she tramped back to Moira and held out the equipment. Setting Lux down, Moira deftly connected the mask's tubes to a tank and opened the valve to release the oxygen; she pressed it to Jim's face.

One second. Two seconds. Three. And then Jim gasped so suddenly that Sophie gasped with him, and his chest began to rise and fall. Her heart fluttered, and the tension in her own chest rushed out of her in a loud exhalation, and then she jumped when she heard Lux do the same. Her twin's face had finally relaxed. She stared at Jim greedily, timing her own breaths with his as if she could somehow transfer air into his lungs by sheer force of will. Sophie watched her, transfixed.

"He's coming back to us," Moira said, sounding relieved herself, and Sophie wondered if she'd forgotten that just hours earlier, she'd been ready to sacrifice Jim for Sophie's sake.

Dr. Hashimoto and the bodyguards appeared down the hall, trailing a posse of shamefaced doctors. Moira didn't even look up. She set her mouth in a hard line and focused on bringing Jim back to life. The other doctors silently went to work, fetching oxygen, and moving the Vitros onto gurneys they wheeled out of the elevator.

Sophie's thoughts strayed to Nicholas. Where was he? It seemed that no one had seen him since Moira sent him to undo the damage he'd wrought on the newborn Vitros, but obviously he hadn't followed through. It made Sophie nervous, not knowing what he was up to. But they couldn't very well launch a search party now; they had to focus on resuscitating the Vitros.

One by one, all the others awoke and were taken away by the doctors, who were wearing surgical masks to protect them from the gas. Jim's eyes finally opened, and he moaned, but Moira hushed him and kept the mask on his face.

Behind them, the elevator door opened and the doctor named Rogers tumbled out, shouting for Moira, his surgical mask puffing in and out as he yelled.

"What *now?*" she called, her face weary.

Dr. Rogers rushed to her. "It's not good!" he said.

"What a shock. What is it?"

"It's Strauss. She's not happy. She's got all the guards outside, armed, and she's ready to make a statement. You've really pissed her off, and Moira." Dr. Rogers winced and dropped his gaze. "I think she means to make an example of you."

THIRTY-FIVE
JIM

Jim leaned on Sophie and Lux leaned on Jim; they made their way out of the building like a trio of wounded soldiers, flanked by Moira and the Vitros, who were being pushed on stretchers or supported by the doctors. Events were moving too quickly around him, leaving him disoriented. He was still weak and dizzy from the hydrogen cyanide, and tasks as simple as navigating through a doorway took all his concentration to accomplish.

Sophie's eyes were fixed on Jim as they walked—well, *limped*, more like. He seemed to be recovering steadily, now that he was breathing cleaner air. "You're alive. I can't believe you're alive."

"Crazy, right? I'm as shocked as you are." He was trying very hard not to think about what had happened in the basement of that building. Everything else that had happened on the island—that had ever happened to him in his life—paled in comparison to the horror of being trapped in that room.

The bitter, almond scent of the gas seemed to cling to him, assuring that every few seconds his mind slipped backward into the gas chamber and a feeling of panic swelled in his chest. He had to fight it back each time, and the effort was exhausting.

"But your plane—I saw—it exploded and I thought you—"

"Oh. That."

"Yes, *that*. Did you forget you were nearly blown to pieces?"

"Hm. Must have slipped my mind between being nearly shot and nearly gassed to death. In a freaking *gas chamber*. Like this is some kind of fascist prison."

She looked away, her face scarlet. "I'm glad you're not dead."

"Makes two of us," he said with a crooked grin. "And I'm glad *you're* not dead. From what I can tell, you saved our lives."

"Well. Me and . . . and Mom."

He scrunched his eyebrows inquisitively; there was too much underlying weight in her tone for him to believe that was the whole story. She shook her head at his look and said, "I'll tell you later. Listen, what I said to you on the beach back there—I didn't really . . . I just want to say . . ."

He studied her face, his throat tightening when he thought of their fight. He'd been shocked at how deeply her words had pierced him—he hadn't realized how much power she had over him, to be able to hurt him like that. *I care about her more than I knew.* Overcome suddenly with a feeling that terrified him as much as it excited him, he took her hand and squeezed it tight. "I know. Me too."

They crossed the atrium, flanked by Moira, a crowd of

doctors, and a man with two bodyguards who Sophie pointed out as Andreyev, the Russian investor. Jim examined the man sidelong as they walked; he looked weary and slightly shell-shocked, much like Jim felt. Though, of course, Jim could easily add to his list of ailments the side effects of hydrogen cyanide and near suffocation. He felt as if his brain had been reduced to sludge and was currently sloshing painfully around in his skull. He checked on Lux; she was pale and barely lucid, but faring better than he was.

When they stepped outside, they all froze, like a crowd of war refugees. Strauss was waiting with a dozen guards in a line behind her. Each one had a rifle pressed to his shoulder, and the barrels were all aimed at the doctors and those with them.

The gurneys bearing the more helpless Vitros sat on the grass, with a few doctors moving frantically among them, their eyes glancing worriedly at Strauss's guards. Andreyev's body-guards smoothly slid in front of him, their hands straying to the lapels of their coats, but even if they managed to reach whatever firearms they had hidden, they would be no match for Strauss's men. Several of the doctors raised their hands in immediate surrender.

"Moira." Strauss's voice was soft, dangerous. The flood-lights turned her white pantsuit a sickly yellow. "This little drama of yours has gone on long enough. Constantin, I cannot express how disappointed I am in the way you have been treated on this island. I assure you, Corpus will make reparations."

"Hm," Andreyev said, his face expressionless.

"We won't let you kill them," Sophie said, stepping for-ward—a poorly planned move, Jim thought, since it left him swaying on his feet as the world spun; he was dangerously close to toppling over and taking Lux down with him. "The Vitros have done nothing wrong. They need help, not a gas chamber."

"Are you going to get your pet under control," Strauss said to Moira, not once looking at Sophie, "or shall I?" She raised her handgun threateningly.

"She's right," said Moira. "I won't let you harm them."

"This place, all of it, belongs to Corpus, not you. *I* make the calls."

"And I'm telling you I won't let you harm them."

"If I have to forcibly remove you, I will."

"Then you'll have to forcibly remove me too," said Sophie, stepping closer to her mother.

"And me," said Dr. Hashimoto unexpectedly. She joined Sophie and Moira.

One by one, then all in a rush, the other doctors stepped forward. Even the bespectacled one who'd turned on the gas after Strauss conferred control of the project to him—what was his name? Michalski. His hands were visibly trembling, but he stood beside Moira and held his ground.

The doctors, with Sophie in their midst, formed a protective hedge in front of the Vitros. Strauss looked angrier with each one's pronouncement of support for Moira, and her skin seemed to grow tighter and tighter over her cheekbones as her opposition swelled.

"Each and every one of you is expendable," Strauss spat. "I have no qualms about removing you all. Once I shut this place down for good, you will all be fired. No relocation, no reassignment, no pension, nothing. In fact . . . I could have you all shot here and now. There is no law on Skin Island but what I make. You know I can do it."

Sophie reached out and took Moira's hand. Then Moira took Dr. Michalski's. Down the line, the doctors grasped hands and stared silently at Strauss and her guards, daring them to fire.

All except Sophie, who looked over her shoulder at Jim.

Jim sighed deeply. The last thing he wanted to do was get tangled up in some Gandhian protest. *He* didn't want to get shot for the sake of some miserable lab subjects he didn't know. But he did know Sophie, and now Lux, he supposed. If he had to get shot over something, it might as well be for the sake of a friend.

Maybe getting involved was the stupid thing to do, but it had never stopped him in the past. And if Skin Island had showed him one thing in the brief time he had been there, it was that the world had plenty of heartless, detached bas- tards—and it could really use a few more idiot heroes.

So he took Sophie's hand and stood beside her with his other arm wrapped around Lux. She was still shaking and a little wobbly on her feet, but she was proving her resilience. She looked at him with clear eyes, eyes less innocent than they had been an hour ago. The world had given Lux a cruel reception, and she was growing up fast.

Jim drew a deep breath and turned to face Strauss and the dozen rifles aimed at him. Sophie squeezed his hand; he squeezed hers back.

For a long moment, Strauss said nothing. He imagined her running a hundred different responses through her mind, trying to find a way to cow them into submission. The guards glanced uncertainly at her, waiting for an order.

Together, in silence, they waited.

Only one person stood apart from it all—well, three, if you counted Andreyev's bodyguards. The Russian stood a short distance ahead of the line of doctors, between them and Strauss's men. He seemed unperturbed by the amount of firearms being brandished about, and looked lost in thought, as if he were sitting in the back of a movie theater watching with halfhearted interest as they all played out their drama. His bodyguards, on the other hand, were tensed like a pair of panthers, ready to spring at the first sign of gunfire.

Jim realized Sophie was staring hard at Andreyev, her eyes pouring pressure onto the Russian's shoulders. Why? What did she want him to do? Is this what it came down to—one man whose decision could tip the scales for or against them?

"Constantin," Strauss said slowly, "come with me. I am afraid what I must do next will not be pleasant, and it would be best if you were not caught up in it. These employees have proven too insubordinate to be trusted, and so Corpus must act."

"As one of Corpus's foremost investors, Miss Strauss," Andreyev said, his accent almost a purr, "I believe I have a say in what Corpus will and will not do, wouldn't you say?" He slowly shifted into motion, crossing the grass to stand on the other side of Lux, completing the defensive line against Strauss.

Her eyes widened slightly when she realized he had chosen his side—and it was apparently not the side she had predicted. "I don't understand."

"Understand this, Miss Strauss. Young Sophie here has

apprised me of some very interesting facts regarding Skin Island's past—and its original purpose. In light of this information, I would like to double my current contributions to the Vitro project, under three circumstances. One"—he lifted a finger. "Full control of the project will go to Dr. Crue. And by full control, I mean I don't want *you* to have a say in so much as the color of the wallpaper."

"*Mr.* Andreyev! I—"

Two," he continued steamrolling right over Strauss's angry interjection, "I want every possible effort to be made in reversing the mind control you have put over these poor children, and I want my funds to be channeled not into the making of Vitros but into utilizing the neurotechnology that has imprisoned them to explore its therapeutic and curative abilities. There is a great deal of potential in that, I think, and I am curious to see what Dr. Crue can make of it."

Strauss's eyes bulged, but she said nothing. Down the line, Moira Crue let out a soft cry, and she turned to stare at Sophie with wide eyes. Sophie looked up at Jim and gave him a small smile. He returned it and squeezed her hand again.

"And three." Andreyev turned to Sophie and Jim. "I want these young people to be given their freedom. They must be allowed to leave this place with no harm done to them."

Jim resisted the urge to crawl across the ground and kiss the man's thousand-dollar golf shoes. He wondered what the Russian words for "can I buy you a drink" might be.

Strauss cocked her head and studied him with a bemused look, as if she was wondering where the punch line was, as if she couldn't believe he was actually serious. But the look he gave her in return was cool and smooth as Russian vodka.

"If this is your decision," Strauss said, "to reject everything I have offered you here, why did you come in the first place?"

"I came because I was curious. And because I cannot afford to have weapons such as these"—he gestured at the sedated Vitros—"in the hands of my enemies. I will admit, at first I was intrigued when I read the dossier you sent me last month. Only a fool would not consider the advantages of the particular services your company offers, and I wanted to see these Vitros for myself, to see whether this imprinting could really be done. Still. You think that because I deal in arms, that because I fund your weapons research and your . . . special project in South America, that I am a coldhearted bastard who would sit by while children are turned into robots, made to serve with no capacity for their own choice?" He shook his head slowly. "I am a businessman, yes. But I am not a monster."

Jim was surprised Strauss's death grip on her handgun hadn't already dented the metal. Everyone seemed to hold their breath as they waited for her to speak. The silence was filled by the rushing surf and windswept leaves of the palm trees. Even the moon, suspended high above them, was poised in suspense.

At last, Strauss relented. Her capitulation was evident even before she spoke; she folded visibly, like a tent robbed of its supports. "So be it, but this is entirely on your head, Constantin. I will take no responsibility when this plan of yours fails."

He nodded amiably as everyone breathed out in relief. The guards behind Strauss seemed very grateful to be lowering their weapons. Andreyev crossed to Moira, took her hand in his, and kissed it. "Dr. Crue, I should be honored to invest in your technology. I think you will find I can be a very resourceful supporter."

Moira actually blushed. "Constantin, I . . . I don't know what to say. Thank you."

"Don't thank me, Moira. You must thank your bold and persuasive young impostor," he said, ignoring Strauss and shifting his gaze to Sophie. His back was now to Strauss, as if he'd dismissed her already. "Miss Crue. My regards." He gave her a small, stiff bow—and then it was Sophie who was blushing.

Jim gave a soft, impatient grunt, and Andreyev's eyes flickered his way.

"Not to be rude," Jim said, "but now that we're all sorted out, I wondered if we might discuss the issue of my plane? Now, the way I see it—and the way my insurance company might see it—someone here is responsible for it being *blown up*. So I was just wondering if—"

Sophie elbowed him hard in the ribs. "*Jim.* This isn't the time."

"What? All I'm saying is—"

"If you want to talk to the person responsible for your stupid plane," said a voice behind them, "perhaps you'd like to talk to me?"

They all turned to see Nicholas leaning the doorway, absently tapping a device against his leg. In his other hand was a sleek black pistol. "Or perhaps you'd like to talk about the bomb I have planted inside."

THIRTY-SIX
SOPHIE

"Nicholas . . . What is this?" Moira was white as a ghost, but she stepped forward and faced him.

"Good God, Moira, he doesn't have a *bomb*," Strauss said, approaching.

"If you really believe that," said Nicholas, "why don't you tell them to shoot me now?" He wiggled his eyebrows at the guards and gave them a Cheshire cat grin.

"Nicholas." Moira's tone could turn grapes into wine. He stopped taunting the guards and turned to her. "What is this about? What do you want?"

"Finally," he said, with an exaggerated groan. "Someone who speaks reason. I want the helicopter." He pointed at the Corpus chopper. "I want a pilot to fly it—Lux will do. And lastly, I want Sophie."

"And what if I call your bluff?" Moira asked.

Sophie was only half listening. Her mind raced up and down the corridors of the past twenty-four hours, collecting stray bits of information like a trail of bread crumbs. *I know every corner of this island, down to the forgotten rooms and the spaces inside the walls themselves,* he had boasted to her. He'd said that he'd lost his bomb when he used it on Jim's plane, as if he didn't have any others . . . but then what was it he'd added? *Well. I can always come up with something.* He wanted to destroy the Vitro building, one way or another. Escaping wasn't enough for him, oh, no—he had to have it all: Sophie, his freedom, *and* his revenge on Corpus.

"He's not bluffing," she found herself saying.

Everyone turned to stare at her as she went on. "*You* sabotaged the gas lines. That's what this was all about, from the very beginning. You woke the Vitros and sent them to the cliff; you knew the Vitros would distract everyone but Moira, who would come to investigate. *I* was just there to distract Moira while you sabotaged the gas chamber equipment inside the walls, because you knew Strauss would shortly use it to try to kill the Vitros you'd *also* sabotaged. He has a bomb," she said, turning to Moira. "The entire building is his bomb, thanks to Strauss."

Nicholas's smile could melt an iceberg. He gave her a mocking bow. "Brilliant, Sophie Crue. You truly are your mother's daughter. Oh, wait . . ." He straightened and gave a sardonic frown. "No, you're not."

The only thing stopping her from slapping the false pity off his face was the detonator and the gun in his hands.

"I imagine the control you're holding sets off a spark somewhere in the basement, to ignite the hydrogen cyanide," said Moira carefully, as if the wrong word might somehow ignite the gas on its own.

"It was so easy. There are *tanks* of the stuff down there. It's like you wanted to blow this place up from the beginning. You have to admit—it's so brilliantly simple that it's simply brilliant." He beamed at her, as if he expected applause.

"Think about what you're doing," Moira said. "We are not your enemies, Nicholas. We're your family."

"I don't have a family and I don't want one."

"We raised you, taught you." She held out a hand, her eyes sorrowful. "Loved you."

"Your sentiment may ensnare the likes of her," he said, flicking a scornful look Sophie's way, "but I'm smarter than that. You try to build cages out of a false sense of obligation and affection—flimsy materials, *Doctor*. If you really wanted to control me, you should have built a cage of steel. I've been your pet for too long. But no more." He held the detonator above his head. "I hold the keys now."

"Oh, good *God*," said Strauss. "You little bastard. You're nothing, do you hear me? You're a laboratory failure, a pet I let Moira keep simply because you were too pathetic to kill. Do you want to know why I let you live all those years ago when we discovered what you were? What Moira had made of you? I let you live because you're not a threat. Not to anyone. You're not even *half* as smart as you think you are, and you're delusional and dramatic and stupid if you think I'm going to let you just prance off into the sunset. You think you're special? Tell him, Moira. Tell him about Isaiah."

"I . . ." Moira shut her eyes. "Oh, Nicholas."

His mask of triumph slipped just slightly as his gaze honed in on Moira. "Isaiah?"

"Your Control, Nicky."

Laughing, Nicholas waved the detonator, making them all flinch. "I don't have a Control! Sophie is the only one!"

"His name is Isaiah Cartwright," said Strauss, "and he lives in Wyoming on a ranch with his adoptive family. He is *not* a psychopath, but a decorated rodeo rider. Am I right, Moira?"

"Shut *up!*" Nicholas swung the gun toward Strauss, who stared him down.

Opening her eyes, Moira looked sadly at Nicholas. "She's telling you the truth, Nicky."

"No, she's not—she's lying! You all are! You always have!" he screamed. Spit sprayed from his mouth. "*Stop it!*"

"He has two parents and a sister who love him dearly," Strauss went on, pouring acid on the wound she'd opened. "He has friends. He goes to school. He's *normal*, Nicky, and he has a real life. He's a real boy. Not like you—you are nothing. You're just . . . just a shade, a shadow of what he is. You'll never know what he's known. You're not a threat. You're an echo of someone else."

If this was Strauss's method of calming Nicholas down, then Sophie was extremely unimpressed by her approach. Nicholas howled, his face going deathly white. His cheeks turned to pockets of shadow as he sucked in a breath. "I'm not a threat? I could blow you to hell with a flick of my thumb!"

"And kill yourself in the process? Ha! Look at where you're standing! You are much too fond of yourself to do that."

"I would," he said. "Even if it was the last thing I ever did, it would be worth it, the revenge. The knowledge that I'd be dragging you into hell with me!"

"You lying son of a—"

"I'll do it!" He raised the detonator. "Say one more word, and I swear I will."

Strauss studied him, her eyes thin slits. Then she turned to one of the guards. "Give him the chopper keys. Okay, Nicholas, you win."

The man tossed the keys; they glinted as they arced through the air. Nicholas, caught off guard, reached to awkwardly catch the keys with his gun hand. Strauss took advantage of his momentary distraction to fire.

Nicholas screamed as his other arm exploded in a spray of crimson. The detonator dropped to the ground. Strauss advanced on Nicholas, firing again, but he twisted aside, still screeching in pain and clutching his wounded arm to his stomach.

Moira spun around. "Get them out of here! Away from this building—*now!* The gas chamber is located beneath the atrium, and we're practically standing on top of it. Go! A few feet of dirt won't stop that blast, and every moment we waste makes it worse!" The doctors immediately began wheeling and carrying the Vitros down the hill toward the resort. The moment Strauss had fired, Andreyev's bodyguards had pulled out their weapons, twin revolvers black as jet. One trained his on Strauss, the other on Nicholas, but Moira told Andreyev to help get the Vitros down the hill. He nodded and ordered his men to help him. They shot him mutinous looks, and kept their guns in hand as they helped push stretchers down the slope. Moira whipped her own gun out and directed it at Strauss. "Victoria, *stop!*"

Nicholas tripped and fell into a heap in the grass,

whimpering and snarling like a rabid dog, swinging his gun wildly at everyone who came near him. Sophie took the chance to dart across the ground and pick up the detonator — but someone got there before she did.

The Vitro girl, Mary. She held it up in triumph, her eyes flaming.

"I got it, Nicky! Do you want me to do it?" She stood with her legs spread and her curls bouncing in the wind, her thumb leaning against the little metal switch. Sophie froze in horror.

"You'll kill yourself, Mary!" Sophie hissed. "Do you really want that?"

Mary looked down at her.

"Just listen to me," said Sophie. Moira and Strauss were still in a standoff, but she knew they were watching Mary — or rather, Mary's thumb. "Nicholas was going to leave without you," she said. "He had it all worked out. You're his friend, right? You're one of the ones who didn't imprint. One of the lucky ones, I think. And yet he was going to leave you behind. Why would you die for his cause?"

The fanatical light in Mary's eyes faltered. She lowered her gaze to where Nicholas crouched in the grass.

"Give it to me," said Sophie, holding out a hand. "Please, Mary. You don't want to throw your life away for him."

"Do it," Nicholas hissed. "Light it up. We'll burn together, you and me, Mary."

"Mary, *no*. Give me the —"

Craaaack!

Mary flew backward, the detonator falling from her hands, a bullet planted between her eyes. She landed heavily on the grass and lay still, her eyes stretched open, her mouth contorted in a scream she didn't live long enough to give. A thin line of blood drained down her face and pooled in her eye socket.

Strauss smiled. Actually *smiled*.

For a moment, everyone stared at the body in shock. Sophie gagged on a surge of bile.

Then, with a roar of rage, Moira fired at Strauss and missed, and everyone left on the hilltop sprang into chaos. The guards took up firing stances all over the place, but seemed uncertain whom to fire at. Nicholas crawled toward the detonator with fiendish speed despite his shattered, bloody arm, and Sophie scrambled in an attempt to beat him to it. Meanwhile, Moira and Strauss ducked behind palms and took wild shots at each other that sent splinters of wood flying; one of Strauss's bullets hit the glass doors to the atrium, and they shattered in a magnificent, glittering crash.

Nicholas reached the detonator first, but Sophie was a breath away. She slammed into him, sending them both hard into the dirt. He threw her off and lunged away, but she grabbed his long hair and yanked him back.

Jim charged toward them and slid in as if they were sitting on home plate. He collared Nicholas, trying to get a stranglehold on him, when Nicholas clamped his teeth onto Sophie's hurt shoulder. She howled and fell back, giving him the chance to deliver a cutting elbow jab to Jim's jaw and breaking Jim's hold on him. He leaped for the detonator, but not before Lux scooped it up. She danced backward, out of Nicholas's reach, then tripped over Mary's body and toppled down. Before she could get back on her feet, Nicholas was on her. She caught him in the stomach with her feet and threw him over her head, then rolled smoothly into a crouch. Nicholas landed heavily, howling at the pain in his arm.

"Whoa," said Sophie, her eyes wide.

"I know, right?" Jim's voice was hard. "Talk about teenage mutant ninja blonde. Lux, don't let him touch that detonator."

She nodded, clutching the detonator in both hands. Behind them, they heard a loud click.

"Ha! You're empty!" Moira cried, and Sophie spun to see Strauss standing in the open, her gun at her side. Moira advanced on her. "And I've still got one left, Victoria."

Strauss rolled her eyes. "Fine. Your round, Moira. But the board will have the final say."

"Oh, I'm sure they will," said Moira. "I'm looking forward to telling them all about how you shoved my Vitros into a gas chamber."

"I hope you'll add that one of those same Vitros turned that gas chamber into a giant bomb." Strauss dropped her gun and held up her hands. "If it's all the same to you, I'd rather not be around when that thing goes off. And it will. Whether or not your little psychopath sets it off, it *will* go off. The place is full of explosive gas, and all it will take is a spark. This whole hilltop will go up in flames."

She turned her back to Moira and walked briskly down the hill to where the others stood, without so much as a backward look.

"She's right," Moira said, turning to them. "Let's go, Nicky. Let's—"

"You have one shot? Well, I've got eight." He waved his pistol.

"Enough," she said impatiently. "You're bleeding out. Let me help you!"

"No, let *me* help *you*!" He struggled to his feet, wheezing and pale. "Let me help you understand what's going to happen here. First, you're going to back up, all three of you. *Now.*"

Moira, Sophie, and Jim backed away, hands raised.

"Toss the gun, Moira."

She dropped her pistol.

"I've reached a decision," he announced. "Do you want to hear it? I've decided to shoot all three of you. That's right. No more games, no more talking, no more surprises. Just *pop, pop, pop!* And then Lux and I fly off into the sunset—oh, no, precious. Don't even think about moving." He held up a hand in warning to Lux. She was several paces away, just far enough to be out of reach.

"You act like you don't care," said Moira. "You tell yourself that—and maybe, for the most part it's true. But you're not as lost as you think you are. You *do* care, don't you? You care about Sophie." She looked at her daughter, then back at Nicholas, her eyes moist. "Your trouble isn't that you *can't* care; it's that you don't know *how* to care. Luring her here, these games you're playing, this is your way of expressing that deep down you do feel a connection. You did all of this for her, right? To be with her? To find some way into her world?"

Nicholas sneered. "I did all of this for me. You see what you want to, that's all."

"I'm trying to make *you* see it! You aren't beyond saving, Nicky! Maybe we assumed too much about you when we called you a psychopath. Maybe there is still time—"

"I'm tired, Moira," he said, and he looked it. Bags under his eyes, shadows beneath his cheekbones and over his temples. "I'm so very tired. Tired of this place, of this life, of your constant *nagging*. Just . . . enough." He raised the gun, and Moira threw herself to the side, but not before he fired; the bullet caught her in the back, and she fell with a cry of pain.

Sophie's chest seized; she felt herself begin to hyperventilate. *No, no, no, got to stay focused!*

"Stop it!" she yelled. "Just stop! You don't have to be this way! You don't have to be this—this *monster*."

"Well, that's the thing, isn't it? Everyone always blames the monster—but no one ever blames the one who created it. Isn't that right?" He sneered at Moira's limp form. "Tell me, who is the monster? The creation or the creator? It has to start somewhere."

"You can't blame someone else for your own actions," Sophie said, her eyes slipping to her mom. *She's breathing! Now if I can just keep him talking.* The guards below must have heard the shot. Surely they'd come running.

"Oh, fine. Blame whoever you want. While you can. Which isn't for much longer. Hmm . . . who's next?" He swung the pistol steadily until it was pointing at Jim, who stood with clenched fists and a scalding glare, but he said nothing.

Sophie looked from the gun to Jim, and everything he had once been to her—friend, protector, partner in crime—roared through her head, a maelstrom of memories and emotions, as if the last ten years had never happened. But it was different now, the way she felt toward him. He wasn't just a boy she'd take the blame for when he put grapes in the microwave to watch them explode. He was a boy she'd take a bullet for.

The thought struck her like a punch, leaving her breathless, amazed. She reached out and took his hand, stepping closer until they were shoulder to shoulder. She felt him stiffen, then his fingers tightened around hers, and, ludicrously perhaps, she felt safe. Calm. Whether this sudden surety flowed from Jim or from their entangled fingers she didn't know—all she knew was that she would hold his hand no matter what came—bullets or explosions or poison gas—and she never wanted to let go.

If Nicholas's eyes were burning before, now they raged with reckless abandonment as he stared at Jim and Sophie's interlocked hands. He was beyond reason. He craved revenge and blood. What could you say to someone like that? What words could possibly mend the wrongs he felt had been done to him—especially when she knew that in a dark, twisted way, he was right?

She couldn't look at him. Couldn't bear the fury in his eyes, so she looked back at Jim and saw that his angry mask had slipped away and been replaced by horror—he wasn't looking at Nicholas or the gun pointed at him, but at Lux.

Sophie saw what Jim saw.

Her heart suspended in midbeat.

"*Lux*," Jim said, "don't you *dare*. Listen to me! You have to do what I tell you—so *don't you dare*."

THIRTY-SEVEN
LUX

"*Don't you dare,*" he said.

She fought it. The urge to obey was overwhelming, consuming, a roar in her skull. Her finger trembled on the switch. Her brain vomited images of fire and burning and heat and all the things that would unleash if she flicked the switch. She knew the words: *bomb, explode, fire, pain.* They sent a torrent of images through her head, images so terrible they made her want to claw out her own eyes.

But if I don't, Nicholas will shoot him.

He'll die.

She had seconds. Not even seconds—milliseconds.

Her mind was a battlefield. She stood still as a statue but inside she rioted. She raged against the chip, against the endless, infinite stream of numbers, the ones and the zeros that began and ended every thought, that burned on the inside of her eyelids and beeped in her ears. She could *hear* the chip in her brain, hear it whirring and processing, spitting out words, gathering data into neat packages and storing it away, reaching out with electric hands to every corner of her brain, scouring her from the inside. It clicked and murmured, hissed and sang; it had been there all along, every moment of her brief life, but until Moira had mentioned it she'd never known it was there. She'd thought the chip was *her*, and she was the chip. But no. If she concentrated very, very hard, she could find the line between them, fine as it was.

She pried at that line now, fighting back, pushing with everything she had within her, battering at the impulses it sent zinging through her body. If she weakened for the slightest breath of a moment, it would take control of her and she would obey Jim and she wouldn't flick the switch and then Nicholas would shoot him—she could see his finger tightening on the trigger now—because she was moving, thinking, seeing at a speed outside human capacity, processing the way a computer processed, drawing in data and spinning it around and translating it at the speed of light.

It was *so strong*, the urge to obey. It pushed at her from the inside, battered at the lining of her skull, pushed at her eyes.

Don't you dare don't you dare don't you dare Lux you have to do what I tell you so don't you dare.

She fought it.

Tears sprang into her eyes with the effort.

She bit her lip so hard that blood ran over her chin—no, it came from her nose.

"Lux!" Jim yelled. "You're bleeding! Sophie—why is she bleeding?"

Nicholas had turned around now. He looked at her hands, at her trembling finger, and his eyes widened. He knew. He met her eyes and—she saw it, she knew she saw it, but that didn't mean she could believe it—he nodded, a tiny eyelash of a nod.

You can be your own person, Sophie had said. Sophie. Her sister. *I can help you. Please—let me help you be free.*

And even Jim had said it, so long, long ago: *Lux, you don't have to obey me.*

But he didn't understand. None of them did. They thought it was so easy, so simple to just say no but it wasn't like that at all it was like it was like *it is like pushing back the ocean like swallowing the sky like turning yourself inside out and it hurts hurts hurts—*

Her vision blurred. Dark spots dotted her eyes. Her throat clogged, stopping air from flowing in and out, and her ears rang with a high, irritating buzz. But she pushed back. She fought, struggled, screamed aloud, her mouth stretching wide and she tasted blood and tears as she screamed to the sky and when the scream had all gone out of her she said it:

"NO."

A click. A sigh. Her brain ran backward. The chip was shutting down. Her mind was shutting down. Her thoughts blinked out one by one. She felt her very cells turn inside out, wither, implode. *I can turn it off*, she thought. *I can turn it off.*

She smiled.

She looked up and saw the stars, a million billion sprinkles of light.

She was free.

She looked down at the two people she loved best in the world, and she said one last word to their astonished faces:

"*Run.*"

And then she flipped the switch.

THIRTY-EIGHT
JIM

Before he could move, before he could react, before he could even comprehend what had happened, Sophie grabbed his arm and pulled him toward the cliff's edge.

Seconds passed in the form of years. He saw everything with dazzling clarity: the blood running from Lux's nose, the swift, slight brush of her finger over the switch on the detonator, the sudden look of peace in her eyes.

But Sophie pulled him away from all of it. She sprinted to the cliff and dragged him with her. It seemed to take years to reach the edge. *But why . . . ?*

"Sophie!" He skidded to a halt, just in time, pinwheeled on the edge, and grabbed her to keep her from toppling over. "Are you—"

"JUMP!"

She leaped, arcing into a swan dive.

"—CRAZY?" Jim yelled after her.

Then the blast caught him.

He weighed no more than a scrap of paper. The wave of heat flung him outward into open space; he flipped through the air like a paper clip from the flick of a giant index finger. Through space and darkness, moon and sea wheeling over each other in a dizzying, sickening blur until at last he crashed into the ocean.

The collision drove the air from his lungs with a shattering smack. His chest and stomach and face stung. The dark water sucked him down, pressed him against the ocean floor. He struggled to turn himself upright, managing to plant his feet on the sand and then push himself upward. He exploded out of the water in a fit of coughing to find the sky was on fire.

"Sophie!" he gasped, casting about. Burning debris rained from the sky like a shower of tiny flaming asteroids, littering the water around him. The blast from the explosion had thrown him far from the cliff, possibly saving his life. If he'd fallen to the foot of the cliff he'd have been killed on the rocks.

Sophie had dived before him, though. She might not have landed as far out.

He swam with all his strength toward the shoreline. Watching for any sign of her. The water burned orange around him as if he were swimming in a pool of fire. He kept calling her name, over and over until he was hoarse, choking on ash and salt water.

He dived underwater and searched, but saw only a confusion of light and sand and patches of darkness. When he broke surface again, he was much closer to the shore.

"Sophie!"

The body was floating a few yards away, facedown. He swam hard toward it, grabbed it, and turned it over—then yelled and let go. It was the dead Vitro boy who'd fallen over the cliff. His eyes were still open, and the side of his head was bashed in where it had hit the rocks. Jim's stomach somersaulted and he gagged. He swam in the other direction, letting the body float off to sea.

The waves tossed him and crashed down on him, pulling him beneath the water. When he finally reached the shallows he stood up and wandered back and forth, bracing for each wave, coughing so hard his chest ached. Burning embers rained from the sky; would they never stop?

Lux had defied him.

She had looked as if she'd half killed herself in doing it. Her face white, her eyes nearly popping from their sockets, blood running from her nose.

But she did it. She broke free. Somehow, though sheer willpower, she broke the thread between them, snapped his hold on her. He could have cheered, could have celebrated with her— but she'd blown herself up, and Nicholas with her.

He cursed Lux as he searched for her sister. It wasn't until he dragged himself, weary and aching, onto the shore that he realized the salt he tasted on his lips wasn't entirely from the sea. The current had swept him around the island, tossing him onto an unfamiliar shore, on the eastern side if he was reading the sky correctly. Most of the stars above were blacked out by the plume of smoke pouring upward from the Vitro building. He could see where the smoke began, off toward the west, behind the trees. This shore was deserted save for an old broken pier and the flock of gulls sleeping on its rotting posts.

He lay on the sand, panting, chest heaving, mind struggling to come to grips with the world around him. *Surely this can't be real.* The night had a surreal quality to it, half dream, half hallucination. He felt too disconnected from his senses for this to be reality. The colors were too dim, the sounds too distant, the sand beneath his hands too coarse and hot. Like ashes and embers.

He jerked to his feet, then stumbled across the sand like a drunk as the world spun around him. He blinked repeatedly to wash the ash from his eyes and to make the whirling lights and colors stop long enough for him to get his bearings.

He tripped over a rock and landed heavily on his face, getting a mouthful of sand. Propping himself up on his elbows, he spat out the grit and looked back.

"Sophie!" It wasn't a rock at all. She was lying in a crumpled heap; the surf rushed around her, slurping and nibbling at her hungrily. The same current that had left him here must have carried her also.

Jim gently turned her over, called her name. She groaned and tried to push him away, but she was alive. Dizzy with relief, he pulled her against his chest and murmured into her hair, feeling the pounding of her heart against his own. "Wake up, Sophie. Please."

"*Umph.* You're squeezing too tight!"

Embarrassed, he released her at arm's length.

"You okay?"

"Oh, *God*," she moaned. "That was a bad idea."

"You must have hit the shallows. You're lucky to be alive. You're completely insane."

"Yeah . . . What about Lux? Did she get away?"

"I don't know." But he feared that he did. She had been too near the building, too far from the cliff. He kept an arm around Sophie and hid his grim expression from her, afraid she'd see the doubt in his eyes. She murmured something unintelligible, her eyes slipping shut. He made sure she was breathing normally, then leaned against a rough, pockmarked rock and tried to find within himself the energy to climb up the beach and trek back to the site of the explosion.

But when he opened his eyes, dawn was beginning to spread across the sky before him. The horizon line glowed hot orange, as if a distant fire were devouring the sea. Behind him, in the trees, a gull screamed repeatedly, annoying as an alarm clock. *Wait.* It wasn't a gull—it was a human voice, calling his name and Sophie's.

"Here!" he called out, his voice throaty and dry, startling Sophie, who jolted in his arms.

"Where are you?" cried the voice.

"Down here! On the beach!"

"What's going on?" Sophie mumbled, her eyes bleary.

"How you feeling?" Jim asked.

"Hurts," she moaned, and a wave of shock washed over Jim as he dizzily recalled waking Lux just forty-eight hours earlier, and her saying the same thing when she opened her eyes.

"You're alive!" a voice cried, and they turned and looked up. Andreyev stood over them, his face haggard. As ever, his silent bodyguards flanked him. They looked a bit worse for the wear, lacking their sunglasses, white ash on their shoulders.

"Carry her," he said to them. One of them scooped Sophie up as if she weighed nothing, and they followed Andreyev over the beach and through the resort. They'd been closer to the Vitro building than Jim had reckoned, and Andreyev told him they'd been searching through the night for any sign of him and Sophie. "We saw you jump from the cliff," he said. "After that, nothing. We looked but it was so dark, and there were so many hurt by the explosion. We had to help them first."

"My mom . . ." Sophie moaned.

"She lives. She'll recover, but she may never walk again. It is too early to tell. The doctors have her."

"Nicholas?"

"Nothing left of him."

"And . . ."

"Lux," he said softly. "We found her. But it was too late."

Sophie shut her eyes. Tears leaked from their corners.

When they reached the area below the Vitro building, he saw the crowd of doctors and Vitros and guards, who were gathered beneath the restaurant with the thatched roof; some of them ran to and from the still-burning Vitro building, trying to put out smaller fires. Jim saw no sign of Strauss. The big, grand building still stood in skeletal form, but from the look of the flames, it would be burning for a while. A column of smoke coiled into the dawning sky and hung over the island like a dark, malevolent spirit. All the palms around the building were naked, smoking pillars, their leaves blasted away. How Moira had survived, he did not know.

When he saw Moira, he saw that her survival had come at a cost. She lay on one of the tables beneath the restaurant's thatched roof, her face and arms covered with blistering burns.

Sophie demanded to be put down, but leaned on Jim for support as she limped toward Dr. Crue.

"You're alive!" Moira cried, then she fell into a ragged cough.

"Mom," Sophie whispered, gently brushing her fingertips to Moira's hair, the ends of which were singed.

"Why . . ." Moira coughed. "Why do you still call me that?"

"You're the only mom I ever had," Sophie said simply. Andreyev pulled up a chair for her to sit.

"Lux is gone," said Sophie abruptly. Jim lifted a hand to hide his face.

"I know." Moira turned her head and stared at a still form covered with a sheet on the next table. Sophie went to it and slowly pulled back the cloth.

Lux could have been sleeping, except for the trail of blood from her nose, already dried on her face. Jim lowered his hand and felt his knees give out. He sat abruptly, his eyes fixed on her frozen face.

"She was thrown clear of the blast," said Moira. "Her legs were burned pretty badly, but that isn't what . . ."

It wasn't what killed her, Jim thought. Sophie, her hands trembling, took a corner of the sheet and wiped her sister's face clean. "Jim told her not to set off the bomb, but she did it anyway."

Moira's breath stopped, then she breathed out in a rasp. "That's impossible."

"I saw it." Sophie's voice was flat, emotionless. "She broke the bond. Went her own way. At the very end, she was strong enough. Do you think that's what it was? Do you think in breaking the chip's hold, she did this to herself?" Her eyes met Jim's briefly, guiltily, and then it was he who looked away.

"I don't . . . We've never seen this before. . . ." Moira fell silent for a long moment. Jim leaned against the table, his arms folded across his chest. He could feel his heart racing like a frantic animal in his chest. He watched Sophie as she leaned down and kissed Lux's cheek, leaving a few tears on her skin before she raised the sheet over her face. For a brief, wild moment, he wanted to rip the sheet away and tell her to get up, to see if his influence on her reached beyond death. But he stayed still and lowered his eyes, fixing them on a beetle that was scurrying in circles beneath the table Moira was lying on.

"She broke the bond," Moira said at last. "But then, of course she did. She was your twin. She had your strength."

"Ha." Sophie's voice turned bitter. "Not strong enough to save her."

"But strong enough to save me." Moira lifted a burned hand, winced at the effort. "And to save every other Vitro on this island. You did this. Not *that*." She glanced at the flames at the top of the hill. "This." She gestured at the doctors and Vitros around them.

"Does it matter?"

"Of course it matters. Don't you ever get cavalier about life, Sophie Jane Crue. Don't you ever think it doesn't matter. Each and every one of them owes their life to you, and you owe your life to Lux. Don't take that for granted."

Sophie closed her eyes and nodded.

"We could toss blame around till the sun goes down," Moira went on. "And I think you'd find that each and every one of us has a piece of it to bear."

Jim turned away, his eyes smarting. He knew he bore more than just a piece; he wore his guilt like a chain around his neck. *If I hadn't woken Lux in the first place . . . If I just stayed away . . .*

"Jim." He turned around. Moira was looking at him. "Little James Julien. Was it only yesterday you two were running around under the palms, raising hell and laughing all the way? Happy days. Happy memories." She sighed. "That goes for you, too, Jim. If you must trace blame to its source, look to Nicholas. And if you look to Nicholas, you must look then to me. He would never have become what he was if not for me."

Tell me, who is the monster? The creation or the creator?

"But if you chase blame back to me," Moira continued in a rasp, "then you have to ask why I did what I did. I did it because Corpus paid me to. Are they to blame? Where does it end? Listen to me, the both of you." They each turned to reluctantly meet her fervent gaze. "You will walk away from here and you will leave all of this behind, do you understand?"

They exchanged guilty looks.

"Let it go." Moira let her head drop, shut her eyes wearily. "Let it go."

Sophie burst into tears. She laid her head on the table beside Moira and sobbed. Moira looked down at her, her eyes watering, and then up at Jim beseechingly. Of course. She couldn't hold Sophie, not in her state. So Jim pulled her into his arms and let her weep onto his shoulder.

"Let it go," Moira whispered, tears coursing over her burns.

They sat thus for several long minutes, until Sophie's tears subsided. Jim sat stock-still and held her tight. All around them, doctors were soothing frantic newborn Vitros; they seemed lost and confused without Nicholas. They would have to find a way to break the bond, Jim thought. If Lux could do it, so could they. He finally glimpsed Strauss, standing under a palm tree in the distance, talking to a few guards. The morning took on a dreamlike tempo: crackling fire, rushing sea, whispering wind. The smell of salt and smoke.

After a while, Moira said, "Andreyev. You should go."

He stirred from where he'd been leaning against one of the roof supports. "Come," he said to Jim. "Can she walk now?"

"Where are we going?"

"I will take you back to Guam. We must go now. I want to get a head start on Strauss. I need to reach Corpus before she does, to tell them of what happened here. I feel if they hear her version of these events first, they will not be as accommodating of the changes I wish to implement on Skin Island."

Sophie sat up quickly. "I can't leave my mother like this," she said.

"The doctors will care for her. They have already proven their loyalty when they stood up to Strauss. Never fear, child."

"Sophie." Moira turned her head. "Go. If you don't leave now, you may never leave at all. Strauss will do everything she can to contain this. She'll trap you here if she can as one of the Vitros. I won't have it. You go and live your life and leave this place behind."

Sophie assented, her shoulders squaring as if a great weight had been lifted from her. "There's just one more thing," she said. "Something you should know." She ran a hand through her hair, then bent over Moira. "I love you. You lied to me, used me, abandoned me—but I love you anyway. Not because I owe you or because I feel obligated to—that's not really love anyway, is it? I love you because I want to, because I choose to. I love you, but I can't . . . I can't live for you anymore. Do you understand that?"

Jim looked away, embarrassed to be watching such a private exchange, but he heard Moira softly reply, "I have a lot to answer for in my life, and I've done a lot of things I regret— but you are not one of them. If there is any one thing I can point to and say I *am proud of that*; *I would never change a thing*, it would be you. You're the one thing I got right, however unlikely that is. I brought you into this world, and though I am not responsible for any of your virtues, I can at least say I had a hand in giving you a chance. I love you, Sophie."

When Sophie joined him, her face was dry.

"Let's go," she said. "I'm ready."

They followed Andreyev and his bodyguards up the hillside; the chopper was covered in ashes but looked relatively unscathed.

"Wait," Sophie said. "The keys! Nicholas had them. How will we—"

Andreyev held up a glimmering key ring. "The ones Strauss had her pilot hand over were not the helicopter keys. I believe she intended to shoot Nicholas before he ever reached the chopper."

Jim stared at the keys. "Why do I feel as if the *real* psychopath is still running loose?"

"Because she is," Andreyev said darkly. He jumped into the helicopter and offered Sophie a hand up. Jim climbed in with them, and they settled into the backseat.

"Uh-oh," said one of the bodyguards, his accent shockingly Irish. "She's seen us."

"Go, go, go!" Andreyev said, slamming the door shut and

slapping the back of the pilot's seat. The Irishman laughed, a deep, warm laugh that put a small smile on Jim's lips, it was so infectious.

The helicopter churned to life. Jim looked out the window to see Strauss hotfooting it up the hill, waving a gun and shouting, though her words were lost to them.

Jim gave her a little wave as the bird lifted into the air, and she stopped and stood still, a glowing white figure in the midst of ashes and chaos. The look on her face sent a chill down Jim's spine, and he turned away.

Sophie leaned her head on his shoulder; she was still shaking. He put his arm around her. "Going home," he said into her ear.

"Wherever that is."

"You'll find it." Of that, he was confident. If there was one thing he could say with certainty about Sophie Crue, the one thing that she'd always been, even as a child, it was that she didn't back down and she didn't give up.

"Yes," she said. "I will."

Her hand slid into his, surprisingly familiar, and he held it gently, staring at it with no small amount of wonder and bewilderment, both at the events that had transpired to bring them back together and at the burgeoning sense that even as all the terrible events of Skin Island were growing smaller and smaller below, something new was beginning, something unexpected and fragile and terrifying . . . something he wanted more than he could have ever imagined.

They turned for one last look. The Vitro building smoldered in the morning light, growing smaller and smaller until it became a tiny red eye in the large black beast that was Skin Island. Then Sophie turned her head and shut her eyes, breathing in deeply until her body ceased to tremble.

But Jim watched the island as they rose higher and turned northward, until it melted into the dark sea and faded from sight altogether.

from: ghkg874a@mcnwr.com
  to: misdefyingravity@gmail.com
date: 10 October 08:46
subject: update

We have reversed the Imprima Code, thanks to Lux.

Remember how I told you trying to override the code on the chip would be like inventing the bicycle before the wheel? Lux invented the wheel. We were able to retrieve her chip, and found it undamaged—and filled with a new code, a code written by Lux herself. A lengthy technical description would take pages to write, so I'll cut to the chase—in rebelling against Jim at that last crucial moment, she reversed the flow of information fed to her brain by the chip, overrode it with her own force of will. All this time, we've been translating code into human thought, but Lux did the opposite: She translated human thought into code. We are only beginning to scratch the surface of the full ramifications of this. So far, we've been able to use this new code, the Lux Code, to cure the Vitros—yes, cure them. Even Wyatt and Jay. We are able to communicate with the mind in ways unprecedented even in theory, reading thoughts, accessing memories, not just in the Vitros . . . but in anyone. We've stumbled into a new frontier, but we proceed with caution. None of us wish to repeat the mistakes of the past.

I cannot express the delight with which this discovery was received by our new investor. Corpus . . . they have remained ambivalent. They are not pleased with us, and it will take more than this to sway them, I think. At the moment, all that is stopping them from shutting us down is Andreyev, but I hope that in time our advances will regain their support.

Speaking of which, I will not be able to contact you again for some time. They are closing in on us, tightening security, after what happened here with you and Jim. And there was another incident, something in South America from what Andreyev tells us—anyway, they've turned paranoid lately and despite all our success here on Skin Island, I am worried about what they will do. They are tying off every loose end. The Vitro Project is just the beginning.

Sophie. Be careful.

Do not reply to this e-mail. I will cut off all contact for a while. I suggest you do likewise. Lay low for a while, and tell Jim to do the same.

Be ready, the both of you.

They are _always_ watching.

Yours,
Mom

ACKNOWLEDGMENTS

This book would not have been possible without the talent and inspiration provided by these individuals:

Laura Arnold, who walked with me through *Vitro* page for page, draft for draft, and whose belief in this book inspired me to dig deep and grab the heart of the story. Lucy Carson, who is a champion among literary agents, and the whole team at the Friedrich Agency.

Jessica Almon, Ben Schrank, Rebecca Kilman, and the rest of the Razorbill/Penguin team who applied long hours and valuable input to this story and its process. Greg Stadnyk and the Penguin design department for creating *Vitro*'s stunning cover—seriously, you guys are art wizards. Marisa Russell, Anna Jarzab, and all of Penguin's super-savvy publicity folks for their hard work in promoting the book in so many creative ways.

My grandma, whose early conversations with me about neuroscience and ectogenesis provided much of the inspiration for the Vitros (my grandma's really smart, you guys). My dad, who pointed out all the impossible things I tried to make Jim's plane do and told me how it should actually happen, and whose love for the sky was my inspiration for Jim. My Benjamin, who puts up with my crazy writing habits and who always believes in me even when I don't believe in myself. You make my dreams worth living for.

And of course, all of my readers, whose kind words, e-mails, and letters inspire me anew each day. It's all for you guys!

COMPLETE THE CORPUS TRILOGY

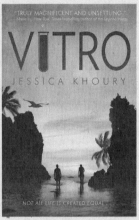

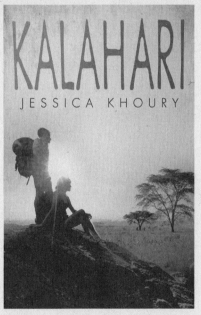

Turn the page for a sneak peek of *Kalahari*!

ONE

The lions were napping on the runway again.

I held up a hand against the blazing African sun and stared at the small silver plane that was just minutes away from touching down. I'd have to move the pride before it landed.

"Theo!" I called. The Bushman was sitting on the hood of the Land Cruiser, and when he looked my way, I pointed at the three lionesses and two cubs sunning themselves on the hard-packed sand. Laughing, he leaned backward and honked the horn of the truck, his way of saying we'd have to chase them off. I nodded and ran back to the Cruiser, tossing my folder of papers in the backseat.

In a moment, I had the engine roaring and we were off, rattling down the runway toward the sleeping lions. They yawned and chuffed at me in a lazy attempt to scare me off, but I bore down on them. I recognized the pride; the lionesses were sisters, used to us rambling around the bush. They barely opened their eyes as the truck trundled up to them.

I stopped the Cruiser, leaving the engine running, and climbed onto the hood. From there, I shouted and waved my arms, to the amusement of the cubs, who rolled and yowled and stretched. At last, their mothers lifted themselves up huffily and ambled off the runway. They were soon lost in the waving golden grass, their tawny coats blending into the dry savanna. Just the black tips of their tails showed, flickering slyly above the foliage, and then those too vanished.

I drove the truck back to the other end of the runway and parked it, then grabbed my folder out of the backseat. The plane was dropping lower in the sky, lining up with the runway.

Theo glanced at me sidelong. He was part Bushman, with the lovely golden skin characteristic of his nomadic ancestors, and though he was older than my father, he was no taller than I was. He had found a praying mantis somewhere, and the insect was crawling over his hands, from one to the other. As soon as it crawled onto one hand, he lifted the other and placed it in front, so that the mantis was continually crawling forward but getting nowhere. Theo could charm any creature that walked, crawled, flew, or slithered.

"You look like you got a toothache, girl," he said.

"Two weeks," I murmured, my eyes still on the plane. "What are we going to do with five teenagers from the city for two weeks?"

"You're a teenager." He grinned, taking far too much delight in my dismay. "I am sure you will have a grand time."

"Yeah. A grand old time." I sank lower in my seat and flipped open the folder, riffling through the documents inside. "I went to school for three months in the States once, did you know that? The kids in my class called me Mowgli and threw bananas at me during lunch."

"What is the problem? At the end of the day, it was you who ended up with all the bananas." Theo turned in his seat, and though he was still smiling, his dark eyes were serious. "Tulum-sa, it will be good for you. You cannot live your whole life with only animals for friends."

"I can try." I sighed and shut the folder. "Here they come."

The plane touched down in a cloud of dust, its silver sides reflecting golden grass and blue sky. It taxied down the short length and then turned, the propeller whipping up a whirl-wind of sand. Theo and I got out of the truck and walked toward the plane, and I held my scarf over my mouth and nose to keep from breathing in the dust.

After the engine died and the propeller wound down, the pilot ran around the front of the plane and opened the passenger door. I drew a deep breath and put on what I hoped looked like a welcoming smile.

"And here we go," I muttered through my teeth.

An Asian boy with a bright red baseball cap cocked sideways over his long, shaggy hair tumbled out of the plane. The pilot, a young Frenchman named Matthieu, was standing at the door and tried to help him out, but the kid ignored him and fell to the ground, where he promptly puked onto the hard-packed sand.

I winced and consulted the papers I was carrying, quickly putting a name to our first guest's greenish face: Joey Xiong. From California. Seventeen years old, Hmong American. Listed Sasquatch as his favorite animal. I hoped his sickness was due to the plane ride and not a sign of something worse.

The last thing we needed was flu or malaria in our camp. The nearest hospital was an hour's flight away.

Next out was a tall, graceful girl with springy dark hair. She paused in the doorway, half bent over, and stared at the spot where Joey had deposited his breakfast. For a moment it seemed as if she would turn around and go back inside the plane, but Matthieu offered a hand and she gingerly stepped down, her expression a mask of disgust. While Joey lurched to his feet, she pointedly stood a few steps away from him and stared in the other direction. Avani Sharma, her profile paper read. Canadian, of Indian and Kenyan heritage. 4.0 GPA. The list of her academic achievements, recorded there for no apparent reason, was long enough to put some college professors to shame.

I let out a little breath, trying to force my thoughts to stay positive, as the next two guests exited the plane: a boy and a girl so entangled with each other that it was hard to see where one ended and the other began. They were both dark haired and pale skinned. They had on khaki from head to toe, but they wore it as if they'd just arrived for a Burberry photo shoot—his shirt was partially unbuttoned, her beige scarf was arranged in a complex knot, and they were both sporting manicured, immaculate hairstyles. There was no denying they were both drop-dead gorgeous and deeply obsessed with each other.

They could only be Miranda Kirk and Kase Rider of Boston, Massachusetts. They had come together and they were both seventeen. Other than that, the profiles they had filled out were scant on information. The space asking why they were here at all—*Please state what you hope to gain from this experience*—was blank on Miranda's, while Kase's form said only *wildlife photography portfolio.*

They jumped to the ground without taking their arms from around each other, then stood between Avani and Joey, whispering in each other's ears and regarding the surrounding wilderness with suspicious looks.

Last out of the plane was a boy who must have been, by process of elimination, Sam Quartermain, our final guest: shaggy dark blond hair, a plain white tee tucked messily into his jeans, carrying a tattered Adidas duffel bag. The moment his shoes hit the ground, his head was up and his eyes were wide, scanning the trees around us and finally settling on me.

"Hey!" he called out, the first of them to even acknowledge my presence. "Sarah, right? I'm Sam!"

"Hi, Sam."

"Mind if I take a picture?" said Kase, pulling out a camera roughly the size of a lawn mower engine.

"Um, no?"

"Sweet." He held up his camera and the shutter clicked. Then Kase cursed and fiddled with the dials. "Crap. Settings are all screwed up."

Miranda shielded her eyes from the sun as she whipped out her phone, her fingers a blur as they navigated the touch screen. "Ugh! No service? Are you *kidding* me?"

I suppressed a sigh and nodded to Matthieu. "*Salut,* Matt. *Bon vol?*"

He grunted and began unloading the boxes of food and necessities I'd ordered from our supplier in Maun. "Je ne t'envie pas vraiment dans cette situation. C'est aussi amusant qu'un panier de serpents." *I don't envy you with this lot. They're about as much fun as a box of snakes.*

Easy for him to say. I was the sort of person who, upon arriving at someone's house on a social visit, ended up making friends with his or her canary instead. I'd take a box of snakes over these five any day. But as Dad was fond of saying, "We must soldier on, eh?"

"Hello, everyone," I said, clearing my throat. *They're just people. Get it together.* "Um, I'm Sarah Carmichael and this is Theo. Welcome to the Kalahari."

Beside me, Theo flashed his brightest smile and said, "Hello, hello," in his soft accent. I was glad I'd brought him along to meet the plane, because he immediately began putting everyone at ease, shaking hands, taking Miranda's and Avani's bags and pretending they were too heavy for him. Avani smiled a little, but Miranda rolled her eyes. Only Sam and Joey laughed, and Theo gave them a grin and a shrug as if to say, *Girls, eh?*

"Climb aboard," I said, waving at the battered green Land Cruiser. "It'll be a tight fit. You'll have to hold your bags. We're about a ten-minute drive from the camp."

As the group climbed into the Cruiser, I made a quick check of the supplies Matthieu had brought and then left Theo to stand guard over them until I returned with the car to load them up.

The Cruiser choked to life as I turned the key, and the whole thing began vibrating like it was about to fall apart. I heard a little shriek from behind me but couldn't tell who it was.

"This is Hank," I shouted over the engine, slapping the dash. "He sounds like a trash compactor, but he's the only thing that'll get through this terrain."

I turned the Cruiser around and rumbled down the track to the camp. The sides were all open and the canvas roof was rolled back, allowing the passengers a 360-degree view of the Kalahari semidesert.

A dry wind blasted my face, pulling my hair out of its messy braid and nearly sucking the wide-brimmed sun hat off my head. All around us, the graceful acacias and stocky *Terminalia* swayed and rustled, and a lone chanting goshawk cut the air above, hunting for mice in the tall golden grass. Behind us, Matthieu's plane grunted to life, and moments later I saw him climbing into the sky ahead of us, destined for Maun and his next group of tourists to ferry through the cloudless Botswana sky.

When I looked down again, I realized there was a face hovering beside mine and I jumped, gripping the wheel harder and biting back a curse. It was the one named Joey. His baseball cap was now backward, and a sprig of his black hair sprouted over the Velcro strap.

"I'm Joey," he said. "Nice wheels. Very rugged. I like a girl who can drive manual. And on the wrong side of the car too."

In response, I kicked the Cruiser into third gear and gave him a tight smile.

I desperately wished we didn't have to do this, but my dad's conservation research needed all the funding it could get, and in return for babysitting four American (and one Canadian) students on a conservation exchange program, we'd receive a research grant from the Song Foundation. We might even be able to buy another vehicle, which we sorely needed. It wasn't a good idea to be this far out into the Kalahari bush with only one form of transportation readily available, not with the way the terrain around here destroys cars. We'd had a second car, until Mom's accident.

I turned to Joey and smiled a bit wider. "Have a good flight over?"

"Ugh! Dude, did you see me hurl?" He laughed and elbowed Sam. "You totally shouldn't have let me eat all those sausages in the airport, man."

"You guys know each other?" I asked.

"Nah, met on the plane from JFK. Totally bonded though. We did a *Die Hard* marathon on the flight over, but my man Sam here conked out halfway through number three. Yippee-ki-yay!"

Joey's chatter continued, most of it blasted away by the wind, but I nodded and pretended to listen as I navigated the Cruiser through the treacherous sand. There's not a single stone to be found in the Kalahari, just endless deep sand, white in the north and fading to red in the south, the nemesis of every vehicle that attempts to cross it. I'd lost count of how many times Dad, Theo, and I had had to dig this thing out. It was the reason why I had "muscles like a rugby fullback," according to my dad. He's from New Zealand, and in his view, everything on the planet can be analogized to rugby.

We startled a pair of tall gray kudu, and they froze in front of the car, their huge dark eyes fixed on the great gray-green monster that had interrupted their grazing. At once, everyone behind me was leaning forward, and I stopped to let them get a better look. Kase's zoom lens extended over Joey's shoulder as he snapped a ream of photos. Avani suddenly spoke up, identifying the "two young female kudu, called cows, scientific name *Tragelaphus strepsiceros*" and rattling off a stream of kudu-related information as deftly as any safari guide.

As the car approached them, the kudu leaped into fluid motion, disappearing into the brush in three steps. They weren't called the "gray ghosts of the bush" for nothing; despite their size—they stood as tall as horses—they could vanish in moments into the dry vegetation.

The group let out a collective sigh and then they all fell silent, now on high alert for more animal activity, but we reached the camp without seeing anything more exciting than a few sparrows and fork-tailed drongos.

My dad was waiting. He stood with a warm smile and an armful of bottled water, outfitted in his usual khaki gear, rugged and faded like a worn photograph that's been handled too many times. He looked older than he was, tanned and leathery from spending all his time underneath the suns of a dozen wildernesses, from the Burmese jungles to the Australian outback and now the Kalahari savanna, charting migratory patterns and documenting the myriad ways humans were destroying the natural world. His long graying hair was tied in a ponytail at the back of his head, though a few wispy strands had escaped.

As soon as our guests' feet touched the ground, my dad introduced himself, his strong Kiwi accent booming across the grass. "Welcome to our little corner of the Kalahari, boys and girls! My name's Ty Carmichael, and I'm the head researcher here at Camp Acacia."

You're the only *researcher here,* I thought, shaking my head a little.

"Camp Acacia" wasn't much of a camp. There was my tent, Dad and Theo's shared one, and then there were the two new ones we'd put up that morning to accommodate the guests—one for boys, one for girls. The tents were large enough. You could stand up straight if you were right in the middle of them, and they kept out rain (for the most part), if not bugs and the occasional snake or wildcat. There was a fire pit in the middle of the camp, surrounded by logs for seating, and a portable shower was set up in the trees nearby. It was about as crude a camp as you could ask for, but it had been my home for the past five years, more or less, and resembled every other camp I'd lived in as my family moved from one remote location to the next.

"Where's the lodge?" asked Miranda.

Silence fell. We all stared at her. She took off her designer sunglasses and gave my dad a bewildered look through mascara-laced eyelashes, then turned to her boyfriend.

"Uh . . . Mir . . ." coughed Kase, looking a bit pale.

"You said there would be a lodge," she replied to him, quite loudly. "You *distinctly promised* there would be a lodge! The only reason I agreed to come on this—"

"Miranda, listen, I might not have mentioned . . ." Kase reached for her hand.

She slipped her shades back on and folded her arms, resisting his touch.

"Baby, don't—" Kase kept whispering apologies.

"I'm sorry if there's been a misunderstanding, mates," my dad interjected, looking only slightly rattled as he started handing out the waters, "but you'll soon see that staying in a tent brings you closer to nature than any lodge could. Now, girls will be there in the blue tent, and fellas, you'll be there in the green. There's an outdoor shower behind that tree—don't worry, we'll put up a privacy screen. We're close to an old borehole, luckily, so there's no end to freshwater." He kept casting anxious looks at Miranda, who glared back at him as if being "closer to nature" was synonymous with "closer to hell."

Dad's description of camp life and its scant luxuries continued as I fired up Hank for the return trip to the runway. By the time Theo and I had loaded all the supplies and arrived back at camp, the girls had disappeared into their tent and the guys were beating around in the bushes, Kase busy photographing every leaf and spider within a hundred-foot radius with his massive camera. Dad met us and started unloading boxes before I'd even properly parked.

"God help us," he said in a low voice as I helped him carry a cooler of meat into my tent, where we kept most of the provisions. Above us, the shadows of the trees danced over the beige canvas, like the reflection of rippling water. "What did we agree to, Sarah? Why are we doing this?"

"Just keep smiling and think of all the fancy equipment you can buy with that grant money."

Dad groaned. "Your mother would have known what to do with them."

The blood drained from my face. For a moment, I couldn't move, couldn't breathe. In an instant, frost crackled over my heart. It had been four months, and still the simple mention of her crushed me.

Dad's hand went to my cheek, the warmth in his rough palm shattering the ice inside me.

"Chin up, love," he said softly, and he kissed my forehead. "We must soldier on, eh?"

I couldn't talk about her, not even in passing. Every time her name rose in my throat, I choked on it and fell apart. Dad knew that, and so he didn't press me but held me to his chest for a moment while I pulled myself together. His rough cargo shirt smelled like all the things familiar to me: gasoline, camp-fire smoke, the lavender-scented laundry soap I used when I washed our clothes under the pump. I used that scent and his quiet strength to steady myself.

"All right, then?" he asked, stroking my hair, and I nod-ded. "Good girl. Because I don't think I can manage this lot without my Sissy Hati."

Oh, now he was really fishing for a smile, pulling out that old name. When I was three, I'd thought the Bengali term for a baby elephant was Sissy Hati. Close, but not quite the right words. The village we were living in had turned the mispro-nunciation into a pet name for the little white girl who ran wild through the jungle with their own children, stripped to the waist and without a care in the world.

Another kiss on the top of my head and Dad was gone, striding back to the truck.

It took me a minute to catch my breath, and when I stepped outside again, I saw Sam helping to unload the truck. Kase had disappeared into his tent, and Joey—it took me a moment to locate him—had climbed to the top of an umbrella thorn acacia, which was a remarkable feat considering the two-inch thorns that covered it. I watched him for a moment, incredu-lous. Sam caught my eye and gave an exaggerated shrug, shak-ing his head at Joey's antics.

"You should have seen him on the plane," he said. "I think the flight attendants were plotting to sedate him."

I showed Sam where to put the box of muesli he was carrying and held open the tent flap for him to duck inside.

"This your place?" he asked.

"Home sweet home."

He set the box down at the front of the tent with the others; my cot and the sum of my worldly possessions were at the back, behind a wall of boxes and crates. I had a shelf made of crates and boards, and it was cluttered with Bushman artifacts and crafts I'd bought from the children in the village markets. A worn stuffed elephant I'd had since I was three sat on my bed, alongside a stack of Agatha Christie books I was reading through for the third time. The mosquito net draped around the bed was decorated with tiny beads I'd painstakingly sewed on.

I felt a sudden flare of embarrassment at this invasion of my privacy. Everything in my tent suddenly seemed shabby and odd. I moved between him and my "room," feeling far too exposed.

We didn't normally get visitors, and though I used to love seeing new faces around to break up the monotony of my remote life, lately it seemed as if every new face I saw only reminded me of the one face I loved most, the one face I would never see again. *She would have known what to do with them.*

Sam brushed his fingers over a delicate dream catcher hanging from the poles that crossed at the apex of the canvas roof. "Nice place."

"Thanks. We can handle the rest of the boxes," I said.

"Nah, I don't mind." His smile was easy and quick, like a strike of lightning. He picked up a book from my small folding desk and stared at the cover; it was a copy of *Dreams of Afar*, the memoir my mom had written about our family's travels.

His lips twitched as if he was about to say something; then he put the book down and moved on.

As he slid past me and back outside, I pulled the papers out of my pocket and scanned his file again. Sam Quartermain, from Pittsburgh, Pennsylvania. Age: seventeen. Favorite animal: wolf. His statement for being here simply read *Keeping a promise*. There wasn't much else, besides his medical needs (none) and allergies (peanuts).

When I reached the Cruiser, I saw that Dad had stopped unloading the boxes and was occupied with the radio on the dash. The incoming voice, fuzzy with static, could only be from Henrico, the South African warden stationed south of us. He was the only human within communicable distance of our camp, unless we used the heavy, awkward satellite radio that was currently gathering dust in the back of the truck.

Dad's face was thunderous; whatever Henrico was saying had gotten him unusually riled. My dad was normally as easygoing as they came.

"Theo, what is it?" I asked. The Bushman made a shushing noise. He was also listening in. I stepped closer, trying to overhear Henrico's words, but at that moment Dad said into the speaker, "I'll look into it and let you know. Give a call if you hear anything more." He dropped the radio onto the seat of the car and turned to me, his face flushed.

"Sarah. There are reports of poachers in the area. A white lion's been spotted just west of here, and Rico thinks they're after it." The mere mention of poachers sent my dad into a blind rage. I didn't know how many times I'd fallen asleep at night listening to him rant about the declining rhino population, the uselessness of antipoaching NGOs, the apathy of the world toward the cause. Only my mom's death had elicited a stronger emotional response from him.

My heart dropped. "Dad. Dad, no—"

"It might be the same outfit who slaughtered those rhinos up in Chobe last year. They slipped past us once—we can't let them do it again." Dad had spent the better part of that month helping Botswana's antipoaching unit track the poachers, only to lose their trail in the end. The poachers had cut right through the area we'd been researching, and Dad had been angry about it for months, swearing that he wouldn't let it happen again.

"Dad, *please*," I said, leaning into the word, "you promised you wouldn't do this. Not after—We had a deal, remember? We stay together. Always."

Dad paused, the crusader's fire fading from his eyes. "I remember, kiddo. You're right. But if this is the same crew . . ."

I sighed, seeing the anguish in his eyes. I'd been the one who'd drawn that promise from him, terrified as I was that the past would repeat itself and I would lose him too. But letting the poachers slip away again would wreck him.

"Promise me," I said slowly, wilting beneath my own sense of guilt, "you won't get involved. You'll just find them and send their location to the government. If you don't see anything by dark, come home, okay?"

Dad's face relaxed into a grateful smile. "I swear. Cross my heart." He drew an imaginary X on his chest, then took my shoulders and quickly kissed my forehead. "Thanks, sweetie. I'll be back tonight. Everything will be fine. It's just a few hours, and I have the radio. Got yours?"

I tapped the radio clipped to my belt. Dad sighed at my expression of unease. "If you really want me to stay—"

"Just hurry," I said. "And don't do anything stupid or heroic, all right?"

His grin did little to soothe the constricting knot of worry in my gut. He climbed into the Cruiser and cranked it. "You can look after these guys for a few hours, honey. You'll be fine," he said. Sam stood a short distance away, watching solemnly, and I could see that even from up in his tree, Joey had heard what was happening. The tents behind us opened, and the other three emerged curiously to see what the fuss was about.

Dad leaned out far enough to grip my shoulder. He had that look in his eye, the one that could stop a lion in mid-charge. "Love you, Sissy Hati."

Theo returned with bottles of water, jackets, and my dad's old shotgun, and he jumped into the passenger seat.

"What? You're taking Theo?" I grabbed hold of the windowsill, standing on the footstep below the door.

"Hey, now!" said Theo. "Can't keep me out of the action!"

"He's the only one who can track them," said Dad. "We'll be back before dark, I promise!"

He stomped the gas, forcing me to jump back from the vehicle. Hank seemed to have caught my dad's anger, chugging like a locomotive. Theo threw me a wide smile and a cheery wave. You'd have thought he was going on a picnic.

"Be careful!" I yelled, but he was already gone, churning up a whirlwind of dust and sand, massive tires crunching over the dry brush as Hank hungrily devoured the land in his path.

Sound travels extraordinarily far in the rolling Kalahari. A minute later, I was standing in the same spot, still hearing the Cruiser's roar. Then I turned on my heel and froze. Five pairs of eyes stared back at me.

For a moment, my brain went blank and I had no idea what to say or do. Dad was supposed to have taken the group out on a drive to spot the nearby animals while I made a light lunch. That was The Plan. We'd been working on it for days—sectioning these two weeks into carefully premeditated activities designed to give our guests maximum exposure to the gritty, unglamorous face of conservation fieldwork, so that they could return home with their cameras loaded with shots of themselves saving the planet.

Instead, there I was in the middle of the Kalahari wilderness with no Dad, no Theo, no Hank, and no Plan—with four Americans (and one Canadian) wholly unsuited to this place and this life. I looked at them, they looked at me, and I think we all came to the same realization:

This had been a bad idea.